A Universe Against Us

Us

Marc B. DeGeorge

MUSEMARC STUDIO

Cover Design by: SeventhStar Art

Author Photo by: MuseMarc Studio

ISBN: 978-1-956487-19-0 (digital), 978-1-956487-20-6 (paperback)

First Edition: **March 2024**

9 8 7 6 5 4 3 2 1

Contents

Acknowledgments

A story may be written by one person, but it takes many to turn it into a novel. To that end, I'd like to thank the following for their contribution to turning my typing into reality.

First, my dedicated and awesome reading group, Ben Pick, Tracey Canole, E. Marie Robertson, Michelle Darnell, Joe Creech, and J. Logan Rice. Thank you for your critical commentary, positive support, and friendship.

My amazing editors, Joanne Machin and Ariel Anderson. Your skills have kept me from making one too many plot holes. Thank you.

Also to my wife and family, for your support and love.

ESCAPE

FANA

THERE IS NO REASON to say goodbye. No one left would miss us. We, the destroyers of our own planet.

Nature will struggle to make a lasting world with the poisoned earth that remains. And we continued to burn and contaminate everything, even as we made preparations to leave. Now, our ship, the *Devant*, is the last in a thousand-year exodus. We are running away from the disaster we created, and my short legs cannot move fast enough.

"Fana, hurry!" Raey waves with such force she must jump along to balance herself. "Commander Azazhi is closing the hatch soon!"

Raey is what I would define as a classic beauty. Luscious lips, eyes to get lost in, and cheekbones to make royalty jealous. She's half a head taller than me, putting her at just above the average height for a woman. When she wears the traditional seven rows of braids in her curly brown hair, she seems even taller, but today, because we're in a rush, she's just clipped her mane back.

"Maybe if you helped me with these last loads, I could!" I shout back as I balance the last stack of portable med kits on my sled. The sky was getting dark, and thunder rumbled in the distance. We would need to be inside the shuttle long before it arrived. The rain could be deadly for those without proper protection. Raey and I have none.

As it is, Commander Azazhi's going to skin us alive for being late. We can't allow for any more complications, but that is no excuse to leave these behind. I'll take getting yelled at once for ensuring we're prepared.

"Why do you need to bring those?" Raey stamps her foot and throws her hands out, her mass of curls bouncing with her excited gestures. "We have two hundred years of medical supplies already!"

"Don't be a child. You know these kits are better than any we have on the *Devant*. And if I remember correctly, *you* are the medical officer, not me!"

She throws a nervous eye at the sky and rushes toward the sled, snatching up the two kits remaining on the floor.

"The beta kits we've stocked on the ship have upgraded medicines to handle all the side effects of waking up from stasis," Raey explains and slaps the kits on the top of the pile. "And, trust me, after the first time you wake up from it, you're going to be begging me for ten doses!"

"But these kits have the auto calibrating anti-viral doses. The new ones don't. New tech isn't always better tech."

"These are from the expedition fifty years ago! They don't need them because they can't wake anyone until they arrive. And we'll get there a hundred years before they do. We may be the last to leave but—"

"Hey, silly, you're talking to the chief engineer of the ship. If there's something I know better than you, it's interstellar travel. And yes, we'll arrive on Asteria well before any other expeditionary craft."

The kit on top of the pile pops and hisses. A second later, another kit makes the same noise as a wisp of smoke rises from it. I swallow as I stare at the small hole forming in the kit's packaging.

"Oh, hell," Raey groans as her eyes roll up to the sky. It has gotten dark faster than either of us noticed.

"Don't look up!" I race to the front of the sled and use the weight of my compact body to shove it toward the shuttle. It moves, but slowly. Too slowly.

"Forget the kits! We'll never get them loaded!" Raey throws her arms above her head as she races ahead.

The occasional pop turns into a steady tick as rain lands on my uniform. Not every drop is corrosive, but once this turns into a downpour, it won't matter. I lean hard on the sled and fight myself to keep my head down. Eyes can be repaired, but there's nothing to stop the agony I would feel if they got wet.

"Fana! Come on!" Raey is in the hatch now, waving me over. I'm moving as fast as I can with this sled that must weigh ten times more than me.

I'm breathing hard as my feet slip on the ground, forcing me to make the extra effort to push the sled. I don't know why I didn't put in a logistics request. Oh...yes, I do. Adding the extra weight onto our shuttle without notification is against regulations. But if I asked, I wouldn't get them onboard. Most judge priorities differently than I do.

I jolt as my foot hits a puddle, splashing water on my leg. The moisture soaks right through my pants and touches my skin. I let out a whimper. It stings. Badly. I don't want to imagine what the caustic reaction is doing to me. I'm jumping into a shower the moment I'm in the shuttle. It's not far now.

Then the sky unleashes a downpour. Raey screams as I hurtle into the hatch, releasing the sled from my grip and clawing at the zip on my uniform. Every part of me burns. My arms feel like someone's branded them with molten metal. I writhe as fire torches my head and back.

"Get it off! Get it off!" I cry as I rip my shirt off. Raey ushers me into the nearest cabin. It doesn't matter whose it is. Water. I need water now, or I will dissolve. Literally.

She lifts me into the shower and engages the cold rinse, soaking us both in its chilly stream. I don't care. It's this baptism of ice that eases my suffering. I crash to the ground as Raey sponges me off, her lungs wheezing from the unexpected exertion.

"What the hell are you two doing?" Commander Azazhi bursts in, stopping short as he catches the sight of my bare figure huddled in the stall's corner. One of us should remember our modesty, but this is an emergency. I'd rather my commanding officer see me naked than let the corrosive rain melt my skin. Still, something about being so vulnerable forces me to pull my legs up tight and wrap my arms around them.

His eyes widen as he realizes how mottled and black my legs are. If my skin was a lighter tone, it'd be far more shocking. As it is, I'm preparing for a serious outburst from him. And I deserve it.

"We've neutralized it, Commander," Raey says with a sigh of relief. She wipes her soaked hair out of her face and drops next to me. "We'll let the water run a little more, just in case."

The Commander grabs the edge of the doorframe as the shuttle's engines ignite. We're already past our launch window, and now we'll be late to rendezvous with the ship and off schedule to leave orbit. The delay is worth it. The tongue lashing I'm about to get is worth it. My body burned all over might not be. Still, I have no regrets. Yet.

"How bad is it?" Commander Azazhi asks Raey.

Raey rubs the tip of her tongue across her lip and side-glances at me. I duck my head a little, not wanting to show her just how much I want to beg her to lie. I could get demoted for this.

"She got lucky," Raey says. It's not a complete lie. "Though we'll need to get her over to medical and get those burns covered as soon as possible."

The commander leans his head to the side and reaches up to scratch his lip. I'm thankful he's trying not to look at me. Either that, or he's so angry that he can't stand the sight of me. A chill runs across my skin just thinking about that. Or is that the ice water pounding on my head?

"Might be better to put her in stasis until we're out of orbit," Commander Azazhi says.

The cry that comes from my throat makes Raey jump. She's breathing as fast as I am, but for a different reason. It still makes her reach up and turn the water off.

"Commander! No!" I shout, squeezing my arms tighter across my legs as I shiver. "We've got to tune the engines and do all the run-up tests for interstellar travel. I can't be asleep for that!"

"You should have thought about that before you broke regulations. I'd well be within my rights to turn you into a passenger and let you sleep through the entire haul." He turns to Raey. "Get her a blanket or something before she freezes to death. Take the one off my bed if you want."

His bed? Holy hyuk, this cabin is his! Maybe if his wife had found us, I'd be escaping this threat.

Raey returns with a thermaweave sheet and covers me with it. The impermeable material heats me up the moment I'm bundled up in it.

"You know," Raey says to the Commander, "it might not be a bad idea to let her sleep through our departure. Even with everything we can do to help her body recover, she's still going to be in a lot of pain. At least in stasis, we can use the pod's recombinant tech to heal her."

My jaw drops open. "You are not my friend any longer!"

Raey lower lip pushes out. "That's mean, Fana. I'm trying to help you."

Commander Azazhi tilts his head in the opposite direction and looks away. Whatever it is he's considering, I expect it is not to my benefit.

"Commander, please!" I beg, even as my burns sting again. "If you put me in stasis, I won't get to see the planet from our departure angle! And I need to calibrate the hydrogen collection tanks!"

"There's at least ten people that could do that," Raey says. I throw a glare at her. Raey only shrugs.

"All right, Chief," he says, straightening and facing me. "I'll let you decide. Either you heal up in stasis, or right here and now, you absolutely certify that whatever pain you feel won't affect your ability to do your job."

"Commander, that's cruel," Raey says. "She'll need medication for that pain. We can't deny her that."

"I'm not denying her that." He folds his arms. "The amount of medication you need to give her, and the side effects from it, are part of my calculations. If Fana believes she can keep her efficiency up, even on whatever drugs you stuff into her body, then I'll accept it. But I'll demote her the moment she screws up."

I must look as pathetic as the last canine to walk the Earth. But my expression only affects Raey. She gives me a sympathetic smile and coos at me like I am her child, then drops to a crouch as she faces me. I remember to push my lips into a smile, trying to show her my appreciation for her efforts—something I've always been bad at. Maybe that's why we couldn't make our relationship work.

The shuttle shakes as it achieves orbit velocity. The rumble of atmospheric pressure dies away, and the shuttle jerks, shifting the blanket across my wounds. I wince and suck in a sharp breath. Raey better hop me up on the best stuff medical has, or I'll be useless in engineering.

I sigh and hang my head. "I'm sorry. I'm only thinking about myself, aren't I?"

"That'd be about standard operating procedure for you," Raey mumbles. But the commander hears it and smirks.

"Okay...okay. You're right. You too, Commander."

"I'm always right, Chief. Just remember that."

I offer an upward curve of one side of my lip. He's only half-joking, and he knows I get that.

"So, just for official purposes, I need to hear you give me your decision, as it's got to go down on record."

"Fine." I swallow. "Commander Azazhi, for the benefit of all aboard the *Devant*, I, Chief Fana Neridi request to be put in stasis until my wounds heal or until you require my expertise. That good enough?"

The commander nods. "Acceptable. Have a good sleep. Now get the hell out of my cabin."

LIMBO

— • —

CERI

I PUT MY WEAPONS away nine months ago. There was no reason to carry them. On the *Stratford*, we're all friends now. Lovers. Family.

There are still fights. Still battles to be won. Instead of a gun, I use words. Sometimes my hands. Though often, when I struggle for the right thing to say, I wish I had kept my pistol.

All I want is to save my parents and the thousands of others that lie in stasis, unaware they're hurtling toward forever, never to reach their new home. I've done little toward that end. They trained me to be a soldier. To kill. Not to solve technical problems. Though I never wanted to be squad leader, either. The situation forced me to accept the assignment, and now I fight to do anything but. The adults may have put us through hell, but as much as we've grown, we are still children. And children will always get themselves into trouble.

"Keep her still," Efa says as she glares at me, then draws the needle and the thread up to prepare another stitch. "I'm almost done."

I sit with Efa in the medical bay on level fourteen, my arms wrapped around Dru, one of our many children, as she whimpers in my lap. We've propped her leg up on an exam table so Efa can sew up the horrific gash on her ankle. My arms lock her shoulders back to make sure she doesn't jerk and cause more damage to herself. It's bad enough that she was climbing in the hull where we told her not to.

I wouldn't do this for everyone, but at twelve years old, Dru never had the chance to train as a soldier. That's both a blessing and a curse. She'll never know the horror of battle. Never know what it's like to end the life of someone the same age. Though, if she knew a few tips about pain management, she wouldn't be shaking in my arms. I will teach her. I just haven't had the time.

"Alright, Dru." Efa pats the girl's leg and gives her a smile before wrapping a field dressing around Dru's ankle. "No more excursions, okay?"

I release her arms, dropping mine around her waist. Yet Dru only slouches into me more, and I can't help but let her. She may have chosen to stay on board the *Stratford*, but she had no idea what she was getting herself into. And just like the rest of us, she only found out after the adults left. I don't regret allowing her to stay. No adult would care for her the way we do. I just wish I knew how to stop her from being so curious.

"It's going to get better, right?" Dru asks, hesitation in her voice.

"It will," I reply. "Efa's the best field medic we've ever had. It's a good thing—"

"Then why didn't you replace the part?" Seren, my fifteen-year-old former squad member, throws her hands up as she barges in. Dirt and grease cover her face, matching her duty uniform's soiled appearance. She throws a glare behind her and continues until she stops before me, arms crossing.

The target of her anger is just behind her. Rhys. Former F Squad member and sometimes subject of Seren's infatuation, but more often her annoyance. He's equally dirty, black goop stuck in the tangles of his shocking blond hair. The extended frown on his face makes me think they've been arguing for a while. They better end it quickly. I have little time to spend on another argument.

"It didn't need to be replaced," Rhys grumbles. "The contacts were just dirty."

"Yeah?" Seren spins on him, hands on her hips. "But you didn't clean them good enough, did you?"

He looks away, his cheeks reddening.

"Hyuk. Sometimes I wonder why I saved your life."

Rhys ducks his head and looks at her.

"Hey," Efa says. "Come on. No need for that."

Efa may be attempting to calm the situation down, but in the back of her head, she must know she's partly to blame for this minor would-be lovers' spat. Though, I likely am as well. I never warned Efa not to make her relationship with Merek public. I was too naïve to know to do it. Seren and Rhys are the result of my ignorance.

Dru elbows me in my ribs as she squirms. I murmur an apology as I realize how tense my arms are around her. With a gentle lift, I slide her down to the seat and stand with a sigh. There's no way I can relax with these two bickering like this.

"Alright," I say. "We're fixing this now. What's going on?"

"You know that console that we found partially working in control?" Seren asks. "The one you ordered us to get working again?"

"Of course I know it." I shake my head. "But I don't order you to do anything. I'm not your captain or your field lead. Not anymore."

Seren tosses a hand and shrugs, then motions to Rhys. "Well, bish-head over here thought it'd be a good idea to just clean it out before we started changing parts. There were so many sparks, it nearly caught fire!"

"Fire?" Efa's eyes widen. "It's out, right?"

I squeeze my lips together to hold back the fury that's about to explode from my mouth. Fire on a ship is a serious problem. That they were careless enough to allow one to happen means I can no longer trust them to work together unsupervised. And it'd have to be me who watched them. Perhaps I can forego a meal to make it happen, though I was getting to enjoy the only free moments left to me.

"What do you have to say about this?" I ask him. It's only fair he gets to speak.

"Better you just see for yourself," Rhys replies.

Efa motions to me as she puts a hand on Dru's shoulder. It's a permission I don't need but appreciate. One less person I have to worry about.

"Okay, let's head to control," I say.

As we make our way up to level two, I watch the silent inter-actions between Seren and Rhys, the once in a while lovers. I doubt they even understand what it means to be that. I don't. All I know is that I saw them kiss once, and I nearly beat them for doing it. We can't have complications like that in our team, yet I don't know how to stop it from happening. I almost don't want to, because then I'd be involved in managing yet another thing I don't have time for.

When others, including Dru, told me Seren and Rhys have done more than just kiss, our response was to separate the boys' nests from the girls'. But that's not working. Some children are so curious, they'll try to kiss anyone, and that's led to a few misunderstandings and a fight or two. One boy even locked himself in the outside hull. We barely saved him before he froze to death.

The adults were right to suppress our natural inclinations. All it's done is cause problems.

"It's not my fault," Rhys says as we complete our twelve-level climb. "I thought it was good enough."

"Good enough is the problem, idiot," Seren spits back.

"Stop it," I growl. "That won't solve anything."

"The only solution—"

I grab Seren's arm before she finishes and give her a serious stare. Seren's mouth closes, and her body deflates. I don't enjoy being harsh on her, but I can't play favorites. Not if I want things to run smoothly.

"Just show me the console, okay?" I say as I squint from the glare of the overhead lights.

Seren sighs and nods, then pulls herself from my grip and moves to stand on the opposite side of the console's rear panel from Rhys. He shines a beam inside the open compartment and points to the section they were working on. Two rows of circuit boards, easily accessible, line the bottom of the metal console frame. There, in the middle of the top row, is a board, blackened by the unexpected heat applied to it. The carbon char has spread to the two nearest of its neighbors and likely has destroyed them, too.

A gigantic pit forms in my stomach as I motion for Rhys to turn his beam off. With every part we've replaced, I grew confident that we could fix our ship, that we could achieve our goals and bring our passengers to their new home. But it was just luck. That was it. Now we may never get this done.

I never thought I'd ever say this, but we may need to wake up some adults. Perhaps my parents, if only to let my mother rock me gently in her arms as I closed my eyes and pretended I was still ten years old. Of course I wouldn't, but anything would be a welcome escape to the harsh reality of now.

"See?" Seren asks. "He's completely messed it up."

Rhys' jaw drops open. "I wouldn't have needed to clean it if you had gotten your lazy ass down to storage and back in a proper amount of time!"

"What are you talking about?" Seren steps toward him, fire filling her eyes.

"Bish!" he says as he waves a hand toward the nearest ladder. "We used to do twenty levels in thirty minutes! You took two hours to come back!"

She swears and gets in his face. "That's because I had to find the part, stupid!"

I sigh. If only my mother was awake right now...

"Cut it out!" I shout and shove them apart. "If the two of you can't work together, I'm going to send you to work on opposite sides of the ship and chain you there until you finish your task. Seriously! What the hell is this bish all about?"

They both go quiet and drop their gazes to the deck as I wait for an answer. Likely I already have it, judging by their reactions.

But I don't know how to solve a lovers' quarrel, and Merek and Efa, the only ones who have experience in this area, have been little help. All they've done has been to encourage any would-be couple to talk through their problems. How can they do that when none of us even understand what it means to be together like that?

It's stupid we're pretending to be mature. All of us agreed to stay here to take care of the thousands of people in stasis, not play husband and wife. Or wife and wife. Or whatever. And only Niah seems to agree with my assessment of things, yet she's been spending all her time in the far reaches of the *Stratford* when I really need her help. She's nearly ten years older than me. She's bound to have at least a suggestion.

"For hyuk's sake already!" I throw a hand in the air. "Whatever personal disagreement the two of you have had, just get over it!"

"It's not like that," Seren tries to continue her explanation but falters.

I turn to Rhys. "Did you say some dumb-ass thing to her?"

"No, he..."

I blink as a tightness forms in my chest. So much is being unspoken that I feel as if I've trespassed into a situation that doesn't concern me. All I care about is fixing the console.

No. That's not true. I care about the both of them. Maybe I look out for Seren more because she was on my squad, and she's younger, but we're all on the same team now. We all have the same mission. And even if I feel a little left out of some of this nonsense, I just want all of us to have the best life we can while we're here.

"Just tell me. If you can't work together anymore, I'll pair you up with someone else. Then no more problems, right?"

Quiet again. For the second time, my feet want to turn and walk away from the two of them. Whatever their conflict is, I don't need nor want to be a part of it.

"Don't separate us. Please?" Rhys says, a hint of despair in his voice. Seren shifts then. She glances at him and wrings her hands together as she clutches them close to her body. I don't know what that's about, but I've got a feeling. I've seen Efa give Merek that look, and I know where it leads. These two might be too young to figure each other out long-term. I'm not so concerned about that. It's what happens in the near-future that gets my stomach twisted.

Damage to *Stratford* control and communications aside, we've had it relatively easy. Plenty to eat and drink. Working showers. More medicine and supplies than we'll ever need in our lifetimes. That's why these two have found free time to be with each other, as little good as it's done them. If they can get beyond their differences, we might be okay for a while.

"Fine," I say. "Whatever. Can we just agree to push the distractions aside and get something done? How about this system over here? This is the ship's communications. If we can get it working, we'll be able to send out a distress signal. And then, if we're really lucky, another ship will receive it."

"What's the chances of that?" Seren asks.

"Hyuk if I know. But it's still more than what we've got now."

The two of them lock gazes then and even attempt to smile a little. I suppose the shrug of Rhys' shoulder is his attempt to apologize. If it is, then I'm not needed here any longer. I should go.

There are a thousand other problems on this ship that need fixing.

DISCOVERY

FANA

MY FIRST CONSCIOUS THOUGHT is that I am home, in my bed, waking up from what was likely a rough night of hard play. An invisible hand grips my intestines and twists them until they feel as if they're going to give up anything that might be inside. A sharp object pierces my skull, and the most abrasive material on Earth rubs against my throat. It's a good thing I've experienced this before.

Raey and I were notorious for our reckless evenings, drinking deep of any sensual pleasure that came our way. It didn't matter who or where. As long as we were together, we knew it was going to be a riot. Of course, that was only until it became dangerous for humans to go outside. That was when we began to build the *Devant.*

My next thought is to remember I am not home. More than likely, I am light-years away, traveling at a speed never achieved by humankind. The *Devant* is my home now and would be until my hair turns gray.

Gloved hands brush against my skin, bringing my attention back to a reality that will shortly smack me in the face.

"Easy, Fana," Raey says, rubbing her hand on my arm. "Your body's still in the process of waking up. We've still got to complete the desalinization of your bloodstream. Give it a moment, and I'll take the patches off your eyes and get you some water."

The tone of her voice is deeper now. More mature. A little husky too. I like it. Mine would be the equivalent of a frog's once they pull the tube from my throat. That has better be soon. The moment my body is aware that something is there, I will wretch hard until it's gone.

"We're going to give you a few shots," a man's voice says. "It'll help with the sickness and get your cardio-pulmonary system moving again."

Once the throat tube comes out—not without a long moment of panic when I couldn't breathe—Raey's hand slides under my back and sits me up. The process speeds up then. I get poked and prodded in a thousand ways, but before I can protest, the promised cup of water touches my lips.

"Sip slowly," Raey says. "Your stomach will want to reject it, but it'll stay down."

I do as instructed, and someone peels the patches from my eyes, but fingers press on my eyelids and hold them down. I don't think I could handle visual stimulation at the moment, anyway.

"Listen, Fana," Raey says. "The commander's ordered you to Control the moment you're on your feet. No, just hold on. Your legs won't work for a while. We may need to stimulate the muscles back into action before you get on your feet, and even then, if the head med-tech thinks you can't, we'll put you in a powered assist."

"Raey...you," I croak, "sound...sexy."

She chuckles. "You had your chance. Besides, you're too young for me now."

I cough and double over. Raey's hands are there to catch me. Her...older hands. But just how old? A shudder runs through me as I imagine what she must look like now. Wrinkles? White hair? My time in stasis wasn't supposed to be longer than fifteen years. Was I down longer?

"Let me see you," I say.

"Not yet. Your eyes aren't ready."

"Please. I want to."

Raey sighs. "Fine, but don't laugh."

Her fingers come off my eyelids. I struggle to open them with any kind of control. Light stabs my pupils, and I react, squeezing them shut again.

Eventually, I find a balance, and my eyes attune to the brightness in the room. My vision is blurry, but it doesn't stop me from searching the room for Raey.

She's there, next to me, her hand on my shoulder and a hesitant smile on her face. Her cheekbones are more prominent. Lines spread from the edge of her eyes. A hint of gray peeks from the top of her head. She might be around the age my mother was when we left. But my parents won't ever grow older than that last memory. They both died in a shuttle crash on their way up to another colony ship. Raey is the only familiar person to me now.

As I take in her matured face, a tightness forms around my heart. Time has taken my friend and turned her into someone I should speak to in honorifics. I'm torn between the awe I feel at the woman she's become and the longing to be with my friend and former lover as I remember her.

"I'm glad you're back, Fana," she says, stroking my cheek. "I've missed you."

I mash my lips together. For whatever amount of years she's been on duty, they must have been lonely.

"Don't worry," I say with a smile. "I'll have the chance to catch up to you soon."

I reach up to touch her face, but before I can, Raey stops me by catching my hand in hers.

"Not just yet," she replies, setting my hand down on my lap. "We've received a distress signal from an unknown source, more than definitely human. Commander Azazhi ordered the current crew to remain on duty until we figure out where it's coming from."

An hour later, I am in Control, staring at the aged commander as Raey holds me steady on my mobile assist device. I refused it at first but let the med techs strap my legs into it when I made a fool of myself by falling flat onto the floor and bloodying my nose as it smashed into the deck.

If time had made Raey more beautiful, it had made the *Devant's* top officer an exaggeration of himself. Wrinkles creased his face, and what remained of his hair had long turned gray. Azazhi had opted to grow a beard and had left it to its own devices—it hung down to his belly. If regulations on appearance still existed on the *Devant*, the commander had ignored all of them.

"About time, Chief," Commander Azazhi says, a bit of sarcasm in his tone. "Not sure if we could have done without you for another seventeen years. Hope you get out of that assist device soon. You're going to be very busy."

"I'm ready to work," I reply. "What's this about a distress call?"

"Yes, that." The commander strolls to a console and flicks a switch. Control is filled with the sound of a synthetic voice, repeating a standard message. "We were hoping you might tell us what it is or where it comes from."

"Attention to all ships of the commonwealth. We are in need of assistance. Focus your array on the following coordinates and transmit the standard acceptance immediately. We will reply with direction, velocity, and destination information."

I listen to the message a few times before I motion to him to turn it off. Whatever it is, and wherever it came from, it's old. I can tell by the dialect the automated voice uses. No one has spoken like that in a long time. How long is beyond my expertise, but I could care about that less than the question at the forefront of my mind.

"Where's it coming from?" I ask. "Do we have a direction?"

"That way." The commander points right down through the deck, around the thirty-degree point from the forward direction of the *Devant*. "It's getting stronger, so wherever it's coming from is on a vector that is parallel to ours, or we're getting close to the source."

"So, apologies, Commander. What do you need me for?"

I am overdue for my shift, so I'm not complaining about that, but this message is straightforward. I could be looking over what's likely to be a very long list of tasks that engineering needs to complete and hasn't yet because I wasn't on top of them to get things done.

"We need to decide whether this is a legitimate call for help or if it's just an automated call that isn't worth diverting our course for."

Of course he is putting the responsibility of this on me. Commander Azazhi may be older, but he's still the same man he always was. He's only content when he can pressure others to make the hard decisions for him. Why they've chosen me as the scapegoat this time is beyond my current brain's capacity to consider.

"Have you ever heard anything like that before?" Raey whispers into my ear.

I shake my head. But then I realize the commander is asking me a different question. We know the message is legit. We just don't know if it's worth going after.

It would be easy to remind him that regulations require us to investigate any distress signals we receive. The age of the transmission isn't a consideration. If we can receive it, it means whoever is sending it is still capable of doing so. And that's the real question.

"Commander, there should be a secondary carrier signal with data rather than audio in it. That should tell us who this is and if we should respond."

"We've received nothing additional."

"Let me check."

"Before you do, Fana, just remember we have a responsibility to the 7,652 colonists on board the *Devant* to get them to their new home. Any deviation from our path puts them at risk of never getting there."

I want to roll my eyes, but I'm feeling dizzy, and that could cause me to lose my sense of position. The assist device would hold me up, but I'd be dry heaving all over Raey as she tried to steady me.

The commander is warning me not to look too deep into this, and I get why. Still, my curiosity is stronger than any implied directive from him. His sense of duty may have softened after so long, but my life has just continued from the moment I lay down in the stasis bed. I want to know where this is coming from. And who sent it.

"We can triangulate the transmission," I say. "It'll take a bit of trickery and a few calculations, but we can do it with the multiple receiver arrays we've got. I'll only need a few minutes...and, uh, maybe a little help to sit down in front of a terminal."

Commander Azazhi inhales, then nods and motions to an open station just under the large transparent dome in the ceiling. I've always liked that feature, and now that I see it in the dimness surrounding us, the view is breathtaking. A hundred thousand stars light the blackness of space, with the occasional hint of a larger astral body filling the void. If I had the time,

I'd just stare up into the dome and take in the vastness of the beyond.

Raey takes me by the arm and leads me to the station, helping me to get into the seat. I give her my thanks, even though I'm embarrassed that she needs to help me.

As stiff as they are, my hands and fingers fly across the terminal interface, calling up the trajectory information I'm looking for. There's got to be a few nearby celestial bodies that the signal is bouncing off of. Once I understand where those are, and the angles involved, I can make my calculations.

Commander Azazhi comes to stand over my shoulder as I work, an intense reminder of his agenda. I use whatever active brainpower I have to push his face from my mind. All I want to do is find out where this message is coming from. After that, it's not my problem.

"Well?" Commander Azazhi asks.

"Hold on, I'm looking for a fourth angle."

The answer comes up faster than I expect. And it's more interesting than I ever would have guessed.

"Okay," I say. "Looks like the transmission is coming from a distance of about seven light-years away. It's just leaving the TOI-1136 system, which isn't on the list of habitable ones, but there could be a planet that's liveable there."

"But you said it's on its way out of that system. Where's it going?"

"I can find out, but I need a moment to gauge vector and velocity."

The thump in my chest grows as I tap out the new commands. There are other humans in deep space, for sure. We've always known that, but this is actual proof another ship is out there. The question now is which one is it?

Two expeditions left just before us. The *Eldridge* and the *Akbar*. They were the best that humanity could build back then. It's unlikely to be them. They move nearly as fast as the *Devant* does, so there's no chance of us catching up, even if we weren't on a completely different vector from them.

So if it's a human colony transport, it's got to be older. Maybe a lot older. Ships were leaving Earth hundreds of years ago and likely will be just hitting the middle of their journey.

A gasp pops out of my throat. We could meet people from the past. How amazing would that be?

I dig into the *Devant's* log of known expeditions, attempting to cross-reference the data I have with the destinations of each expedition. If I can gauge where they might be, based on their speed and direction, I might figure out who it is. Even if the Commander doesn't want me to.

The log takes a long time to respond. There are nearly a thousand possibilities it needs to run through. And the longer it takes, the less I expect to find anything. I might have done my calculations wrong. Maybe the transmission is from somewhere else. It could be hundreds of years old already. Our predecessors likely have solved any emergency they might've had already. Or they perished from it.

"What are you checking on?" Commander Azazhi leans in to get a better look at the screen. "You searched for a ship? That's unlikely, Chief. Let's not waste any more time on this.

Then the terminal beeps. All of us lean in to read the search results.

"But it found one," I reply, my mouth hanging open. "It's the *Stratford*."

LOSS

CERI

I REST ON THE desk in Captain Daga's former office, my back against the wall and one foot on the desktop while the other dangles off the side. Efa faces me, sitting cross-legged on the opposite side. The two of us are comfortable in our restful silence, content to spend the time doing little more than being in each other's company.

For the first time in many days, I have an hour to be idle with her. The space is only large enough for the two of us, and that's to our benefit. We can shut the doors as a message to everyone that we don't want to be bothered. After near-constant supervision of the younger crew, I needed a moment alone. Having Efa here is only an extension of that desire. She and I have spent so much time together, we are often like one.

Except for when she brings Merek into the equation.

"You want to...what?" I stare at her, my forehead getting tight.

"Have a child." Efa smiles, her cheeks turning rosy. "We'll need to ensure we have a custodial crew to care for the passengers when we're gone."

I chew on my lip as I consider. "True, but Efa...you're—"

"What? Too young? Too inexperienced?" Efa grins and leans forward, her eyebrows waggling. "Don't know how to get pregnant?"

"Keep that information to yourself," I say, feeling my face get warm. "I'm not interested. And no, that wasn't what I was going to say. Young children need attention. They need education. They need time none of us have right now. I'm too busy to look after a baby, and so are you. Even if we knew how."

Efa twists her mouth and wrinkles her nose. "If we can't maintain this ship, our families are as good as dead. You know that."

I won't stop her if she's determined. I'd have to lock her in a room on level one and Merek in machine access a hundred and twenty-three floors away if I wanted to stop any chance of it happening. But Efa is right. None of us, not even twelve-year-old Dru, will live forever.

"I'm just saying wait a few years," I say. "Once we've got things running smoothly, then you can do whatever you want. In the meantime, you better scour any working system on this ship for information about babies."

A pounding on the door makes the two of us jump. Before either of us can speak, it rips open, and Merek stands there, an intense look in his eyes. I stare back with bated breath.

"We've got a problem," Merek says. "Tal is sick. We're not sure what it is, but he's got a high fever. Sayer's trying to give him medication, but..."

"But what?"

"Better the two of you just come and see."

Efa and I share a glance. Merek wouldn't be interrupting us if it wasn't serious. I nod and motion for him to lead the way.

Tal is a former Fahrasi solider, just barely old enough to be one. He was lucky to avoid deployment to the massive battle on ninety-five that killed half of all soldiers on both sides. It was such a disaster that the chiefs of both factions came together to create a truce.

And then they ran away, taking all twelve of the *Stratford's* emergency pods to a new world that I'd found. But I'm glad the adults are gone. As much as our freedom has been a challenge, it is still far better than what we suffered under them.

Merek slides down the ladder to fifteen and darts toward the boys' quarters, C Squad's former nest. Efa is less than a second behind him, with me a distant third, already panting hard. I never recovered from my months locked away. One of these days, I'm going to remedy that.

Sayer eyes us as we enter, his face blank.

"He's getting worse," he says, glancing at the three of us. "Not sure all of us should be in here at once."

"How do you know it's contagious?" Efa asks. She looks down at Tal, moving to him, but Merek grabs her shoulder and spins her to face him.

"Efa, you wait outside," Merek says.

"What? I'm the one with the most medical training!"

"All the more reason for you not to catch whatever he has."

"Bish." Efa shakes her head and sighs. "Don't stop me. I can help him."

Their debate leaves room for me to slip in and kneel next to Tal's nest. He lies in it, mouth open and eyes unfocused. His breathing is shallow and quick. I put a wrist to his forehead—fever for sure. A bad one. My fingers find his pulse on his wrist. It's there, but it's faint. And the fact it reminds me of someone who's been wounded in battle makes my heart race.

"Did you give him anything?" I ask Sayer.

"Yes. But it hasn't helped." Sayer drops next to me. "And look at this."

Sayer lifts the bottom of the blanket covering Tal to expose the boy's feet. I gasp. His skin is purple and spotted with bumpy white patches. In a few spots, the bumps have cracked and black puss oozes out, along with a smell so putrid, it makes my stomach wretch the moment it touches my nose.

"What the hell is that?" I hiss and draw back.

"What?" Efa says, trying to push past Merek.

"No, we're leaving," Merek says and wraps his arms around her to move her out. "And the two of you should, too. We're scouring this room clean and blowing all the nests out the airlock."

Merek's statement sends a chill across the back of my neck. We've never had to do a shock sterilization before. Not even when the adults were here. Everyone knows the procedure. We've just never had to melt or incinerate any invasive microbes that were discovered.

We've neglected air filter maintenance, and I blame myself. I did as much as I could to run through all the manuals and procedures I found in Chief Generys' former office, but there are just too many for any one person to learn. And no one else had the time.

Efa wants to bring a baby into an environment like this?

"What have you given him so far?" I ask.

Sayer inhales and looks up. "Something for the fever, a shot of the antimicrobial stuff. The usual."

I bite my lower lip. "Is he in pain?"

"I don't know. He hasn't spoken in hours."

"Bish and a half. We've got to move him into medical."

"And risk contaminating that room, too?" The watery gaze he gives me matches the tightness in my gut. We need to use the diagnostic equipment—the ones we know how to use—in the med bay. But how do we justify one life over many? In times of combat, the rule was what's best for the squad is law. Sure, we broke it often, but this is different. Back then, we had the safety net of experienced medical staff to fall back on. Now it's just us.

Tal moans and gurgles. His back arches, and pain rips across his face. That's it. I can't sit here and watch this boy suffer.

"Go ahead of me," I say, leaning down to scoop Tal in my arms. "Create whatever isolation space that you can. Use one of the operating rooms if you have to."

Sayer just holds his stare. His stillness is acid in my throat. How could anyone who can match me in a fight freeze like this? I don't have time to ask. So I jab an elbow into his chest.

"Hyuking move! I am not letting him die!" I shout.

He shakes his head and pushes up. "Alright, alright! I'm go-ing! Just wait until I tell you before you bring him in."

As he races from the room, Merek and Efa fire questions at him he's got no answer to. Neither do I. That's why we need the diagnostic machines. They should help him get them ready. And quickly. Tal's body is fire in my arms.

Tal coughs, and black ooze drips from the edge of his mouth. I curse and lay him down, grabbing the corner of the blanket and wiping it off. That'll need to be incinerated, along with everything else in this room, including my uniform. I won't miss it if it helps save him.

He sputters and moans again. I'm at a loss at what to do, so I stroke his hair, as if that might help. I doubt he's even aware I'm here.

"Take it easy, kid," I say, feeling stupid for saying it. "We're going to get you to medical. It'll just be another minute."

Ten minutes later, and I'm still waiting. Tal's body is writhing. Mine is screaming to move.

With a groan, Tal's head falls to the side. Black stains his shirt, and now there are white spots on his right hand that weren't there before. I force myself to stay next to him, even as the thought of my catching whatever the hell this is sends a chill as cold as space down my spine. It's likely too late to do anything about it, but it doesn't stop me from covering my mouth and nose with a torn sheet from a nearby nest.

Two minutes more, and I'm shaking from the need to save him. This boy is dying in front of my eyes.

"Hyuk it." I pick him up, dash out of the room, and yell down the hallway, "I'm coming!"

"One more minute!" Efa replies. "We're almost ready."

But something's wrong. Tal's chest isn't moving. His body goes limp. A cry bursts from my throat.

"He's stopped breathing!" I shout as I rush into the med bay.

The three of them meet me with eyes wide. Merek pulls Efa into a side bay while Sayer motions me into the smallest of the three examination rooms. I put Tal down on the nearest table and rush to tug the nearest diagnostic machine over him.

A sickening glug, like that of stasis fluid flowing from the tube, echoes inside of Tal's body. Both of us freeze, our mouths dropping open as his arm slides off the side of the bed and hangs there.

"We need to resuscitate him!" I say. "Get the mask!"

Once again, Sayer just stares. But this time, the look in his eyes is grim as he shakes his head.

I pound a hand on the table. "We are not losing him to some hyuking infection, dammit! Move, Sayer! He's just a kid! You want him to die?"

"He's already gone," Sayer replies, his voice going soft. "There's nothing left to save."

"No! I'm not backing out like that. I'm—"

He grabs my arms and locks his gaze with mine. "Ceri, you and I need to worry about ourselves. I'm not turning into a puddle of black bish like that. We need to use the machine to check our exposure!"

"But he was still—"

"Ceri!" Sayer shakes me. "I told Merek to lock the door behind us! We're quarantined in here until we can prove we're clean. Get it?"

I stare at him, my throat getting tight. It takes a minute for my heart to stop pounding before his words hit my brain. When they do, I push him away and fall into a chair.

Poor Tal. He was barely two years out of a stasis he should have never been woken up from. Not until we reached our destination. Sayer and I, however, our years on the *Stratford* have been hell, and now this.

"I hope you've got your gun with you," I say. "We may well need it."

Sayer takes a breath. "Better pray to your Ancestors we won't."

SILENCE

FANA

COMMANDER AZAZHI STARES AT me, his face blank of understanding, so I repeat myself.

"The *Stratford*," I say.

He shrugs and shakes his head. "Is that name supposed to mean something to me? Or even you?"

I turn the terminal screen toward him so he can read it and spin in my seat to do the same. I don't know why I want him to look. Maybe it's just curiosity to see how he'll react. It certainly piqued my interest. I've never had the chance to examine the older technologies used to hurl humans as far away from Earth as possible. How they could create anything that could do it completely baffles me.

"A bard-class colony ship," the commander says, reading the screen. "This is an automated signal. We don't need to check on it." He makes a move to walk away, then something catches his eye, and he scans the data.

"What is it?" Raey asks, leaning in.

"It left seven hundred years ago with...Interesting. Their destination is Asteria."

"The same as us?" The edges of my lips curl upward. We could rendezvous with them. Possibly. They'd need to be not too far off our current trajectory, and they'd have to want us to visit. I hope we'll be able to communicate with them to arrange it. After that long, who knows what language they speak?

It doesn't matter. My heart thumps faster every time I think about meeting one of my ancestors. I'd ask them so many questions. What was life like for them on Earth? Was the sky still blue? Could they swim in the oceans? I don't know which I'd ask first, but...just imagining the possibility of it is making my breath come up short.

"Commander," I say, "I'm going to pass my triangulation coordinates to the navigation crew. Maybe we can locate this ship."

"For what purpose? I just said we don't need to check on them. They could have been sending that signal for a hundred years. More. Our help isn't required."

"Even if everything is fine, wouldn't you want to meet them? Or talk to a forgotten relative? They'll be colonists on the same planet. We could share some current tech with them, too. I bet they don't even have a gravity generator on that ship!"

His glare stops me from continuing, but I could. There are a thousand reasons to investigate a ship that old. Their custodial crew has got to be on their twenty-something-th generation. They could teach us a thing or two about long-distance space travel. And, in the chance they still need help, the *Devant* is more than capable of providing it.

"Fine." Commander Azazhi waves a hand. "You're still recovering from stasis. Take ten minutes and humor yourself. But afterward, I want you cleaned up and ready for duty. You got me?"

"Yes, Commander!" My hands are already sending the message to navigation as my acknowledgment comes out of my mouth. He turns and walks away, heading to complete whatever standard routine stuff he needs to do.

A message returns almost instantly. It's from Scan. The *Devant's* optical and infra-red sensors have already spotted it. And they've attached an image!

"Raey! Look!" I point to the object on the screen.

Raey plants her hands down on the console and leans over my shoulder to examine the picture. A tingle explodes in my ear and runs down my body from her closeness, and I remember an intimate moment long gone. The memory is welcome, and I smile as a warmth fills me. It's an added plus to this exciting moment.

"It's just a big black stick," Raey says. "Why would they build it like that?"

"Not sure. Maybe to create gravity through their inertia. Imagine that. It must have taken geniuses to figure out a system like that. At seven hundred years old, actual chemical engines could be powering that ship!"

My heart is in my throat as I imagine a conversation with their chief engineer. It'd be like getting a lesson from the godfather of ion drives. I could tell him about the working model I had made when I was a child. He'd be so impressed!

"Okay, enough play," Raey says and stands up, her hands finding my shoulders. "Let me take you to your cabin, and then I've got to get back to waking the rest of the next shift up."

"No, wait!" I tap out another message, this time to Communications. Before I have to focus on my work, I want to know if they'll reply to a query. "Just give me five more minutes."

"If the commander finds you here when he gets back, he's going to incinerate you."

"Just five minutes!"

"Do you ever stop being stubborn?" Raey sighs and squeezes my shoulders. "Fine. Have it your way. I'll be back in five."

I lick my lips and stare at the message screen, squeezing my hands into fists and hoping that the *Stratford* will be as curious about us as I am about them. We've got so much to learn from each other. It'd be stupid just to continue on our way without even a quick chat.

I'm not afraid of Commander Azazhi. And work can wait. My team may be aging by the second as they wait for me to relieve them, but days, even weeks or months, won't hurt them. The doctors made calculations for all of us on how long we can be awake and have modified our body chemistry to extend our lives a bit. No one will arrive on Asteria too old and feeble to appreciate a new world.

But as the minutes tick down, the message screen remains as it was since I made my request.

And Raey, as punctual as she has always been, returns nearly to the second the timer clicks down to five minutes. As I hear the gentle clip of her deck shoes echoing in the corridor, I accept my unwillingness to step away from this. The *Stratford* is far too important to only give it five minutes of our attention.

Raey won't let me stay. She hasn't released me into full duty yet, and even though I'm third down in the chain of command, my rank means nothing while I'm still under her care. She has the authority to stuff me back into a stasis pod if she wants to.

I rack my brain, trying to come up with a reason or a plan before she comes around the corner. Too late. There's her leg, and then her smile, as her eyes connect with mine. But only until she realizes I'm up to something. Then she presses her lips together and lowers her eyes at me, ready to lecture me on my failure to act appropriately to my position.

I've got to make a move.

"Commander!" I shout, risking the chance I annoy him too. "Come here, please!"

"Fana." Raey puts her hands on her hips. "Knock it off. I may have gotten older, but you're still the same, and I haven't forgotten about your tricks."

"Commander Azazhi!"

"What do you want, Fana?" The commander stomps through the door from his office with narrowed eyes.

Raey mutters a few choice curses and shakes her head. If she was mad enough to say it, she'd be telling me this kind of behavior is why she broke it off with me.

"Sorry, Commander. I just think we need to investigate the *Stratford* more, and I wanted your permission to—"

"Yeah, okay." He waves his hand at me again, dismissing my concerns as if I was a child rather than the person responsible for all the systems on this ship that keep us moving and alive. "Tell Scan to take some images and run them through the spectrograph. Are you headed back to engineering now?"

I swallow. I'm going to press my luck here, and if I fail, it's going to be some time before the two of them forget why they're annoyed with me.

"In a moment. Scan has already sent back images. I was thinking something more direct."

"Yeah?" He crosses his arms. "What did you have in mind?"

"So, they're only seven light-years away. Their destination is the same as ours, and..." I hold up a hand to stop him from commenting. "They're on a completely different trajectory. Why?"

Commander Azazhi considers for a second, then shrugs. "Bad computations? Who cares?"

"Well, assuming everything is fine onboard the *Stratford*, what if they know something we don't? They've been out here for seven centuries, and that entire time, they've only had one celestial object in their sights. They've got to have a ridiculous amount of data on Asteria."

"Oh, hell, Fana," Raey hisses and rolls her eyes.

"That's quite the conclusion jump, Chief," Azazhi says. "Have you even considered how much fuel we'd use getting over to them?"

"No, but honestly, it can't be much. We're moving so fast, all we'd really need to do is tap the maneuvering jets, and we'd be on a direct intercept. It'd take less than a month to rendezvous with them."

"Let's just call them," Raey suggests, to my irritation. "Then we'd know for sure if they were in trouble, and it'd save us the time needed to recalibrate our trajectory. Not to mention our crew, who are all eager to get into their stasis pods."

"We called them already," I shoot back. "They didn't reply."

The commander's eyes dart between the two of us as he evaluates my proposal and Raey's counter to it. He's well aware of our past relationship, and even though both of us swore it would never compromise our actions or decisions as officers of the *Devant*, Azazhi is likely including it in his calculations. I need to show that I'm mission-focused the whole way.

"Commander, the regulations state—" I start.

"Don't go there, Chief Neridi," he replies, his voice snapping back to its strict cadence. "Your expertise in the standard regulation book is about as good as my knowledge of our unified field drive. And there's no point in those regs anymore. Our mission is to get to Asteria and nothing else. You can bet all the expeditions are thinking the same way. It's every ship for themselves out here. So for the next three hundred years, I'm the ultimate authority in what we do."

I dip my head. I should have chosen a better tact. Something that I actually know how to talk about.

"Now if you have nothing else," he continues, "Raey is right. We've got to get the crew into stasis, or they're all going to look like me soon."

Panic runs through me as I glance back at the screen, scouring the information there for something—anything—that will delay the crew changeover. The number of people on my shift is half that of the commander's and Raey's. There'd never be enough personnel to get it done.

"Just one more thing, Commander," I say. "The *Stratford* is carrying three times the amount of excavation equipment we are."

"How do you know that?" Raey blinks, then peers at the screen, searching for the information. It's not there. I'm just making a guess based on what I read and hoping I'm right.

"Bard-class ships were the vanguard of their fleet. Their crew and passengers would be the ones to build the colony, so they'd be loaded with machines. And if I'm not mistaken, we pulled some of our units out of the cargo hold to make way for the extra load of passengers and all the additional stasis pods, didn't we?"

"So." Commander Azazhi sniffs and runs a finger down his beard. "You're suggesting that we rendezvous with the *Stratford* on the pretense of replying to their distress call, make sure everything is okay, then ask them to give us their excavation equipment?"

I nod.

"Well, as you just pointed out, Fana, we don't have the space for it, so there goes your idea."

"We do a swap," I reply. "Their excavation equipment for our surplus of pods. We could even ask for volunteers to go over there, set them up, and stay there to get them up to speed with all the new technologies we've got."

"You are completely out of your mind," Raey says. "I should have done a brain scan on you."

The commander snorts, and my shoulders droop. Leave it up to her to tear the last life remaining in my idea. It was farfetched, I'll admit. Ah, well. Time to get to work.

But as Commander Azazhi considers it, his eyes light up.

"Our chief is sometimes a little questionable, Raey. I agree," he says. "But she might be onto something here. More excavation machinery gets the colony up and running faster, and fewer mouths to feed means lower risks during our founding. I bet some would be delighted to have the option to switch. Not all our passengers are cut out for the strain of building our new home."

"So you're going to just push them off on another ship?" Raey gawks.

"As I was just saying, we have one mission. Anything we can do to ensure it happens is acceptable in my mind."

As Raey smolders, a renewed rush of energy surges through me. I should get rid of the mobile assist device now. It'd just impede the hundreds of micro tasks that I am mentally assigning myself.

Then Commander Azazhi turns to me.

"Alright, Fana. I'm game. We'll change course to intercept." He lifts a finger and points to the door. "Now both of you have a lot of work to do. Raey, you'll need to poll the crew before you put any of them under. And Chief, I want to know for an absolute certainty that what we're going to divert for will be worth it."

"Of course, Commander." I smirk, attempting to hide my hard gulp. "I guarantee it will."

DENIAL

CERI

Yesterday, I was sharing the top of a desk with Efa. Today, I am sharing a room with Sayer. The difference is that she and I enjoy each other's company, while my current roommate and I could think of many other things we'd rather be doing. All we have are beds to lie in and each other to stare at.

At least they took Tal away. I shudder at the image of his lifeless body slowly decaying not two paces away from me. Forget the fear of contagion. What would crush me would be to see him lying there while I wondered if I could have done anything differently. If I had known of his illness a day, or even an hour, before, then maybe we could have saved him.

"I need to get out of here," I say and lower my gaze at Sayer. "No offense, but this room doesn't bring me fond memories. And it smells like...death."

"Not everything bad happened in here." Sayer lifts a finger and points it at me. "And don't tell me you're not blaming yourself for everything that did, because I can see it in your eyes."

"So, are you supposed to be my best friend now?"

Sayer makes a rude noise with his lips. "We've saved each other's lives more than a few times. Doesn't that count toward something?"

I look away and make myself busy, covering my legs with the sheet. It's not that I dislike him. Being locked up in here is bringing up memories I'd soon just forget.

"Hey." He leans forward to get my attention. "We're all we have. If that doesn't make us friends, then what are we? Family?"

A hard snort comes from me. But Sayer is right. Squads were like family. We looked after each other as brothers and sisters would. We embarrassed each other like siblings did. And some of us acted as parents to the junior squad members—all while our actual blood relations slept in stasis.

I open my mouth to reply, but before I can answer, Efa knocks on the large window, which covers most of the front wall. She's covered in a full-body isolation suit, one that offers the highest level of safety this side of an airlock. I only feel bad for her need to wear it for a few seconds. After that, my excitement for nourishment overwhelms any guilt.

"Mealtime," Efa chimes as she opens the door and brings in a tray with four green boxes on it. Adult food. The stuff inside may not look like anything I remember from Earth, but it certainly tastes like it. The gray slop the adults forced us to eat had the taste and consistency of carbon fiber. I'd slurp it down anyway, as it could have been the only chance to put food in our stomachs that day.

This is an unexpected pleasure, and I smile as she puts the tray down on a table near me. Then I spot a small cup with a dome of brown in it and my mouth really waters. Ice cream. This must be a peace offering for making us wait in here. I accept.

"Proper nutrition first," Efa says with a waggle of her finger.

"But it'll melt!" I counter, snatching up the cup. With a smile, I lean my head back, open my mouth, and drop the singular scoop into it. Even though I have open access to this sweet delight now, I would have raided the Fahrasi headquarters had I known about it before. Merek may sometimes irritate me with his overprotectiveness of Efa, but I'm truly thankful to him for introducing ice cream to me.

The cold creaminess fills my mouth. The lush texture, mixed with the sweetness and the bitterness of what I'm told is called chocolate, touches every taste bud. I swirl it around with my tongue as it melts, letting the liquid drip down my throat as I close my eyes and let out a contented sigh. It is pure refreshment, unlike anything I have ever had before, save for my prior indulgences.

"What an exaggeration," Sayer mumbles and reaches over to grab a box. "That stuff was good, but it was never that good."

"Try never having it for nineteen years," I shoot back, then turn to Efa. "Thank you, but are you trying to soften the blow of something you need to tell us?"

Her shoulders drop, and she looks down. The pleasure I just felt hardens in my stomach as if the cream had frozen again. If she tells me I've tested positive, I'm busting out this cell. I won't be locked up anymore. Not after the adults put me in that closet for so long. My hands get shaky just thinking about it.

"There's another who's taken ill," Efa says. "Elis. We're keeping him in a storage room on six, which is near the Fahrasi medical space."

"Why not bring him in here?" Sayer asks as he licks his fingers. I throw him a glare. Only Efa catches it.

"In case we're not infected," I reply. He looks up then, his eyebrows going up as he catches my intensity. Then I turn back to Efa. "Which would be nice to know soon, yeah?"

Efa sucks in her cheek. "Yeah, about that..."

"Oh, hell, no!" The air goes out of my lungs. I grab the bed's railing and rattle it. Efa's eyes widen as she leans back.

But when understanding hits her, she shakes her head. "No! The test we did was inconclusive. Maybe we did it wrong."

"Then do it again!" My hand makes a deep thud as it pounds on the mattress.

"I'm sorry for keeping you in here for so long, but another test is going to take time. There are no instructions on how to do this right. And I'll likely need more blood from the both of you."

"Well, I don't feel sick." I throw the sheet aside and slide off the bed. It's not a valid argument, but my mood makes me want to behave like a six-year-old. "And I'd like to be out of here as soon as possible."

"Be patient. Maybe one more day." She attempts a sympathetic smile. "It'll get done."

"You and Merek can't handle everything by yourselves."

"Niah will help."

I tighten my jaw, not wanting to say the truth nobody wants to hear. Niah is more comfortable on her own than she is with us. She was never an adult, but she's not a child either, and none of us have any idea how to make her feel more welcome and accepted than we've done already. It's only because I've spent the most time with her I see what's happening. If there was a way off the *Stratford*, she'd take it.

"Just bring us anything you can't do," Sayer suggests. I roll my eyes. He's trying to help, but I won't remind him how infections work. He should know. Other than battle medicine, infection control was the other health-related thing the adults drilled into us. Especially the boys. Girls didn't think every dark corner on a lower level was a toilet.

Efa cants her head as she looks at him, trying to not to react. We both know Sayer won't get it. Instead, she sighs and looks at me for help. When I just stare back, she only does the same until she can't handle it any longer.

"I need to get back," she says. "Tegan's got her hands full."

I nod and drop my gaze to my hands as she closes the door behind her. There's nothing she can do or say that will ease my desperation to get out of here. As problems increase out there, Sayer and I will have to find patience somewhere.

Sayer grabs his second meal box and falls back into his bed to stuff his mouth. I pace the open space in the room instead, which is little more than three paces forward and back. After a few repetitions, I grow irritated and scan the room for a way to release my frustrations. Exercise might help.

But when I attempt to make enough floor space to do push-ups, I find don't even have that. I grab at the door frame, thinking it would work for pull-ups—not a chance. Something heavy enough to use as dead weights? Not that either. I end up just wrenching my hands around the bed rail again and use that as something equivalent to an exercise, even though there's not enough space to make it effective.

And all my efforts do is wind me up more.

"You're going to drive yourself crazy," Sayer says, then mutters, "if you haven't already."

"You don't know what it was like, being locked up like that." I push up from the rail, increasing my repetitions as I brace my feet on the bottom edge of a cabinet. "I felt like I couldn't breathe half the time."

"Well, you're breathing fine now, so just relax."

My heart thumps as my pulse speeds up. I jerk myself down on the rail, then shove back. Faster. And again. I'm trying to focus on the blankness of the white sheet in front of me, but my eyes go blurry. I grit my teeth and move faster. The rail shudders under my force. I press so hard the bed slides into Sayer's with a thump, the rails clanging together.

"Ceri! Cool it!"

He's up on his bed now, kneeling. My head is pounding in time with my pulse. My chest gets tight. I fight to get air. I don't know if it's just a mental reaction or not. My skin is on fire. My lungs burn. I've got to get out of here. I need to be free. If I don't, I'm going to—

"Hey!" Sayer shouts.

I release the rail and fly back, slamming into the cabinet. We stare at each other as I force air into my lungs. Sayer's jaw is slack, and for a moment, I think he may actually be worried about me.

I'm not waiting around to find out.

"Hyuk this," I say, pushing off the cabinet and heading toward the door. "I'm getting out of here."

"You know you can't." To his credit, his tone remains low and steady. He's talked Merek down once or twice when he was about to do something stupid. Maybe he thinks he can do the same with me.

I grab the door handle and jiggle it to test its strength. Like most things on the *Stratford*, it's built to survive a thousand-year journey. Even at my peak strength, I wouldn't be able to knock it down. Sayer likely could, but he won't.

He hops off his bed and approaches. I flash him a warning. It stops him, if only momentarily. Long enough for me to look for another option.

The window.

It's large enough for me to get through, and even though it's reinforced with thin metal wire, I might still be able to smash my way through it with something heavy.

I rip open a drawer. Only a few medical tools and some bandages. The one below has vials of medicine. The third, still nothing. How about the entire cabinet, then? I size it up to see if I could lift it—unlikely. What else?

"What are you doing?" Sayer demands.

Yes. The scale. I grab it and rip it from its base. It's weighty, alright. Perfect.

"Ceri, no!" Sayer grabs my wrist. I spin and jam the device into his chest. He stumbles back. I turn, take two steps, and hurl the scale into the window.

It hits with a resonant thump. The composite of the window cracks but stays intact.

Sayer is on me then. He gets under my right arm and locks it back. I twist and shove at him, but he's got me in an awkward position. I can't get any force behind my thrust. He turns, bringing me down to the floor.

"Hyuking cut it out!" he yells.

My hand grabs his ankle, and I yank him off balance. Sayer topples in between the bed and the side cabinet, releasing me to protect his head with his arms. I spring up and dart over to the scale to grab it and force my escape.

Whatever fight I have left in me goes into pounding the window over and over. Sayer's up behind me, but it's too late. With one last hit, the window crumbles and the wire bends under the beating I gave it.

"Ceri, don't!" Sayer cries. "You'll kill us all!"

That stops me. A vision of Tal's body flashes through my mind, and I imagine everyone that way. Efa. Merek. Seren. Tegan. Even Sayer, who is doing his best to end my madness.

Efa returns, freezing the moment she notices the window. She takes in the scene, blinking as she looks from me to Sayer and then at the window again.

"Stay back!" Sayer warns.

"What the hell?" Efa shouts.

"Talk her down, Efa! She's putting everyone at risk!"

She catches my eyes, a mix of concern and anger in her gaze. Heat comes to my face then, and I get a sudden urge to drop my eyes to the floor. I've been a real bish-head.

"I'm sorry," I say as I drop into a crouch and hug my arms about me. "I just couldn't take it."

Efa sighs. "Well, other than the busted window, there's no real danger. We figured out our issue with the test. Both of you are clean."

Sayer grabs my arm and yanks me up and around so he can look at me. His eyes are incendiary as he shakes his fist in my face. I tense, expecting an attack, but he holds back. I watch and wait. Whatever he wants to say, I likely deserve.

"You are hyuking insane," he hisses. "We need to have a talk. The four of us."

Efa huffs. I nod. We probably needed to even before this. And now we will.

RISK

CERI

I WIPE THE SWEAT from my forehead as I take a moment between rounds to catch my breath. The cartons of freeze-dried meals are heavier than I expected. But this is good. This is what I wanted—to be doing manual labor, down here on level one-thirty-one, to rebuild my muscle strength.

And to be alone.

After my hysteria up on fourteen, everyone, save Sayer, gave me a lot of space. Even Efa made excuses to be with Merek, as if she needed them. The message was clear. I am a live grenade that no one wants to handle. Not until they've figured out what to do with me.

I suppose I see what Niah finds appealing in this solitary work. We keep the lower levels dark, so they remain cool, and by some unfounded fear the light would wake everyone in stasis. But there are no pods here. This level is all storage. Stacks of crates and boxes, piles of sacks and packages, arranged in logical order, giving the floor an urban sprawl. Lanes are broad boulevards crisscrossing the building like pallets of supplies. It's my micro city, and I am enjoying being its mayor.

With a smirk, I squat down and lift three sacks onto my shoulder. I'll do three sets of squats with them and then move them into the automated rail car to send up to our living spaces. I won't be going with them. At least not for now.

My legs burn as I raise up to complete the last round. Fire fills my lungs, a reminder of just how out of shape I am. It's my fault, just like that smashed window in medical. In my push to get things moving and to look out for the younger crew, I've neglected myself. I had to. It was the only way to get work done. Though now we've established a routine, I have more time to live with my thoughts. I wish I didn't. The horrors that come into my head are better off buried.

I grunt as I re-balance the load on my shoulder and move to the rail car doors, reaching out for the call button to open them. When they don't, I frown, then notice the light's remained on. Someone called it to another level, which means they might come down here and ruin my time of self-reflection.

When the car stops at my level, I step back and tense. It's a reflex, hard learned and long ingrained into my psyche. No solider would be stupid enough to stand directly in front of an opening door. That is a guaranteed way to die.

"Ceri," Efa says with a small smile, until she gives me a once-over. I know I'm sweaty. I must be filthy too. Dust and grime pile up on a ship after hundreds of years. Especially when there is no one to clean it away.

I nod, but the tight-lipped look on Sayer's face stops me from smiling. Merek is also with them, which means the conversation they were demanding to have with me is about to happen.

The sacks come off my shoulder, and I toss them into the rail car in front of Sayer's feet. He glances down at them as they thump on the floor, then hurls a glare at me. I return it and Sayer huffs. He's received my message.

"Uh, yeah," Merek says, stepping from the car. "We heard you were down here. Can we talk to you?"

"Do I have a choice?"

"Ceri, it's not like that," Efa pleads. I'm glad I'm not the only one that wants to avoid the argument that's coming.

"You come down here with superior numbers and expect me to believe that?" I cross my arms and scan each of their faces, watching for their response.

"Hey, come on." Efa rests her hand on my arm and looks at me with earnest eyes. "This isn't a squad intervention. We're not even a squad anymore."

"And we're not soldiers anymore," Merek adds, stepping out of the way so Sayer can exit the rail car. "So there's no need for one."

"We just want to talk because we're worried about you," Efa says, rubbing my arm.

"That is exactly how a squad intervention starts." I pull away and head back to the pallet to pick up another three sacks. As I make my return to drop them in the car, I catch Merek shift and purse his lips. Efa looks to him, lost.

Perhaps I'm reacting too hard. My defenses went up the moment I saw the three of them. They do care for me. I shouldn't be questioning their motives for wanting to talk.

But before I can offer an apology, Sayer blocks my path.

"Maybe it should be an intervention," he says. "Since all you seem to remember is how to be a hard-ass."

"Sayer, come on," Efa pleads.

"No." He thrusts a finger in my face and grits his teeth. "You are out of control, Ceri, and you're a danger to everyone. We were lucky an infection didn't hit us this time. But with the way you reacted, I know you're going to hurt someone, and I won't stand around and let that happen."

My cheeks are getting hot, and the tension in my body is pushing me to consider aggressive action. It's a good thing none of us carry guns any longer. If Sayer keeps this bish up, mine would already be out of its holster, and it might not go back until I used it.

I exhale and move past him to drop off my load. Better to focus on moving supplies than to open my mouth and say something I'll regret. This is why I came down here. I needed to clear my head. Only then could we have a realistic discussion about what's happened. The way things are, I'm ready to punch him in the face.

"Aren't you being a little harsh?" Merek challenges Sayer.

"You weren't there," Sayer replies and points at Efa. "Did she tell you why Ceri smashed the window?"

Efa ducks her head, but Merek consoles her with an arm around her shoulders.

"She did," Merek says. "And I can't blame Ceri. She's been under a lot of stress. That's why we're here, isn't it? To help take some of the pressure off her?"

I stop and turn to face Merek, feeling my eyebrow raise. He might not be in my face with accusations, but what he's suggesting isn't far off from what Sayer just said. What expectation they have of me, I don't know. I thought we were all in this together.

"Let's just try to make a few decisions together," Efa offers. "That might help."

"What decisions?" My fists are tightening. I better keep to my work.

"Sayer's suggesting we turn off the emergency beacon," Merek replies. "At least until we figure out how to control this virus."

"I'm not suggesting," Sayer corrects. "We go dark until we get it, and her, under control. We're a danger to anyone who contacts us otherwise."

I spin on him. "How is that my fault?"

"You broke quarantine! Literally! You smashed a window because you freaked out!"

I back away, inhaling slowly before I pound his face. They're getting on me for breaking down under pressure when it would have happened to any of them. The beacon is just an excuse to take control. I'm not so sure I care. Merek is right. All of this has put more pressure on me than I ever had as squad leader. And I'm not even in charge. I'm not sure I'd want to be if they begged.

"Whatever." I throw up a hand and turn to enter the rail car. "If you want to decide things without me, go ahead. You could have saved yourselves a trip and had that conversation up on fourteen."

"Ceri, no!" Efa pushes herself into me and blocks my exit. "We're not trying to do that at all! This is bigger than any of us. That's why we have to talk it through together."

Efa doesn't realize it, but her arms are up against me in a standard grapple. If I tried to move around her, she could put me on the ground in an instant. So much for doing things together.

"This is some serious bish," Merek says, leaning on the edge of a tall crate. "None of us should choose what to do by ourselves, but honestly, Ceri, if anyone could, it's you. You're the one who got us here."

"Yeah, and now you're wishing you weren't, right?"

"No!" Merek slaps the crate, then takes a breath and a moment to calm himself. "No. We want to be here. With you. With our passengers. And our crew. There's no doubt in my mind about that."

"Mine either," Efa says. Her arms slide down, and she takes my hands with a smile. "And you need to know, Ceri, how grateful we are to you. For everything."

I fight a sniffle as I squeeze her hands back. This would be the worst time for tears, yet I always seem to be extra vulnerable where it involves Efa. She always knows how to pull my emotions out of me, whether it's deliberate or not. Maybe it's because our feelings for each other run deeper than any family members' ever would. Efa has saved my life a hundred times.

And I have done the same—would do the same—a hundred more.

"Alright, enough," Sayer growls. "Sure, she did a lot of good bish for us. But that was before. Now it's all our asses on the line. And anyone else's that decides we're pathetic enough to answer our call. We can't ask them to help us if all we're going to do is make them sick."

"But whomever they are," Merek counters, "they might be better equipped to stop this infection before it...before it gets really bad."

Sayer shakes his head. "I'm telling you that's wrong. We've got no control over this. And no guarantee anyone else would, either. It's not like another expedition would get to us, anyway. If there are other ships out there, they're a thousand light-years away. We're on our own, just like always."

I won't say it, but he's right. No one's coming to our rescue. The beacon is just there to give us some kind of hope, even if it's false. Without it, we'd tear each other to pieces. Like the adults did. We'd start disagreeing over the smallest things. And if that gets violent, we're more than capable of killing each other.

And we would.

"What do you want to do, Ceri?" Efa asks.

"Leave it on," I say. "If no one's coming, there's no harm in it."

Sayer steps back, his face intense as he attempts to reassess a thing he didn't consider.

"No...no," he says. "We're turning it off!"

"If we're following the plan you created, you don't get to decide that for yourself." I turn to Merek. "What do you want to do?"

Merek glances at Efa and mashes his lips together. Now he doesn't need to say anything at all. If he's worried about disagreeing with her, I already know what his answer is, because I already know what she'll say. Efa will support my decision, just as she always has.

"I...uh...agree with Sayer," he says. "We don't know just how serious our situation is yet, and even though we could really use some medical support from another ship, I think it's just too risky. Better we try to solve this on our own."

"Okay," Efa says. "If that's what you think is best."

I blink, looking between them. Did she just give in to him so easily? Is Efa so attached to Merek now she can't make her own decisions? This is more wrong than I can even say. But I'm going to try.

"No, Efa," I say. "That's not what you want."

Efa frowns. "What do you mean?"

I wave my hand at her. "Stop joking. You want to keep the beacon on!"

"No, I don't."

"Bish and a half!" I throw my hands up. "Why are you so willing to give in?"

Efa only shies away from me. And after she put herself in my way to keep me down here. It's clear that I've got no idea how a relationship works, unless it means one person just forgets their option to appease the other. If that's the case, then I hope I never have one.

"Well, that settles it," Sayer says, heading to the rail car. "Majority wins, and we're shutting it off."

No. That doesn't settle it. But as when they came down, I'm outnumbered, and I won't win if I fight. At least not now.

CHOICE

— · —

FANA

MY LUNGS ARE TIGHT. My body tenses. I can't believe I'm seeing this with little more than my eyes. To have an optical sight on a seven-hundred-year-old-ship is simply...breathtaking. The *Stratford's* streamlined and lengthy black hull is a complete departure from the *Devant's* bumpy oval design. To me, it doesn't look dated at all. It looks alien, and I can't stop thinking about it.

Which is why, after fifteen days of speedy travel, a continuous period of rest evades me. Raey's given me medication to help me sleep, but unless she wants to tranquilize me like an animal, I remain awake and edgy through every third shift.

It matters little. Time is relative and has no real meaning for those in transit. There is no reason to enjoy the trip, anyway. It's all the same: this many set hours of work, this many set hours of break, this many set hours to put nutrients into our bodies and a small number more for recreation. Except I spend most hours scouring the database for information on the *Stratford*, all the while pushing navigation to give me time on the scope, so I can lay my eyes on my current infatuation.

That is what I am up to now, squeezed into the *Devant*'s optics control room, annoying the piss out of the junior officer in charge of it and stealing as much of her hydration and nourishment as she's tolerant of. I may not be able to sleep, but I'm more ravenous than ever. It could just be my ovulation cycle, but I expect not. My hunger is to see that ship.

"Did you get the images you wanted?" the junior officer asks, trying to be polite. She already has one foot out the door, and a quick glance at the clock on the wall shows its nearly the end of her shift.

"We're about to be within an astronomical unit of it. Don't you want to see it?"

Her forehead goes tight. "Not really."

"This ship could have your ancestors on it! Wouldn't you want to meet them?"

The officer does her best to stop her eyes from rolling, but her opinion is clear. I can't really blame her. By the time we had left, we had already said goodbye to our friends and family, and even though our destinations were the same, most of us expected never to see them again. It was better to put our loved ones out of our heads so we could focus on getting the *Devant* moving. It wasn't good to dwell on people who were already gone.

"Listen, I know you need to go," I say. "I promise not to break anything. And I'll find a way to pay you back for your, er, generosity."

"Oh?" The officer perks up. "Have something of value to trade?"

I shrug. "Maybe?"

Before she can reply, a tech comes in, his eyes darting between the two of us.

"Which one of you is Chief Neridi?" he asks the officer.

"Do I look like a chief to you, bumble brain?" She doesn't wait for his answer. With a quick glare at me and a two-fingered motion at the boy, she stomps off, leaving the two of us alone.

"Where are you from?" I ask.

He goes blank for a moment before answering, "Communications."

"What can I do for you, then?"

A pause. Then, "The commander told me to come here and tell you something."

I stare at him, waiting for the message for about ten seconds before I get fed up.

"So? What's the message?"

"We've lost contact with that legacy ship. Their emergency beacon's cut off."

When I start swearing enough to cover the entire crew for a year, the tech claps his hands over his ears. It's enough to make me stop. Not all of us were spacers before this. Some are just a little more sensitive to rough words than others. I'll have to remember that.

But first, I need an explanation. His news is too vague for my liking.

"Is that it?" I ask. "What else you got?"

"I have nothing else. My chief couldn't explain it, and neither could the senior techs. I'm sorry, but that's it."

I press my lips together, considering the next step as I take notice of the stasis rings around his eyes. He's been awake less than a week, and by my guess of his age, this is likely the first time. He'll have that spacey look for another five days, and his brain will be mush for two more after that. Which means he's little help to me.

"Alright." I get up and take him by the arm. "Let's go talk to the commander."

We find the boss man right where I'd expect him to be: in command and control, managing the crew there by watching them over their shoulders and terrifying them into a high level of productivity. I put myself at risk of a similar torment, being this close to his prowling grounds, though my place of work on shift is a far walk from here, and I'm glad about it. The commander seldom comes down to engineering.

"I can bet I know why you're here, mistreating Specialist Abbas like that," Azazhi says. "Unhand my subordinate, would you?"

With a smirk, I pat the boy on the shoulder and give him a gentle push. He skitters away, likely looking for a terminal to lose his head in. Not that it'd take much.

"I can't provide any more detail on the lost signal from the *Stratford*, if that's what you're about to ask. We've done diagnostics on every receiver. Twice. Our systems are all working well. Which means either the *Stratford* has turned off their transmission, or they've had an equipment failure."

"We're within an AU of them now. Maybe they turned it off because they're aware of us. Have we tried a direct link?"

"Chief, a ship that old likely has nothing more than the RF communications we've been receiving."

I wrinkle my nose. What an idiot I am. I should have realized that. It's only been a hundred years since we discovered we could send a signal through warped space. There's just five ships that have the technology, including the *Devant*, and those ships don't need to talk to us.

"What about—"

Commander Azazhi holds up a hand. "Before you start making suggestions I can't answer, let's get Chief Jawsana, and the two of you can swap tech talk."

I'm wary of the fact he didn't include himself in the conversation. But Katari Jawsana has every bit of my respect. He's sharp and knows almost as much about the *Devant* as I do. With his expertise, we'll figure out how to talk to the *Stratford*.

"Chief Neridi, good to see you out of stasis," he says as I knock on the wall of his comm room. "Still got the twitch?"

My forehead wrinkles. "No. Do I look that bad?"

"Sorry, I thought—"

"Fana's been out about two and a half weeks," Commander Azazhi explains, then eyes me. "Though I suspect she's not doing her regulation sleep shift, as is *required*."

Chief Jawsana grins as he watches me. "I bet I know why that is. But really, you can get rest now. In another day, we'll be alongside the *Stratford*, thanks to you."

"But we can't talk to them!"

The chief shrugs. "It's likely no big deal. Once we're in their visual range, they'll reach out. And trust me, Chief. The moment we get their call, I'll let you know, alright?"

I get that no one else is as over the top excited about this as I am. Everyone wants to help a ship in distress, certainly. But for them, it's just an inconvenience to be handled, and then that's it. Chief Jawsana doesn't know about the commander's plan to clear some space for the *Stratford's* excavation equipment. Maybe he should. It may motivate him more if he was aware of the commander's agenda. I couldn't care less about it myself, other than how it currently coincides with mine.

"What if we can't get a hold of someone over there?" I ask, somewhat thinking out loud.

"We'll just knock on their door," Commander Azazhi says with a smile.

Jerk. He's just joking. It makes my ears burn. There's a serious lack of consideration going on here, and it's not just for me and my interests. The *Stratford* could be in big trouble, and he's treating it like all they are is a minor curiosity.

"Well, Commander," I say, giving him as much seriousness as I can, "if we're going to do that, I volunteer to be part of the first team to go over there. If something's broken, I can offer expertise and tools that they won't have. I'll get them up and running before you can even get the pods out of the cargo hatch. We'll be on our way in only a full shift rotation."

Chief Jawsana frowns as he continues to use his tongue to search for something in the side of his mouth. The commander's reaction is more of what I was expecting. He crosses his arms and gives me a look of disapproval.

"Fana, I can appreciate your zeal for this, but you're the chief engineer of this ship and an extremely valuable member of this crew. It's common logic to say that officers like you or Chief Jawsana don't go on excursions. And we definitely don't visit ancient wrecks like the *Stratford*. So, whether you were joking or otherwise, just know my official position is that I'm denying your request."

I tighten my jaw to stop the chuckle from coming out. Now that I've said it, I realize I've got to go. Any hint from me I wasn't being serious, and he'd never give me permission.

"Commander, I understand your point." He smiles, then sets his jaw when he sees I'm about to continue. "However, no ship, no matter how old, makes a request for help if they weren't in serious trouble. As to how valuable I am, well, I appreciate you saying that, but if the last seventeen years of smooth travel isn't proof that my team is more than capable of doing anything I can, then I've already failed at my job, and you should just throw me back in stasis."

The commander's eyes grow large and intense. Chief Jawsana turns away to hide whatever reaction he's having. That's appreciated, since I don't need both of them arguing against me.

"Fana, your humility is not appreciated or welcome in this situation." Commander Azazhi's finger comes thrusting out at me. "You have a duty to this ship, and you don't get to simply walk away from that because you want to go play. Now, are you going to follow orders, or am I going to confine you to quarters?"

If my fellow chief had any level of interest in supporting me, he'd be giving me not-so-subtle clues about shutting up. Or he may know I don't need them. I've pushed this as far as I can go with the commander, anyway.

I sigh. "No, Commander. That's unnecessary. I know my responsibilities. Don't worry about me making sure the *Devant* is in perfect working condition."

"Good." He nods. "I know I can count on you, Fana. Now, why don't you try to get some rest before your work shift starts?"

"Good idea. Thank you, Commander."

He offers an upward curl of the side of his mouth and motions that I'm dismissed. Chief Jawsana looks up then and offers his silent approval of my choice. I give him a tight-lipped smile back and turn to leave.

Sure, both of them are seventeen years older and more experienced than when we departed, but I'd expect that'd make them more open-minded. Instead, it's turned them into old men who look at me like a child when I'm just the same person who'd launched with them all those years ago.

And it's their fault if they can't see through my fake compliance. The moment we match the *Stratford*'s velocity, I'm heading over there. And they won't know I did it until I return.

DISOBEDIANCE

FANA

I STARE AT THE black mass of the *Stratford*, a mere excursion line's distance away, and my heart stops for an entire second. Maybe more. At least it feels as if it does. I'm not sure if I'm still breathing. I can't feel my body anymore. Only my consciousness exists, and it's screaming to return to a safe place.

What the hell did I talk myself into?

They did as much as they could to familiarize us with the vastness of extra-atmospheric work, but that was when the Earth, along with the nearby station, took up a large part of our view. The all-enveloping darkness I see before me isn't something I want to remember in my dreams. It's not anything I want to remember ever.

Three seconds ago, the airlock hatch had yet to be opened, and I was shaking then. I checked my pressure suit three times, starting with the seal on my helmet, then the oxygen and re-breather system. Then the locks on my gloves. And just like five seconds before, when I had checked everything the second time, all signals were green.

There are plenty of legitimate reasons to never attempt solo space travel. I'm experiencing one of them right now. If I panic out there, there's no one to save me. Yet here I am, doing exactly what I shouldn't be, all because Commander Azazhi forbade me to do it.

I'm glad the beauty of *Stratford* helps to ease my fear, at least. The images in the archive don't come close to what my eyes take in. Space dust and micro-radiation have spent hundreds of years scraping up against its semi-illuminated hull, bringing the black skin to a cloudy luster. What was once matte in appearance is now shiny, like polished onyx—deep and sensuous. I almost blush from taking such a long gander.

It's also longer by half than the *Devant*, though much thinner through its entire length, with the aft being the largest in width. And that violet glow from the engines brings a smile to my face. I can't wait to get my hands on its equipment. If I was still dating Raey, I would feel bad for cheating.

I put my foot on the airlock's frame, taking a few deep breaths as I prepare to launch myself across. My target is the nearest hatch, marked by an obvious yellow outline and a pair of steady blue lights. We've matched our speed with the *Stratford*, and while I'm not an expert on interstellar travel, I think I've got the calculations right.

Okay. One last breath. Here I go.

No! Wait! I don't want to do this!

My hands clamp onto the airlock door, and I turn away. I'm close to hyperventilating—I should return inside just for that reason. Still, I can't. There will only ever be this chance. After that, there will be too much going on for me to try again. I've got to go now—or never.

I swallow hard and face the *Stratford* again. No more delaying. This time I mean it. I bend my knees and count down. *Three...two...one...*

Go!

My eyes suddenly cross, and I become so dizzy that I fall back into the airlock, landing on my air pack. A warning sounds in my ear, and my heart pounds. With a sharp grunt, I launch myself up and pound the hatch close button, falling back to the deck with a whimper.

The hatch shuts as I lie there, gasping and coughing. If I tore my suit, then that's the end of my micro-trip. Not that it would matter. I've just proven that I'm too much of a wimp to go out there on my own. I'd need help if I wanted to try again. And the possibility of that is about equal to my ability to traverse the distance between ships alone.

As the airlock cycle light turns green and my suit's diagnostic returns as all-clear, I shut my eyes. Raey would roast me if she knew what I was doing, and the commander would demote me to permanent passenger and put me back in deep freeze until we arrived on planet.

I pop my helmet off and suck in a breath. The recycled air tastes fresh compared to the sweat-heavy humidity of my suit. It calms my nerves and gets me thinking about how I can get across.

Do I even know any of the crew with excursion experience? Or if I do, are any of them out of stasis?

I should get out of here, anyway. Someone in control is bound to notice the airlock cycled, even after I set a notification delay timer. What I should have done is disabled it completely, but that would come up on a systems report.

My body shudders as I push myself up. This is too soon after waking from stasis to be doing a space walk. Three months is the prescribed time for humans in normal health. Only people specially conditioned, like the ship's security team, are capable of less.

The more I think about this, the more I realize how thoughtless I'm being, and yet I don't care. My minute of terror is just a setback, and as soon as I can wrangle someone, or more than someone, into going with me, I'll be on my way.

It takes only a few minutes to take the suit off and hang it up. My nose wrinkles at the amount of perspiration on the inside. I knew I was scared, but I must have been in denial about how much. I should chug a good amount of water to rebalance the amount my body just lost. And take a shower.

With a quick check of the corridor, I open the inside door to the airlock and slip out. Now I can just stroll down to my quarters and change while I consider who I need to kidnap.

"Hello, Chief," a man says from behind me. I jump and spin, not recognizing the voice. He grins, then lowers his head in apology as he takes notice of whatever petrified look I've got on my face. "Getting in your physical activity for the day?"

"Oh, hi." My eyes dart to his name tag, but it's not there. And now I remember. There are none. The rotation staff is so small that no one needs them. Except for me, apparently.

"Specialist Baati," he says with a nod. "I'm maintenance. Part of your team. Sort of, anyway."

Maintenance crew aren't under my supervision, but Specialist Baati isn't exactly wrong. His team uses the reports my team creates to schedule their work. I'll take the fact that he's attempting to connect with me as something I can use.

"Right." I smile back. "You're on my rotation, aren't you?"

"Yes, Chief. Just woke up last week."

"Oh? And how are you feeling?"

"Good, actually. I have a friend in security that gave me a few tips before we left. It's really helped."

I run a finger across my lower lip as I size him up. "Say, Baati, have you ever qualified for EVA maintenance duties?"

"Of course. All of us have. It was a requirement."

My hands ball into fists. Of course it was. And I knew that. The only question in my head now is, how fast will he agree to come with me? Well, there are more questions, but I'll put off answering the one about how stupid and selfish I'm being in favor of learning more about this guy.

"Are you on work shift now?" I ask, forcing down any sense of anticipation boiling up inside of me.

"Not yet. I'm on third shift with my senior."

"Oh? Who's your senior?"

"Specialist Taye."

I catch my breath. Taye is better than skilled. I did some pre-launch work with him. The man knows his way around the outside of a ship, that's for sure. And if he mentors Baati here, then I've found my help. These two should follow my orders, and even better, they're more than qualified to make the excursion to the *Stratford*. They might even be excited about doing it.

Conscience, don't get in my way. I'm doing this.

"Ah, Taye. I know him well." I pretend to consider something. "You know what? I really could use the two of you for a special task."

Specialist Baati straightens as his eyes light up. Wonderful. I've flicked the right switch. Hopefully his senior will be as enthusiastic. If he's not, then I'll have to decide if Baati will be enough. With the level of sheer panic I just experienced, likely not. My body is still shaking from it.

"I'd be glad to help, Chief," Specialist Baati says. "Just let me call my senior and let him know you're requesting our help."

"No!" I wave a hand at him. "Let's not gum up the comm with unnecessary chatter. We can just go get him ourselves. Where is he?"

Specialist Baati shrugs. "Likely in his quarters. He enjoys watching old cinema during his rest shift."

I motion to him to lead me there and then follow. Taye won't be as agreeable or as quick to agree just to gain my favor. Just like me, his responsibility is to the ship, and any departure from the schedule that he created will be met with questions. I don't know if I'll be able to come up with answers that will satisfy him, but I have to try. The vision of the *Stratford* still hangs in my head like a pinup poster from the war.

"Chief Neridi!" Specialist Taye jumps to his feet as his door slides open. He's still in his sleep jumper and seems as if he might just have been dozing just a minute ago.

"Sorry to bother you," I say, doing my best to pretend as if I have something important going on. "I wouldn't be here if it wasn't absolutely necessary."

"The chief needs our help to complete a task," Specialist Baati says, making no attempt at all to lessen the wide grin on his face.

"Oh?" Specialist Taye looks at me, then back at his junior. "What is it?"

"An extra-vehicular project," I say. "One that requires a little discretion. I need you to come with me right now. As soon as you change, that is. We're going outside the *Devant*."

"How long will it take?" Specialist Taye asks, scratching a finger in his curly hair.

"Not sure, honestly."

That I can't lie about. They need to be prepared for any situation. I may be deceiving them a little about the reason I want them to go outside with me, but I'll be straight with them about the dangers involved.

"Well, Chief, we've got a heavy load on our schedule this upcoming work shift, and if we take too much time with this, that'll push some mandatory work to the next shift, which we can't have happen. As you know, my chief is back in stasis already, so responsibility for everything falls on me."

"Hmm, yeah, I understand. But this could be a life-or-death matter," I reply. "I wouldn't ask if it wasn't critical."

Specialist Taye nods. "Okay. We'll help then."

I curl my toes in my boots and throw my hands behind my back to squeeze them together. This was easier than I thought. I'll be on the *Stratford* in a matter of minutes.

"Let me just inform Commander Azazhi of the change in schedule and we'll be good to go."

"No!" My eyes fly open before I can stop them. "I mean. That's unnecessary. I've already informed him."

"Oh, thank you." Specialist Taye's brow furrows. "You're amazing, Chief. Honestly, I didn't think the commander would allow it."

"It wasn't an issue." I force a grin onto my face, even as I fight to hide my fear. "Commander Azazhi trusts me to do whatever I need to, mostly."

My stomach is growing ill over the frequency of my fabrication of facts. And there will be quite a few more before I can open the *Devant's* airlock again. If I wasn't dying to get inside the *Stratford*, I would've ended this before I put my suit on the first time.

Specialist Taye excuses himself to use the toilet and throw on a work coverall, and Baati retreats to his nearby room to do the same. It may be socially awkward to wait in his room like this, but I'm not letting either of them out of my sight for more than a few seconds. As it is, my body is screaming to get out of here and go hide in my bed until the next work shift and forget about this insane desire I have of seeing that gorgeous ship.

After ten minutes of me tapping my fingers and hands on any solid object in his quarters, we're off and headed to the airlock. I'm wary of seeing anyone who might ask questions as to our destination, but luckily few would.

And then we meet Chief Jawsana, and I freeze.

"Chief," he says and nods.

"Hey," I reply and kick myself for being so casual. It stops him. I push against the wall of the corridor as my pulse pounds in my head. He's well aware of my shift schedule, and if he realizes I'm doing work outside of a specified shift, he'll tell the commander.

"Listen," he says, then stops, taking notice of my two un-orthodox companions. He raises an eyebrow and looks back at me. "What are—"

A lump forms in my throat. This can't be the way my tenure ends. I've got to at least try to get away from him.

"Oh, we're just on our way to do something," I explain.

"Sure," Chief Jawsana says, holding up a finger. "But just wait a minute."

The lump grows and presses against my ribs. I've got to force myself to take breaths. If he notices, it's all over.

"W...What? Why? I mean, what do you need?"

He frowns. "Are you okay, Chief?"

Oh, hell, he's looking at me funny. He knows, he knows! Keep it together, Fana!

"Fine."

He presses his lips together and sighs. "Listen, I just wanted to say, I know how exciting this is for you, and if I were you, the first thing I'd want to do is slide down a tether to that ship. When I promised that I'd tell you the moment we hear from them, I meant it. This could be a monumental moment for the colony. And you were the one who sparked it to happen."

For longer than is comfortable for either of us, I stare at him, too terrified to reply with anything other than a stiff nod. He gives me a tight smile then, and this moment becomes clear. If I wasn't so freaked that he was suspicious, I would have noticed it earlier.

"So I hope you don't feel any animosity toward me. That's all," he says.

"Nope. Not at all."

"Okay then." Chief Jawsana claps me on the shoulder. I jump. "Hope for some good news soon."

I give him a tight smile and lean against the corridor wall before I collapse. That was just about the most terrifying experience I've ever had, save for those few minutes in the open airlock.

As the chief walks away, Specialist Taye slides toward me and leans close. "Chief...this EVA...are we going to another ship?"

My eyes slide up to meet his. He's guessed it. And I've got to put his safety before my secrecy. They'll be finding out soon enough, anyway.

I offer a guilty smile. "Oh yeah. It's going to be amazing."

DEFIANCE

CERI

Level two. With a tightening of my jaw, I pull myself up the last rung of the ladder and step onto the charred decking. It's silent, and only the single work light that we've installed illuminates the space like a star in a black sky. I am its sole companion, and I plan to keep it that way.

Even though Sayer and Merek, through Efa, asked me not to come here, it's my right. They've no authority to keep me away from the communications system and the beacon they shut off. And what irritates me most is that they used Efa to deliver their warning. She can't lie to me anymore than I can to her, and as gentle as she tried to make their message seem, Efa avoided my gaze too often during that conversation.

I take a few soft steps toward the console, but the flakes of burned metal and plastic still crunch under my feet louder than I want them to. Just because I feel within my right to be here doesn't mean I want anyone else to know. The last argument the four of us had almost turned violent, and despite our disagreements, we don't want to pound each other into the walls as we've done with others.

As I continue forward, micro-sized chips of the ceiling fall down around me. It reminds me of snow, and I feel a wistful hand wrap itself around my heart. I must have been eleven the last time I saw the real thing, though the ashes from burning buildings often replaced the pure calm that winter's precipitation created.

Nine years ago in my memory seems more like the hundreds it has been. Where I am now is half a galaxy away from Earth. And I don't really know how long I've been awake. The adults kept everything other than a clock away from us. The only way we knew a year had passed was when they would mark the passing of our birthday with a salute. Then it was back to war.

A foot on the ladder. I drop and listen. My hand goes for my blade. My eyes target the access point. A hand appears. It's female.

I reach the ladder in two steps and grab the wrist attached to it, yanking up hard. Its owner yelps and struggles to break free. Too late. I've already got them up onto the deck.

"Seren," I hiss and return my blade to its sheath.

"C...Ceri?" Seren lifts her head to look at me with fearful eyes. "What are—"

I clamp a hand over her mouth. Seren jumps.

"Noise discipline," I whisper. "Remember how to do that?"

She nods, and I remove my hand to pat her on the shoulder, then motion to the communications console as I offer her a hand up. We move to the far edge and sit down in the equipment's shadow. If anyone comes up, we'll have plenty of warning, though I might be overreacting. There is no reason to come here, unless...

"Who were you meeting here?"

A pause. "No one."

"Not Rhys?"

Seren drops her mouth open. "No!"

"Why not?"

"He's a jerk."

I reach out to brush her hair from her face, but Seren pulls away and ducks her head. It starts a fire in me. If Rhys hurt her, I will slice his kneecaps off. Slowly. He needs a reminder that I will always protect my squad.

"Sorry," I say and stroke her cheek instead. But her brow furrows as she looks at me.

"Why?" Seren inquires.

"Well..." I shut my mouth. Even if my estimate of what happened is right, this conversation will go nowhere. I won't force her to confess her relationship to me, and I've no advice to give, even if she did. I've misread her, and now I should change the subject. "Does anyone know you came here?"

"No. I just wanted to check my work from yesterday, and then I was going to sleep."

"Anyone see you on your way here?"

She shrugs, but I take her by the shoulders and catch her gaze. These are standard questions the adults burned into our minds. Seren shouldn't have forgotten them so easily.

"Think hard, Seren. It's important."

She presses her lips together as her focus folds back into her mind. "I think I passed Sayer on my way here."

My grip on Seren's arms goes tight as bile creeps up into the back of my throat. If Sayer found me here, there would be more than a punch or two thrown. We may work together for the benefit of our crew and our friends, but our history has been rough. And without Efa or Merek to intervene, one of us would wind up with more than a serious wound.

"Ceri, that hurts," Seren whimpers.

I gasp and pull my hands away. She was struggling to get out of my grasp, but I was so caught up in my panic I failed to notice.

"Forgive me. I didn't mean to." I reach out to touch her, but she shies away again, her gaze on me full of suspicion.

"What are you doing here, anyway?" she asks.

"Good question." I clasp my hands together and curl my lips in. There's no reason I should be wary of Seren's loyalties. But I don't want her getting involved with this, either. My actions will start trouble, and the last place I want her to be is in the middle of it.

Of course, I have yet to do anything, and now that she's here, I'm less determined to carry out my plan.

"So?" Seren pushes up to slide her legs under her body and then leans to one side to put a hand down on the deck for support. Her other hand pushes a lock of her hair back as she tilts her head and watches me.

"I'm here to turn the beacon back on," I say, watching her.

Her eyebrows crash together. "Why'd we turn it off in the first place? And why are you doing all this covert action?"

I drop my gaze, fearful she might see something in my eyes and get the answer on her own. But if Merek and Sayer haven't told anyone they were doing it, that's to my advantage. They don't want to frighten the younger crew, and I agree. We don't know enough about this virus to just make snap decisions. Of course, that's why I'm here. To put an end to their hasty reaction.

But I can't tell Seren any of that.

"Help me out, would you?" I stand and brush the dust and ash from my uniform. "You know this system better than any-one."

"Sure, but"—Seren springs to her feet—"what's going on, Ceri? Are we in danger?"

I snort. "You remember where you are, don't you?"

"Yes." She goes to shake her head but winds up throwing her hands up instead. "Of course, but I meant are *we*, like as in the crew, in danger?"

The bile circulates in the back of my throat, and I swallow to push it down. It's good that I'm facing away from her. She'd know instantly that there was trouble. We explained away Tal's death and never brought up Sayer's and my quarantine. Perhaps Seren would be more fearful of me if we had.

"No," I reply, even though I want to warn her. Having Tal's deteriorating body in my arms was a moment I'll never forget. I don't want to repeat the same with Seren.

"Then what?"

I motion for her to switch the power breaker on and drop behind the console to check the connections. As expected, Sayer was thorough in his shutdown. He knew I might try this and pulled all the power leads from their sockets and a few of the circuit cards, too. I'll need Seren to help me. Thank the Ancestors she's here.

A chill runs across my back as Sayer's angry face crosses my mind. I haven't forgotten about what would happen if he shows up. I will wish for Seren to be far away at that moment. She'd attempt to stop us, and that would get her hurt.

"That one goes there," Seren says and points.

"Thanks." I slide the card in and then yank her arm toward the deck. "Get down."

She watches me work as she sits on her haunches with her arms about her knees. It's innocent enough, but I can feel the hair on the back of my neck standing up. Seren's mind is likely working through everything I've told her. Even the lies.

"You have a disagreement with Sayer?" she asks.

Bish, this girl is sharp.

"Nothing you need to worry about."

I hand her the next card. Just two more to go, then we can power the console up and be gone.

But when she takes it, our eyes meet for a second before I look away.

"But you're worried," Seren states, her voice tightening.

As much as her persistence is grinding on me, I know that I've only myself to yell at. I taught her that kind of steadfast determination. Before, that'd mean the relentless pursuit of the enemy until we eliminated them. Now I'm the target and unless I put a stop to it, Seren will continue to push for an answer.

"Listen to me," I say and put a hand on hers. "This is nothing you should get involved in. It'll all get settled soon enough."

Seren searches my eyes for something more. I'm doing my best not to give her anything else. The lie I just told will only be exposed if I try to be deceptive again.

"Now let's finish up so we can go to bed, yeah?" I say, pressing in the relays on the power distribution box. The console lights up and runs through its diagnostic. Lights flash across the top in sequence, screens glow, and the software boots into a ready state.

Once the system is up and running, I eye the screen, then fold my arms and wait. Once we get confirmation everything is working, we can go, and Seren can get the sleep she deserves. I won't be able to. Not until I know the beacon is staying on.

"Why's it taking so long?" I ask.

Seren scans the console. "Oh! We've got to reenable the beacon. The power down would have reset our commands. It'll just take a second to put them back again."

Her hands find the controls, and she taps out bits of syntax on the keyboard below the screen, humming a tune while she works, one I can't place. It's happy and upbeat, and I'm glad that she can think of it in a dark place like this.

Then her humming stops.

"Ceri," Seren says, frowning. "Do you know what this means?"

I lean forward and read the message on the screen she's pointing at.

Request...8.4GHz...accept? (Y/N)

Suggest uplink at 7.2GHz, PCM standard.

I read the message. And read it again, my chest tightening as I consider what it could mean. It would be a miracle if...no...it'd be too soon for anyone to pick up our signal. Wouldn't it?

Even as my desperation to confirm my hope increases, I push it away. This can't be. We put one circuit back wrong. That's got to be it. But if we got it straight, how would we—

Hyuk. This is impossible. There's no way—

Yet there it is.

"Seren, get Efa. Wake her if you have to. And tell no one else."

"What does it mean?" She turns to me, her eyebrows raising.

I catch her gaze and put my hands on her shoulders. "Go. Get her now."

"What is it?"

I run my tongue across the back of my teeth and breathe. "I think we're receiving a message."

ACCESS

— · —

FANA

MY PULSE IS RACING as fast as it can go. I do my best to control my breathing. The only sound is the static from my helmet's comm. Everything is dark. But that's because I'm squeezing my eyelids shut. Even though I am on the verge of an amazing achievement, I couldn't bear to look.

We're just mere seconds from rendezvous with the *Stratford*'s hatch.

Baati, Taye, and I have tethered ourselves together, but that wasn't enough to shake my fright. So Baati holds my gloved hand in his, and he counts down the remaining time remaining so I can prepare myself for touchdown.

"*Two...one...thruster on,*" he says with a load of calm in his voice. I feel a jolt as the maneuvering jet he's got fires off a blast to slow us. "*And...landing.*"

With my eyes still closed, I reach out, hoping to touch the past.

And jerk back as my fingers meet metal.

It's cold. No. The *Stratford*'shull is freezing, even through my glove. Hundreds of years of exposure to the deep chill of interstellar space have brought the skin of this ship almost to absolute zero.

I risk opening an eye and catch a bit of the yellow strip that outlines the airlock's outer hatch. Blue lights on the far side of the hatch temper its color. In a muted sort of way, it's beautiful, and I have to stop myself from staring too long.

A glint catches my eye, and I look down. *A window!* I shove away from Baati and fly across the hull to peer through it. Inside will be everything I've been dying to see. Maybe someone's nearby!

"Woah! Chief! Don't do that!" Baati shouts through the comm, his excited voice overloading the mic.

"No need to shout," Taye chides. *"If you bust your comm, we'll have to scrub the mission, and then we're all headed back before the chief can complete her work."*

"It wasn't my fault. I didn't know she was going to let go like that. I almost lost my grip!"

His complaint barely registers in my mind. I'm too busy pressing my visor against the portal and squinting as I try to hold myself in place.

But if I had hoped for a well-lit and clear view into history, I just ran out of luck. All that's there are a few glowing status indicators just inside the airlock and a cloudy perspective of what could be a corridor beyond. Still, just the thought that I will soon walk through a ship that left Earth hundreds of years before my great-grandparents were born is making me shiver. Or maybe that's just the chill radiating off the ship.

"Do we know how to open the hatch?" I ask.

"Working on that," Taye answers. *"There's no clear access pan-*el."

"Maybe no one needed to go outside," Baati suggests.

"That could be true. But I doubt it. In an emergency, the custodial crew would have to get outside."

"Sure," Taye agrees. *"Then how'd they get back in?"*

As I continue to stare through the window, my mind drifts. I imagine the people on this ship moving through the corridor, entering the airlock, and exiting the ship to float among us. It couldn't have been a difficult procedure. The designers would have to consider the non-technical crew in the operation of things.

Which means I can figure this out with ease. The technology at work here is older, but the concepts are the same. Sure, we now use bio-enhanced circuitry for our quantum qubit-based processing engines, but all that really means is that they can do more. Like pull people in and out of stasis.

"Think simple," I suggest. "There's going to be more manu-al operation involved here than on *Devant*. And security isn't likely a priority. These people aren't expecting invaders."

"What do you mean, Chief?" Baati asks as he moves down to check the lower half.

"I mean, the only thing we're looking for is a mechanical or electronic switch. Forget biometrics, or even old-fashioned RFID, IFRID, MFID, or even motion sensors."

Baati whistles. I bet he's only heard those terms in passing.

"Well, whatever we're going to find, we need to do it soon." Taye spins to invert himself so he can join Baati on the lower half

of the hatch. *"Our breathable air is just above our minimum safe level."*

"That's my fault," I say. "I assumed we'd be inside already. Just set a monitor and an alarm. We don't want any surprises."

"Aye, Chief."

Taye will make sure we don't go below the failsafe, but I still get a strange feeling running through my body thinking about it. We have to get inside, and I am ready to risk as much time as possible to do it, even if the acid in my stomach is churning up a storm.

So I should stop daydreaming about the *Stratford* and help my team figure this out.

I push off the hull, just far enough to take in the entire hatch. Since they're nearly sucking the paint off the ship, I don't need to be so close. In fact, a high-level view might just be the thing that solves this. Now, to consider the mechanics at work here.

The hatch likely unlatches from the bottom and swings upwards. At least that's what I'd think. Or if it was the opposite way...No. It doesn't matter. Just because the ship is oriented in a certain—

Again, no. I've got to think simple. The *Stratford* has no artificial gravity. It's just using basic physics to keep the crew and everything else inside from floating. The decks are perpendicular to the length of the hull. Down for them would be—

"Taye! Upper left quadrant! About forty-five degrees if the fore of the ship was zero."

Right on the edge of the seal is a depression just large enough for the finger of a pressure-suit glove to fit into. That'd stop the latch release from being engaged if something hit it.

"Got it! Good eyes, Chief." Taye flies across the hatch and lands right next to it. He inserts his finger, and a panel opens, revealing a screen and a dial connected to a handle large enough to manipulate in a suit.

But the screen is dark.

A beep sounds in my ears. I mutter a curse under my breath. We're down below the safety margin on our air. Regulations state we end our EVA now and head back, leaving a wide margin in case of unforeseen circumstances. It's the safe way and the right way. But all I can think of is finding the person who came up with such a conservative rule and giving them a fat lip. They weren't thinking of this moment when they came up with it.

"Chief?" Baati queries, his voice pitching up.

"We're almost there. Keep going. We can refill our supply once we're inside."

I attempt to sound confident, but I'm hardly that. The air could be unbreathable. Maybe that's what their distress call was about. Their atmosphere became contaminated, and they need to evacuate. If that's the case, this could become a very short trip.

Great. Now I'm scaring myself.

"Taye, any luck?" I ask.

"Negative. The airlock has to cycle before I can open the hatch, but I don't know if it has because the screen is dead."

"You're certain of that?"

"I can't be certain of anything if I can get a readout on the screen, Chief."

I groan. If I followed others in worship of their respective deities, I might wonder why those omnipotent beings were making this so difficult for us. All I want is to help these people if they need it.

Well, that, and to spend endless hours exploring every level of this museum in space.

"Are you sure you want to break regulations like this?" Taye asks. *"I'm fine with reasonable risk, but this is going beyond that."*

"We still have time."

I push myself next to him to examine the screen. It's a diode-based organics device. I recognize it because I built a few when I was a kid. This was cheap tech, even back then. Why would they use it on the outer hull like this, where it's guaranteed to corrode long before the *Stratford* was even a century into its journey?

The one good thing about it is that I think I can fix it.

"Baati, give me your arc torch, any tool that's flat, and a clamp."

"Chief." Taye's tone is way more insistent than it was before. *"We don't have time for you to be playing around like this. I'm recommending we go back."*

"This'll just take a minute."

With a flick of the torch's power switch, I press it against a panel below the screen and engage it. The panel glows red hot, then cracks. I push the flat tool into the crack and pry back the metal to reveal the insulation beneath. That gets pried back, and I set the clamp in place to keep it away from the electronics underneath. Then—

"Chief, if you won't go back, then give me permission to return with Specialist Baati."

"No way!" Baati cries. *"We can't just leave the Chief out here by herself!"*

"Better we go back and refill our supplies than wait here. At least then we can return to rescue her."

"That could take too long!"

I should send them back. The only reason they're here is because I'm a terrified little child when it comes to navigating outside a ship. I'm fine while I'm staring at the tiny space this circuit takes up.

Of course, they'd need to return to get me. I wouldn't make it back on my own, air or not. Which means the only way I survive is to get inside the *Stratford*. I'll take that motivation and use it to ensure I remain alive.

"Permission to go," I say. "Do it now, while you still have reserve."

"What about you?" Baati asks.

"I'm about to get in."

"Specialist." Taye's voice maintains his insistence. Only now his tone is an order. *"We'll be back as quickly as we can. Now secure her tether to the ship and let's go."*

"I promise we're coming back," Baati says and puts a hand on my shoulder. I keep my lips tight, as any words I say may betray my determination to stay here. As it is, my head is screaming

not to let them go. But it's the right plan. They'd just be waiting around to suffocate. And they'll come back. Baati thinks I'm irreplaceable. Even though the *Devant*'s crew proved for seventeen years, I'm not. They'd only need my experience if something seriously bad happened to the ship. And nothing will.

There. I've found what I'm looking for. A pair of broken leads coming off a processor. That little gray chip is unrepairable, and I don't have a replacement for sure.

My suit beeps a critical warning, and I suck in a slow breath and hold it. In a few minutes, the air recycler in my pack will struggle to supply me with enough oxygen. I'll lose the ability to think straight long before I lose consciousness.

Time for drastic measures.

The torch goes against the processor, and I light it up. It gets soft as it heats, and once it's a bright orange, I pry it out and send it hurtling into space. Now I need something to fast wire it. But all I have are the three tools Baati left me.

My suit beeps again, and a warning light comes on in my helmet. All I can do is concentrate on my work, even as I feel a headache is coming on.

With no other options, I put the pry tool against the circuit board, connecting it to the leads I think should be right. A quick shot of the torch fuses it into place. It's a weld job so bad, my elementary school teacher would fail me on it.

But it works.

My head spins as I grab the switch and turn it. And wait. Maybe now would be a good time to learn why prayer is important. If the airlock hasn't cycled yet, I'll still lose.

"Come on!" I shout with what might be my last full breath.

The hatch opens. Slowly. I race to detach my harness. My sight is going hazy. My hands aren't working as they should. Did I get it off? No time to wonder.

I grab the edges of the hatch and push into the airlock, searching for the control to close it. The big red button must be it. I don't so much as press it as float into it.

A light comes on inside the lock. Something's happening. But I can't read the screen. It doesn't matter. Either I did it, or I failed. I can't think straight any longer.

As my body floats to what is now the floor, I see it. The hatch is closing. I have to stay awake to get my helmet off. My eyes are closing. I'm drifting off.

I hope this crew pays attention to their airlocks...

ALARM

CERI

SEREN GRIPS MY ARM with ever increasing tension. My hands are on the communications console, digging into the wrist pad. We're frozen here, attempting to make sense of what is appearing on the screen. Each letter comes with an agonizing slowness. To read a word is to hold still for an eternity. The possibility of what it could mean torments us, and I long to know where it comes from.

And who.

Stratford. Beacon received. Do you wish f—

The next letter, *o*, appears. *For? Food? Formula?* If the message was in complete sentences, I might have a better chance of guessing.

"Do you know how to triangulate the origin of the target?" I use tactical terms. Seren understands them. I don't know the correct ones.

She shakes her head, then realizes her nails are digging into my arm and jerks her hand away. I don't react. Pain is a sense I'm used to. And nothing will distract me from getting this message.

I remember I told Seren to get Efa. But I can't send her away. Not until this message completes itself. She'll have something to tell then.

Stratford. Beacon received. Do you wish for as—

"Wish for what?" Seren whispers. "Why are we wishing for anything?"

The syntax is odd. Whoever this is doesn't want to us to close our eyes and hope for something to happen like we were five years old.

Hope isn't reliable. Any former soldier on this ship would say that. We didn't wait for some adult to grant us anything. We stood up to them and turned the nightmare they gave us into a better life. It still may be hell, but now we're in charge of it. Save for this message.

"Any idea why it's taking so long?" I ask.

"I barely figured out how to put this console back together. And most of that was just guessing, Ceri."

"I'm not blaming you."

"No." Seren curls her lower lip back. "I wasn't thinking that."

Stratford. Beacon received. Do you wish for assistance? If oth—

I step away from the console, squeezing my hands into fists as I walk to the edge of the level. A quick check down the ladder shows all clear. It's just conditioning. No one, not even Sayer, will be there. By now most everyone, save for those having illicit meetings, will be sleeping.

We used to post sentries, just like we did before, to protect ourselves. From what, I don't know. It was a waste of time and a strain on those who had to fight fatigue to keep themselves alert. That was when we locked our guns up and removed any last reminder of what we suffered under the so-called adults. Of course, the joke was on us. They're now living on a new planet. We're still prisoners of a runaway ship, by our own choice.

"Ceri, come back! There's more!"

I rush back to the console, skidding before I catch myself on its edge. I take a moment to focus my eyes on the screen. By then, another word comes up.

Stratford. Beacon received. Do you wish for assistance? If other, then respond. We await a reply.

"Is that it?" Seren asks.

"I don't know." I stare at the message, attempting to understand it. Its meaning moves back and forth in my head, from clarity to confusion. I tap my fingers on the console and consider. "They're offering to help us, but...why would we respond only if we want something else? Do they know—"

Bish and a half. They can see us.

"Is there anything on this level that can give us a scan around the ship?" I ask.

"Not anymore."

Wait. The top level has a huge port out the front. We might see them if they're close enough. And to see any part of another ship would be a beautiful sight.

"Come on." I grab Seren's wrist and dash to the ascending ladder.

She yelps as she's dragged along. "Wait! What are we doing?"

"Looking."

We fly up the ladder to one, Seren right after me, and waste no time racing around the remnants of the *Stratford's* command level. Here were the stations for the captain, the lead navigator, and the senior pilot. Now all that's left is the pilot's seat and her burned-out console. The adults took the three of them along to their new home. There might be other officers, but without a passenger list, we'll never know.

My hands clap onto the inner window as my face presses against the transparent composite. It's cold against my cheek, but I'm immune to the biting chill. My only focus is finding that ship as quickly as possible.

"See it?" I ask.

"No. Nothing."

"Try the other side."

The two of us rush over and peer out. But all we can see is the glare of the *Stratford's* identification lights reflecting off the panel they're illuminating. An adult in medical told me it's a holdover from when ships were ocean-going vessels. I doubt there's anyone who will ever read the name of the ship from the outside ever again.

I grow more despondent as the seconds move by. Our mystery responder would need to be bright and close for us to see them. Otherwise they'd just look like any sparkling star out there.

"I don't think anything's out there," Seren says, her voice a wistful reflection of my current mood.

"No, I guess not." I put a hand on her shoulder and stare out into the deepness of space, unwilling to let go of this view so easily. It's foolish to put any hope in a message that could be a hoax as much as it could be real. We've got no way to confirm it.

And I've put too much importance on the transmission being authentic. I'm hoping for someone to save us when no one will. This virus has me scared, that's all. Above all other dangers, it's the one that's most immediate.

"What should we tell Efa?" Seren asks.

I remain silent, my eyes lost in the ocean of twinkling lights before my eyes. The only other time I've been up here was when we first tried to finish what the adults started. We had little training and only the massive files of the ship's manuals and schematics to refer to. It's a miracle we—mostly Seren—could get anything to work.

Not that I had expected much. I only assigned it to her so she and Rhys would keep their hands busy with something other than each other's bodies. There was no actual need to get anything up here to work. We'd never repair control to any level of functionality where we'd be able to steer the *Stratford* back to its correct heading.

The moment I chose to stay here was when I had accepted my life would end here, caring for our sleeping passengers. I became like a gardener of flowers that would neither grow nor die. I'm not so sure the others really understand how there will be nothing more than what we have now.

"Ceri." Seren pokes a finger into my side. "We have to inform the others, right?"

My arm goes around her shoulder. "Not yet. Let's just keep looking for a moment."

But Seren wiggles from my hold and turns to face me. "We should check the terminal again. There could be more to the message."

"No, I think that's all they're sending." I run a strand of her hair through my fingers, then sigh as I pull her to me. "Alright. Let's go talk to Efa."

If I had any regrets about remaining on the *Stratford*, it's the thought that I may have unfairly influenced Seren and the others to stay here with me. They've claimed time and time again that it was their choice, but I wonder if my actions haven't doomed them to a miserable life. They all deserve so much better than this.

"Ceri, are you okay?" Seren asks, narrowing her eyes at me. I smile. I rarely put my hands on anyone, but today, for whatever reason, I feel the need to maintain a physical connection to Seren. Ever since she joined my squad, I've considered her my little sister. So much has changed since then. Maybe I'm worried about her more than I used to be.

"Yeah, I'm fine," I say. "Let's go."

It will annoy my former squad mate we woke her up, likely from a relaxing sleep, next to Merek. He might wake up too. That'd be fine. Even though I went against both of them, they need to know.

Seren leads the way, and I follow behind her for a moment before I pause and glance back at the portal, letting the view ease the tightness in my shoulders. I should come up here more often, if for no reason other than to have peace as I consider how to improve the quality of our lives here. I want all of us to live some kind of fulfilled life, whatever that means here.

We slide down the ladder and move toward the access to level three. I consider what I will tell Efa, given we've not been able to confirm anything. She'll listen and then realize what I've really done is turn the beacon back on. I expect a few words to fly then.

A klaxon sounds, and I pause. By the volume of it, it must be at least two floors away. It's not the fire alarm, so there's no reason to be worried. One of the younger crew likely opened something they shouldn't have.

On second thought, I should go check it out.

I motion to Seren to speed up, and the two of us return to moving as we were still at war, sliding down ladders and crossing levels in a matter of seconds. My legs and lungs burn as we sprint across the deck, unused to such a need to rush.

We land on level eight when we spot Deryn at the same time he spots us. He rushes to us as we do the same, and the three of us meet in the center of the floor.

"What's the alarm?" I ask.

My stomach churns the moment Deryn's eyes widen. It's not a fire, but something else is seriously wrong.

"I promise this isn't a lie," he says, breathless. "I swear it's not a joke, either."

"What?" Seren asks. "What's the problem?"

Deryn scans our faces, and my jaw tightens. He may have been a bish squad leader, but he'd never panic over anything minor. Whatever is exciting him is doing the same to me.

"Tell us already!" I demand.

"The airlock on seventeen just cycled," he says. "Someone's entered it from the outside."

INVADER

CERI

WE ARRIVE ON SEVENTEEN in less time than it took us to get to eight. My body is pulsing with intensity, not just from our marathon tear, but from the idea that someone or something was close enough, and intelligent enough, to operate the *Stratford*'s airlock.

No, that's impossible. Seren and I checked. No ship is close enough. Maybe something broke, but that would mean serious trouble. We'd have to seal off the entire level, and that'd cause issues for anyone below. Niah is still down there. If we closed off seventeen, she won't be able to return.

I gasp as I run. The airlock could have just as easily been cycled from inside. That's the far more likely answer.

Bish, did one of our crew do something stupid?

It doesn't take us long to find out. As we arrive, we're greeted by a subset of the crew known to associate together—Tegan, Rhys.

And Sayer.

A lump forms in my throat as I slow. There's no possibility that he'd know what I've done. Not yet. It doesn't stop my muscles from tensing. Still, it doesn't mean a fight. He and

I want the same things. We just disagree on how to achieve them.

As I come closer to the group, I notice a figure on the deck, back propped up against the side of the airlock. I can't tell yet if they're a boy or a girl, or even a human. The helmet that covers their head is dark, and the visor is down. Yet something is odd.

It hits me. That pressure suit is thin, streamlined, and seamless. Our suits are bright orange, clunky, and full of joints and locks. This suit only has one where the helmet and suit meet. And the material it's made from is shiny and form-fitting. There's also a tablet or computer keyboard strapped across one forearm, currently dark.

"Female," I say, taking notice of how the lines of her waist meet her hips. "So likely human."

"Did you think otherwise?" Sayer asks, his voice relaxed yet curious. I'm surprised. We haven't been on good terms since he, along with Merek and Efa, ambushed me.

"Do you see a ship out there?"

"A ship?" Sayer raises an eyebrow. "What makes you think—"

He gasps and jerks as he peers out of the airlock port, his jaw dropping. I glimpse a dark ovular shape only for a second before Tegan, Seren, and Rhys rush toward the airlock, forcing me back. They climb over our visitor in such aggressive fashion it snaps me back into focus.

"Move off," I order, grabbing arms and wrenching them away. "She might be in trouble." And then to Sayer, "How long ago did you get here?"

Sayer shrugs. "A few minutes."

As the others clear the airlock, I crouch before the suited figure, tilting her head to get light into the visor. But like any good design, it's coated with a heavily reflective material. Our suits have a control to turn the mirroring off, and likely this one does, too. But the person inside of this suit would need to be awake or alive to change it. Right now, I don't know which she is.

"Help me then," I say, searching the collar of the suit. "We need to remove her helmet."

"Hyuk no!" Sayer shouts. "We don't know what kind of risk that would be!"

I twist to stare up at him. "That's not the problem. She could be hurt, and if we don't take it off, she could die!"

"And if you do, you could kill her, still. How do you know she even breathes our atmosphere?"

"Oh, come on, Sayer!" Tegan says. "Ceri already said it's a girl. That means she's human. She'd have no problem breathing the air in here."

Sayer didn't mean it like that. The intensity in his eyes tells me so. He's speaking code with me for the benefit of the others. And as much as he's grating on me, he has a point. Just because no one else besides Tal has died doesn't mean the air is safe to breathe.

But if she's dying, then worry about infecting her is a minor issue.

I lift her arm and examine the device on her wrist. The screen is dark, but there's a light on the top left of it, blinking red. On the chance that something happens, I tap the screen.

It lights up, the screen going red. A message with strange characters flashes across it, save for a number at the end followed by a percentile figure. That number is zero.

"Bish! She's out of oxygen!" I cry and run my hands across the collar, pulling and prodding every piece of the collar to open the seal. If it's been a few minutes, her brain could already have suffered damage.

"Don't do it," Sayer warns.

"Don't stop me!" I growl.

"You're putting everyone in danger!"

"Get back! I'm doing this."

Seren screams a warning, but before I can react, Sayer grabs me from under my arms and tosses me into the corridor. I tumble and roll, recovering quickly and getting to my feet in a single beat. I snarl at him as heat rushes through me. If we weren't on the same side now, my next move would be to slice his gut open.

"What are you doing?" Tegan shouts at him. "We could still save her!"

Sayer steps out of the airlock, shutting the hatch and sealing it. He glares at Tegan, then reaches for the cycle switch. My heart stops.

He's going to blow her into space.

In a heartbeat, my blade is out and flying toward his hand. It hits the panel and ricochets, the flat of the blade smacking into his arm. Sayer jerks back, his hand going to his arm.

"Hyuk!" he shouts. "What the hell is wrong with you?"

"You don't get to decide whether she lives or dies," I growl as my eyes narrow.

He meets my stare and matches it. "Try to stop me."

"Sayer!" Tegan tries again. "Just get out of here! We'll handle this!"

Too late. I charge him, my shoulder slamming into his gut. His body pounds into the wall. He grunts, his arms flying back. I twist and throw him to the floor. He hits and rolls, spinning back around to face me, reaching behind his back to pull something out.

A gun.

I step back, my muscles tensing to evade, but with the airlock behind me, I've got little space to maneuver. He might not shoot to kill, but I've never really watched him enough to know. If he's ready to take this to the death, then so am I. I just hope he's not.

"She's dead!" he shouts. "And we don't need any more hyuking complications! If whoever is over there gives a bish about their crew, they'll save her. Now open the outside hatch and let her go."

The ring of metal sliding from composite sheaths echoes through the corridor. Seren and Tegan flank Sayer, dropping into an attack stance, their blades at the ready.

"You fire that gun, and I will make sure you never walk again," Tegan hisses. "You can't shoot her and stop us, too."

Rhys' mouth drops open as he looks from Sayer to Tegan and then to Seren, who glares at him. With a curse muttered under his breath, he draws his blade and points it at Sayer. A frown from Sayer puts Rhys on the defensive, and he gives him an apologetic look.

Sayer huffs, then turns back to me. "You're the one killing people, not me."

"No," I reply. "No one else dies on this ship from anything other than old age. That goes for anyone who's either brave or stupid enough to drop themselves in our airlock. You may not agree with that, Sayer, but you know it's the right thing to do."

He tightens his jaw, his pistol hand readjusting on his weapon. I tense, my pulse pounding through every inch of my body. But not for me. For every second we waste, that girl in the airlock dies just a little more.

"Bish." Sayer sighs and lowers his gun. "Fine. You want to split the crew over this? Just remember, Merek and Efa voted against you last time. And as soon as I tell them what you did, they'll be down here to stop you. With everyone else behind them."

With that, he turns and stomps away. He'll be back. Quickly. It doesn't matter. I'll be done before he returns.

"Ceri," Seren says, her voice nearly breaking as she races toward me. She throws her arms around me and presses her head onto my shoulder. I wrap an arm about her and give her a squeeze, thankful I still have allies in the younger crew.

Tegan wastes no time in pounding the hatch release and opening the airlock again. I spin with a hand on Seren's back, and the three of us drop around the unmoving body.

"Press anything and everything you can," I say. "There's got to be a release somewhere."

Six hands slide around the collar of the suit in a flurry of action. We touch and prod every part of the metal ring in a synchronized dance.

"Found something!" Tegan says. There's a click and a hiss as air rushes into the suit. We gently twist the helmet and lift it off, each one of us holding our breath in anticipation of what we're about to see.

It's a definitely a girl, older than me by a few years. Pink-haired and dark-skinned. The features of her face are soft but strong. Her lips are full, her eyes wide-set, and in between them a nose I can only describe as perfect. She'd be pretty if her jaw wasn't slack with her tongue hanging out.

"Woah," Rhys says, his eyes popping and his voice breathless. It's not lost on me he's still got his blade in his hand. Not that I'm worried. He'd have to get through three soldiers more skilled than him before he could even tap this girl with a single finger.

I huff. Here we are, arguing over smaller matters, when we should try to comprehend the reality that's before us. This girl's from another ship, one that's more advanced than our own, and she may have received our distress call. Which means they may help us.

It's all speculation, of course, but this girl took the risk of leaving her ship to come across and rendezvous with ours. She must have wanted something.

The message we received is making a lot more sense now.

My hand reaches out to touch her face. Her skin is smooth, pliant. It's warm underneath my hand.

"She's still alive!" I hiss. "Quick, help me pull her from the airlock and lay her down."

Rhys backs away as Tegan and Seren turn the girl to lay her shoulders on my hands. With a short countdown, we slide her from the airlock and rest her on the deck. Seren rushes to the storerooms to find something to put under her head. Rhys, not knowing what else to do, goes with her.

I lean down and put my ear to her mouth. Air is moving, but just barely—not enough for her to live on. I press both hands over her heart and press in the cadence that I learned in combat medicine.

Tegan leans over and checks her breathing again. But she listens for longer than I expect, and I freeze. *Am I too late? Has the lack of oxygen to her brain turned her into nothing other than a body with a dead brain?*

I grit my teeth and continue, unsure of what else to do. I press faster, my repetitions increasing as if that alone would save her.

By the time Tegan sits up again, my brow is sticky with perspiration, and I catch a prayer running through my head.

"Good," Tegan says. "I think it's working. Keep going."

Two seconds later, the girl gasps, her back arching as her mouth opens wide to suck in every molecule of air that can fit into her lungs. Tegan throws a hand under her back and motions for me to help, but I can't. My body slumps under the exhaustion of my efforts. At least I can be glad that she's still alive.

Though I may have just negated anything I just did. As I catch my breath, I realize my heavy respiration may just have contaminated the entire area with virus.

Perhaps I've saved her life, but it could be for only a short, and very painful, time.

ANCESTOR

FANA

MY BODY WRITHES IN a shock of terror. My head jerks, twisting my neck. I'm only barely aware there's a hand under my back. It supports me as I collapse, lowering me gently to the deck. My head pounds like I've been banging it on the outside of the ship's hull. Without a suit.

A voice speaks. The dialect is odd, but it's female, and it may just have told someone to sit me up. My body rotates off the floor to press against something cool and flat. Hands put something soft behind my head and move me into a position they must think is comfortable for me.

I'm alive. Anything is comfortable for me.

The person who spoke touches my face with a rough hand. There's a strength, and a grace, behind it. Weird. Who's got hands like that on the *Devant*? Not Raey and not any of the other med techs. I remember them. Hers are smoother than a newborn's butt.

And there's a strange smell, like stale air mixed with the tang of grease and the sweetness of human sweat. Unless the commander has locked me in a machine room to work the rest of my shift in, I don't—

Wait. I'm not on the Devant*! I made it to the* Stratford*!*

I throw my eyes open, and they dart around. Everything is dim. Shadows move before my eyes. The warm, humid air of breath brushes against my face.

"Holy bish," a boy's voice says. "You did it."

"Keep back, Rhys," the female voice, who's closer, replies. I understood a little more that time. But who is bish? And what's a Rhys? It's like they're speaking a version of the common that I've only ever heard in a video.

Light flashes off of something. I turn to look at it, my eyes coming into focus to see a teenage boy in a filthy gray outfit. His black hair is a complete mess, and his eyes are hollow and dark. He's sneering at me as he grips a—

A knife! A long knife! And it's pointed at me!

"No! Don't kill me, don't kill me, don't kill me!" Hands hold me as I panic. I twist to escape, but they're way stronger than I am. My body is heavy, likely from the oxygen starvation and the dose of emergency oxidizer my suit injected into me, and that terrifies me more. I feel a scream building up from inside.

A hand strokes my head, breaking me from my trauma. The female voice from before speaks softly. "Hey, easy. You're safe. No one's going to hurt you. I promise."

My eyes search for its owner. If I could see who is trying to help me, I'd calm down a little. The deepness of her tone makes me think she might even be in charge here.

As her face comes into view, I gasp. Everything about it is intense. Her pale skin is tinted with olive, and a long scar stretches across her cheek. Her cold blue eyes are large yet hard.

Still, there's a freshness about her. She must be just a few years younger than me. And her lips.

Her lips.

I get a tingle through my body as I take them in. Soft. Round. Warm. Slightly parted and beckoning for me to...

Whoa.

I check myself. Of all the things to feel at this moment, desire shouldn't be one of them. Yet the longer I stare at this face, the more I struggle to find my breath. For lack of any better words, this girl is...She's...beautiful.

"Do you understand?" she asks. "We just saved your life. So there's no reason to worry."

I blink as I search the faces of the others surrounding me. Besides the one I'm going to call my savior—at least until she tells me her name and I understand it—there's the boy with the knife and two other girls here. The one who stands by the boy is younger than the other two. She's staring at me with a forehead full of creases.

"You're going to get wrinkles if you keep doing that," I say to her in a raspy voice and smile. It's just a joke, and it's more for me than it's for them. Humor eases my stress.

The teen girl wrinkles her brow more and shifts, glancing at my savior. So she's in charge, alright. That eases my tension by an order of magnitude at least. As warmth returns to my limbs, I lose my fear of those facing me and realize I'm looking at a bunch of seven-hundred-year-old teenagers. Questions flood into my head, way too many to organize with my muddled brain. Maybe a simple approach is better.

"I..." *What's their word for ship's commander, I wonder?*

"What's your name?" the one behind my savior asks.

"Fana. Fana Neridi." My body shakes as I cough. "I'm chief engineer of the *Devant*."

"The what of the what?"

My savior watches me, peering into my eyes as if she can see what's inside of my mind. I get a chill down my back and another tingle through the rest of me.

"Fa-na," she repeats. "Fana. Her name is Fana. Fana, I'm Ceri."

"Keh-ree?"

She smiles. I got it right.

A ruckus down the corridor makes all of us throw a glance in that direction. Two teenage boys, about the same age as Ceri, and a petite teenage girl, maybe a little younger, march down the passage.

With weapons in their hands.

Ceri lays a hand on me as I suck in a sharp breath. She's trying to keep me calm, but I feel the muscles in her arm go taut, so I also tense up and hope those guns are just for show. The ease with which they handle them doesn't make me think so.

"Is one of them your leader?" I ask.

She raises an eyebrow at me, then glances back at the new arrivals. The taller boy, who's quite pretty, is giving me a nasty look.

Ceri chuckles. "No, they're not our bosses."

That makes sense. Too young.

"So where are the people older than you? The ship's officers? You know, adults?"

Ceri pulls back. Her chin lowers as her face goes dark. "No adults here."

Before I can ask what that means, she gets distracted by the approach of the teenage girl, who tilts her head and eyes me with what I'm guessing is a lot of suspicion, though she's trying to hide it.

"Is she hurt?" the new girl asks as she approaches.

"Not that I can see," Ceri replies, then looks at me again. "Are you?"

I give her a smile and shake my head. At least she understands that. I'm catching on to their dialect, bit by bit. Just a few variations in pronunciation and a lovely lilt to the tone of their voices. If they didn't speak so fast, I might understand all of it the first time they say it.

The petite girl crouches next to Ceri, and there's an obvious easing of her attitude. I can trust this girl, too, I think.

"Hi. I'm Efa. I—"

"Hey!" the pretty boy shouts. "Are we all just ignoring infection control now?"

"Give it a rest, Sayer," Ceri fires back.

"There's no rest for anyone until we figure out this virus! Three more, including Beka, Ceri. Three more!"

The three that were here before gasp and widen their eyes. I didn't get all of that, but I get they're arguing about some kind of pathogen contamination on the ship. Raey would know more about that kind of thing than I would, but if they're worried, then maybe I should be, too.

"And now you just infected her!" This boy, Sayer, thrusts a finger at me. "She could have helped us, and now she's going to die!"

Huh?

Ceri's face hardens, and my body tenses again. Did I just take a colossal risk to come here, only to put my life in danger of infection by some microbe? Boy, do I hope not. I want to live longer. A lot longer.

But all this talk about disease is making me nervous. I'd be ill often if I didn't take my immune system boosters. Which reminds me, it's been more than a day cycle since I took my last serum. I've got at least another day or so before I open myself up for problems, but if this is some kind of new bug, I'm in trouble. Running back to the *Devant* could be the better idea.

"Are you sick?" I ask, looking between Ceri and Efa.

"No," Efa replies. "All of us here have tested negative, so don't worry."

"I'm not." That's a small lie. Or a big one. These teens may know something about infection control, but I doubt they know about treatment if one of them gets sick. Pretty boy's angry statements are proof of that. Maybe I need to get Raey over here.

"Put her helmet back on and get her out of here!" Sayer demands. I wince at the volume of his voice.

"Hey, easy," the boy next to him says. "You're scaring her."

"She should be scared!" Sayer's eyes meet mine then. "You may be happy you're alive now, but soon enough, you'll wish you weren't."

Ceri shoots to her feet, facing him. Her body floats into what I think is a fighting position with such speed and ease that my mouth drops open. She's got to be security on this ship, even if she's a little young for the job. Ceri could protect me from a hundred aggressors if she had to, and I'd be more than glad for her to do it. I'm already forcing myself not to grin, as I don't want to cause trouble for her.

Sayer's shoulders relax, and he sighs, while his friend looks to Efa for answers. Oh good. Ceri won that one. Not that I was doubting her. He may be taller and stronger, but she looks like she could beat his ass all the way back to Earth.

"Listen," Sayer says to me. "I don't know how you found us, and I don't really know why you bothered to come here, but this ship is completely hyuked, understand? You shouldn't have risked your life to get on board."

"She came because I asked her to," Ceri says. "I turned the beacon back on."

Her tone is defiant, and if I thought this was just a little disagreement, I was very wrong. A shiver runs though me as I realize I might be the one who needs saving from this group of kids with a potential violent streak in them.

"What the total hyuk, Ceri?" Sayer waves his gun around. Even his friend looks uneasy. "Did you just think our vote didn't matter? Now your selfishness just put this lady in danger." He looks at me again. "I bet you thought you were coming here to help us, didn't you? Now you're going to die!"

"Sayer, enough!"

I duck my head as the volume of her voice pierces my unsteady nerves. There is something very wrong on this ship, and I've dropped myself right into the middle of it. Weapons in the hands of teenagers. No adults. A spreading contagion? What the hell happened here?

"Send her back," Sayer growls. "She can't help us if she's sick."

"No," Ceri replies.

"Hey." Sayer's companion holds up his hands and looks at Ceri. "I know you thought you were doing the right thing by turning the beacon back on, but we should send her back now. It's the only way to guarantee her safety."

"Let her decide," Efa suggests, glancing at me. "She's an adult, and I bet she knows how to make up her own mind."

I can, but I don't know if I really want to. I'm both safe and in danger on this ship, and that naturally makes my heart pound for different reasons, like it does now. How do I even calculate this risk, anyway? There are way too many unknowns for any choice to be accurate. The only thing I'm sure of is that I'm screwed no matter what I do.

But when I look into Ceri's eyes again, I catch her youthful desire shining through, and the more I see it, the more I want to learn about it. There's something amazing about this girl, and I have to know what it is. That might be a selfish reason to stay—okay, it's definitely a selfish reason to stay here—but as much as I think I can get from her, I know there are also things I can share.

And that makes my decision easy.

"I'm staying," I say, reaching out to take her hand. "I can help you...okay?"

While the others share glances, a clear sign of their uncertainty, my savior crouches before me and takes my hand up. Warmth radiates through me at her touch, and I get the feeling that as long as I stick with her, I'm doing the right thing.

"Yes. Please," Ceri says. "We need as much help with the *Stratford* as we can get."

I put my lips together, fearing what would happen if she thought I was about to deny her plea. As much as I'm taking a risk, this girl has got my attention, and I won't let her slip out of my grasp.

My eyes connect with every teenager here. Efa, the three younger ones behind her, that guy Sayer and his friend, and then Ceri. I squeeze her hand as I smile at her and shake my head.

"I swear. I won't leave you."

STATUS

CERI

I DIDN'T WANT TO bring her here. Efa thought it a bad idea, too. Fana had nearly died. Yet the moment Efa completed checking her over this morning, she insisted on seeing the ship. Now here we stand on level four, ready to make the climb into command and control, as Fana eyes the ladder to level three with uncertainty. Perhaps she's realized how she's not ready to push her body into action. Perhaps I shouldn't have given in to her childish pleas, but I'm determined to find out if she can help us rebuild the navigation system.

Her night in medical wasn't without challenges, either. First, we had to verbally spar with her to let us remove her pressure suit, then she fought us when Efa asked her to remove the inner base layer. I've never seen a girl be so shy in front of other girls. We're all the same without clothes.

Fana wears a surplus Fahrasi combat uniform now, though we haven't told her that for concern she might not want to wear it. With no one fabricating clothing for us, it was all we had to offer. At least she's content to wear it and no longer bashful. I will accept that as a battle won.

"Efa, go first," I say, then nod at Fana. "You'll go next, and I'll follow."

Fana glances at the ladder again and pulls her hands to her body.

"Don't worry. I'll be there if you slip."

"We can't take the elevator?"

"The what?"

"I think she means the rail car," Efa explains, then turns to Fana. "The adults welded the doors shut on the top few levels."

Fana crunches her eyebrows together. "Why?"

"Ah, well." Efa looks at me for support. I shrug. I can't just summarize everything we've been through and everything the children who died before have experienced. Nor do I want to relive those moments for the sake of explanation.

"The adults decided it," I reply. "It's not important any longer."

Since she's arrived onboard, I've gotten the sense that Fana is highly intelligent, if a little odd. She's picked up on a few of Efa's and my nonverbal communications and quickly understood the medical devices we used to test her vitals. The second time I used the diagnostic cuff on her, she knew how to use it.

"Okay," Fana says. "I'll go."

It still took more than a few minutes to get her up the ladder. She seemed more concerned with me being behind her than climbing. Halfway up, I had to push her ass to keep going as she completed the last few rungs with shaky limbs and a timid pace.

Level three, like the levels above it, is a blackened wreck. The only remains are the bent frames of the computer systems that covered this floor. Strands of melted wire hang from their tops like black vines in a steel jungle. The floor laminate has peeled apart and curled up from the heat, reminding me of sheets of charcoal art paper I used when I was young.

The adults long ago removed any hardware that was salvageable, and anything they didn't use or ruin was down on level one-sixteen. Only Merek and Sayer have seen what's there, so only they know what's left.

"What...what happened here?" Fana asks, breathless.

"A fire ran through here about seventy years ago," I reply. "We're not sure how it started. We've heard plenty of rumors, though. A short circuit, sabotage, a sloppy repair. Not that it matters."

"We're stuck either way," Efa adds.

Fana steps unsteadily toward the first burned-out hulk of a processor tower. Her hand touches it as her breaths come faster. Efa motions for me to follow her. I agree. Fana's moving like a wounded soldier.

She gasps as her hands caress the broken metal, moving across it as if it was a beloved pet or a toy. She looks out into the dimness of the level, lit by only a pair of portable lights that have become permanent residents of this wasteland.

"No..." Fana whispers, her body shuddering. "No...How? How is this ship...How could you? Oh, you poor...all of you..."

Fana steps backward and falters, her knees going weak. Efa and I both approach as she catches herself on a crossbar in the frame, but she's panting now, her eyes wild as she takes in the complete hopelessness of our situation.

Then she collapses.

I catch her before she hits the ground, gently lowering her to the deck as I kneel beside her. Efa drops next to me and takes Fana's paled face in her hands to examine it, her eyes hardening as she works.

"It's okay. It's okay!" Fana says, pushing our hands away. "I'm fine. I promise!"

Efa pulls back, frowning but broken from her intense focus. "Are you sure?"

"Yes." Fana sighs and takes a moment to look up at both of us with a smile. "You girls really take care of me. I could get used to it."

"Don't," I say, standing and glaring.

Fana squeezes our hands as we help her up, shaking her body with joy as she does. Efa and I share a glance, but I'd prefer to forget it. All that's important is Fana's evaluation and answer.

"So?" I ask.

"I won't," she replies. "I swear!"

"No, I mean, can you fix it?"

"*Fix?*" Fana's eyes widen, and she shakes her head with un-expected vigor. "No. We can't fix this."

Efa lets out a cry as my stomach drops to the deck. A vision of my parents flashes before my eyes. I see them suffocate in their pods, their bloodied fists pounding on the thick glass of the portal. My chest tightens as I watch terror explode on their faces, but I'm helpless to do anything to save them.

"No!" I grab Fana's arms. "No, you've got to do something. There are four thousand people in stasis on this ship, and I swore I'd do everything to save them. So you will too!"

"Hey!" She struggles in my grasp. "I'm sorry! I didn't know it was going to be like this! If I had something, anything to work with, maybe I could do something! But this...this..."

I slam Fana against the frame, and she yelps. My insides burn as I seethe at her. In that moment, I'm as fiery as the blaze that ended our promise of a new world and a hopeful future. We're doomed now. Every child I inspired to remain on the *Stratford*—Efa, Seren, Merek, Rhys, Tegan, even Sayer—has chosen an empty hope. All of us will die here, knowing how our sacrifice, our decision to stay, was for nothing.

"Ceri, ease off." Efa pries my fingers off Fana's arms. "It's not her fault."

She pushes me away from Fana, who only gawks at me as she rubs the spot where I nearly crushed her bones with my bare hands. That is what I imagine is running through her head—how I'm an uncaged animal.

And now here is yet another whom I've hurt.

"I could talk to my commander," Fana offers. "We have plenty of spare pods. I'm sure he'd be willing to take you on as passengers."

Efa's face brightens as she looks at me with hopeful eyes. "Oh, Ceri! The others will be so excited. We'll have a future. A real future. Merek and I could have children. We'd have a home that wasn't some dark maze in the middle of nowhere. And you—"

"No." I drop my gaze. "If that's what you want, then do it, Efa. I'm staying."

"For what?" She points at Fana. "You heard her! This ship is done! You'd be wasting your life for nothing."

The embers of the fire that filled me before glow hotter as Efa's words stoke them.

"My life's not a waste!" I shout, pounding my hand on the wall. "The *Devant* isn't the only ship out there. If they heard our beacon, someone else will, too. I'll wait."

Efa sighs as her body sags, the edges of her mouth drooping when her head does. Neither of us wants me to be alone. Even with as much time as she spends with Merek, Efa and I have been together longer. I could never replace the part of me that would disappear with her. And being alone on this ship would turn me into a creature like Rabbit. That old man may have been half-mad, but he recognized freedom when it was offered to him, and he took it.

"There's no way I can leave, Efa," I breathe. "You may have dreams of a family with Merek, and that's wonderful, but…"

"You could have that, too," Efa says. "Once everyone is awake, you'll meet someone. I'm sure of that."

"No." I shake my head. "I can't let go of this. It would haunt me if I did."

Fana shifts and watches me as she curls her lips in. If she's planning on supporting Efa's plan to get me to leave, she better try something else. I won't listen, and her words will fail. I've survived through too much for anyone to bend my will again.

"What's upstairs?" Fana asks.

"The communications console," I answer.

Fana bites the edge of her lip. "Anything else?"

"Bits and pieces of the navigation system and the pilot's station."

She grabs the back of her arm to rub it, her eyes drifting to the ceiling as she hums an odd tune. I'm not sure I appreciate this interruption. Efa's also confused by her questions, her narrowed eyes verging on a glare.

"What are you thinking?" I ask.

"Help me." Fana motions up and holds her hand out. I take it to mean she wants to see level two, not throw her through the ceiling. Though if she refuses to let us in on her line of thought, I might just do that.

I do as she asks and, along with Efa, a little more than that. I give her a shove from below as Efa yanks her up from her shoulders. Fana is far from heavy, and despite her weakness, we get her to the second level in less time than she took to make it up to the third.

"Oh!" Fana raises her eyebrows and half-stumbles, half-crawls to the communications console. She licks her lips, scans it, then taps a few buttons. "Your crew repaired this?"

"Yes, mostly."

"But none of you are engineers, right?"

I nod, but her question was more likely her thinking out loud.

Fana spins to face us, her hands and body on the edge of the console. She smiles and, with a coy motion, dips her head. My jaw tightens. I won't play games with her. Not here and now. If she doesn't want to take this seriously, then she can return to her ship. The population of an entire town will be lost if we don't fix the *Stratford*.

"I have an idea, and I'd really like to try it. If it works, we could build a rudimentary navigation and control system with very little effort."

"Explain," I say, folding my arms.

"I can't. Not yet. I'm still trying to think it through, but if I can get one of our multiprocessor systems over here and interface it with your ship's navigation, we'd have a very good chance to save everyone and everything on this ship. Just tell me if you want me to do it, and I'll have a go at it."

"Of course we want you to!" Efa cries as she looks for my response.

I run a finger across my throat. Until now, everything Fana's done has proven how she wants to help, so she's not attempting to deceive us. It isn't an impossibility, however. I'll keep an eye on her and make sure she doesn't deviate from her promise.

I press my lips into a smile. "Okay. We accept."

ARRIVAL

FANA

I STAND WITH THE Four—what I'm calling Ceri, Efa, Merek, and Sayer—as we wait for the airlock to cycle. Then we can open the inner hatch and let Raey and two security agents inside the *Stratford*. Without telling her too much, I tried to explain the challenges here. Raey responded with just two words, and now my hands can't seem to find a comfortable position to stay in. Plus, despite being behind Efa and Ceri, the heavy sound of Sayer's breathing is giving me chills.

If I could see Raey's face, or maybe if I could hold Ceri's hand again, I might relax. Neither is going to happen. Raey's still wearing her helmet, and Ceri gave me a suspicious glance when I tried to slip my fingers into hers. Raey wouldn't like that, anyway. Not because she'd be jealous, which she might be, but because she'd think her chief engineer has latched onto a scary set of people.

I can't wait to tell her these teenagers are running the ship.

The airlock light goes green, and the hatch unseals with a sound that reminds me of a person gasping, stopping my heart for at least a second. After what I've seen and learned from my caretakers, I'm amazed the *Stratford* is still in any sort of operating condition. I really need to examine their engine and make sure it's still got life left in it.

Raey steps through the door and pulls off her helmet. She spots me and makes a direct line over. Her gaze connects with mine, and I catch the lack of emotion on her face. But that means she's a total mess inside, which is usually before she verbally whips me for being an idiot.

"Are you okay?" she asks, taking my arm with a bit of a grip.

As I smile and nod to her, the security agents come out of the airlock, their eyes scanning everything multiple times as their hands hover over their weapons. That could be why the Four shift into an aggressive posture. It's a subtle move, but it's hard to miss with them next to me.

"I'm Raey T'ena, a medical specialist on the *Devant*," Raey says to them. "Thank you for caring for our chief. Can I speak to your officers?"

Raey eyes me when I snicker. I do my best to transform it into a cough. It fails.

Efa, Merek, and Sayer all glance at Ceri, possibly expecting her to reply. But she misses it because she's busy staring at Raey. I don't get that she's worried, or even suspicious, but it's hard to tell, and that makes my stomach twist.

"Raey, I'm Efa Kandha. It's nice to meet you. Welcome to the *Stratford*." Efa nearly curtsies and does her best to put on a warm smile. It's awkward at best.

"Yeah, let's get past that nonsense," Sayer adds. "We really need your help with a few of the crew. They're pretty bad."

Raey cocks her head to her side. "Bad? As in ill? Or wounded? Where's your medical staff?"

"That'd be me," Efa replies with a small upward curl of her mouth.

"You? How could you be a doctor?"

"I'm not."

Raey's forehead creases as she takes Efa in. The girl doesn't look like much, but after spending time with her, she's earned my respect. All the Four have, even if Sayer scares me still.

"Fana, what the hell is going on here?" Raey demands.

Before I can answer, Sayer pushes past Merek and Efa and steps in front of me. The security agents tense, and he eyes them back. But to my relief, a second later, he turns to Raey, who is already retreating as she takes him in.

"You need to know that stepping on this ship just put all of you at risk of infection," he hisses. "We have a serious problem here, and none of us know how to solve it."

Raey shakes her head, the wrinkles in her forehead getting deeper. "I'm sorry. I understood very little of that. You have an infection? Could you repeat that again slower? And where's your captain?"

I glance at Ceri, but she's just acting all passive, leaning against the wall as if she is just having some casual conversation. The others wanted her to take charge. Why doesn't she?

Sayer's finger pokes me in the shoulder. I jump as he glares at me.

"Explain to her how hyuked we are," he orders.

"Hey, take it easy," Merek says, motioning to the rifles in the security agent's holsters.

Sayer's eyes drift over them, and they stare right back. Their knees are bent, their fingers ready to fling the flap off their guns and draw them out. Not good. My legs already feel weak with the amount of tension hanging over the moment. Maybe I should act like the senior staff I'm supposed to be and calm this showdown.

I gesture to Sayer that I'll do as he asks, even though he didn't ask, and I'm a little miffed at that. But I'm more afraid of what happens if someone shoots.

Raey runs a hand through her hair and sighs as I try for my best explanation of everything that's happened until now. I keep my voice calm, hoping not to provoke either side, but the more detail I get into, the tighter Raey's jaw becomes.

"Your transmission said nothing about a potential outbreak," Raey says as she glares at the Four. "Doesn't your captain know the regulations? It's been standard procedure for at least a thousand years to warn other ships about the dangers of boarding your vessel."

"Our communication system isn't exactly up to spec," Merek replies, speaking slower to help her comprehend his words. "Fana wasn't able to let us know others might come."

"Well, if she had, that's one thing in a million she might have done right." Raey looks at me and folds her arms. "Get your suit on. We're taking you back."

"Uh..."

The security agents come forward, and the Four move again, ever so slightly, as if they're about to get into some serious work. There's no conscious thought about their reaction. Whatever they're about to do, they've done before. A lot.

Before I return to the *Devant*, I need to know why these teenagers hold calm when a pair of armed security agents with the skill to hurt them—or kill them—are threating serious action if they get in the way. I really need to know where'd they learn to be unafraid like this and why they're so eager to keep me here. Of course, I'd very much like them to do that. I don't want to leave.

"So you won't help us?" Efa asks, her jaw dropping.

"As per my commander's orders, I am returning Chief Neridi to the *Devant,* where we will run a full set of tests on her and now on the three of us as well," Raey replies. "Tell your captain, if we find something, we'll create a serum and send it over."

"And what happens if you find nothing?" Ceri challenges. "What then?"

"We will work with your captain, and whatever senior staff he chooses, to solve your infection issue. The facilities on the *Devant* are the best that humanity has ever developed, and frankly, after seeing just this much of this ship, I would doubt any results that you came up with."

Ceri lowers her gaze at Raey, who frowns as she waits for a response.

"You're not getting it, are you?" Ceri pushes off the wall and moves in front of the others.

"Getting what?" Raey shrugs.

"There's no captain here. No senior staff. No adults at all. We're the crew." Ceri gets in Raey's face. "And if you saw what this virus does to people, you'd wouldn't be thinking about returning to your fancy ship, because by the time you figure out what it is, it'll have infected half of your team."

Raey blinks at Ceri, doing her best to work through every word while Ceri's body remains taut. At least the others have eased down now that she's taking charge. Maybe that's why they were so anxious.

"So who are you then?" Raey asks.

"Ceri."

"Well, Ceri, I appreciate your warning, and I understand about your crew, but as your friend here"—Raey gestures to Efa—"just pointed out, you have no medical staff, so whatever you think of our *fancy* ship, you are not qualified to determine our levels of risk. Now, I promise we'll do everything we can to help, but until my commander gives us new orders, we have to follow the ones we've been given."

Ceri puts her lips together and eyes Raey. It's her turn to consider the words she's just heard. I'll bet she's gauging just how much she can trust Raey.

"Talk to him, then," Ceri says, sticking her chin out. "And get new ones."

Raey nods. "Of course I will. As soon as we get back. It won't take long at all."

Her eyes fall on me, and I know what comes next. But before she can drag me back, I'll try everything I can think of to remain here. I've only seen a few levels of this ship so far. There are at least another hundred that I've yet to explore. And I'm making sure the effort it took to get here is worth it.

"My suit is out of oxygen," I say.

"Yes, we figured as much. So we brought a recharge with us." Raey twists and points to the pair of cylinders resting in the airlock, and I grit my teeth.

"I might have damaged it," I say with a tight jaw.

"So we'll repair it. Don't worry." Raey smiles and reaches out to touch me, but I step back, and she frowns, her hand hanging in midair. When she tries again, I slide out of reach.

"I'm not going back, Raey." I throw my hands up before she can protest. "Not yet. The situation here is dire, and it's not some illness that's the biggest problem. I need to see what I can do for them while I'm here. Then once I have a plan, I'll return."

Now that was a good one. Raey should believe that, even if it is only a secondary reason.

"That's logical," she says, "but it's not up to either of us, and you know that. So come on. Let's fix your suit and go."

Ceri reaches back and pushes me fully behind her while Raey stares in amazement. I'm not entirely sure why she's trying to protect me like this, but it's bringing a smile to my face, and I duck my head close to Ceri's back to hide it. If this wasn't so serious, it might be a little fun.

"Please, children," Raey pleads. "Let's not be irrational. I already said I'd help you."

"So did Fana," Ceri replies. "And you're about to make her break her promise."

"Specialist T'ena," one of the security agents says, "we can handle it from here. You can step away so we can escort Chief Neridi back to the *Devant* or arrest her for abandoning her post."

"I'm not abandoning my post!" I protest, my voice muffled as I speak into Ceri's back. "Our directive is to support any ship that requests help!"

"You can debate that with Commander Azazhi, Chief. Now step forward so we can suit you up and get you back...or do we need to use force?"

"That would be a poor choice," Ceri says, her tone darkening. "Even with your weapons, you're outnumbered and in an unfamiliar environment."

The security agent's eyebrows mash together. He's got no idea what she means, but I do. These kids can fight, or at least they think they can. And Ceri is right. Even with guns, it's four against two. They'd have to be fairly quick to tap out the Four before they got hit, though a battle is the last thing I want to cause. A chill runs across my back, just imagining it. The security agents firing their plasma guns as the Four bear down on them.

Someone could die.

I pop my head out from behind Ceri and give Raey my best pathetic, big-eyed puppy look. It's got a near one-hundred-percent effectiveness rate. Once she sees it, and she will, I can get nearly anything I ask for. I'll have to make it up to her later, but it's usually a good trade.

Raey huffs and rolls her eyes, then she puts her hand on her hip and rubs her tongue across her teeth as she looks away. My heart flutters because it's so cute, and I just want to throw my arms around her and squeeze. But I won't. The security agents would snatch me up in a second if I did.

"Okay, let me examine your sick, at least," Raey says after a few seconds of her silent tantrum. "Then I can give Commander Azazhi a more accurate report about what is going on here. After that, you'd better do as he orders, Fana."

OFFER

——— • ———

CERI

Specialist T'ena is a skilled medical technician. It's in the way she flows through her procedures, almost like a soldier pressing an attack. And the care she shows Beka and the others while running tests on them nearly makes me smile. It certainly makes Beka happy.

Beka could use some joy right now. The graying of her skin is a portent of the pain that follows. I only hope Specialist T'ena is talented enough to cure whatever ails the poor girl. Beka's had little luck on this ship: denied a new life, wounded in combat, and now this.

We'll have to move the girls' nests again. This cramped space is contaminated, and just like the boys' barracks, we'll have to incinerate everything. Perhaps now is a good time to switch to actual beds instead of these weaved jumbles of blankets and foam. I can't remember why we ever accepted them as comfortable. Maybe we never had a choice.

"Okay, you just rest for now," Specialist T'ena—Fana calls her Raey—says. She touches Beka's face and pulls the blanket up under her chin. Beka struggles to smile, but at least she's still conscious and coherent, even if she's not speaking much. I will try to be hopeful and pray that Raey can save her.

There's more between her and Fana than just a professional relationship, I think, though, to me, that's odd. Raey, somewhere in her fourth decade, certainly qualifies as an adult, while Fana often acts more immature than even some of our youngest. I couldn't imagine them being lovers, or even former lovers, despite the similarities I see between them and Efa and Merek's interactions.

"So?" I ask as Raey stands and brushes herself off. She turns to me with a pained look, then motions to the door.

"Talk with me outside," she says.

I follow her out, and we stroll to the end of the corridor toward a secluded part of the level. Efa and I would come here when we wanted to hide from the squad and just chat without the possibility of interruption.

That's where Raey turns on me.

"You are failing to keep your crew safe." Her eyes fill with intensity as she thrusts her finger at me. "Are you that naïve about infection control?"

"Me?" I open my hands. "What makes you think this is my fault?"

"Aren't you responsible for the others?"

I shrug with a half-hearted motion, uncomfortable with her attempt to place blame. Yet she's correct. I've tasked myself to look after Beka and the other children. I just won't admit that to her. She'll use it against me, and my sense of guilt over Tal's death will crush any will I have to stand up to her.

"Don't lie," Raey says. "I'm well acquainted with attempts to deflect accountability, and I see how the others look up to you."

"Nobody looks up to me here. We're all equal."

"That's a load of nonsense, Ceri. You're the leader here. It's more than obvious, so stop denying it." She puts her hands on her hips. "Now what are you going to do to minimize contagion in your crew? I'll be leaving soon, and it'll be on you and the others to care for your crew."

Acid presses against the lining of my stomach as the specter of Tal's diseased body and Beka's ashen face flash across my vision. I wish Raey was staying longer, especially now since she's seen how desperate our situation is.

Fana will go with her when she leaves, and like Raey, she won't return. If I were her commander, I'd never let my chief engineer leave the ship again. She's far too important. Likely she never had the permission to come here.

I need to stall their departure, or we will be back in the same hell we started in.

"How are they?" Efa asks as she approaches with Sayer. His face is a permanent scowl, and he looms over Efa as if he's forced her to come here. He could never manage that, but his anger with me is more than apparent.

Raey shakes her head. "Not well. Without a proper pathology diagnosis and curated anti-viral treatment, these kids are going to die."

Efa fights to stay calm, her fists clenching while the acid in my stomach threatens to scar the back of my throat. Even when

I knew the truth, I still denied it. To watch Beka wither into an agonizing end is more than I could handle.

Raey is still here, so there might yet be a chance to convince her to stay longer. I just need to figure out what will convince her.

"Specialist," Efa says, squeezing her hands together. "You see how badly we're in trouble here. Couldn't you stay longer? We need your help."

"I would, but it makes little sense to," Raey replies. "You don't have the facilities to do the testing, and you have no idea how to manufacture the medicines required to defeat this infection. The longer I stay, the less chance they have."

Sayer curses under his breath and shakes his fists so hard, Raey jumps as she stares at him. He glares at me and walks a few paces away, where he stops, facing the wall. A second later, his fist swings out and pounds the composite material, sending a deep boom through the corridor. It's a good thing that's all he does. We can't afford another standoff. It would force the crew to take sides, and then we're back to where we were before—under the thumb of the adults. Except they wouldn't be around to keep our youthful aggression in check. I fear the result of that.

Despite his threats, I'm sympathetic. He cares so much it tears him up inside when something goes wrong. I'm the same, save that I don't threaten anyone with weapons when things go bad. If he gets reckless again, I'm not sure I'll be able to talk him down.

Raey curls in the edge of her lower lip as her gaze drops. A moment later, she folds her arms and turns to me. "I could take the most critical back with me to the *Devant*. They'd get a treatment much faster, and I'd be able to monitor their recovery."

Efa gasps, a smile spreading across her face as she presses her hands together. When her gaze moves to connect with mine, I avoid it. Hope may be lifting her up, but I will remain cautious. Raey's words to me before were far from charitable.

"But," Raey adds, "I'll be honest with you. That's putting my entire ship at risk. This is an unknown virus strain, and there's no guarantee that we'll be able to synthesize a cure or that my commander would even grant permission to bring them over."

"We understand that," Efa replies, "And we're at your mercy, but if there's any way to appeal to your commander's humanity, we could really use a hand."

Raey tilts her head and shrugs, then takes a moment to consider. Or at least pretend to. My doubt about this woman is increasing by the second. We may need her and her ship, but anyone that speaks first in terms of their own issues won't prioritize ours in any meaningful way.

Still, she's offering to help, and she's concerned about the virus spreading. I know little of how that happens, so I have to rely on Efa and, with reservations, Raey.

"Maybe if I could bring him something in exchange," Raey says, appearing thoughtful. "Something that might counterbalance the risk."

"Like what?" I say.

"Well." She folds her arms. "We've just completed a shift change, and the new crew are bound to be a little mindless after stasis. They'll need a few weeks to get their heads into the routine, and they'll need some help while they're adjusting."

"So?"

"So let me take your crew to the *Devant*. We'll run some blood tests on them to make sure no one else is infected, and once that's done, they can handle some basic tasks for our crew."

Raey makes her suggestion sound as if there's nothing to it. Yet there's something about her offer that's making me tense.

"What tasks?" Sayer asks.

She lifts a shoulder. "Oh, I don't know. Whatever needs doing, likely. The commander will make that decision. Don't worry. I'm sure whatever it is will be reasonable."

The tight-lipped smile forming on her face is sending a chill across my skin. I've seen that smirk before. Too many times. Adults always put one on when they were about to demand something from us.

Now I know what's bothering me.

"So do we have an agreement?" Raey asks.

Sayer scowls at her and plants his feet while Efa looks at me to reply, her eyes big. She'd want nothing more than to me say yes. I want nothing more than to save Beka's life.

But I can't.

Once they had Beka, she'd be their hostage, and they'd force us to do whatever the commander of the *Devant* wished to get her back. The thought alone burns a fire through my chest.

All the pain we've endured, all that we've sacrificed, and the freedom and right to choose our own fate that came from it—adults don't get to take that from us again.

"No," I growl. "We're not agreeing to that."

"Ceri!" Efa spins on me, her jaw slack. "Beka will die if we don't do this!"

Beka's crew. If saving her life was the only reason to say yes to this trap, I would. It's not. I still hate that I've got to put Beka's life up against this bish deal.

Sayer should have spoken up by now, but his lips are tight as his eyes dart between Raey and me. With a glare, I attempt to impress upon him the need to refuse Raey's offer.

But as he debates, I get the sense he's going to give in.

And that's exactly what he does.

"I'm uncomfortable with this exchange as it stands," Sayer says. "But we've got to do anything we can to save Beka and the others. If Specialist T'ena says it shouldn't be too bad, then we'll just take her at her word."

"It wouldn't be her word," I counter. "She's just the messenger in all this. All she can do is bring our offer to her commander. And at that point, Beka and the others would be there. We'd be forced to agree if we ever wanted to see them again!"

"You're overreacting, Ceri," Raey says, holding her hands up. "Commander Azazhi isn't a cruel man. He'll help you. I'm just suggesting you make it easy for him to agree to do so."

"So it's a bribe, then?"

Raey opens her mouth to speak, then sighs, her shoulders going slack. She can play this however she wants, but the truth remains. She's got no way to prove otherwise. And I refuse to let my crew to be slaves again.

"Don't be so hard on her," Efa chides. "She wants to help us!"

"Maybe," I reply as I watch Raey. "But she's also gauging how much she can get away with."

"What are you talking about?" Raey's brow furrows as she shakes her head.

"I think you already know what kind of work the commander wants us to do, and until you tell us what that is, I'm not agreeing to anything."

"You are hyuking out of your mind!" Sayer says, shoving me. "Do you realize your paranoia is going to cost Beka her life? No? Get over yourself already."

Raey steps in between Sayer and me, holding her hands up. "Kids, there's no need to get violent about this. Just talk it over and let me know. I'll be here for another hour."

As she walks away, Sayer clenches his fists and gets in my face. I just stare, not interested in sparking another fight between us. He's allowed to be upset. We all are.

"Are you satisfied?" Sayer asks as he pokes his finger into my shoulder. "You just killed Beka. You got that? Hope you can live with yourself."

He storms off, and the stress seeps from my shoulders, if only a little. Efa is still here, and the disappointed look on her face means this issue isn't over yet.

"Ceri," she says, squeezing my arm. "For everyone's sake, *please*, if you don't want the crew over there, then come with something else to offer them. I don't care what it is. No one else dies, okay?"

I nod, though I'm confused at her plea. We all want Beka to survive. Why wouldn't she care?

As she leaves, clarity hits me. She and Sayer may have protested my refusal, but they have no idea what the right thing to do is.

And now it's on me to figure this out.

COUNTER

FANA

SEREN WATCHES AS I dig my fingers through the mass of wires and circuit boards underneath the communications console. I'm flat on my belly, with a light in my mouth and my arms buried as deep into the system as they can go. She's crouched next to me, a second beam in her hand shining down into the electronics from above so I can get an overview of the circuit topology here.

"How can you know what every one of those wires and cards does?" Seren asks.

"Who says I do?" I reply.

"Well, you move through them like you do. So even if you don't know exactly what they are, I think you must have some idea. Or at least can make a good guess."

"Huh." I chuckle. "You're perceptive. Tell you what, if I can figure out their functions, I'll share that with you."

I'm pouring over some of the design logic that the *Stratford*'s systems use. That way, I can devise an interface between one of our multiprocessors and whatever machines they have left. Then I can either copy the *Devant*'s navigation software or write a few new programs to correct the *Stratford*'s course and put the ship in orbit once it reaches its destination, which, if I'm acting selfishly—and I am—will stay the same as the *Devant's*.

Despite the quality of the build and the skill of the engineers who built this ship, little of it is making sense to me. It doesn't help that every trace in these multi-level printed circuits ends in an archaic-looking flat black chip that I don't know the function of. All I can do is guess, and that means, even with Seren's help, I'm making slow progress.

"Fana."

Oh hell. It's Raey and the security agents. Time to put on my smile.

"Hey." I dust myself off as I stand up from behind the console. "How are your patients?"

Raey eyes me with a look I've seen often, and even though a few lines grace the edges of her eyes now, the meaning of it hasn't changed. This is her cutting-through-my-nonsense face, and I'll bet she's using it now because Raey is about to get very direct with me.

And as I understand why, I get goosebumps across my arms.

"We've fixed your suit," the older security agent says. "So finish up whatever you're doing and get ready. We're leaving."

"But I won't be done here for a while," I say in a causal tone. "What's the rush?"

The man looks to Raey, who sets her jaw and approaches me with that evil gait of hers. I'm in extra trouble now.

"Fana," Raey says, crossing her arms. "The commander has given you a direct order to return and given us an order to subdue you if necessary. If you don't want him to stuff you into a stasis pod for the rest of our journey, think about going to see him and begging for forgiveness the second you set foot on the *Devant.*"

Seren ducks her head and looks for an exit, but before she can slip away, I snatch her hand and keep her from escaping.

"We have an opportunity to help them, Raey," I say, pulling Seren closer. "It's amazing what they've done on their own, but as you can see, without some serious fixes to this ship's command and control, we'd be dooming them to live out their lives here with no purpose. And we don't do that kind of thing."

Raey smirks. I suppose an older and wiser version of herself, who no doubt has forgotten little about me, is much more difficult to argue with.

"If you really believe that," she says, "then go make your case to the commander. Or did you hit your head and forget he's the only one who can allocate the personnel and materials to make anything like that happen?"

Well, she's seen right through that ploy. Unfair, I'd say. She's had seventeen years to gain all kinds of advantages over me, and now I'm getting beaten up by them. It feels more like a full-body ache than a bruised muscle, but the assault is the same.

Seren tugs on my hand and gives me an expectant look. The frown on her face makes it seem like I'm torturing her by keeping her here. I hope not. I still need to borrow her for a bit.

"Say, that reminds me. Seren here said she wasn't feeling well. Could you give her a quick examination? She's feeling a little warm to me."

"It's fine," Seren interjects, pulling away before I can put my hand on her forehead. "I mean, I'm fine. I'm not sick. Anyway, I've got to go."

I lower my head and stick out my lower lip. Seren offers an apologetic smile but continues to step away.

"Let her go, Fana," Raey says. She's sounding more like my mother every minute. I'm not sure whether to be excited or afraid.

"Thanks for letting me watch you work," Seren says as I release my grip on her hand. She does some odd little bow and then moves off in a hurry.

It was probably wrong to use the girl as a shield like that. She's innocent in all this and likely could be a big help in navigating the *Stratford*'s lower levels where all the bio and environmental systems are. I should apologize to her later.

Right now, I need to—how would Ceri say it? Readjust my tactics.

"Okay, I'll make you a deal," I say, coming around to the front side of the console.

"No," Raey replies.

I sigh. "Don't you think this is strange?"

"What's strange?"

"You and me."

Raey shifts her weight and drops her gaze as her cheeks turn pink. We didn't keep our relationship a secret, but we didn't flaunt it in front of the crew, either. The commander would have looked down on that as setting a dangerous precedent between the ship's executive team and lower ranks. As long as we remained low-key about it, he just pretended not to know. I kind of liked that. It really made my blood pump sneaking around to meet with her, and our secret meetings became such a thrill I couldn't wait for the next one. Even now, it puts a grin on my face.

Which gets wiped away by Raey's glare.

"There is no you and me," Raey says. "I wouldn't have a relationship with someone who might be the same age as my daughter, if I had one. And certainly not with someone who's acting like a child."

Her words strike me right in my chest, and now it's my turn to look away. She's had years I didn't have to forget about us. And while time in stasis can heal the physical body, it does nothing for the mind. I have no thoughts about us getting back together, but it still hurts to hear her be so final about it.

If I return to the *Devant*, it'll only remind me of Raey's dismissal every time I see her. And Commander Azazhi will treat me like the child she's accusing me of being. Maybe it'd be better if I went back into stasis.

No. No way. I'm not giving up.

"Fine, I'll go back," I say and wait for the three of them to relax. Then I continue, "On the condition you stay here and care for these children until all of them are at an acceptable level of health."

"You don't care about these children," one security agent says.

"It doesn't matter if I care or not," I fire back. "We are bound by regulations to help any ship that requests it. That's why they gave us the fastest and most technologically advanced ship humanity has ever built."

The man's eyebrows clash, and he looks at his partner. "I've never heard of that. Is it true?"

The other agent shrugs, opening his hands. They both look at Raey, who sighs and curls her lips in.

"Haven't either of you read our operating principles?" she asks.

"Have you studied the self-defense manual like you were supposed to?" the first security agent retorts. When Raey keeps her mouth shut, he huffs. "Then don't accuse us either."

I hide my smile as I sense an opportunity to turn this to my advantage. If they can't get along with her, I might have an easier chance of taking Raey into seeing my side of things. She's likely just acting like this because of the security agents, anyway. All she needs is a reason not to cooperate with them.

"Not knowing what the principals are doesn't excuse us from following any guideline," I say, lifting myself to my full height. "And they say we stay here and take care of this crew."

The first agent's eye twitches. I hold my breath and force down the grin that wants to explode across my face. They should have known better than to go against me, the chief of engineering. I finished secondary school before most of my age had even entered. My advanced certifications cover most of the natural sciences as well as a few of the formal ones. I'm the smartest person on the *Devant*. Out of stasis anyway.

"You don't know when to stop, do you?" Raey sighs and presses her palm at me. "Never mind. I don't need an answer. I've had this same discussion with you a hundred times."

I shake my head at her as I swallow down the bile in my throat. Did I read the situation that wrong? Just a minute ago, it seemed like she was shifting toward my side.

"Stop what?" I ask. "We're doing the right thing by staying here. Now—"

"Who said we were staying?"

My jaw drops open. "What about the regulations?"

"Don't pretend to be naïve, Fana. You heard what the commander said earlier. No one cares about the regulations. Only our survival matters."

All I can do is stare. She's changed so much. My Raey would have insisted on staying here. She would have threatened to report these two agents for failing to abide by everything we stood for.

Huh. My Raey. That seems like someone who died years ago, just like my parents.

The first security agent grins and steps forward. "So are you getting into your suit, or are we arresting you?"

FLIGHT

FANA

As the first security agent presses closer, the second approaches from the side, attempting to trap me against the console. Their beady-eyed stare is sliding ice down my back. In five seconds, they'll spring forward, knock me down, jerk my arms behind my back, and throw me in restraints. And that'll be that.

Raey bites the corner of her lip and fidgets with her shirt as she watches. Even if this is bugging her, there's no chance she'll stop them. Not even if she wanted to. And she doesn't.

So I run.

My head drops as I duck under their arms to charge at Raey. Her eyes pop wide as I rush toward her, snarling. She screams and throws her hands over her face.

And I rush by.

"Fana!" Raey shouts. But I'm already at the ladder, hitting the first rung and sliding down the rest of the way. My mind is racing, and my heart is in my throat. All I can manage is to think of one word. Escape.

Which is why I miss my landing.

My legs buckle. My feet slip out from under me, and I land on my back. Hard. My sight goes blurry as my head slams into the deck. I'm up a second later.

"Stop or I'll fire!" The first security agent jams his gun through the hatch. My brain screams to run. I spin and dash—anywhere.

His weapon screeches. A bolt flies past my head and burns itself into the wall. I gasp. *They're really trying to shoot me!*

"Quit it! This ship is ancient!" the second agent cries. "You'll compromise the hull!"

"But she's running!"

"Get down there and get after her, then!"

The next ladder is just across the level. I fly for it as the thump of boots echoes through the space. They're already down. *Go faster, Fana!*

Almost there. I'm panting hard now. My body is still a mess after nearly dying. But the thought of returning to stasis keeps my legs moving. I'm at the ladder and down it in seconds.

There's a corridor to my left. I take it, rushing down its length until I come to a turn. I dart right.

And run into a dead end.

My legs shake as I stare at the wall. I don't know what I was thinking, running like that. I just reacted. Self-preservation or something, maybe. Raey always said I was good at that.

Though it's not going so well at the moment.

The urgent sound of the agents' voices shocks me into movement. I spin and dash down the corridor again, pounding on any door release I can find. It's the only option. I can't run forever.

Each button chirps as I press it. But the doors are so old they screech as they shudder, then stop, barely open a crack. Bad. I just gave away my location.

I double back and go right at the turn instead of left. This corridor is long. Maybe I'll get lucky here.

And I do. The second door I come to slips open silently. I'm in and pounding the lock enable and any other button I find until the lights go out.

Then I crash onto the deck.

My head is spinning. My throat is dry. I struggle to get air as my stomach twists and threatens to release its contents out of my mouth. They're going to hear vomit if I can't calm down. But my wheezing is the smallest problem. I can't stand. My legs have gone stiff.

They're going to find me for sure.

It's another full minute before my heart stops threating to burst from my chest. My legs are moving again, but I doubt I'll be standing soon. Even if I can get on my feet, I will definitely puke my guts out. And being in the dark isn't helping.

I power on my light and scan around the room. A shelving unit as tall as the ceiling looms next to me. Yellowed sheets stand on their ends in thick bundles, held upright by chunks of metal and other random objects I can't tell the functions of.

There's a desk at the back of the room and a map of the *Stratford*'s levels hanging on the wall. Someone's scrawled red markings all over it, with arrows and boxes pointing to and highlighting certain areas and levels of the ship.

Now that could be useful.

A rumble outside sends me scrambling behind the desk and powering off the light. I flatten my body to the ground and go still. It's easy. I'm so exhausted I could fall asleep.

"She couldn't have gotten far!" The muffled voice of the first security agent comes through the walls of the room, which means if I can hear them, I'd better not make a single noise.

"But we've covered this level already!" the second security agent moans.

"Specialist, are you going to help us or not?"

Silence follows. Raey could be contemplating or refusing him at the moment, and I'm not sure I care which. Though, if I'm being honest with myself, I hope she's giving them her deadly stare of reluctance, the one she's used on me a thousand times. It'd mean she still holds me in her heart the way I do her. But ever since she arrived on the *Stratford*, it's been hard to tell.

"Fine, if you're not going—" the first agent says.

"Check the rooms, agent," Raey replies. "She might hide in one of them."

My heart stops. If they find a way into this room and discover me, it'll be my ex-girlfriend who gave them the idea to do it.

I won't panic. Or cry—well, maybe a little. Raey still cares about me. I'm sure of that. But if I get out of this mess I've put myself in, she and I are going to have some words.

"Good idea," the first agent says. "You start on the other side and—"

"No." Raey's flat tone makes the edges of my lips curl up. "I have to report this to the commander. He's expecting us back, and we're way past our return time. I'd be surprised if he hasn't already dispatched another team to retrieve us."

"She's got a point," the second security agent says.

"Whatever! Let's just get it done! Starting with this one."

I hold my breath as the door switch gets pressed repeatedly. A buzzer responds to each hit. But when nothing else happens, I let it out. All of my button-mashing actually enabled something!

Then the door chimes and opens.

A beam of light shines across the room, creating an eerie glow. My throat goes tight. This is it. Any second, he'll lower it to check under the desk, and I become a prisoner frozen in suspended animation. Possibly forever.

I cringe as the agent steps closer, his light moving to the shelf and then onto the map. It's brighter than my little device, and for a minute, I forget I'm about to be arrested and stare at the rendering of the *Stratford*.

"What the hell is this?" the first agent says.

A line stretches down the left side of the map—the rail car! I can use that and shoot back aft, all the way to the systems levels. They'll never find me there, not even if they bring the *Devant*'s entire seventy-person security team over. All I need to do is get to it. Wherever it is on this level.

"Forget it," the second agent replies. "We've got way too many other rooms to check, and if Miss Prissy-Pants won't lend a hand, this is going to take forever."

"Yeah, right, let's move," the first agent says.

I puff out a breath once the door slides shut, taking a moment to refocus. After a momentary struggle to find the edge of the desktop, I'm back on my feet.

Dizziness hits me as soon as I'm upright. Good thing I'm still holding onto the desk. Getting to the rail car is going to be rough.

I breathe, and with as little stumbling as I can manage, I reach the door and press my ear against it. Only the hum of the ship comes through, so I chance pressing the release.

I squint as my eyes readjust to the brighter light in the hallway. It only takes a few seconds of living through panic before I can see, and then another minute to calm my spinning head. Once my feet feel solid on the decking, I push off the wall and edge my way down to the corner, listening for sounds of movement. They're still close—likely working their way through the rooms on the opposite side of just the main corridor.

With another breath, I go, shuffling across an open area and into the next corridor, past the security agents. As I slip by, I catch the two of them leaning into the rooms. *Ha!* They won't even know I got past them. What a pair of incompetents.

"Fana, what are you doing?"

I freeze. Raey. She's there at the end of the main passage, with her arms folded and a harsh look flashing across her face.

"I thought you went to call the commander?" I say in a casual tone as my stomach twists and threatens to hurl whatever's in it onto the deck.

"I did." She holds up her communicator to show me. "Now stop this childish nonsense and get suited up."

"Er, no."

Raey's shoulders lower, and her head dips. If she ever resembled my mother, it'd be right at this moment. That's fine. I was a disappointment to her, too.

"Hey!" she shouts. "She's here!"

My eyes go wide as my body itches to run. I grit my teeth and shake a finger at her. It's all I've got time for. I will remember this betrayal. Her second.

I rocket down the corridor, hoping I remembered the map correctly—yes! The doors to the rail car are just ahead. I can make it. But I'll need every bit of energy to do so.

"Chief Neridi!" the first security agent yells. "You stay where you are!"

I punch the door release and drop into the rail car. The agents rip their weapons from their holsters and run down the corridor. I roll forward and press every call button I can.

"Stop right now!"

All I can do is watch as the rail car beeps. But the doors still need to close. My lungs go tight. My body tense. *Please! Doors! Close now!*

The agents are five steps away, their eyes full of rage. The doors are closing. I don't know if they'll be fast enough.

I'm shaking. They're going to get me. I know it. I'm done. He'll get his hand in there and shove the car open again. I'm going back to stasis.

Then, with a heavy thud, the doors shut and lock.

The rail car shudders as the first agent slams into it. He lets out a howl as he pounds his fists on the doors. The second agent shouts profanities after me.

But I'm already moving. To which level, I don't know. Wherever I can hide is fine.

This isn't over. They'll scour the ship for me. Maybe by then I'll have seen enough of it to be satisfied. Maybe. I fear what happens if I turn myself in after that. Commander Azazhi isn't a violent man, but he's never had a chief engineer go rogue, either.

The car jerks to a stop at level fifteen, and I curse my luck. Still too close, though that's my fault. I panicked. Now I'll have to race out and hope I can find a place to hide here.

As the doors open, I bend my legs and prepare to sprint. I won't stop until I'm in the clear. It's the only way.

Go!

I spring from the car, pounding my feet into the deck and picking up speed. There's a junction at the end of the corridor. I choose right and skid around the corridor.

And run right into Ceri.

"Bish!" Ceri shouts. Her hands shoot out, halting my forward movement. I yelp as I jerk to a hard stop. She grabs my shirt, yanking me close as she shakes me. "What the hyuk?"

Her eyes narrow when I fail to reply, but I'm still panting hard. When Ceri notices, her glare turns into a wrinkled-forehead stare.

"What happened?" she asks, her voice softening as she lets go to touch my arm. "Are you okay?"

I inhale, slow and deep. She deserves an answer, mostly because she's going to have to deal with the mess I've just created.

But as our eyes connect, I lose my words. We're so close I can feel the gentle caress of her breath across my face and the warmth radiate from her touch. It relaxes me and I feel safe.

Ceri's going to save me again. I just know it.

"Hey, Fana, are you okay?" she asks again.

"Yes," I reply as a smile spreads across my face. "I really need to talk to you."

PROTECTION

CERI

I STEP BACK FROM Fana now that she's calm. So am I. No one's charged at me like that in a long time. I'll thank my lack of recent training for my slower reflexes. If I was still battle ready, I might have broken her arm. Or her neck.

Fana wipes the thick drops of sweat around her collar as they bead on her face and drip down. Her normally well-kept hair is loose, strands of her braid coming loose at all angles. Her breathing has slowed, yet her eyes still reflect some level of former panic. Was she running from something? Or someone? She came from the direction of the rail car. Did she just use it? When did she learn how? And now she wants to talk to me. About what?

Whatever it may be, I get the sense that she's in desperate need of my help.

"Come with me," I say, putting my hand on her back. "You need to sit."

I bring her to an unused storage room and motion her inside. She smiles and enters, but when the door thumps closed, Fana spins on it, eyes wide. It takes a touch of her shoulder to break her out of her fright. Then, shaking her head, she sighs and drops herself onto a pallet. I'll remain by the door. It seems as if Fana is only comfortable with me around her.

"So what's this all about?" I ask.

She curls her lips in and lowers her head, likely debating how or even if she'll say what she wanted to. I expect as much, so I fold my arms and try to be patient. Despite her awkwardness around others, Fana is extremely sharp. She'll figure it out in a moment.

"I…" She swallows hard. "I did something bad, and I need your help."

My left hand grips the opposite arm as I shift. We've been at peace since the adults left, and if she's caused trouble for my crew, she'll learn just how furious I'll be.

"With what? What did you do?" I press.

"Commander Azazhi has ordered me back to the ship. I—" She swallows again. "I disobeyed a direct order by coming here."

Bish. She's going back to her ship? Fana had just begun her evaluation on the *Stratford*'s systems. She couldn't have completed it yet. And I get the sense that if she returns to the *Devant*, she won't be returning.

"He won't let you come back, will he?"

Fana shakes her head. "I'm under arrest."

I let out a slow exhale to avoid snorting. This girl is more complex than I realized, and her actions have likely complicated matters. If I help her, Raey could refuse any deal to save Beka and the others. Then she and her two security agents will seize our one chance at saving this ship. And once they're gone, we'll be on our own. Again.

"So you're asking me to help you avoid capture," I say.

Fana's eyes grow large, and her lips quiver. She's like a child seeking protection, and as odd as it is, it compels me to help. I'm not sure that's wise, but if she was one of my crew, I wouldn't hesitate at all.

"Yes," she says, shooting to her feet. "More than anything. I can't go back. It won't be good for me. Please, can you help me?"

She moves close, staring at me with those helpless eyes. I should lecture her about blind dependance on others, like I have with my juniors. But Fana is unlike any soldier. She has skills and knowledge that could save us...no...*will* save us.

Still, saying yes puts us in danger. I'd be choosing to side with a renegade against a force more advanced, and likely larger, than my own. If the tiny amount of compassion they've shown us so far is any hint, they'll hit us hard to get Fana back.

My hands clench at the thought. I can't handle seeing any more of my crew hurt. Or dead.

"I need to talk with Merek and Efa," I reply, shaking my head. "I can't make this decision on my own."

Fana's forehead creases. "Why ask them?"

"Because they'd be taking a risk, too."

"But you're in command here, aren't you?"

A sigh escapes my lips. I get I'm decisive, and that's why she thinks I'm in charge. But Niah is senior-most, and I very much wish she was here to help me figure things out. The adults of the *Devant* may even listen to her first because she's older.

"No, you've got the wrong idea," I reply. "I was squad leader, but that was before. We don't have ranks anymore."

Fana cocks her head to the side. "You're...all soldiers?"

"Were. That problem is solved. Yours isn't." I offer a hand. "Come with me to find Efa and Merek."

Her eyes fall on my hand as her mouth opens, yet Fana only stares. Perhaps she's thinking of something to say or is searching for the right words. It's unnecessary. All I need is for her to say yes.

After a minute of waiting, with another bout of irritation building inside of me, I snap my fingers in front of her face. Fana blinks and looks up.

"I want to stay here," she says.

"Why?"

"They're looking for me."

Well, bish. That explains her disheveled state.

If two adults, armed with weapons likely more lethal than our dart pistols, are hunting for her, we've got a bigger problem than I understood. They won't leave without her, and they may mess up the ship—or my crew—in the process. Better I should attempt a negotiation, however unlikely it is to work.

"Please, Ceri," Fana begs, clasping one hand over the other. "You can't let them take me back. Commander Azazhi will punish me for sure. He'll drop me back into stasis for the rest of the trip. I want to be here and help you. I can't do that locked in a pod."

Back into stasis? Imagine that. How different our lives would be if we could have woken a few reasonable adults and put an end to all the bish we went through. How many children would still be alive then?

I want to ask more about it, but this isn't the time. If the *Devant*'s commander will do that to his top officers, then there will be no deal for us kids. Perhaps there was never any real chance of one.

But I'm not giving up. The gnawing in my gut won't let me quit. I will save Beka and the others. All I need to do is figure out how.

Fana steps closer, moisture forming around her eyes as she looks at me. Her sleeve brushes across them, and she sniffles. Truly a recruit in every way except for height, though not by much.

"Okay, I've got an idea, but we'll need help," I say. "Let's go find Niah."

"But..."

"Trust me. This is my ship. Your security people will never find us if I don't want them to."

She attempts to curl the edges of her mouth up, but it's a struggle, so I smile for her. Or grin, really. I'd enjoy running circles around those two security agents. But not unarmed. That'll be the first problem I will need to solve.

With a quick check of the hallway, I motion for Fana to stay low and follow me. She nods, and then we're on the move, heading to the rail car.

It's still here, though few would use it today. Most of the others are down in the stasis levels, doing the routine check of all the pods. We found the operator's manual and realized how critical it was to ensure the pods were all running right.

It'll be to my advantage.

Fana keeps tight to me as we slip down the corridor. A little too tight. She's scared, of course, but the top of her head will smash into my back if I stop short, and that will rub on me if it happens more than once.

"Where are we going?" Fana whispers.

"Twenty-five. We need to pick a few things up."

"What do we need twenty-five of?"

"It's a level, not a quantity."

When we arrive, Fana drops back into a crouch and hides behind the edge of the rail car door as she peers out. I just stare. How someone who possesses so much intelligence can be so fearful of new situations baffles me. I suppose it's endearing to some. Not that I have much experience with things like that. Still, I'll enjoy the moment for the lightness it brings to my heart. Things have been heavy here for too long.

"You can stand up," I say and tap her shoulder. "No one's stopping here today except for us."

"Oh?"

I nod and press my lips into a smile. It's the most I've exercised that part of my face in a while, and the muscles in my cheeks protest as I try to keep it on for Fana's sake. It seems to keep her at ease, and she'll need to remain calm once we head all the way down.

The room I want is off to the side of a stasis storage level. They scavenged everything they could from twenty-five a long time ago—well before they woke me up. Now it's just piles of broken crates, torn plastic, and smashed parts someone thought was important to separate out from the rest of the trash by shoving it all along the wall.

As we approach the room, doubt over my decision crashes around in the back of my mind. I push it away. Fana needs protection. Our passengers won't get to their destination without her. Likely the commander of the *Devant* is thinking the same thing. He won't let her remain here for long. I just wonder what he'll do when he realizes she's not coming back.

"Ceri."

I spin.

It's Sayer and Rhys. They're just as surprised to see us as we are to see them.

"What are you doing here?" Sayer asks, throwing a glance at Fana.

"What are *you* doing here?" I fire back.

Sayer's eyes blink wide for a quick second before he recovers. He shuts his mouth then, as do we all. By the open-handed, flat-footed stance he's in, I can tell he's not looking for a fight. So his intentions here are not all that innocent. Neither are mine. But if he's going to put his energy into deflecting any suspicion, I should be safe from any serious questioning.

After a minute, he reaches behind his back and pulls out a pistol. "I'm returning this, because I didn't think I needed it any longer, but..."

He eyes Fana again, who steps back and ducks her head.

"You never needed it," I say, moving in front of her. "No one's a threat to you. Not since the adults left."

"Yeah…" Sayer chuckles.

"So don't let us stop you."

He chews on his lip and nods, as if he's deep in thought.

"What's she doing down here?" Rhys challenges, throwing a finger at Fana.

My pulse quickens. I've got no prop to lie with, and Sayer will catch any weak attempt to evade. I was trying to push an offensive tactic, as it was the only defense I had. Now Rhys has poked a hole in that plan. I should have shot him a long time ago. Then he wouldn't be breaking Seren's heart as well as causing me grief.

"We're going to see Niah," I say. "She should know about everything that's going on."

Sayer snorts. "Good luck. You won't find her. She's got no interest in us anymore."

"That's total bish, and you know it."

"Is it?"

I wave a hand at him. "Just go put the gun away before you hurt yourself."

"I will, but Ceri. You and I need to talk." His voice is earnest. I expect he wants to cool things down between us. But I curse his timing. My reply won't be as sincere, not while I'm hiding my true intentions.

"Fine," I say and turn to head to the down ladder, grabbing Fana's hand to tug her with me. "When we get back."

We'll head down the ladder and hold in the dark there until the two of them disappear. Then I'll get what I need from the weapons locker. Sayer may not need a pistol any longer, but I may soon need two.

"Wait," Rhys says. "How'd you get down here? We came from twenty-one. If you were taking the ladders, we would have seen you cross the level."

Rhys, I will put your head into a wall one of these days.

"Huh?" Sayer says, then growls. "Yeah, that's right. Hold the hyuk up, Ceri."

Bish.

GUARDIAN

CERI

I MUST AVOID A fight. As much as Rhys has inflamed my desire to teach him a hard lesson, I'm outnumbered, and Sayer still has a pistol. I won't get within ten paces of him before he fills my chest with darts. Hardly what I want to accomplish. My goal is downward. And Niah. Getting caught up in a brawl with these two only delays us.

"What do you want?" I say casually, turning back to face him.

"Answer Rhys' question," Sayer growls.

"Why?" I shrug. "What's it matter which way we came?"

"Answer it!" Sayer clenches his fists as his body tenses.

Hyuk. I didn't mean to provoke him. I'd better keep my tone friendly if I want to diffuse this. And if I can't, I'll have to put him on the deck, though I'll need to get within range if I want to do that.

Fana presses close, but I push her back. Even if it comforts her to, she'll just get in my way if I move fast. Better I should tell her to wait by the ladder or, better yet, down it. I'd never forgive myself if she got hurt.

"We took the rail car." I motion a hand to the open doors.

"So why are you about to climb down?" Sayer asks, sharpness coming off his voice.

I move a few steps nearer to him, keeping a relaxed pace. Unintentional, even. But as I imagine him raising his gun, my breath quickens. I can't let Sayer notice. My left hand slides to the opposite shoulder, feigning an itch. It stays there to cover my chest, blocking his view.

"Niah won't see us if we take the rail system all the way down," I reply. "I'm not even sure where she is."

"No way she could even climb ten levels!" Rhys says, throwing a finger at Fana.

"Niah could out-climb all of us with two of you on her back," I respond.

Rhys' eyebrows furrow as he shakes his head. "I didn't mean Niah! I meant—"

He grunts as Sayer knocks a fist into his chest. Rhys pulls back and coughs as he frowns at Sayer, who glares. Rhys wrinkles his nose but remains quiet, rubbing the spot where Sayer tapped him.

I slide forward two more steps before he returns his attention to me.

"Niah's a hundred levels down," Sayer says. "Maybe more. It'd be easier if you went by yourself."

"I want Fana to check out a few things on the way down. Stuff she could fix."

Fana shifts, loud enough for Sayer and Rhys to notice, and I suck in a quick breath. She was doing well by staying back, but she may have given away my intention. My legs bend, ready to strike if needed.

I'm safe. There's still time for words, whatever they might be. Not that I've ever been skilled at using them.

Sayer's gaze remains on Fana, and I relax a little. He's running something through this mind. Something serious. Perhaps he's reconsidering being such an ass to me. It doesn't really matter. I still need to talk him down or take him down.

Two more steps. My hands clench. I'm almost within range.

"Ceri," Sayer says, with an earnest gaze, "just be straight with me, and whatever is going on, let's talk it—"

Bish. He's noticed how close I've gotten.

With a snarl, he powers the pistol on and raises it, ready to shoot. His eyes narrow and turn hard, like any soldiers' would just before a fight. If he's itching for one, I'd better be willing to have it, even if it kills me. Fana is our best solution and our only hope. I won't let anyone destroy that, not Sayer, not Rhys. I will defend her—with my life, if I have to.

But I am not so ready to die as I used to be.

"What the hyuk are you trying to get away with?" Sayer hisses.

"Nothing. I told you what I'm doing."

"But not why." Sayer aims his gun at my heart. "Back up."

A burst of energy pulses through me, even as I tense. He may not have intended it, but Sayer just signaled his willingness to talk. He may yet listen to me explain how Fana's work on the *Stratford*'s navigation system will save us. If he knew that, he might let us go.

I should kick myself for not trying that first, though it would've required my reliance on words, and I'm just not sure he'd believe me, not after I defied his vote, then turned the crew against him while I saved Fana's life. Likely everything I do is suspect to him now.

"Sayer." I put my hands up. "I am not a threat. Let me explain, and—"

"Back up!" he shouts.

I sigh and do as ordered but drop my hands as I move. Sayer tightens his grip on the pistol, checking Fana before returning his gaze back to me. A second glance at her turns into a frown.

"She's supposed to return to her ship," he says. "Why is she still here? What are you planning?"

"If you'd lower your gun, then we can talk, and I'd tell you."

"I don't think so."

So much for words.

I'm four long paces away from him now—too far for a successful direct strike. Either I'll have to distract him or wait for when his focus is elsewhere. I can cover that distance in two seconds, but then I'd better hit him hard, or he will kill me.

Sayer turns his head slightly toward Rhys but keeps his eyes on me. "Go get another gun from the locker. We're going to bring the two of them back up to the new people from the *Devant*. They can decide what to do with their crewmate."

Rhys eyes me with his jaw tight and keeps still. He remembers what happened the last time he went up against me. If Seren hadn't been there, I might have hurt him.

"Move!" Sayer growls. Rhys obeys, if slowly.

No. This is over if Rhys gets that gun. But I'm just as frozen as he was, caught in this impasse with Sayer, and as long as I am, we're all stuck. No chance to cure our sick, no possibility to save our passengers, and no way to save ourselves. I didn't remain on this mess of ship to lose. Not now. Not when there's hope.

"Fana, stop him," I say. "Stop Rhys."

"M...me?"

"He's bish as a soldier. You can take him."

"I...uh..."

Rhys stops to give me a hurt look. I smirk back, and he drops his shoulders. If he wanted my approval, he shouldn't be working against me.

"Get him, Fana," I say, raising my voice.

"No," Sayer counters, swiveling his gun toward her. "You stay put. Rhys knows how to hurt you, and he will if you get in his way."

Fana comes up behind me, glancing between Rhys and Sayer. She's panting, nearly in time to my own breaths, and she's impeding my ability to move. Again. I can't blame her for being scared, but her lack of situational awareness is causing the acid in my stomach to rise.

"Ceri, what do I do?" Fana whispers.

"Kick him between the legs," I reply, loud enough for Rhys to hear.

"That's mean!" Rhys whines.

"Then stay where you are," I counter.

"No!" Sayer twists toward him. "Rhys! Don't—"

I dive to the deck and roll forward, closing the distance between us in a heartbeat. In the next, my legs shoot out. Sayer swings back, but he doesn't realize his mistake.

That's when I strike.

My boots pound him in the stomach as I spring up. Sayer flies back, his arms going wide. He smashes into the wall with a loud grunt, his head lurching forward as it smacks into the edge of a panel.

I'm on him, my fists raised to pummel his pretty face. Blood is pounding in my ears. I will finish what I started and ensure he won't get in my way ever again. Rhys cries out. Fana screams. I bare my teeth, suck in a breath—

And jerk to a halt.

Sayer slides down the wall, his head rolling to one side. His limbs fall limp to the floor as his body sags. The impact knocked him out. It was lucky. For me and for him. The rage inside of me subsides as reason returns to my thoughts.

Ancestors, what did I almost do?

I back away, my stomach twisting at the idea of ending Sayer's life. We were allies once. Friends maybe. How it came to this...

A whimper spins me around. Fana is there, her eyes wide as she covers a hand over her mouth. I wish she didn't have to see that. It must have been terrifying for her. Doubly so to realize I am very much the monster I told her I was.

"How did you move that fast?" she gasps and points at Rhys, who stands not far away, petrified. "Sayer just...looked at him, and then he was in the air."

"Years of training," I reply, my gaze dropping. "Most of which I wish I could forget."

"What...happened on this ship?" Fana whispers.

"You don't want to know," Rhys mutters, his eyes never leaving Sayer's body.

He's another problem I need to deal with. Right now.

"As for you, bish-head." I spin on him, grabbing the collar of his shirt to yank him toward me. As expected, Rhys cowers as I lift him and push him against the wall.

"Please! I'm sorry! I didn't know he was going to do that! I swear." Rhys throws his hands in front of his face.

"Don't, Ceri," Fana pleads. "He's just a kid!"

I give Rhys a hard shake, bumping him against the wall again and holding him there.

"Look at me," I order.

He shakes as his hands come down, his head ducked as he watches me. I better make this quick. Rhys has grown, and he's heavier than he used to be. I'm also weaker than I was.

"I'm disappointed in you," I hiss. "You take his side over mine when you know you can trust me. Anything I do is for this crew. And me being on this level is no different. We've got a proper plan to get the passengers to their new home now, and it's going to happen, but you and Sayer need to stay the hyuk out of my way. Got it?"

Rhys nods, his eyebrows rising a little as his head lifts.

"And one more thing. You either treat Seren with respect, or you keep your little mitts off her. If you make her cry again, I will break both of your legs."

"We're not together anymore! She broke it off! I won't bother her! I promise!"

I let him down as softly as I can, but my arms are tired, and Rhys drops before he's back on the deck, landing on his feet with a thump. I back away and wait for him to recover. As he straightens himself out, his eyes swivel to where Sayer lies in a heap.

"What's going to happen to…" Rhys begins.

"Nothing," I reply. "You're going to get Efa and get him looked at."

"What should I tell her happened?"

"The truth. You know she won't believe anything else."

"She's going to be mad. And she's going to come looking for you."

I shrug. "That's nothing new."

Fana tightens her jaw as she watches. I should feel as much regret as she does. I doubt I ever could, not after what I just did, but it's far from important. Saving the ship is all that matters.

"Now get out of here," I say to Rhys as I pick up Sayer's gun. "And remember what I told you. This is for all of us."

"I believe you," he says, then tries a small smile before dashing off toward the ladder access to twenty-four.

Once Rhys is gone, I motion to Fana that we need to get moving.

"Will it take a long time to get down to the bottom of the ship?" Fana asks as we return to the rail car.

"Ten or fifteen minutes, likely."

"Good, because I want to know everything."

DEPTH

FANA

I CAN'T STOP SHAKING, not after what Ceri's told me. It's almost impossible to believe, though it certainly explains why Ceri has the skills of a master assassin. I still don't understand why the *Stratford*'s custodial crew would decide that children made the best soldiers.

"Because we weren't useful for anything else," Ceri replies when I ask. "The ship still runs whether we're alive or dead."

She looks away, and I cover my mouth to hide my gasp. No one could make this up. It's just too terrible for any imagination to conceive. At least one that's rational.

Now I get why their movements are so controlled or why their gaze pierces my soul, even when they laugh or smile, which isn't often. What should they be happy about? The people responsible for looking after them did everything they could to escape that trust.

"I'm so sorry," I say.

"Why? What did you do?"

"I just don't understand how anyone could be so...cruel."

She stares at the rail car's control panel, her finger tracing the edges of the buttons. For the first time since I met her, she appears as the young woman that she is. I'm not really sure how old—I never asked—but younger than me, for sure. Younger...and hurting.

My desire to comfort her overwhelms my caution. I move closer, my hand reaching out to touch her arm. She might welcome a hug, too. I've seen how they care for each other with a brief touch or embrace. They may be warriors, but they're still kids and still human. They need to protect themselves against this horror of a life.

But as I'm about to reach her, my will falters and my hand drops. What do I know of comforting someone? Raey was always the mature one in our relationship. Now, with seventeen years between the two of us, I'm even more of a child to her. No wonder why she's been treating me like she has.

"By the way," Ceri says, taking notice of my nearness, "when I'm about to fight, you can't be close to me like the way you are. I know you're scared, but it limits my movement, and you don't want to be around if someone shoots. Every soldier's aim here is good, but nobody's a perfect shot all the time."

I swallow and retreat, with her watching me the entire way. My eyes search for something to keep them occupied, and I should do the same for my brain. Too much of a focus on her will drive me crazy. It already is.

"So why did the custodial crew leave?" I ask.

"You mean the adults. We're the crew."

"Right. I'll remember that. So?"

Her only reply is pursed lips and a stare that makes me shrink. I push back into a corner and prop myself up on the handrail there. I want to seem unaffected by her, but I'm so out of my element I'm totally unsure what relaxed looks like.

The rail car jerks to a stop with no warning. I yelp but save myself from becoming a pancake on the floor. Good thing I was holding on. What the heck happened?

Oh. Ceri hit the stop button. It would have been nice for her to warn me first.

"Level ninety-five?" I ask, spotting the number on the display. "Is this where we'll meet Niah?"

"Unlikely. Niah won't come here. I don't really want to be here, either."

"Why? Is something wrong with this level?"

"You'll see."

Ceri opens the doors and stares into the darkness of the level. I sense hesitance from her. Of course, it could just be the lack of light, but something tells me it's not. She's afraid to step onto this level, and after what I've learned, I can think of a thousand reasons why.

She wants me to see something here, something important enough that she's willing to face her fear and push forward. The least I can do is to be a good observer and keep my eyes open.

With a deep inhale, she steps out of the rail car and walks to a panel along the wall. The moment she touches her hand to it, the overhead lamps power on. They flash, then glow a dark orange as they slowly come up to their designed brightness. I blink as my sight adjusts to the change.

And catch my breath.

Four massive tubes fill the double-height space, stretching from the center of the room to the hull. The moment I see them, I understand their use. But the launch tubes aren't what makes my gut tight.

It's all the blood.

Streaks of dark brown cover nearly every surface from the deck in front of my feet to the far side of the level, which must be five hundred paces away. I know it's blood because I've been an unfortunate observer to scenes like this before. Back on Earth, when war came to every town and every city, no one could claim to be just a witness. The only way to survive the brutality was not to be there. The *Stratford*, and other ships like it, were the wisest out of all of us. They left before things really got bad. But it seems a thousand light-years wasn't enough to escape human aggression.

"Oh, Ceri," I exhale as I shuffle behind her. "This must have been a massacre."

"It was," she replies, her voice soft. "This was the largest battle we've ever known. But it was just a waste of lives. Only death can claim victory."

She stops at one of the far tubes, though to me, they all seem the same, dormant and still. Everything here is. It's like time stopped here the moment the last person left. Then again, most of this ship is like that. Ceri and her crew live in an ancient photograph.

"I'm…sorry," I say, struggling for the words that might match this epic tragedy. "No one should have to live through this. Especially child—I mean, teenagers."

She lifts her head and looks up. "You know who Merek and Efa are, right?"

"Efa is the one who took care of me, and Merek is…her…boyfriend?"

"Lover," Ceri corrects. "I've heard your word before, but I don't think it fits. The love the two of them feel for each other can't be defined so loosely. They'd die for each other, if it came to it. They almost did."

She drops to a crouch and tells me their entire story, then, one that sounds like a tale from an ancient past, and an ancient place, back on Earth. Two tribes at war. Two people in a forbidden affair, with poor Ceri in the middle of all of it. She found a way for Efa and Merek to be together, and from what I comprehend of her tale, their adults punished her for it.

As she speaks, anguish pours off her. She's trying to hide it, but I can feel it from my position a few steps away. Her pain is a powerful attraction, and I can't help but be drawn to it. She's suffered so much, and no one has been there to help her through it. I may not be the right person to help her heal, but I want to, almost more than anything else.

"Hey," I say as I sit beside her. "You want to know something? You might be the bravest person I've ever met. What you did for Merek and Efa, I could never find the courage to do."

Ceri snorts. "Yeah? And what did that get me?"

She hangs her head, her eyes finding a spot on the deck to examine, maybe one without dried blood streaked across it. There's few of those.

My hand finds a place on her arm then. She tolerates it for a minute, then her body stiffens. I scramble to find something kind to say. I can talk technical terms forever, but eloquence, I've got no skill for. For Ceri's sake, I'll try, but I'm better off just holding her hand. If she'd let me.

"Ceri, what you've done...it's nothing less than phenomenal." My voice is close to a whisper. "You...you've..."

I moan, clenching my teeth. Everything was clear as crystal in my head, then when I opened my mouth, it comes out like a ship's sewage. All I know how to use is my hands, and if they can't make her feel better, then I should give up.

But when Ceri shies from my words, it makes me continue.

"Honestly, I think you're amazing, Ceri," I breathe.

She shifts, leaning back on her haunches and wrapping her arms about her knees. "Thanks, I guess."

After a minute of her gazing into space, she pulls away and stands, stretching her back a little before turning back to the rail car.

"We should continue down," she says. "It'll take some effort to find Niah."

Oh hell. I made her feel uncomfortable. Now she just wants to run away. I can't let her. I spring up, racing to get in between her and the rail system doors. Ceri pauses, her eyebrows getting tight. I must look like an idiot, but I want to reach her, and I don't mind being the fool if it helps her heal.

"Hey," I step closer. "If you need to, you can tell me anything. I promise I won't share it with anyone. It's not good to keep bad stuff inside. It'll eat you up."

Ceri's gaze becomes hard as she looks at me. It may be intrusive, but I only want to help. She's got so much tension built up it's got to be unhealthy. It wouldn't surprise me if her heart went into cardiogenic shock before she turned twenty-five. Of course, I don't want that to happen, so I hope she'll open up, if not to me, then to someone who cares.

"Ready to go?" she asks.

I blow a breath out between my lips. Failure for sure. But Ceri's not a machine. She won't respond in the same ways a pump in the *Devant'*spropulsion system will.

I'm not giving up. Not on her. She's my savior, and I owe her everything.

CONTAMINANT

—— • ——

FANA

WE ARRIVE ON LEVEL one-twenty-five. By the heat that hits my face and the smell of carbon-based lubricants, I can tell we're in the true guts of the *Stratford*. It's strange the designers of this ship would compact all the critical systems of the ship down here at the aft. The *Devant*'s systems are distributed all over the ship, with multiple redundant units on the opposite side, in case of an impact or some other disaster.

I guess they had other priorities back then, like getting off the planet as fast as possible. I've read that the war was at a critical point back then. Ceri's people likely had to leave or face annihilation. Back then, armies used far more destructive weapons, and after a hundred years of contaminating the environment, the earth couldn't sustain itself. It was only a matter of time before everyone built enough ships to escape the ruin they had brought.

"Stay behind me," Ceri says and puts a hand on my shoulder to position me just back and to her left. "I don't want Niah to have a bad reaction to you."

"Why would she do that?" I ask.

"Because she doesn't know you. And she's been down here a long time."

I can feel my forehead get tight as I imagine what that means. Ceri seems to have an idea, though I don't want to ask her for fear of her describing someone who'll terrify me. Yet, when Ceri speaks about her, I get the idea Niah is someone she has a lot of respect for. If that means she's more of a killer than Ceri, I should absolutely be afraid.

"How are we going to find her in the dark like this?" I ask, glancing around. "Can't we turn on the lights?"

"No." Ceri glances up at the ceiling. "Niah will find us."

As if emphasizing her words, the doors of the rail car shut with a thump that echoes throughout the level. The darkness covers over us like a thick blanket, and the hum of the machinery is so constant, it blocks my sense of space. I'm so lost, I forget Ceri's instructions and slide closer to her. But even that's not enough, so I reach out and grab a loose piece of her shirt.

"What are you doing?" she hisses.

"I can't see!"

"Let your eyes get used to the low light. You'll be able to catch more than you think."

I stare into the wall of black, trying to follow her suggestion, but I keep a hold on her. Becoming disoriented and getting lost down here would throw me into a panic. The rail car is behind us, and I could find it even if I was blind, but as the heat from her skin sends a calming warmth through me, I push myself to follow.

Honestly, I should be ashamed. I'm the chief engineer of the most advanced ship in Earth's newest fleet, yet I can only feel safe next to a girl younger than I am. Sure, she's a soldier, and I'm little more than a mechanic with advanced knowledge of multidimensional physics, but I'm one of the senior-most officers on the *Devant*. A little dark shouldn't frighten me.

"Who the hyuk is this?" a woman's voice hisses from out of the black.

I yelp and press against Ceri, who nudges me back with her shoulder. She's not trying to force me, but I get the point.

"Fana," Ceri replies to the darkness. "Chief engineer of the *Devant*. Her ship answered our distress signal."

Could it be Niah? Ceri seems to know. It'd be nice if she told me. Maybe she thinks it's obvious. Or maybe she's waiting for me to ask.

"How many more of them are on board?" the voice asks.

"Four," Ceri answers. Her eyes search for the source of the voice. She might not know who this is then, but Ceri always has her defenses up, and I'm beginning to understand why.

"Get them to leave. Immediately. And don't come down here again."

Ceri goes tense, and so do I. This woman's tone was harsh before. Now I feel threatened.

"You're going to listen to her?" I whisper into Ceri's ear.

"It's for your own safety, bish head," the woman snarls.

I jump, my eyes scanning the area for any sign of her. *How did she hear me?*

Ceri pivots to her right and stops, peering into the distance. So that's where this woman is. Why won't she come out? Does she have some advantage hiding in the shadows? Are they even shadows for her? Past the length of my fingers, it's still black. If my eyes were supposed to get used to this amazingly dim light, they've failed me.

"Niah, what's wrong?" Ceri says, her voice almost pleading. There's an edge of worry there, too.

"Nothing. Just forget about me and go back. That's it."

So it is Niah.

"Is that why you've stayed down here?" Ceri asks, stepping toward Niah's alleged position. "Because you think you're a danger to us?"

"Not think. I know."

After seeing Ceri fight, I'm not surprised Niah believes that. Maybe she's the one that taught Ceri how to be so deadly. Which means she's even tougher than Ceri.

That's a chilling thought.

No, wait. Ceri would know just how skilled Niah is already. What if she meant to say she's a danger in some other way?

My heart nearly stops. "You're infected!"

"What the hyuk do you know about that?" Niah charges.

"You're not the only one." Ceri takes another step into the darkness. "It took Tal. Now Beka and two others are sick."

The hiss of curses that come out of the dark are so harsh and varied, I don't understand most of them. I don't need to. I've seen how much this crew cares for each other. They're like a big family, brothers and sisters with no parents. Except for the few that have paired off, of course.

"Niah, the *Devant'*smedical team will cure you," Ceri says.

"No. And I told you to keep back. I won't be responsible for killing you."

"Don't be like that. Come back up with us. I need your help. Fana said she can give us control of the ship again."

My curiosity has become stronger than my fear. I need to see this Niah and understand why Ceri thinks so highly of her that we had to come all the way down here and remain, even when Niah's telling us to run.

I move next to Ceri and peer into the shadows. For a second I think I see a shape move, but when I blink and squint more, the apparition is gone. Despite that, and despite all the background noise, I feel that someone is there.

"You don't need me," Niah says, her tone softening. "You're doing a good job, Ceri. Don't doubt yourself."

"No. I'm not." Ceri's voice is tight. "Tal died in my arms, Niah. And he suffered so much before he died. I won't let the same thing happen to you."

Niah chuckles, but it turns into a cough, and she fights through it as she speaks. "You'd have to get me first, and you were never skilled enough for that."

Why is Niah refusing our help? We've told her we can cure her, though there are still a few details to be checked off before that's a reality. But even if that's the case, that's a minor problem. And she doesn't even know that.

"Why are you making this so difficult for her?" I say. "Ceri already said she needs you, and she already told you we have a treatment, so what's the problem?"

Ceri drops a hand on my arm to keep me from continuing. Did I say something wrong? I'm not being cruel, right? If Ceri cares for this lady, then we should try to help her. I'm not worried about getting infected. Raey may be irritated beyond belief at me, but she'd make sure she treated me quickly if I got sick.

"What's her name again?" Niah asks, her voice raspy.

"I'm standing right here," I fire back. "Why don't you ask me?"

"Because I don't need to talk to you."

I gasp. She's got to be ill. Nobody's that rude to someone they just met, not unless they're a complete jerk, and I seriously doubt Ceri would care that much for anyone who hated everyone.

"Send her back up, Ceri," Niah says. "You and I can talk awhile before you have to go."

"No!" I say, my voice louder than I expected. "You're coming with us!"

"Fana." Ceri pushes me back. "I got this, okay?"

"Yeah, that's right. Go away," Niah adds.

Ceri taps a finger on my arm. *Oh!* She's trying to tell me something. Should I acknowledge I understand? I don't want to mess her plan up, whatever it is. Maybe I should go pretend to be interested in a piece of machinery. It wouldn't be pretend, of course.

"Niah, please," Ceri says, turning back in her direction. "At least let Efa check you out, okay?"

"I'm not going back and risking the crew. That's final."

Ceri shakes her head. "I won't accept that."

"Do you want me to hold you in my arms while I watch you die? What makes you think—"

Ceri shoots forward. Two bodies thump together. Niah grunts and coughs, then growls. I jump as the powerful boom of something heavy slams into the panel of a machine, echoing about the level. Ceri shouts. Feet pound on the deck. Someone shrieks. Metal hits metal and sparks fly.

I step back. The violence in front of me overwhelms my ears. I slap my hands over them and cringe, fearing the worst. They'll murder each other, and I'll be powerless to stop it. I can't even see what's happening.

Until the fight comes to me.

Two bodies explode out of the darkness, slamming into me. My feet lift from the deck, and I fly into something hard. A cry comes from my throat as fire shoots up my back and a flash crosses my eyes. I twist in pain and slump down a hot wall. It's searing my skin, but I'm in such agony my body won't respond.

"Fana!" Ceri yells and reaches for me.

"Idiot!" Niah cries. "Don't touch her!"

But before Niah can stop her, Ceri grabs my arms and yanks me away from the heat. We all slump to the deck, breathing heavy. Niah doubles over as she wheezes, her hand going to her chest.

"Are you happy now?" she says between forced breaths. "I saw your bish move coming five minutes ago, and you did it anyway. Now you've infected yourself, and her, with your hyuking stupidity. Hell, Ceri, why do you always have to protect everyone?"

"Don't worry," I say, still wincing from what will probably be a third-degree burn across my back. "Raey will heal us."

But even as I say it, my voice wavers, and I realize even I'm not so sure about that. Raey and the *Devant*'s doctors are talented, but until they know exactly what they're dealing with, there's a possibility they won't be able to defeat this virus.

Oh boy. I really hope this isn't the way my life ends.

THREAT

CERI

FANA HUDDLES IN THE corner of the rail car, her arms wrapped around her legs and her chin on her knees. She said it was the least painful position. I offered her a painkiller, but she took one look at the needle of the dispenser and refused it with every bit of energy she had. Her response was so violent, even Niah stepped back.

Niah. I am thankful that she's well enough to put up such a fight. She nearly sliced me open, though it took a lot out of her to try. Now she leans her head and her shoulder on the wall, her arms folded and her eyes shut. How she remains standing while she sleeps has always been a mystery to me. That she can while she's sick is simply astonishing.

I don't know if she's infected us or not. My first exposure to the virus was lucky. Perhaps this one will be as well. I've no way to tell. The moment we get back, we'll need to get tested, and Niah will go isolate with Beka and the others. She might prefer it—looking after them will keep her mind off of her illness.

A deep boom rumbles through the rail car's passageway, vibrating the deck below our feet. Curious, but nothing to be afraid of, I think. I've experienced an explosion on the *Stratford*, and it shook the ship so violently, it knocked us off our feet even twenty levels away. Still, I'm curious about this sound.

And as soon as we arrive on fourteen, I find out what caused it.

"Ceri!" Deryn says as he catches me coming out of the rail car. "The *Devant*! It's docked with us!"

"Docked?" A chill runs through me, but I try to suppress it. The maneuver means little until I understand the reason for it. Raey could have requested it to ease the transfer of Beka and the others to the *Devant*, though I wonder why she would. We have yet to agree to any deal, and if Raey sees me with Fana, there won't be any.

It could also mean the transfer of things from the *Devant*. That could be equipment. Or people.

Niah stumbles out behind me, coughing into her arm. Deryn gasps and backs away, his hand covering his nose and mouth. His eyes widen as Fana follows, doubled over and panting.

"Keep away," I warn with an outstretched hand.

Deryn backs against the wall, continuing to stare at Fana. "They've been looking for her everywhere."

"And you haven't seen her either, got it?"

"Yeah."

I can trust his silence. Deryn's grown into a reliable crewmember and helps look after the younger boys. I'd say he's learned from his mistakes as a squad leader. He'd be near perfect if he didn't annoy the hyuk out of Aidan. If I had to guess, Deryn's got an interest in him. I'm not sure it's mutual.

"Find Efa and tell her to meet me on seventeen. I want to see what's happening."

"I'm coming," Niah says.

"Like hell you are. Get yourself to the medical bay and drop yourself in a room. Take Fana with you."

"I'm coming too," Fana adds.

I spin on them with a glare, but it might be a useless gesture. Neither can keep their heads up for longer than a few seconds.

"Didn't you just fight me because you refused to come back up here?" I charge.

"And you lost." Niah turns and heads back into the rail car. "Let's go."

I shake my head and follow. She'll be smart and keep her distance from any of the crew. Likely I should do the same. And if Fana is strong enough to assert her will, she can't be in much pain. Besides, I may need some support. Efa and Merek will be raging mad about what I did to Sayer, and they'll want answers.

When we arrive on seventeen, there's already a mass of people outside the airlock. Three or four of them are a good head taller than the others who face them. They wear black suits, with what appear to be armor on the shoulders and rifles slung on their backs. Only one of them has his helmet off—a man easily in his fourth, possibly fifth decade, sneering and thrusting a finger at Efa and Merek as they stare back at him.

Adults.

"Oh, bish," Fana says. When I glance at her for an explanation, she shrinks. "Did I use it right?"

"You did. What's the problem?"

"That's Captain Yelekal. He's head of security! But he's not on this crew rotation." Fana glances at him again. "He might be here for me!"

Captain. That word makes the hair on the back of my neck stand up. And this man's gestures are all too familiar, as is the way he looks down on everyone around him. My chest tightens as I realize it. He's too much like the one person who I've feared for so long.

Daga.

My stomach is turning, but I must face this man. He's reprimanding Efa and Merek as if they were his subordinates, or worse. If I don't stop him now, he'll stomp on us like we were vermin. And enjoy it.

"Who is this?" Captain Yelekal growls, throwing a glare my way. I freeze, even as I fight to keep calm. This man has no authority over me, and if I want to avoid panic, I must keep reminding myself of that.

"Ceri!" Efa's face is a mix of emotions. She may be glad to see me, if only to help protect her from this brute. The rest will have to wait.

"Where's the captain of this ship, Ceri?" Captain Yelekal demands as if I'm here only to serve him answers.

"I already told him none of the adults are awake," Efa says.

"What about her?" He points to Niah but blinks when she lifts her head. Efa's breath gets caught up, and her hand rises to hide her shock, but Merek lowers it, even as he stares at

Niah. If he's trying to avoid suspicion, it's too late. The *Devant*'s security team is watching them already.

"I'm no adult," Niah replies, "but I at least know you need to state your intentions before we grant you permission to board our ship."

Captain Yelekal shakes his head. "I'll state my intentions to the captain of this ship. So clear all these kids out of here and go get them. Now."

"I don't take orders from you."

His eyes narrow at her. "Is that the way you want it?"

Niah purses her lips and stares back with arms folded. He waits for a moment, then gnashes his teeth and turns to one of his team.

"Bring the rest of the squad over," he says, then glances at us again. "Bring second squad too."

A poke on my back reminds me Fana is still here. If this man is here for her, then she needs to escape now. Four adults, we might handle. Two squads...unlikely. Our dart pistols, if we had more than one here, won't penetrate that armor. That means close quarters fighting, and they'll have a weight and strength advantage there.

"Niah," I whisper as Captain Yelekal gets distracted by a protest from Efa. "Get Fana out of here. We can't lose her. If she leaves the *Stratford*, she's not coming back."

"So?"

"She can give us control of the ship!"

But I say it too loud, and it catches the attention of the cap-tain, who shoves Efa away from him and turns to pound his way down the corridor toward us. A tremor runs through me as he approaches, followed by a twinge in my right hand. It's sharp, just like the knife that nearly severed my finger from it.

No. He's not Daga. He's not Daga.

"Who's behind you?" His hand comes up and points past my shoulder.

"You have no permission to come aboard," I say, my voice wavering. "Turn around."

"I don't need it. You've abducted an officer of my crew, and I will scour this ship until I find her, and then I'll decide which of you is responsible."

"You have no right!" Efa shouts. "We're a sovereign ship!"

"You're a bunch of panty-soiling brats. And I'll do what it takes to protect my crew."

This bastard may not be my former commander, but he's a hyuking adult, just like all the rest. And he's turning my fear into rage. I've had enough of adults treating me and my crew like the dirt on their boots. I may have been fearful of this black-clad hulk before, but the fire that is rising inside of me has burned that chill away.

"So will we," I hiss, stepping up to him. My heart is pounding in my chest so hard it's making it difficult to breathe calmly. We haven't fought an actual battle in a long time, and never against adults. I fear what will happen if I need to make good on my words.

Captain Yelekal frowns and looks me up and down as if he's unsure what he sees is real. I crack my knuckles and size him up. With all that weight on him, he can't move fast, but his armor leaves few unprotected areas where I can make an effective strike.

"Listen, you skinny little sprog," Captain Yelekal hisses. "If you don't get out of my way right now, I'll make sure you never talk back to another adult again."

His face turns red, and he bares his teeth as my eye twitches. He must not be much of a warrior if he lets a small statement like that upset him. Still, I'm worried about what happens next. The three junior crew that flank Efa and Merek have no training. They'll get hurt if a fight starts.

Maybe just a hard punch to his face would be enough to get him off our ship. I wouldn't want to kill him, even if I thought I could. His squads would bring all of their firepower down on us. All I want them to do is leave.

"You have no authority on this ship," I reply, "and unless you want to start a war, you'll leave. Now."

He thinks his move toward the gun in his holster goes unseen, and he shouldn't have turned around to glance at his team, either. Now the back of his neck is exposed. A quick slice will make him reconsider taking us on. Yes. That'd be the way to avoid a battle.

I tense, my hand sliding down my hip to my knife. My fingers wrap around its hilt, and I draw it out. Slowly. My eyes never leave his back. He's still distracted. This should be easy. Yet the lump in my throat threatening to suffocate me says otherwise. I can't stop. No matter what. I've got to protect the others, Fana included.

A hand grabs my wrist. I freeze. Did I miscalculate? Did he see me?

No.

It's Fana. I recognize its feel from the multitude of times she's grabbed me. *But why is she stopping me?*

Niah notices my jerky movement, and her eyes dip to motion to my knife. She catches my glance and makes a minute shake of her head. A second later, the captain turns back to us.

My opportunity to strike is over. I won't get another. Now we'll see what the Captain Yelekal does when he's got all the advantage.

ARREST

FANA

I DID IT. I just don't know if it was the right thing to do. But the vision in my head of Ceri dying was too much. She's just trying to protect me and her crew, but it's impossible. She can't use a knife against a plasma weapon.

Ceri pushes my hand away and slides her knife back into its hidden holster on the inside waistband of her pants. Her body's still taut, pulled tight like a suspension cable that's ready to snap. I'm glad she's not on the offensive anymore, but that could change, along with the situation. And there's a hundred ways it could, especially for the worse. I don't want to be here when that happens.

I should have listened to Ceri and remained in the medical bay, and I should have backed out of here when she told me to—she's only trying to protect me—but I've fowled that up. I can't help it. I feel safest next to her.

Maybe I could still run. Alone. If I can bring myself to part from her.

Captain Yelekal's hand rests on his pistol. He's still, but his eyes continue to move, scanning Ceri's face, then Niah's. Both of them are unwavering against his challenge, shoulders back, body leaning forward. They're ready to deliver aggression equal to anything he's got.

So this is how battles start.

Without warning, he goes straight, his gun hand sliding up to the comm piece in his ear. His gaze turns vacant.

"Yes, Commander. Understood," he says and drops his hand to resume his hard-eyed stare at Niah and Ceri. "Well, isn't this your lucky day?"

Ceri shifts her weight to her back foot, forcing me to move. I press against the wall and slip back, attempting to get Niah's attention. If I can get her to distract the captain for a moment, maybe I can escape.

"Our commander, in all of his generosity, is offering you a deal. Turn over Chief Neridi to me, and we'll take the sick kids with us. They're guaranteed to be saved on the *Devant*. I doubt they'll get the same chance on this wreck."

If I thought Niah or Ceri would agree, I'd run. But I'm too busy fuming over Captain Yelekal's insult to even consider it for more than a millisecond. I'm the only one, however. Neither Ceri nor Niah do more than stare. How they can remain so unaffected is a mystery. After his slander of the *Stratford*, I'm ready to throw a fist into his face.

He has no idea of the history he's standing on. Without ships like this, we couldn't have built the *Devant*, at least not to the level of near perfection our designers and engineers attained. Everything their ancestors innovated here on the *Stratford* became the foundation for the systems I manage.

Well, maybe not anymore. Commander Azazhi won't trust me to run anything anymore. Which is why I should have run the second Ceri tells me to.

"So do we have an agreement?" Captain Yelekal inquires, though it sounds more like an ultimatum than an offer.

To all the credit I've got to give them, Ceri and Niah remain silent. *Okay, time to go.* I pivot and dip. If violence happens, I should be far away. I remember Ceri's request. She'll need as much space as possible to fight, and I'm happy to give it to her.

"Or am I going to plow the two of you down and take the chief myself?" He sneers. "That's right, Fana Neridi. I know it's you back there. I can see your legs."

Oh hell.

"Threats won't gain our agreement," Niah says.

"There's no deal now I know where she is, so move or I will use whatever means I want to retrieve my chief."

Well, no need to hide any longer. I could still escape, but if I run, Niah and Ceri will try to stop him from chasing me, and they'll get hurt. And the thought of that keeps my feet planted on the deck.

Still, I won't let him catch me. I'm far from done with this ship. I've barely examined the *Stratford*'s navigation and control systems long enough to have an inkling of an idea of how to develop the interface code.

"Fana!"

Oh no. Raey!

I spin to face her as she approaches from down the corridor, her two security agents forming a wall behind her. Great. I'm stuck between a monster and an ex-lover who's acting like a monster.

A young crew member rushes past me, heading toward Raey. As she watches the girl approach, her face goes still. Her agents get tense, too.

But the young girl waves, and in a moment of amusement, Raey offers a small smile and lets the girl pass by. The agents also relax. They appear more hesitant to use weapons against a twelve-year-old than Captain Yelekal and his team. I am very glad about that.

"Time to go, Fana." Raey returns to scowling at me. "Get your suit on and don't fuss about it, and I'll forget that little scene you made on the ship's bridge."

"The ship doesn't have a bridge. It's a full level, not a super-structure."

Raey rolls her eyes. "Whatever. Let's go. Now."

Captain Yelekal makes a motion to his team, and they turn to prepare the airlock while Ceri and Niah watch with their predator stillness. Efa runs a hand through her hair, and Merek takes a big breath. I'm not sure if that means they're relieved they've maintained the peace or they're frustrated about los-ing me.

I make a show of my sigh, then stand straight and approach Raey.

"Fana, don't," Ceri warns, but she knows she can't help me. I can't help myself either.

Or can I?

Raey's eying me like a disapproving mother. She thinks a little scolding me will get me to snap into line and be a good robot.

But it won't.

With a growl, I dig my toes into my boots and charge. My hands come up, pushing out in anticipation of my collision with Raey. Her mouth drops open, her arms raising in defense. I yell as loudly as I can, my voice breaking at the peak of its volume. Raey turns her head. I close my eyes.

And dive past her.

I hit the deck with a grunt and scramble to my feet. A huge grin forms on my face. I'm getting out of here, headed straight for the rail car. It'll be easy to pick any floor at random, but I already know where I'll go. Only Ceri will know where to look. And when Captain Yelekal gives up, I can get back to work.

Ceri is going to be so happy with—

Something sharp hits my back, and my body jerks. My knees go weak, and I crash to the ground, shaking as I slam into the deck. I can't see. My sense of direction vanishes. I fight to regain control of my limbs, but all they do is seize.

Moments later, I'm flat on my back, staring up at the dark gray of the ceiling, with my head still reeling. Hands grab my arms and haul me, putting me face-to-face with Captain Yelekal. He gives me a once over, then nods to the two security agents holding me. I cry out as they not so gently yank my arms behind my back.

"Chief Fana Neridi, I am placing you under arrest for dereliction of duty and for disobeying orders," he says. "As per the

Devant's statute of operations, which you already know and I won't bother to repeat, you will be confined until the commander demotes you."

I can barely keep my eyes from rolling back into my head. That stun bolt hurt. A lot. And if I could stop my head from spinning, I might lodge a complaint. It wouldn't matter, of course. I'm done. Commander Azazhi will sentence me to suspended animation for the remainder of our journey.

I glance past Captain Yelekal's shoulder and catch Raey shaking her head at me as her lips mash together. Moisture wicks at the edges of her eyes, and I know I've hurt her. She was just trying to do what was right. I'm a jerk for forcing her to take action against me.

The one benefit out of this is I'll still be the same age when we arrive. It's a slight consolation for the growing ache in my chest. I will miss so much, including Raey, and I won't get to do all the things I was looking forward to. My work on the *Devant*. Exploration of the *Stratford* and the challenge of solving its control problem. The chance to look out of the observation dome in the *Devant*'s bridge and see the universe passing by. I'll miss it all.

Ceri takes a step toward Captain Yelekal's back, a powerful determination in her eyes. Her chest rises and falls with increasing speed as she raises her arm, reaching out for me. But before the security agents can notice, Niah takes hold of it and folds it back down against Ceri's side and leans against her so she can't move closer.

A whimper escapes my lips. My body trembles. I realize just how much I will miss her. *My savior.* Ceri will miss me, too, I think. Perhaps not. Maybe all she cares about is saving her ship and her people. Maybe the only thing she'll miss about me is my ability to fix her ship.

I hang my head then and stare at the deck below my feet as I bite my lower lip and shut my eyes. Ceri may not realize it, but she made my life better. Happier even. She's someone worth knowing and caring for.

But I will never have that chance.

"Return her to the *Devant* and find a dark place to lock her up," Captain Yelekal says. "She needs to get comfortable seeing the insides of her eyelids again."

The security agents drag me toward the airlock, with Raey walking next to them. Silence hangs over the entire corridor, though there's the shuffling of a few feet around to let us by. Someone produces my pressure suit, and Raey helps me into it with gentle force.

As the airlock cycles and opens, a squad of security agents pours in, and we have to wait until they're clear before we can enter. I try to take one last look at the *Stratford* and its crew, but before I can turn my head more than a few degrees, a security agent grabs my head and twists it forward.

Raey attempts to give me a supportive smile, but her lips barely move. So instead she uses my helmet as a distraction, examining it as if she's doing a safety check. There's no reason for it. They've pressurized the tube that connects the ships together. The suits are just a precaution. I guess it must be better than looking at me.

She lifts it over my head and secures it to my suit. And then, just before she shuts my visor, she mouths something. I don't catch it, but by the look on her face, I think she wanted to express her regret. That's certainly the way I'm feeling.

I've been such a fool.

RAID

— • —

CERI

I watch as the one hope we had to repair the *Stratford*'s control system disappears behind the airlock door. They treated Fana like a criminal, like her rank and title had no meaning. All she wanted to do was help, working within the guidelines set for her. Then her friend turned her in.

My eyes scan the corridor, and I spot the betrayer. Raey. She's to blame for our misfortune. Yet she has the gall to be upset about it. Likely she's pretending. I doubt she's conflicted at all.

I will give her something to be conflicted about.

"Whatever you're going to do, stop it now," Niah hisses in my ear as she leans on me. Hard. Her breathing is raspy too. I seethe as I recall Raey's warning about infection control. Just another irritation for me to be angry about.

And because of it, my rebuke of Raey will have to wait.

"You need to be in medical," I say to Niah. "I'm getting Efa."

I search out Efa, and once our eyes connect, I motion at Niah with a tilt of my head. Efa observes her and frowns. A curt nod to me and a brief word with Merek sends them and the junior crew toward us. But no. That's not what I wanted.

Panic hits me as I wave them off, signaling only for Efa to come. She's one of the few that hasn't gotten infected, even after being near so many sick children. Perhaps she's immune. Or lucky. Either way, she's the only one I trust to get close to Niah. I've already been exposed to her a hundred times, and I couldn't care less about the *Devant*'s security team.

"What's going on?" Merek whispers. When Efa indicates Niah with a subtle point, his jaw goes slack.

"Hey," Efa says gently to Niah as she puts a hand on her back and another on Niah's shoulder. "Let's get you to a bed, yeah?"

"I can take her," Merek says. "The two of you will be better off negotiating with them to get Fana back."

"No." Efa shakes her head. "You've had no exposure to the virus. Keep away. Please. I'm not letting you get infected."

Before Merek can protest, we're interrupted—by the very last person I'd want in the middle of this conversation.

Raey.

She offers me a smile, which disappears as soon as she realizes I won't be returning it. If she annoys me further, she'll get something else entirely.

While I'm distracted, Merek grabs Niah and ushers her off before either Efa or I do anything about it. There are more than a few eyes from *Devant* security on us now. Abrupt motions and loud voices from Efa or I would be unwise.

"What do you want?" I charge, lowering my gaze at her.

"As promised, we'll make good on our side of the agreement. I'll be bringing your sick to the *Devant*, and we will absolutely do everything we can to heal them," Raey replies. She presses her hands together and opening her eyes wider to show her sincerity.

I stare back. As much as I want Beka and the others to be cured, I can't trust this woman. Maybe she'll do as she says, and maybe—

"Change of plans," Captain Yelekal says in a booming voice. "We're taking everyone. Commander's orders."

Every muscle in my body gets tight. *Adults. Trying to control us?*

"No," I say. "You won't be doing that."

"Our commander has determined that a bunch of kids aren't capable of running a ship. We're bringing you under our supervision for your own benefit. Now come along so we can transfer all of you over, starting with your sick."

There's no way adults will reign over us again. They ripped us from stasis, trained us to murder each other, and treated us like tools. Then, when they found an escape from their responsibilities, they abandoned the passengers to a frozen existence they would never wake up from. I will die before giving in to adults again.

"Get off our ship," I growl. "You never had permission to be here. And the longer you remain, the more danger you bring down on your team."

Captain Yelekal huffs and tilts his head as he stares at me. I didn't expect my words would send him running, but with no weapon other than my knife, I can't be very intimidating. The only advantage I have is that he's naïve of our battle training, which I fear I'll have to use. I'm nowhere near my peak fighting skill, but it's all I have.

After a moment, he turns to his second. "Go round up the other kids. I'll deal with this brat."

And there it is.

As the security squad passes by, I lean into Efa and whisper in her ear, "Get weapons. We're going to need them."

Efa gasps before covering her mouth. She eyes the captain, then turns back to me. "How many?" she asks quietly.

"Every last one you can find."

She grabs the remaining junior crew and dashes off, leaving me outnumbered, two to one. I may make quick work of Captain Yelekal's second, but the captain himself will test my skills to the limit. If I had the advantage of surprise, and a lot of luck, I might get them both, but only if I had a pistol.

"I've known plenty of punks like you," Captain Yelekal says, leveling his gaze at me. "You're all the same. You think you're smarter than anyone, but you haven't got a clue."

I should be glad that he's underestimated me by so much. If he thinks I'm exactly like one of his fresh-face recruits, then he's got an enormous shock coming. Perhaps taking him hostage will put us in a better position to negotiate.

"Last chance," I say.

He chuckles and shakes his head. "If you keep that up, I'm going to have to teach you a lesson."

The knuckle of my thumb pounds into his second's windpipe. The man chokes and grasps at his throat as he stumbles back. I slam my knee into his stomach, and he collapses.

A blast fires from the captain's gun, missing me by the width of a finger. *Bish!* He's fast! I gasp as I lose focus, spinning away to recenter my attack, my breath coming fast. He's got the advantage now.

The next shot comes before I can reset. I drop, rolling to the ground to get behind him. My hand grabs my knife, and I slide it out to strike his calf. I grimace as the point of my blade slams into his leg.

And has no effect.

I roll again as another shot strikes the deck, sending a spray of melted composite into the air. A piece strikes my face. I wince and duck, coming around to counter. The captain spins and aims. I'm faster.

My knife slices his hand, and he cries out, but only for a second. He swings to bat me away, and I drop, my head spinning.

The captain fires, barely missing me as I tumble into a wall. He fires again, this time just over my head. I can't keep this up. His next shot will hit me for sure.

I need cover. Now.

"You brought this on yourself!" he shouts and fires as I fly around a corner. The captain follows, running at a faster clip than his large body seems like it could. There's no time to wonder. I've got to keep moving. If I stop, I'm dead.

His shots keep coming. A white-hot bolt skips off the wall and rockets down the corridor. Another buries itself in the ceiling, hissing as it dissolves the metal above my head.

I duck and run, attempting to put as much distance between him and me. A ladder is down the next passage. I could get to it, but I need to lose him first. I'm just not sure if I can.

"Surrender, you stupid girl! You can't fight me," he taunts. "And if you don't, I won't have an issue with shooting to kill."

I tighten the grip on my knife to keep it from slipping from my clammy hand. He'd enjoy killing me, alright. So I redouble my efforts and pick up speed, the desperation to stay alive surging through me.

Ancestors, protect me.

I catch the edge of a doorway and swing myself inside. My back presses against the inside wall. I lift the knife above my head with a shaky hand. He's coming. I can hear the scrape of his boots along the floor. The beating of my heart drowns out nearly every other sound. I've got to get him this time, or for sure he'll get me.

But all goes quiet. I swallow a breath and hold it. He might hear. *No.* I'm letting fear take hold in my head. I grit my teeth and force it away, attempting to regain focus. He's just one person. Even with that weapon, I can handle him.

No. I should run. It's suicide to fight.

With the slowest of movements, I slip to the edge of the doorway and place my ear just outside. But I can't hear. The pulse in my ears is deafening.

I've got to make a move. Hiding isn't a strategy. If I remain here, he'll find me and end me and won't think twice about it. I'm nothing to him.

A final inhale, then I fly from the storage bay, sprinting toward the ladder as I push my legs to give everything they've got. I can make it. I'll dive through and suffer the pain of crashing into the deck floor below. Better that than death.

"There you are!" Captain Yelekal shouts and fires. The bolt screams past my head close enough to singe my hair.

All I can think about is escape. I must live, if only to protect my crew. Three steps more, and I'll jump, leaving whatever happens to the will of the Ancestors.

I bend my legs, my eyes targeting the port. I gauge the angle, clench my fists, and leap. My guess is good—I'll make it! I'm diving into my salvation.

A searing pain strikes my abdomen. I scream out as an inferno spreads below my ribs. I'm blinded as fire flashes across my vision. My arms collapse as they hit the lower deck. I slide flat and smack into the floor with a thud. The impact forces the air from my lungs. I struggle to breathe, even as I roll for the cover of shadow. An inferno is filling my side, but I've got to keep running. I'm not safe yet.

But my knees buckle when I try to stand. My body is weak. I'm fighting just to keep conscious.

Keep going. I've got to keep going.

I scramble. Crawl. Slide. Anything to get to safety. The rail car could provide it. I just need to get there.

Ten steps away.

I'm struck with nausea from the pain. Every moment is agony. I pant hard, forcing myself forward. Stopping isn't an option. Slowing is just as bad. Only sheer reflex keeps me moving.

Five steps.

A boot rings on the first rung of the ladder. My body screams to move.

Three more steps.

But my body fails. There's nothing left. All I can do is collapse and roll into darkness. My eyelids are heavy, my breaths weak. The captain arrives on the level, taking a few steps, pausing, then taking a few more. He's near. He'll spot me in no time. I've got nothing left to defend myself. One shot into my head, and it's all over.

I'm sorry. Efa. Merek. Seren. Everyone. I failed you.

"Sir?" Captain Yelekal says. There's a pause. Then he says, "Yes, Commander. Returning immediately."

A few seconds later, he's gone. I can only smile as I lie there, quickly losing consciousness. He won't have the pleasure of watching me die.

It's over though. He got me good.

INCARCERATION

FANA

My teeth are chattering like mad. Squeezing myself tightly to get warm hasn't helped. The air in this storage room must be half the ship's standard setting. Commander Azazhi is doing this on purpose. He's torturing me with a reminder of my first moments in a stasis bed, when the refrigeration process has begun and I'm still waiting for the hibernation chemicals to kick in.

I've been sitting on top of this crate for hours, unmoving, staring at the door, waiting for them to take me to my sentencing. And that's all it will be. There's no reason for them to pretend it'll be a fair trial. We all know it won't be.

There's been little to do except stare at the line where the wall and ceiling meet, its dull metallic gray as exciting as the rest of the neutral-tones crates and bins in here. They've given me no food or water to speak of. No way to get clean. Nowhere to sleep. Though I won't need any of those things soon enough. The digestive system has to be cleared before stasis, and once I'm under, I'll sleep for hundreds of years.

The one useful thing I have done since being locked in here is reflect on my actions. Some, I now realize, were kind of stupid.

Well, idiotic, really. I overdid it, pushing Raey like that. And it was wrong of me to drag Ceri and her crew into this. They'll resist, I know it. Once Captain Yelekal gets his orders, he won't stop until they're carried out. And the *Stratford* kids won't like that one bit.

Oh, I really hope none of them get hurt...

There's a knock on the door before it slides open, revealing Raey. She's in her deep blue medical uniform and cap. Our eyes meet for a moment before she glances behind her, then steps in and shuts the door.

"Why are you wearing a respirator?" I ask, tilting my head.

Raey folds her arms and watches me from just inside the door. That she's not coming to embrace me, or even get closer to her ex-lover, is putting a lump in my throat. I don't want to believe she's that angry with me. She came to see me, after all. Still, something's wrong, and that transparent dome over her nose and mouth might have something to do with it.

"Raey," I say. "What's the respirator for?"

More observation. And then she asks, "How are you feeling?"

"Like the commander forgot I'm human and need to eat. And sleep. Can't I get a pillow or a mat at least? I want to lie down."

"Do you feel ill?"

"No! I feel exhausted! This has been a really long day. Or a couple of days." I shake my head. "I don't even know how long I've been in here!"

"Forty-six hours. Are you sure you don't feel sick?"

Oh. So that's what the mask is for.

I sigh. "Raey, just tell me already. Am I infected? Because if I am, I don't feel a thing."

"Your blood sample came back positive for viral RNA. Not one that's in our catalog." She leans back against the door. "I'm sorry, Fana."

My forehead gets tight. What is it she's sorry about? She didn't infect me. Did she? Maybe my proximity to Niah did it. Whatever it was doesn't really matter. Raey and the doctors will develop an anti-viral, and that'll be problem solved.

"Because of this, the commander has suspended your trial until we can generate a cure. We'll also be moving a medical bed in here, along with some monitoring equipment. I promise you, we'll make you as comfortable as possible."

"Well, that's nice of you, but why do I feel you're going to keep me in here for a long time?"

Raey locks eyes with me, and a chill runs down my back.

"This virus is proving difficult for us to defeat. It may be a while before we can create an effective remedy."

So this will be my prison. I'll be lonely, but anything that delays my return to stasis is a good thing. Even if it's an illness. I'd prefer that over limbo in a can any day. Maybe Ceri could even come visit.

"Okay. I understand."

Raey takes a deep breath. "No, I don't think you do."

"Of course I do! This will be—"

"Fana, one child died before we could do anything, and now more are in critical condition. With the speed at which this virus attacks the body, you could succumb to it before we come up with a solution."

The lump in my throat threatens to close it off completely. I slip off the crate and land on shaky legs and take a moment to catch my breath. I was feeling fine before Raey came in. Now every microscopic irritation is sending me into a panic. I would take stasis over this. In an instant. Unlike death, I can wake up from stasis.

"What about putting me in stasis until you find a cure?" I try.

Raey shakes her head and looks down. "Your body in stasis doesn't mean the virus will be."

"Then what about a full endocrine reset?"

"Not possible."

I pound my fists on the edge of the crate. "What the hell are the doctors doing, then? I won't wait around in this freezing closet just to die!"

She sniffles and hugs her arms to her body. "Oh, Fana. Why'd you have to go over there?"

We go silent then. There's nothing more to say. All we have now is the reality of life without each other. If I die, Raey mourns me. If I don't, I will grieve for her, gone for a hundred years after I wake from stasis.

"I will get the bed," Raey says. "You should at least sleep comfortably."

And before I can respond, she's out the door.

I shuffle across the deck, wrapping my arms about me as I remember the last time we ever embraced. Just before I went into stasis, we held each other for a moment that could never have been long enough. I miss her touch, that gentle yet firm press of assurance that always kept me grounded. I wish I could feel that again. Just once more. Before I'm locked in stasis or...otherwise.

Something comes over me then, a powerful urge to live. It might be my attempt to deny the possibility of dying, or it could just be fear forcing me to move. No matter what it is, energy surges inside me, and suddenly I'm desperate to escape this cold and dark space.

I'm getting out. And once I do that, I'll figure out what comes next.

But other than a few stacks of pod-sized crates and the shelves full of gray goods, there's little else here. Maybe that's why they put me in this dreary room. If there's nothing here I can use, there's no chance I can get out.

I grin. Even as Commander Azazhi labels me a deserter, he still respects my skills. He should respect them more. I've barely taken three steps, and I've already discovered two potential ways out. One would require a few tools, which likely aren't here, but the other...

The other gets me in between a pair of shelving units, stretching my arms and legs to prepare for a climb. I take hold of a top shelf and put my foot on the second lowest, pushing up. My body lifts, and I secure my other foot to the same shelf. I repeat the process until I'm kneeling on the top.

There's a ventilation duct up there, but I'd be stupid to try that. Even if I could remove the vent cover and squeeze myself inside, I'd either get lost or stuck. My target is something much simpler—an access hatch with finger-tight bolts. I can crawl through the maintenance space until I get to a room that leads me to where I want to go, wherever that is.

The access hatch is a little higher than I estimated. I'll need to stand on this top shelf to reach the bolts, then use a box or something to raise me high enough so I can pull myself up into it. No problem. I'll get this done with ease.

But as I reach down for a box on a lower shelf, a wave of dizziness hits me. I fall forward with my arms out, barely saving myself from falling a distance nearly twice my height. I shut my eyes and hold on with all the strength I've got until it passes.

I push back and sit on my heels with a sigh—that was close. I might be sick after all. There's no time to waste then. I grab a pair of boxes and stack one on top of the other. It's a sketchy pedestal, but it's all I have to work with. I take a quick breath, clench my teeth, and climb onto the boxes. They shake as I move, and I take a jittery pause until they stabilize before I can stand.

Phew. Okay. Here we go.

Even with the extra height, I grunt and stretch well above my head to grab the first bolt. It takes effort to turn it, too, but once I've got it loose, it spins out and drops to the floor. There are two more after that one. The middle is next. It comes loose with barely any effort.

One more to go. I should use my left hand to undo it, but instead I use my right, opting for speed over force. To steady my balance, I press on the ceiling and brace my feet. This one is tough, maybe because of the angle I'm attempting to turn it at. I reset my feet and try again.

With a growl and a hard wrench of my wrist, the bolt comes free. A few more turns and the hatch will fall open.

Nope. I've got to pull it down, though that could be a plus. It might make it easier to climb up, using the slats in the hatch as a place to grip and pull myself up. All I need to do is apply a little pressure on the hatch and—*crap!*

Before I can react, the hatch swings down, pulling me with it. My feet slip off the box, and I go face forward into the top of the next shelf. I groan as my stomach smacks into its edge.

Then I'm falling.

My arms flail out, grasping for a handhold, but my fingers slide off everything I reach. I fall backwards, smacking my head into the opposite shelf. Sparks cross my eyesight. I tumble, my limbs searching for anything to stop my fall. I grab the edge of a box, only to yank it off the shelf, sending it dropping after me.

A wail blasts from my lungs as my tailbone crunches onto the deck. My head impacts the bottom shelf with a heavy thump, and the box I brought down with me breaks open and dumps its contents across my body. The world around me goes in and out of focus as my back arches and every part of my body cries out in pain. I may have broken something. More than something. I attempt to lift my head, then lower it as nausea grips me. I'll just lie here a moment. As if I had a choice.

Once my sight's cleared up, I dig myself out of the colossal pile of small packages I'm buried under. Raey will return soon—I'll need to clean this mess up and close the hatch before she does.

But when I examine one bundle out of curiosity, I gasp and sit up, staring at the square box with rounded edges. It's a med kit. No. It's *the* med kit—the kits that I brought aboard. The ones with the auto-ranging antiviral in them. The ones that the med team forgot about after them sitting in here for seventeen years.

Could they work? Could they cure me and the dying kids from the *Stratford*?

I need to find out.

QUESTION

FANA

I DIG THROUGH THE pile of med kits, my body aching and my breaths becoming heavy. Each one I examine and toss away sends my pulse racing faster. I calculated for this. I definitely considered the length of the journey. But the more I check, the more I struggle to explain what I'm seeing.

They're all expired.

Maybe it's because they've been in this dusty, frigid, stale-air closet. Maybe they needed to be stored at a certain temperature. That'd seem unlikely, but I don't know. I'm not a medical expert. My scouring of the instructions on the package only shows how to use the tools and medicines inside. If temperature regulation was critical, it'd say so, wouldn't it?

I spot a miracle. At least I think I do. My hands toss kits everywhere just so I can get through the glut of red-tabbed packages to grab the one that caught my eye.

Yes! This one has a green tab! I nearly scream in excitement but end up with a hacking cough instead. It doesn't matter. In my hands is the means to save my life. And if there's one, there could be more. This pile is just one carton. I remember four.

With a grunt, I pull myself up to examine the shelf it fell from. None of the other boxes are marked, so I grab one and dump it out. Then the next. And the next. Med kits plummet to the deck, landing with a light *thunk*. A few bounce off my legs, but I'm so ecstatic about discovering the one kit, I barely notice.

When I'm up to my knees in kits, I grab packages with renewed excitement, ignoring the sting from the burns on my back and the dull throbbing of my head. I may be dizzy, but I've got a mission. That's all that matters. Expired kits fly toward the far side of the room while any good kits, if I find them, go on the shelf next to the one I found. It's tough work, and even in this chill, I build up a sweat. But I've got to find more. I can't risk my life on one kit working after seventeen years, even if its tab is green.

My adrenaline kicks in when I spot another. That's two. One more and I'll take my chances that one of the three works. The grin on my face widens. *I'm such a genius to have brought these.*

I revel so much in my self-greatness, I don't notice Raey return until she screams my name.

"Fana!"

I jolt, glancing up as she wades through the kits toward me. Even through the full-face respirator she now wears, I can tell she's furious. Of course it's my fault. It's standard operating procedure for me to enrage her these days, even if it's never intentional.

"What..." Raey takes my arms and shakes me as she catches her breath. "What are you doing?"

I smile and grab the good kit to show her. "Look, Raey! Remember these? I've found two of them! One's bound to be good. That means you can cure me!"

"That's great, but…" She looks around, her mouth hanging open. The moment she spots the hatch door hanging down, a moan comes from her throat. "Oh, Fana, why? Where did you think you could go?"

"It doesn't matter," I reply. "If I hadn't opened it, I wouldn't have fallen and found the kits!"

"Fallen?" Raey examines my face and body, then spins me around. "Your head is bleeding!"

"Yeah. It hurts a little, but we can take care of that after." I grab the other kit and push them both at her. "Here! Let's try one now!"

Raey narrows her eyes at me, then drags me toward the crate I was sitting on before. "I'm going to get a sec skin kit to fix that laceration. You are going to do nothing else but sit here until I get back, got it?"

"Forget the cut. This is going to cure me! That's more important, right?"

"The doctors will cure you. And everyone else that's sick. So there's no need to waste time on an ancient med-pack."

When I go to respond, Raey covers a gloved hand over my mouth and locks eyes with me. I get her message, so I keep my mouth closed and nod, pretending to be chastised by her gaze.

But the moment she walks out and the door shuts, I'm back at it, working faster than ever. I hope I find a lot more, but three will be enough. And Raey's right. The *Devant*'s doctors will find a cure for Ceri's crew soon enough.

Ceri. I pause for just a moment and smile. For someone so young, she is so amazing to have taken command of an entire colony ship, especially one that's a few accidents short of becoming derelict. I really want to talk with her again, to get to know what's behind that hard shell she's forced to wear. I bet, under that, she's an amazing person. With dreams and—

"Yes!" My eyes go wide when I spot a third kit. It goes on the shelf next to the others. I should try to find another, just in case.

But when I look over the remaining kits, my heart sinks. The rest are expired. I run my tongue across my lips. Could I have missed one? It's possible. I'd have to go through them all again, with a more focused and deliberate approach that I don't have time for. Raey will be back in a few minutes, and if she catches me disobeying her, her next motion will be to fill my bloodstream with a tranquilizer.

It wouldn't be the first time.

I could still escape. There's more than enough time to get away. I'll bring the kits with me and return to the *Stratford*. Then I can repair their control system—oh, I'll need a multi-processor box—and Ceri will be overjoyed. She'll treat me like a queen for saving her passengers. Well, maybe not, but it beats waiting around here to be sentenced. I might even negotiate with the commander for a return with no consequences.

That open hatch is calling me. It's time to go. With more caution this time.

I toss the three med kits up to the top shelf and climb. This time, I use both shelving units to support me, and it takes half the time to get to the top. This time, I stack three boxes, one on top of the other two, for a sturdier base. Now I can just step up like I was on stairs. The hatch opening is just an arm's length away. I reach for it.

And pause.

My gut is tightening. No, my chest is too. Why? The reason is there, just beyond my grasp. It's like Raey scolding me for something I don't remember doing, and the more I think about it, the worse I feel. The choice I've made is wrong. I'm running away when I should be standing up for...someone?

Those kids.

Oh hell. I'm being a total ass, aren't I? I get to live when the *Stratford*'s crew—children half my age—are still at risk. Am I that scared to die? Well, from an unknown virus that'll turn me into a wretched heap of purple puss...yes. But Ceri sacrificed her life to look after an entire ship of passengers she has no way to save. What am I compared to that?

I can't be selfish. Not anymore.

Raey returns just as I'm reaching for the hatch to shut it. The moment she notices me, she charges up the shelf, swatting at my leg to seize hold of it.

"Fana! Don't you dare!" she hisses. "They'll shoot you dead! Is that what you want?"

"No...but maybe I shouldn't be so afraid of death." I take a seat on the edge of a carton and sigh, a sudden lightness of being coming over me.

"What?" She shakes her head and frowns. "What are you saying?"

I smile. "I found three good med kits. Take them for the *Stratford* crew. I'll wait for a cure."

Raey blinks as her jaw goes slack. But the moment she understands, she swallows hard, as if she's in desperate need of water. Her shoulders slump, and I catch a small tremble of her lips.

"Come down, Fana. Let me take care of you." She reaches a hand out to me. "I've got a bed waiting outside. You can be lying down in it the moment I move it in. I promise you'll be comfortable, and I won't let the commander bother you."

Okay, I'll be selfish for ten more seconds. I don't mean to make her worry about me, but it warms my heart that she still does, especially after everything that's happened. One day soon, I will show her how much it means to me.

"I will, but not yet," I reply. "I've got to close the hatch. The bolts are somewhere down on the deck. Could you try to find them for me?"

"No. Forget it. I'll have Taye put it back up. He was asking how you were. I'm sure we can trust him to have a little discretion."

"It's just three little bolts. I can close it in less than a minute if I have them."

Raey sighs and tugs on her ponytail. "Dammit, Fana, just trust me for once, would you?"

I duck my head and smile an apology. Here I go, falling into old habits again. It wasn't always like this. Our relationship was full of so much joy. Anytime we were together, it was like we could have blasted off tEarth on our own, just the two of us. I would have gone anywhere she asked me to.

"You may not feel bad now," Raey says, "but you will. And the last thing I want is to watch you suffer. So please, for old time's sake, come down, and I will do everything I can to make you comfortable."

Wow. She's serious. And right. It could be our last time to be close. Our last chance to ask for forgiveness—me especially—and remind each other of just how well we used to get along.

"Okay." I take her hand but pause and say, "Thank you, Raey. And...sorry. For not listening."

She nods, a soft smile lifting her lips even when her eyes get misty.

Once down, Raey wraps her arms around me and lays her head on my shoulder. I do the same, though my motions are stiff. I want to show her my appreciation, but my body isn't cooperating. And I get why.

I'm not ready to say goodbye to her.

COMMAND

CERI

"CERI!"

A hand, one that I am all too familiar with, shakes me hard. I moan and wince as a searing pain strikes my side, and I roll away from the assault. But it persists. She persists. Efa was never one to leave things be when she would have been wise to do so.

"Stop," I mumble. "I'm hit."

Still, I'm thankful she found me. And thankful to be alive.

"Where?" Efa asks. She grabs my shoulders and lays me flat on my back. The vibration of my body impacting the deck sends a shock through me, inflaming my wound. I cry out in pain and jerk away from her hold.

"Sayer!" Efa shouts, likely into her comm. "I found Ceri! On eighteen. Get down here. I need your help!"

No. Not the person I want to see. Likely Sayer feels the same way after what I did to him. Efa may provide some buffer between us, but she'll be busy caring for me while she does it. All I want is to find out what happened and then figure out what to do about it. He will only be a complication.

"Lay down, Ceri," Efa orders. "I'll wrap your wound."

As she opens my shirt, she gasps and stares. But Efa's experienced plenty of combat damage, and two seconds later, she blinks and continues her examination. She's gentle, but I suck air through my teeth every time her fingers prod my abdomen. With the way the pain stabs my side, I can only imagine the damage. Better yet, I won't. I don't want to know how horrible it is.

As she works to treat me, the blurriness in my eyes clears, and I take in Efa's weary form. How long has it been since she slept? Too long likely, which means she's been caring for the others.

"Anyone else wounded?"

"No."

Efa's curt answer gives me pause. She could be angry with me, though she's always vocal about her feelings. Especially if I've messed up. This is something else.

"The crew?" I ask. "Where are they?"

"Besides you, me, Sayer, and Mari?" Efa's lips get tight. "Gone."

My heart freezes for a beat, only to return with a heavy thump. "What do you mean, gone?"

"The *Devant'*sagents took them. Merek. Niah. Everyone. They're all prisoners now."

"No! We're getting them back. As soon as you're done, let's—"

Efa presses down hard on the last bandage, and I wail, knocking her hand away and pushing back. My hand goes to my wound as I reel, collapsing against the wall behind me. My side is throbbing, and soreness runs through my hip and knee, reminding me of the crash landing I made coming down to this level.

"Stop being a baby. I'm almost done."

I give her a hurt look. "If you wound me more, I won't be able to go with you."

She puts her hands on her hips and just stares.

Before I can ask why, Sayer comes out of the rail car, his face a grimace. He half limps, half stomps his way toward us, bent forward, his hand covering over his stomach.

Is he exaggerating? He has to be. I couldn't have hurt him that badly.

"Was she shot?" Sayer asks as he gets to us.

Efa nods. "By one of their advanced weapons. It's bad."

Sayer's eyes fall to my side, his nose wrinkling before he sneers. "Good. I hope it hyuking hurts."

I tighten my jaw, holding back my words while I come up with something reasonable to say. This isn't about our grudge. We need to work together.

"Listen, Sayer. I'm sorry about hitting you," I begin, my voice turning raspy. "But we've got—"

"Go to hell, Ceri. You think you did this to me? I had to fight an entire squad of those bastards when they grabbed Dru. And where the hyuk were you when that was happening?"

"Down here, dying." I motion to my wound. His face sobers, and he backs off, though the fire in his eyes remains.

"You know you're to blame for all of this," Sayer mutters.

"Me?"

"Sayer, stop. We don't have time for that." Efa moves in between us as she goes to grab my arm. "Let's take her to medical and get prepped."

"Prepping first," Sayer says. "She can crawl up there for all I care."

Efa eyes me, silent, perhaps expecting my reply, and as her words register in my brain, I get why, and I'm not happy about it.

"No. I'm coming with you," I say and slide against the wall to stand. "I won't sit this one out."

But her hand on my arm moves to my shoulder and stops me from rising. "You're not doing anything but going to medical and staying there."

My eyes narrow at her, ready to argue. This is hardly the time. I'll sacrifice my irritation for some squad cohesion. "I appreciate the concern for me, Efa, but—"

"This isn't concern." Her eyes pierce into me. "This is you staying out of the way. Sayer and I will figure out what to do."

I stare at her as my brow presses tight, trying my best to understand her reasoning. I'm wounded. So is Sayer. And Efa seems ready to drop any second. My body is begging for rest. I can't. I won't. We've all got to go. Four of us are already too few to accomplish this mission.

"Listen, Sayer," I say, keeping my voice calm. "I get you're mad, but we've got to work together on this."

"Work together?" He frowns and tosses a hand at me. "What the hyuk can you do? You're less than useless."

I grit my teeth and push myself up to sit. Sayer may take me more seriously if I can prove I can stand. If I can.

Efa shakes her head, warning me not to try it, as if it was a choice I could make at my leisure. With a breath, I squeeze my hands into fists, then stretch them out, planting them on the wall behind me. I press my feet down and try to get up. I grunt with the effort to move, but my legs shudder and give out, and I crash back to the deck with a whimper, my side burning with the blaze forced against it.

"Let's go," Sayer says, reaching out for Efa. "Who knows what those adults are putting them through."

"Just. Hold. On." I shut my eyes and strain to push up again, but my hands slip off the wall, and I go nowhere.

"Forget it, Ceri," Efa says. "You can't. And we wouldn't take you even if you could."

"You can't go!" I shout, even as I rest my arms on my knees and hang my head. "You've got no intel! No reserves. How will you even get over there without them spotting you?"

"We'll figure it out." She digs into a pocket and holds out a pair of ampules. I wave her away, but she thrusts them at me a second time. I sigh and snatch them from her hand, dropping the vials next to me.

I'm shaking from anger or from shock. It's hard to tell. Perhaps both. Sayer's words have made the acid in my stomach rise into the back of my throat. *Adults have my crew.* And with no one to protect them, those hyuking bastards will do whatever they wish.

Still, I can't just let them go over there and get killed. Neither Efa nor Sayer has led a squad. They may think they understand what to do. They don't.

"Who's going to lead?" I ask.

"I am," Sayer replies.

"Didn't you just get done telling me how the *Devant*'s squads beat you?"

"Do you think we've got a choice?" Sayer hisses, leaning down to thrust his finger at me. "And after what you did, you've got no right to complain about my condition."

I likely deserved that. It's my fault he's got a big gash on the back of his head. And he won't listen to me tell him how he overreacted as much as I did.

"All I'm asking is that you wait," I try. "Not long. Just help me get to my feet, and we can plan together. I'll support you anyway that I can."

"We don't need your *support*," he spits back. "You've caused enough problems already."

I shut my eyes, even as heat rises in my body, fueled by the raw irritation in my side. I've little strength to maintain my calm, and soon enough, my ire at his stupidity is going to explode. For their sake, and their lives, I will try one more time.

"Sayer, even if you were combat ready, you don't have the experience to pull this off. And as good as the two of you are, the *Devant*'s soldiers outmatch you in nearly every way. I know it's grinding on you to think about our crew over there. I feel it too. We'll get them back. We just have to be strategic in our planning."

"You didn't see what they did to Tegan," Efa says. "Or Merek."

I press my lips together. "No, I didn't, but that—"

"We're done talking." Sayer grabs Efa's arm. "Time to go."

"Dammit!" I pound my fists into my legs. "You're going to die!"

"That's our choice."

I just stare. I've heard less nonsense from a fourteen-year-old fresh out of training and eager to prove themselves to their senior squad members.

"Efa, are you going to just let him lead you to your death?"

"At least he leads," Efa fires back.

Perhaps I'm weakened, or maybe it's because I expected Efa to listen to reason and side with me, but her words drive ice through me, turning my body numb. It's not the first time she's done it, but every time it happens, I want to believe it's the first. That way I can pretend we're as close as we've always been and not at such odds that she's willing to kill herself just to spite me.

I shake my head. "You can't do this. Please. Just wait. Whatever you're mad at me for, you can't let it affect your decisions."

"Like Sayer said, we've no choice."

"So you're going to end your life because of some stupid sense of fate? I didn't save you from that stasis pod just for you—"

My mouth shuts the moment her face turns pained as I realize how cruel I've just been to my best friend. But I've said it, and there's little I can do to take it back.

"Efa, I'm sorry…I didn't mean that."

Efa holds her hand up to Sayer before he can pound on me. I should be thankful for that, but I fear what she's about to say is going to be much worse.

"This is all thanks to you, Ceri," Efa says. "You say we're supposed to decide things together, but you went and acted on your own. You created this mess, and now Sayer and I have to fix it. It'll be on you if we die."

My jaw drops open. "That's total bish, and you know it!"

"Do I?" She folds her arms and leans her face close to mine. "You wanna know what else is hyuking bish? Someone who denies they're the leader, even when everyone else looks to them for guidance, and then goes and does whatever the hyuk they want without even considering others."

If my body wasn't already full of aches, I may have noticed the one forming in my heart. If Efa was aiming to kill, she may have just succeeded. Her words make me realize how much I hated the idea of being leader. Now I recognize the things I did to deliberately sabotage my authority or counter the decisions of others. It was wrong, but it didn't bring us to this point.

"Why do you keep making me be the one at fault here?" I ask as my voice breaks.

"Because when we had a crisis, we looked to you for guidance, and you let us down."

I slump, my head rolling to one side as my gaze drops to the ground. All I can think about is Tal's broken body, Beka's graying skin, the terror in Fana's eyes when they led her away.

I failed her, just as I failed my crew, even when I thought I was doing the right thing.

She straightens then. "Make your own way up to medical. Or don't. It doesn't matter to me. Go hide away like Niah did for all I care."

All I can do is stare at my hands as they walk away, perhaps trying to make me feel the same way they felt.

Abandoned.

SERVICE

— • —

CERI

I LIE IN THE same spot for what must be hours. Perhaps even days. My throat is so dry, it hurts to breathe. I could quench my thirst with the water recycler ten steps down the corridor, yet I have little will to move or survive. There is little reason for it. I'm unwanted. Unneeded.

Perhaps somewhere in the back of my head, I was hoping she'd return. Without Sayer. Then we could talk, and I could beg her forgiveness. Even if she wasn't ready to accept my apology, her simple act of coming back would be enough to hold on to.

But she hasn't. And likely now, along with everyone else, she's dead.

That thought shakes something in me. I press up to kneel, taking a moment to let my head get used to being vertical. Other sensations take over—the weakness of my limbs and the soreness in my side battling with the tightness in my stomach. My body is demanding nourishment, even as my heart and brain refuse it.

I could be the only caretaker our passengers have left, and I am nothing against a galaxy of impossibility. Efa's parents.

My parents. Sayer's and Merek's families. It's a good thing they aren't aware of what's happening around them. I wouldn't want to look my mother in the eyes and tell her how I've failed her. Her stasis is naïve bliss, and there is no reason to destroy it.

With a hand on the wall, I push up, but my legs shake and give out. I slam into the wall, letting my face take the brunt of the impact rather than my wound. With a groan, I quickly find an indent in a doorway, a place to grip my hands and keep me upright.

I shouldn't have denied myself water. Now my body pleads for it. It's just another agony piled on all the rest, and the need seems small. It's not. I will die if I do not drink. I cannot give in to selfish desires if I'm to care for everyone as I'd promised to.

A cough comes from down the corridor, breaking me from my self-created misery. Is it Efa? Did they save everyone?

"W...who's there?" I croak.

Seren comes from out of the shadow, her cautious gaze watching me. She's got a gun in one hand and a blade in the other. *Good girl.* I always thought she was a sharp student. No one will ever sneak up on her. Other than me.

Her eyes widen once she takes me in. She rushes to my side, only taking a moment to holster her weapons before putting her arms around me.

"Ancestors, I thought I was the last," Seren gasps as she presses her cheek to my shoulder. "I'm so glad to see you. Are you hurt?"

"Water...please..."

I collapse. Only Seren's fast reaction saves me from crashing to the deck. Still, I'm dead weight in her arms, and all she can do is ease my fall.

"I got some." Seren fumbles for her canteen and spins off the cap in a near panic. She lifts my head and puts the canteen's spout to my lips. Water spills down the sides of my face and into my shirt as I gulp as much as I can get. Now I'm soaked but no longer thirsty.

"Ceri," Seren whispers as she kneels next to me. "Where is everyone? Did those soldiers take them all?"

"Not all. Sayer, Efa, and Mari went after them."

"No!" Seren coughs again. "Why'd they do that?"

I have no answer, but something else has my attention. Seren is sick. For how long, I'm not sure. And I just drank from her canteen. If I get infected, the virus will overcome my weak state much quicker than it will take Seren down. Then she will truly be alone.

"How long?" I ask, leveling my gaze at her.

Seren frowns. "How long what?"

"How long have you been sick?"

"I'm not sick. I...oh, you mean the cough? I got dust got in my throat, that's all."

I sit up so our eyes can connect. She needs to see just how much I don't believe that. Seren shrinks from my stare as she gets my message, pressing her hands into her lap. She may be a good soldier, but she'd make a poor spy.

"Really. I'm not!" Seren throws her hands up and grins. "See?"

Her sudden motion sends her into a fit of coughs. She doubles over, and I have to hold her until it's over. Seren is one of mine. I trained her, and if there is anyone that I'd want to care for, it'd be her. A smile forms on my lips. Perhaps I'm not as useless as I feel. Seren needs me, and I am more than glad to help.

"It's alright, I've got you," I whisper.

She looks up at me from her hunched-over position and gives me a weak smile. "Aren't we a laugh? You, wounded in battle, and me..."

A sudden wave of anguish floods over me when her gaze drops, confirming what I suspect. I can't help her, after all. I can only ease her suffering until there is nothing left for me to do but watch her die.

Efa was right. I have failed everyone, Seren included.

I shut my eyes, doing my best to escape reality. I'm desperate to run away from Seren's naïve worship of me. That spell needs to be broken. I'm no one to hold in any level of regard. She should know how weak I truly am, and I should be the one to tell her. But I can't. Not even that.

Instead, I pull her close, embracing her as if she was my child. It's more for my comfort than hers. Seren is strong, much more than me. Even if I told her the truth, she wouldn't cry. Not like I would. Even if I told her it was okay if she felt like it, she wouldn't. Our life here has created a shell that covers each one of us. It protects us from every cruel moment we encounter. Should it crack, then we would, too. Yet Seren's shell is tougher than most. I should know. I taught her how to strengthen it.

Seren pulls back to sit on her feet as a warm glow surrounds her face. The edges of her mouth curve upward in a gentle acknowledgement of my action.

"Thank you for always taking care of me, Ceri," she says, touching my arm. I force a smile and look away. She may think it, but I know it's not true, and I don't want to destroy that illusion for her.

We sit in silence for a long time, a comfortable, if uncommon, occurrence. We've all trained in ambush tactics, where we would sit for hours, not speaking, not moving. If one adult caught us doing either, we'd get a crack from the instructor's whip. We all learned quickly.

"Ceri?"

Seren's meek voice turns me toward her. The despair in her eyes shakes me, and I fear I already know what she will ask me before she does. I try my best to keep the emotion from my face.

"How long...do you think I have?"

My mouth freezes open. My lips lock in place. How can I give her any answer that wouldn't destroy her? How could I let my words be a sentence for ending her life? It wouldn't matter what number I picked. Seren would take it as fact and live as if that was the absolute time she had left.

"I was just hoping it'd be at least a week," she says, shrugging. "I want to have time to do a few things I never got to do. Like find which level my parents are on. Or just take an hour to do nothing but look out the port on level two. I'd like to have that week, if I could."

But as Seren lists off her wishes, a resistance grows within me, a refusal to accept the only option as being one where she slowly expires until there is nothing left of her but a corpse. And not just her. The entire crew. I can't sit in my self-made misery while all of them once again fall victim to the will of adults.

My hands reach out to cup her face and turn it so I can meet her eyes once more. Seren jerks in surprise, turning a curious gaze up at me.

"No," I say. "You are not doing that. Not while I can still breathe."

She reaches up to take my hands from her face as her jaw goes slack. I'm not sure if it's hope I see filling her face, but Seren is listening, perhaps even wanting, and that alone empowers me to continue.

"I'm going over there, to the *Devant*. I'll find our crew and bring them back. And along with them, a cure."

"But"—Seren shakes her head—"how will you do that? You can't even stand."

"That's a problem, but I at least know how to solve it."

"And the rest?"

"I'll have to figure out, but I still need time to prepare. I can do it then."

Thoughts are flying through Seren's head, fast and furious, as her grip of my hands gets tighter. Her eyes lose their focus until she blinks and looks at me.

"I'm going with you," she says with a determination I've never heard from her before. My gut goes tight as my brain screams, *Never.* I've already failed to protect her so many times. This would just be another way I would neglect her.

Yet I can't refuse her. I need her help, if only to watch my back. And for me to deny her this one chance to fight for herself would be more than wrong. Seren may be my junior squad mate, but she has never been a lesser fighter in anyone's eyes.

I squeeze her hands and nod.

"Okay," I reply. "We'll do this together."

ACTION

——— • ———

FANA

A SCREAMING SIREN WAKES me from my medicine-induced sleep. I'm slow to respond. My brain is foggy, and my limbs feel like someone stuck them in mud. It's all because Raey soaked my body in her magical sleeping potion. As much as I want to find out what's going on, it'll be half an hour before I can get out of bed.

I almost don't want to. I'd go back to sleep if it wasn't for this piercing sound bouncing off the walls and slicing into my eardrums like knives. And Raey must have given me the best bed in medical. It's so soft the dead could rest on it. Maybe they have.

The first motion I manage is to cover my head with the pillow. The next is to remember what this alarm means. It's not a systems emergency, that's for sure. Even in my disconnected state, I'd recognize one of those warnings. They're just as loud but less cutting. This has got to be a security klaxon. Only they would choose a sound so blatantly painful. It's not my problem, so now I can close my eyes and try to fall back asleep.

To my delight, the siren shuts off a few seconds later. I breathe a sigh of relief and slide back into my immobile slumber. There are issues I need to sort out, but they'll have to wait. I'm not up to handling them right now.

"Attention all crew. This is Commander Azazhi. We have an unauthorized entry through the airlock at location B-12-A. This intruder is unidentified and may be dangerous. Secure your doors and shelter in place. Do not open for anyone without approval from me or Captain Yelekal. This is for your own safety."

"Shut up," I moan. I don't want reminders of my impending trial. Not while I'm trying to sleep.

But the words "unauthorized entry through the airlock" and "intruder" light up in my brain. And the location. That's the port where the *Devant* connects to the *Stratford*. Someone's come over—without permission.

There's a sound at the door. Someone's trying to get in! It sounds like they don't know the security code. Then the door slides open. It's Raey, and she's terrified. Why? A second later, I get my answer. Someone with black hair and a dirty gray uniform shoves her through and slips in behind. *Stratford* crew, for sure. But who is it?

My jaw drops. *It's Ceri!*

With one hand holding Raey's arms behind her, she shuts the door and locks it, ordering Raey to sit down and face the shelves. She's bound Raey's hands behind her back with a pair of hose ties, so Raey can only flop on the bed's edge and bend over.

Why is Ceri treating her like this?

In my medicated state, I take longer than a minute to realize she's the intruder. And another half-second to remember I've got a virus inside of me.

"No…no, you can't be here," I warn, but I slur my words when I speak. "I'm…"

"Infected," Raey adds. "And now we are, too."

Ceri steps back, her brow crushing together. She glances between Raey and me, then shakes her head.

"No, I don't think so," she says. "I've been exposed multiple times, and I'm fine."

Raey twists to stare at Ceri with an eyebrow raised. Her mind is running through how or why it could be possible. I know, because I'm thinking the same thing.

"It doesn't matter," Ceri replies. "I'm taking you back with me, and you're going to help us like you said you would."

My pulse quickens. She came all the way here and is risking her life for me? Before I learned what she'd been through, I might have thought that was crazy. But now, I've got my hopes up that she'll be able to pull off whatever she's got planned.

"Your crew is here," Raey fires back. "Why would you take her instead of them?"

"I'm taking them too."

Raey huffs. "Impossible. The security agents will never let you get anywhere near that airlock."

"I'm prepared for them."

I smile at her confidence, then blush when she turns her eyes on me. It's the medication, of course. I'd be more in control of myself if I wasn't on it.

"I really want to try your idea to repair control," Ceri says, licking her lower lip. "So will you come?"

"Fana, no," Raey says, her tone insistent. "You can't. You could infect others."

I shrug. "I'll wear a mask."

Raey turns on me then, ignoring Ceri's warning to turn back to the wall. Our eyes connect, and I sense one of her lectures coming. I'll listen, but that's about all I'll do. I'm tired of her chiding me about every little thing just because she's been the more mature of the two of us. So no matter what she says, I won't do it.

"Now that she's invaded our ship, she's the enemy. If you go with her, the commander will consider you a traitor," Raey says.

"So?"

"Fana!" Raey jumps off the bed to face me fully. "Don't you realize? They won't arrest you again. They'll shoot her on sight. And you too!"

My jaw drops. As much as I know I'd be deserting my post again, the commander would never order my execution. Sure, he'd be raging mad and threaten to lock me in the engine annihilation chamber, but he'd be stupid to off such a valuable resource. Raey's just trying to scare me into staying.

Still, I feel a chill run down my back, thinking about it. My first trip to the *Stratford* was worthy of a court martial. My second might be unforgiveable.

"Sit down," Ceri orders Raey.

But instead of following orders, Raey only shakes her head.

"Do you even know what you've gotten yourself into?" Raey charges. "You may have fought some battles with the other children, but the people coming after you are adults, and they're experts at what they do. Commander Azazhi won't go easy on you just because you're young. If you hurt one of his crew…"

Ceri shifts and tugs at her shirt, dropping her gaze. But if Raey thinks she's intimidated her, she's about to find out what kind of metal Ceri's made of.

"If he hurts one of my crew, you mean," Ceri growls as she looks up. "How much combat experience has Commander Azazhi had? How about his security?"

Raey shrugs. "What does that matter? They're highly trained."

Ceri rushes Raey and grabs her shirt, pressing her against the side of one shelf. Raey yelps as her eyes go wide. She tries to pull away as Ceri gets in her face, but Ceri just smirks and lets go. Her action had its intended effect. Now she just keeps her face close to maintain it.

"The adults that turned us into murderers had no problem with ending one of us," Ceri hisses. "Can your highly trained agents shoot a child? No? We were unprepared for your raid, but this time we won't hesitate to show your agents just how deadly we can be."

Raey swallows hard. She wouldn't want to see anyone on either side die. All life is precious to her. That's why she's a medical specialist. The thought of violence makes her physically ill.

Ceri puts her hands on my shoulders and looks me in the eye. "We really need your help, Fana. Without it, every sacrifice we've made will be for nothing. I'm risking my crew to come here and get you. Please, make this worth it for us."

When I look at Raey for any kind of reaction, her face becomes pained, and she turns away with a sniffle. My shoulders slump, and my head lowers, but Ceri squeezes my shoulders and holds me up, trying to reconnect her gaze with mine.

I keep my eyes locked on the bed. As much as I want to follow her anywhere, this is more complicated than Ceri's making it seem. I'm not sure if I've even got the entire story of what's happened since I've been in here. It must have been a lot if Ceri's taken such a risk to come here.

And what if Raey is right?

"I don't know," I reply, slumping. "This is all really uncertain. I mean, I want to help, but..."

A shiver runs through me, and my hands turn clammy. It could be the fear I feel, or it could be the first stages of my illness, and that thought makes my stomach tight. How I got to be here—to this point—I'll never know. But now that I am, I have to find a way forward.

"I'll protect you," Ceri says. "I promise you won't get hurt."

"You can't promise that," Raey retorts. "You don't even know what happens once you open that door and step out."

"Do you?" Ceri fires back, narrowing her eyes. "Don't pretend like you care about her like you used to."

"You have no idea how I feel about Fana."

Ceri doesn't, but I do. Raey's made it clear. We may not be what we were, but the connection we have now isn't something I want to simply throw away. That'd be what happens if I agree to go.

"Help me and I help you." Ceri's confident tone shakes when she speaks. Maybe she's doubting me. Or herself. For the first time, I see her as just a girl, fearing her world is about to implode.

"How?" I ask.

"I'll get your commander to drop any charges against you."

Raey huffs. "You're just a girl. You have no idea how to do that."

"And you've no idea what I know how to do."

I like Ceri. I really do. Her passion and strength are so very attractive. I wish I was that confident when I was her age. It's no wonder every one of her crew looks up to her as their leader. And that she continues to deny that she is also amazes me. That much worship would go straight to my head.

But as much as I want to get to know her more, that's not enough of a reason for me to put my life at risk. I've been selfish long enough, and everything I've done wrong has gotten me where I am.

"I'm sorry, Ceri," I say. "I can't do this for you."

Raey's smug reaction brings heat to my face and hands. I should tell her off for celebrating Ceri's sorrow.

Except Ceri isn't sad. Her eyes widen, and her mouth opens as she shakes her head.

"No," she says, shaking me. "This isn't for me. None of this is for me. We've near four thousand passengers on board the *Stratford*. My parents, and the parents of every crewmember, are with them. They're expecting to sleep a thousand years and wake up on a new planet. I've given them my life so they can have the future I never will."

I just stare at her, my mind struggling to comprehend how she could make such a sacrifice. No wonder she's desperate to have me complete my work there. Ceri couldn't live her life knowing that she failed to achieve the one goal that gave her purpose. Not on that ship.

Four thousand is a big number. Maybe not in the universe's scope, but as a small society of humans, it is. By the time the *Devant* left Earth, there were no cities or even villages with that size population. Sure, some people remained, but that was their choice. The *Stratford*'s passengers made a different one, and they're expecting to continue their lives somewhere new.

I sigh. Ceri and her crew have such a burden on their shoulders. Without help, the *Stratford* will continue until its engine cores died out. With no way to navigate, they might as well be dead already. I can't let that go, knowing I could have changed their fate.

"Okay," I say. "I'll go. If it gets your passengers the future they're waiting for, then I'll do it."

"Fana, don't be foolish," Raey says, but her protest is weak. She knows I've decided, and she won't change that now.

Ceri beams, and once again, the pure spirit of her youth explodes from the tough barrier she surrounds herself with.

It's beautiful, and for a moment, I remember I'm also not that old and share in her joy. But Raey, negative to the last, makes a rude noise and folds her arms. It catches Ceri's attention, and she turns on Raey, energized and empowered by my decision.

"Don't look so sad," Ceri says to Raey. "I won't be separating the two of you."

Raey frowns and cants her head at her, seeking an explanation Ceri is all too happy to give.

"You're both coming with me," Ceri adds with a smirk.

BREAKOUT

CERI

I WILL NEVER FORGET this moment. My heart blossoms at the possibility of what Fana will do for us. Her agreement justifies everything I've done and everything I've sacrificed. I want nothing more than to wake my parents and tell them of this moment. I can't, but the letters I will leave them will hopefully explain what their daughter has been through.

We've not yet achieved our goal, however. We must rendezvous with Seren and get off this ship. Once we release the transfer tube from the *Stratford*, there's little the *Devant*'s crew can do to stop us. That's when I will pay back everything Fana has earned.

Despite Raey's fussing, I help Fana down off the bed and help her stand. She's shivering, but she's only wearing a medical gown. That would make anyone cold.

With a few cuts of my blade, I fashion a short robe from her sheet and tie it around her shoulders. She smiles at me, grabbing the edges of her makeshift clothing as if it was the newest fashion. I'm happy as long as she can move silently, and quick, inside of it.

"You will never get off the *Devant*," Raey says.

I smirk and pull out my pistol and show it to her. "This is a flechette gun. It fires darts at a range well suited to interior ship combat. It is near silent, and with the right aim, it is as deadly as any other weapon."

"Why are you telling me this?"

"Because you think your highly trained agents have some advantage over me. They don't. Now turn around."

Raey frowns, perhaps not understanding my message. I grab her arm and spin her back to face the wall. She yelps and flails as I drag her across the bed backward and drop her on her feet on my side.

"And another thing," I hiss into her ear. "You've made your interest in my failure obvious, so I'll be watching you. If you even so much as look the wrong way, I will knock you out and drag your body behind me. Got it?"

She swallows and nods. Raey may still attempt to save herself, but at least now she knows the potential consequences of her actions. And she knows I can make good on my threat.

I unlock the door and slide it open halfway, checking the corridor for threats. Dim overhead lights line the ceiling every three or four paces, causing small reflections in the windows of each sliding door. Unlike the *Stratford*, the walls are a light tan, with long multicolor lines running down their length, likely to help the crew navigate the ship. They'll help me too.

Once I'm sure it's clear, I motion for Fana to follow and glare a warning at Raey before allowing her to come out. Likely she'll only cause a problem if she senses an opportunity. I'll need to ensure that she finds none.

I'm hoping Seren's also on her way, though I wonder how many of our crew she can rescue. My directions to her were simple. Find and free Niah, Efa, and Merek. They'll get the others out, then all Seren need do is bring them to the airlock. It's a serious task, but I must trust that she'll get it done.

I nearly went with her, then realized my mission would be half done if I didn't get Fana. Raey was just walking by me when I grabbed her. It was pure luck, and I thank whichever of my Ancestors made it happen. Without her, I'd still be searching for Fana.

We slip down the corridor, me in front, Raey in the middle, and Fana in the back. None of the positioning is ideal, but as long as we keep moving, there should be no issues. And if there is, I know how to deal with them.

Two hundred paces from Fana's makeshift prison, the corridor splits. The left side is quiet and dark, ideal for making safe progress. The right is well lit and direct. It's dangerous, but I've little choice other than to go that way. With no backup and no scout, I need to stick to the shortest distance between me and the airlock in order to avoid as many of the *Devant*'s crew as I can.

My muscles tighten as we move—an unexpected complication. I stop to catch my breath as my pulse pounds in my head. It's my wound. I've misjudged our risk, and I've put poor Seren into a dangerous position. She could be in trouble, and I've no way to know for sure, yet I feel it. I shouldn't have split us up.

A security agent rounds the corner so quickly, my shoulder nearly smash into his chest. I curse and spin to avoid the collision, recovering quickly. With no time to think, I swing my gun and smash it into the side of his head. He goes down with a grunt.

Raey cries out, and I turn on her. She stares, eyes wide and mouth open. My hand flies up and covers it as our eyes connect. She may react strongly to violence, but I still warn her to keep silent.

We move on, but progress slows. I don't want another situation like the one that just occurred, but this corridor is too bright to make that easy. With no support, I've got to cover every direction. Fana points out a colored panel with sets of letters and numbers with arrows underneath them. The lettering is strange, but I remember the red from before. We're heading in the right direction. We just need to do it faster.

Voices echo from down the corridor ahead of us. I motion for Fana to get down as I press on Raey's shoulders. She drops with me, panic and confusion crossing her face. I ignore it. My attention has to be on the approaching threat.

Another voice comes from the passage we just left. It's getting closer, but the tone is calm. Whomever it is hasn't discovered the guard I took out a ways back. Good. I'll be grateful for my luck once we're back on the *Stratford*.

"Follow me," I whisper, "and keep down."

The entrance to another passage branches off from this one, across from our position. It's darker than this one, but it's far from a safe bet. I have to chance it. I grab Raey by the arm and slip into the corridor, pressing her to the wall once we're far enough inside.

"Let go," Raey hisses as she struggles to pull free from my grasp. My hand tightens as I lean on her to keep her in place. She'll only fear my warnings if she's next to me.

"Raey, please, keep quiet," Fana pleads. "If they find us, they might think you're helping us escape."

"She is," I say. "No more talking."

Just in time. Two security agents pass another in the corridor we were just in. I push Raey and Fana back into the darkness as they pause and exchange information. I freeze. They're close enough to hear us if we make a sound. My gun on Raey's head ensures we don't.

The moment they're out of range, we're up and moving, continuing down the passage. Another colored panel catches my eye—it's the one I want. I breathe a sigh of relief and push on toward our goal, hoping Seren and the crew are not far behind.

It's been quiet ever since we left Fana's room. Too quiet. A tightness forms in my stomach. If Seren had gotten them free, there'd be alarms blaring and announcements over the ship's comm. As much as I praise her skill, there's no possibility she could slip over twenty people through the ship without being noticed. I really shouldn't have left her.

Bish! Another guard! I jerk to a halt. Raey crashes into me. My raised hand stops her from making noise. At least the woman has her back to us and seems to be more interested in something happening across the corridor from her. And we're still in shadow. I can take her out in one move.

The moment I raise my weapon, Fana catches the back of my shirt and ruins my focus. I spin on her, anger surging into my fists.

"This won't work. We're going to get caught," Fana whispers. "I know another way."

I tighten my jaw and glare. But I should trust her knowledge of this ship. Likely she knows it better than anyone, and I've only been thinking of her as helpless when it's me who's quickly becoming incapable.

Fana watches me, expectant. I blow a breath out and consider. We've little time to change routes. If I want to follow her suggestion, I'd best do it now.

I bite my lip and nod to Fana, who gives me a supportive smile. I can't return it. Not yet. Once we're safely about the *Stratford*, I'll think about being happy about it.

My hand takes Raey by the shoulder and rotates her to face in Fana's direction. She looks back at me with an eyebrow raised, but a small push gets her moving. Fana's point now, and though she's got no experience in how to do it, I've got to trust her. I still check my gun before following. This may be the safer route, but there's bound to be trouble along the way.

Fana leads the three of us down a back passage, around a few turns, and down a long, dark hallway she claims they never use. This is a great deal longer, but the blackness is comforting to me. Even after months of working in the illumination of the *Stratford*'s overhead lighting, this puts me more at ease.

"There are no cameras or motion sensors on the ship?" I ask as we hide in a maintenance storage room, waiting for someone to pass by. There was little reason to, with this much dark. I just felt the need for caution.

"For what?" Fana replies, then grins. "There's no reason for anyone to steal anything, and the *Devant*'s designers never considered there'd be intruders on board. You cycled the airlock. That's the only reason they know you're here."

I allow myself a small smile. It makes sense. The adults on the *Stratford* only put up low-light cameras around our base. They came out of the equipment meant for the new colony, but when the adults were leaving, they ripped them from their mounts and brought them along. It didn't matter. We had no need for them, and I'm glad to know the *Devant* doesn't, either.

"How much farther?" I ask. "Seren must be getting close. We want to be near when they arrive at the airlock. Then we all go through together. That way, no one gets left behind."

"Not far," Fana replies. "We'll be free soon."

"Okay. Let's go."

I count down to three, take a breath, and open the door. The corridor remains quiet, so I slip out and motion for Fana and Raey to follow. Fana points in the direction where the passage ends in a dimly lit junction. I give them both a signal to wait and move to scout the area.

Clear.

As I return, I see Fana and Raey bickering. Their voices are low, but as the argument becomes heated, Fana's voice rises, and a lump forms in my throat. I skate back toward them, waving my hands to get their attention. This can't be the problem that ends our escape. I've got to stop this. Now.

But I'm so focused on silencing them, I miss the door sliding open between them and me. It's only when a person steps out do I take notice. By then I'm moving so fast, I can't stop. I brace myself and drop as low as I can.

And plow into Captain Yelekal.

CLASH

— · —

FANA

RAEY AND I STARTLE as Ceri shouts, putting a hard stop to our spat. We jump again when a man grunts and a heavy thud shakes the deck beneath our feet. I spin as Ceri hits the floor, rolling to the wall. She tries to get up, but she's gasping and wincing as she holds her side. I rush toward her, hoping to help.

Woah! What's he doing here?

I skid to a halt as my heart shoots into my throat. No way am I getting close to him! If he spots me, Captain Yelekal will shoot first and then decide if he wants to throw me back into my tiny prison.

The captain's aide rockets through a nearby door before I can retreat. *No!* He's got a gun, and he's aiming at Ceri! With all the breath inside me, I cry out a warning.

Too late. For him.

Ceri fires her weapon, squeezing the trigger three times. The pistol whines, and the air fills with a sound like someone spitting. The captain's aide barks, his gun falling from his hand as he grasps his chest. He's down on the deck a second later, lying motionless. I gasp and stare, but he's not my priority.

"Ceri!" I dash toward her. "Are you hit?"

Raey sticks her foot out in my path. I stumble over it and smash hard on the ground. She goes to help the aide, but in a single motion, Ceri springs from a crouch, plants a hand on Raey's chest, and shoves. Raey yelps and flies back, slamming against the wall.

Heat burns one side of my face as I sit up with a groan. When I touch it, I wince. It stings, and there's blood on my fingertips. All I can do is focus on it as heat rises in my body. Raey did this to me, and she meant it. This is what it means to take sides.

Captain Yelekal recovers. Two seconds later, he's on his feet, growling at Ceri. She backs off, her hand still covering her body. He takes advantage of it and charges at her but stops short when she raises her weapon.

"Impressive that you survived my shot," he says, sneering. "But by the look of you, just barely. You can't even hold your weapon steady. Do you really think you can fight me?"

Ceri is leaning over more than a little, and her face mirrors the pain she must feel. But trying to help her now would be a bad idea. Maybe. I've never been in a battle before. How is it supposed to start? Someone shoots first? Or they agree on a time? I just don't know. All I want is to get Ceri out of here.

Captain Yelekal take a step towards her. "You should have stayed on your own ship. I'm within my rights to imprison you for trespassing. Then you tried to abduct my crew. Again. And now you've shot my lieutenant. I'd be furious if I thought you might have killed him. Not with that little gun, though."

"You're welcome to find out if my little gun can kill or not," Ceri hisses. Her voice is raspy, and she's breathing hard. I'm holding mine, hoping she's better than she sounds. If I knew how to stop this, I would. I don't want her to get hurt anymore.

Raey skitters toward the aide, drawing Ceri's attention. As she swings her gun, the captain lurches forwards. His fist comes down on her wrist. She cries out, her pistol flying out of her hand.

But she spins, her foot coming around to pound the captain on the side of his head. He shouts and stumbles back. Ceri drops and rolls toward her gun. It's farther than she thought, and she has to dash after it. He's there first, planting his foot and punting it down the hallway. She kicks his leg, and he drops to one knee.

The captain's fist shoots out and slams Ceri's lower back. She shouts as her arms fly into the air, stumbling toward the wall to stop herself from falling. All of it happens too slowly. Before she can turn, he's up and chasing her down.

I gasp. *She doesn't know he's behind her!*

"Ceri, look out!"

He swings a fist at her. She blocks it with both arms, her legs bending under the weight of his attack. Captain Yelekal takes advantage of her struggle and kicks her hard on her wound.

My heart skips a beat as Ceri screams, her hands reaching toward her side as she tumbles over, rolling until she hits the wall. I start toward her, then freeze, then start and stop again. *What can I do to stop this?*

"Captain Yelekal, please! She's just a girl!" I plead, but he only shoots me a glare.

"You stay where you are," he snarls, thrusting a finger at me. "I'll deal with you next."

As Ceri writhes on the floor, the captain steps toward her, reaching down and grabbing her ankle. He braces his legs, and with a deep grunt, he tosses her against the wall. Ceri lets out a high-pitched moan and crashes to the desk.

Adrenaline is hitting me. I can feel it in the pounding of my pulse and the heat in my chest. I have to do something. Anything. *But what?*

I'm so desperate, I look to Raey for support, but with her arms bound behind her, there's little she can do. She's too focused on the captain's aide to pay attention to me, and I doubt she'd help me at all, after what she did.

A loud curse returns my attention to the fight. Ceri is up, holding a long blade out as Captain Yelekal bares his teeth at her. He's holding his arm as blood seeps through his fingers. There's rage on his face and an inferno in his eyes.

Ceri's hand over her wound matches his, though her shirt is stained well beyond where she's got her fingers. She's struggling to stay upright, and the moment Captain Yelekal figures out how to get past her blade, he'll make sure she won't get up again.

A shiver runs through me. *I can't let this happen. He's going to murder her.*

"Raey," I beg as I slide toward her. "Let me help him. Just stop this fight. Ceri's going to die!"

"*She's* going to die?" Raey catches my gaze as her eyes narrow at me. "*She* abducted us and shot him, and you want *me* to help her? Go to hell, Fana."

My jaw drops open. How could she not want to stop the violence? I even offered to help her! Why can't she just act like she used to?

"You took an oath to save lives!" I cry.

"And if my hands were free, I could live up to that oath. Maybe you should remember that before you accuse me of betraying it."

I grimace and turn away with a pain in my heart. My eyes are getting wet even as I try to deny the change in her. Something has broken between us, and if there was time, I'd ask her why. But there isn't. Ceri's only hope to remain alive is me, and I'm no fighter. No heroine.

What can I do?

Captain Yelekal swings his fists, throwing one punch after another, but he can't reach past Ceri's blade. She lunges forward to stab him and misses. He dodges to the side and snatches at her wrist. Ceri pulls away just in time. He follows through with a swipe at her knee. Again, she evades. Barely. She's moving slower than before. Her face is agony. The captain isn't even breathing hard. This won't last much longer.

What do I do?

I scan the corridor for her gun, giving up soon after. It's impossible to find in this dim light. And even if I found it, it's useless to me.

A boom echoes through the passageway. Ceri's leaning against a door as Captain Yelekal raises a fist about his head.

"Captain! Enough!" I shout, rushing toward him.

He hesitates, and Ceri slips past him, staggering clear of his attack. The captain roars and swings at me. I scream and jump back, shrinking against a wall, my breath racing. If he was really trying, I'd be out cold.

"Keep your mouth shut, or I will pound you into the deck!" he shouts. As if his fist wasn't warning enough.

Ceri struggles to keep her blade up and her legs underneath her. Her body doubles over, and she winces with every breath. It's a miracle she can keep fighting for so long. I'm shaking just looking at her.

Captain Yelekal checks the long cut on his arm and then squares off against her. He watches Ceri like a ravenous animal. My body becomes tense, fearing his final attack.

I've got to make a move. Now.

"Run!" I cry at Ceri as I spring up and charge the captain, my hands out. I'll knock him down and flee with her. If I can.

"I told you to—" But as the captain turns, he sees me running for him, and his eyes pop open. He tightens his jaw and pulls his arm back.

Oh hell.

A second before I can touch him, the back of his hand slams into my face. A bright light flashes before my eyes, and the corridor does a complete revolution before my body smashes onto the deck. The air rushes from my lungs as my eyes cross.

For a moment, I lie paralyzed on the floor. It's like I'm outside myself, only to get sucked back in again when the pain hits.

"Fana!"

Ceri's voice is distant, but her footsteps are thunder in my ears as she roars toward me. I shake my head. At least I think I do. *Why is she still risking herself for me? She's got to escape before he kills her!*

"Ceri, no," I say, my voice just a croak.

"Not so fast!" Captain Yelekal shouts. There's a scuffle. The sound of objects cutting through the air surrounds me. The deck rumbles over and over. Something shiny flies past my vision. Raey screams.

And Captain Yelekal laughs.

Everything goes quiet. I struggle to lift my head to see what happened. All I catch is him grinning as he bends over and picks up Ceri's blade.

Her blade!

I strain to see more and catch Ceri leaning on the floor and staring up at Captain Yelekal as he shakes her weapon at her.

This is my fault. Ceri would have run if I had stayed out of it. *What was I thinking?*

"Did you really think you could fight me again?" he asks. "You're just a kid. You should have learned you can't beat an adult. But now you won't get the chance."

No...

VICTOR

— • —

CERI

I'm losing blood. Too much. Too fast. My head is spinning, and my limbs are getting weak. Soon I won't be able to stand, much less fight. There's no obvious way to win. He's too strong to overpower, too quick to get past, and now he's got my blade. I shudder as I consider my end, as it's one slip next to becoming real.

But I've been here before.

The captain tests me, teasing a step forward. I hold still as much as I can. If he sees how poorly I move, he'll know I'm done and will dive in for the kill. Perhaps he knows already. Raey said her security agents were well trained. I don't doubt it, not after the pounding he just gave me.

"Captain Yelekal," Raey says. "I need you to call for medical help. Your aide is dying."

My eyes shift toward the man on the ground. His chest rises and falls, but the movement is slow and ragged. I didn't think I got him that badly. Maybe I did. He came out so quickly, I only had a fraction of a second to aim. It's his fault he charged me. Not that I wanted it that way.

"He won't die," the captain replies, maintaining his gaze on me. "And I'm not done with this one yet."

Raey huffs and stares at him, unconvinced by his answer. She glances at the aide, considers something, and turns back to the captain.

"Then at least cut my hands free so I can do it," she offers.

The captain's nostrils flare, and he grips my blade tighter as his feet shift. So he cares about his people after all. That only motivates him to kill me more.

"Please, Captain!" Raey pleads.

"Hold on!"

"He doesn't have time to hold on!"

Captain Yelekal glances back, and in a heartbeat, I shoot forward, aiming to reclaim my knife, but he pivots, and I fly past him. *Foolish.* He brings the blade down, and I get a searing pain across my back for it. My legs give out, and I take a dive, barely finding it in me to tuck my head down so I can roll. I recover and turn to get to my feet, but I stumble and hit the wall as a fire races across my back. It's only by luck that it keeps me upright. At least the cut's not deep. I think.

Fana cries out and makes a move to go to me. He stops her with a single stroke across her path. Fana jerks away from the blade and falls, her back crushing the aide's legs. Raey barks and pushes her off the man with her feet.

"Stay out of it!" Raey yells at her.

"No!" Fana yells back. "She doesn't deserve to die!"

The captain glances at his second again and growls, taking a swing at me. I roll away as the blade strikes the wall, sending sparks into the air. He attacks again, stabbing downward at my shoulder. I evade and get a knee into his side. He counters with an elbow to my face.

I kick out as I go down, my foot impacting on his hipbone. He groans and drops the blade, throwing a hand out to the wall to keep his balance. The weapon bounces off the deck and lands with a hard clatter just out of reach.

As I go for the blade, Raey pushes to her feet and runs. *Hyuk.* I pivot and knock her legs out from under her with a spinning kick. Raey cries out and goes down, her shoulder pounding into the deck with a thud. I release a breath even as I fight through the pain to take another. This is far from over. I need to stay conscious to survive.

"That was a stupid choice," Captain Yelekal says as he saunters over to the blade and picks it up. He bares his teeth at me and stomps forward, the weapon rising over his head.

This is it. He's going to end me. With a cry, I kick away from him, refusing to let it happen. It's futile. I can't move faster than he can walk. My heart shoots into my throat, my breaths coming so fast I can barely keep air in my lungs. I'm blacking out. Maybe it's better that way. I don't want to see my end coming.

The captain grins, and he drops a boot on my ankle. I gasp as fire shoots up my leg. Blackness covers my sight. I struggle to regain it, even as I wait for the blade to end my life.

A wail fills the air. *A weapon discharged!* The captain yells out, and I feel his weight come off my ankle. I blink as my sight returns, searching for the sound.

Fana stares at the captain from her spot on the floor. In her hands is the aide's gun. She cradles it like it was a drill, her fingers under the barrel as she presses her shoulder into the stock. The weapon quivers in her shaking grasp.

Captain Yelekal just stares at her, unmoving. His face is stony, and his hands hang by his sides.

Did she hit him?

Then I see it, a charred spot on the wall, just behind him. Not even close. What's he waiting for then? Does he think she's going to fire again?

"Do it," he orders Fana. "If you think you can hit me."

Fana goes still, her eyes widening. The captain chuckles and puts his hands on his hips as he watches her. Even as I fight to keep from blacking out, my brow gets tight. This is Raey's highly trained soldier? He's taken his focus away from his opponent.

Talk about stupid.

With every bit of strength remaining in me, I lurch up, slamming my palms together. I thrust them into his knife hand and shove as hard as I can. The edge slices across his leg, tearing a wide gash through his pants. He yells out in pain and stumbles back. The blade falls from his hand. I catch it and, in a single motion, drive it deep into his belly.

The captain stumbles back, his hands dropping to his abdomen as I withdraw the blade, pulling it back to strike again. He's in too much agony to defend himself. This may not be the only way, but ending him will stop the *Devant* from abducting my crew ever again.

"Don't!" Raey shouts. "You do that, and the commander will kill your entire crew!"

I freeze, my fists clenching. She's right. Captain Yelekal may be the force, but the commander of the ship is the direction. Only he can end this assault on my crew. For now, I just need to escape.

My jaw tightens, and I swing, dropping my hand as my elbow comes out. It strikes him across the chin, and his head jolts, his eyes rolling back into his head. A second later, his legs fold and his body slides down the wall and crumples to the ground.

"That might just have been the smartest thing you have ever done," Raey adds. "Now keep thinking like that and release my hands so I can save their lives."

So that's her motivation. Why Fana doubted that earlier, I don't know. I should let her do as she asks. I've got Fana on my side, and that's what I came here for. Not to start a war.

I take a step toward her and open my mouth to reply, but my muscles refuse to do anything more. My knees buckle, and I drop, landing on my side with a grunt. I feel my eyelids get heavy as my body grows cold. I pushed myself too hard, and now I'm paying the price. Not that I had a choice. If I'm going to die here, then I'll go out the way I choose to.

Fana dashes over, kneeling next to me as she puts a hand on my cheek. She gasps and looks at Raey.

"Save Ceri first," she orders.

"I can't," Raey replies. "There's no way I can save all three of them."

"Yes, you can!" Fana nods at her. "You know how to do this! I've seen you work!"

Raey shakes her head. "It's not about knowing, Fana. There's just not enough time."

My arm is moving before Fana can raise another protest. I slap the hilt of my blade onto her leg. She jumps and looks down at it, then glances at me with eyebrows raised. I pat the hilt to confirm my wish. There's no sense in three people dying, and if saving the others protects my crew, then that's all I can ask for.

"See?" Raey says, motioning with her head. "She's telling you to release me. So hurry! Every second is critical!"

"No," Fana whispers to me. "Come on. Don't just sacrifice yourself. Your ship needs you. Your people need you."

I catch her gaze then and shut my eyes for a moment. It should be enough of an answer. It has to be. I doubt I have the strength to speak.

"What if I helped you?" Fana asks Raey. "Then we could, right? Save the three of them? Or just give me enough time to get her away, and you can call for help."

"You're not going with her," Raey says. "But if you help, then maybe we can. No promises though."

"Fine."

Fana motions for her to turn around and then puts the edge of the blade under the strap around her wrists. With a single yank, she cuts through the strap. Raey wastes no time in checking on Captain Yelekal and his aide before moving next to Fana and me. Her hands move quickly as she opens my shirt and removes the bandage there. A quick order to Fana gets her to roll me over to look at my back.

"Look!" Fana says as she pulls a pack from my belt. "Ceri's got a med kit!"

"Quick then! Hand it here!"

Raey rifles through it, pulling out all the bandages and frowning at the can of cauterizer before her eyes open in understanding. She wastes no time applying it to my wounds before covering them over with bandages. The moment she's satisfied with her work, she moves away to care for the captain and his aide, reminding Fana of the promise she made to help.

As I lie there, watching them work to save the two men, I realize I won't be unhappy if they live. But only if my crew makes it, too. We deserve to live as much as they do, if not more. They are only two of a massive crew. If they die, their passengers still get to their destination. Our ship needs every child that remained behind. Without them, we all fail.

Once they've patched up the captain and his second, Fana comes to me and grabs me from underneath my arms.

"Well?" Fana says to Raey. "Come on! Help me!"

But Raey just stands there, shaking her head. Fana glares at her, then puts me down and picks up the aide's gun, slapping it in her hand to emphasize her point.

"Raey...Help. Me."

Raey sighs. "Fine. But first I'm making a call."

ACCEPTANCE

CERI

WE MADE IT BACK. Barely. I didn't believe that I would see the gray passageways and dim lights of the *Stratford* again. And once I can stand on my feet, I will pay a visit to my parents in stasis, if only to see their faces. I know doing so will fill a hole in my chest that's been widening for some time.

Raey and Fana have done an amazing job getting the three of us past security and through the *Devant*'s airlock, Though I suspect Raey's call for help had something to do with that. Once Captain Yelekal's agents heard he was wounded, they must have broken discipline to get to him. At least that is what I want to believe. No matter what the reason, I am glad to have made it back. If only my crew could be here, too.

"Put her down here," Fana says as they move me into the rail car. As she lowers me to the deck, she pants. "Wow, she's heavy."

"That's muscle," Raey replies, "which is the reason she could keep up with two men twice her size. Still, she's a little lean. What they've had to eat here doesn't count much toward nutrition. It won't be much help in assisting her to heal...Where does this go, by the way?"

"Um. There's a medical bay somewhere up a few levels."

"Fourteen," I croak.

Fana's face lights up, and she smiles at me, though in a matter of seconds, her face twists back into the look of concern it had before. I do my best to put some cheer on my face—and fail. My attempt to get more comfortable only results in a jolt of angry pain shooting across my back and side. I gasp and writhe, trying to stop the burning from reaching my fingers and toes.

"Quick," Raey says. "We need to get her up there. Select the level."

The airlock beeps and cycles. Fana freezes, her gaze finding Raey's as their eyes widen. Both hold their breaths and wait.

Did the Devant*'s agents follow us that fast?* Despite the weariness in my body, I push up to a crouch. They won't catch me lying down. If it's them, I'll make it as difficult as possible for them to take me.

"We know you're here!" It's Efa! "We see your suits! Show yourselves, or we'll shoot first."

"Make noise," I gasp, motioning for Raey and Fana to follow my directions. They stare at me until what I've said registers in their brains. Fana is the first to move, slapping her hand on the wall and sending a boom echoing down the corridor. If Efa doesn't hear that, she's gone deaf.

"We're here!" Fana shouts. "In the rail car!"

Silence follows, a sure sign she heard. I would be cautious, too. All we can do is wait until she's made her way here. She's likely scouting the area to ensure no one has laid a trap for her.

It hits me that Efa said *we* and not *I*. It could be a tactic, tricking her opponents into thinking they face more than one combatant. Or she could have brought the entire crew with her. Efa here means Seren freed her. Did she free anyone else?

Efa appears before us, her gun up, aiming at Fana and Raey as she checks for targets. A streak of dried blood crosses her cheek, and part of her sleeve is blackened, likely by weapons fire. Her eyes are intense as they dart between the three of us, only relaxing once her gaze falls on me.

With a grin, I collapse from my crouch to lean on my side, propping myself up with my arm. But between the shaking in my limbs and the pain running through me, I struggle to maintain my position and my smile.

"Oh, you idiot." She sighs as she drops next to me, throwing her arms around my neck. "What did you do?"

I would hug her back if I could. It's enough for me to press my head against hers and close my eyes. I am glad to feel a familiar closeness. Her embrace is also keeping me upright.

"I brought back our salvation," I whisper. "We're getting control back of the *Stratford*."

She pulls back to connect her gaze with mine, keeping her hands on my shoulders. In her eyes, I see her desire to tell me something, but it'll have to wait. I nod with understanding. Then she turns to look out of the rail car.

"All clear!" Efa shouts into the corridor.

A second later, Merek shows up with Niah leaning on him, her forehead hanging low enough to rest on her arm. He moves to come closer, then stops, eying Fana and Raey with hesitation.

"Sorry," he says, motioning to Niah. "I didn't know it'd be all of you."

"It doesn't matter," Raey says. "We've all been exposed. Probably more than once. Count your blessings none of us are more ill than we are."

"I'm fine," Fana says. She wants to move closer to me, but Efa's blocking her.

Merek looks to Efa, who motions him on. "We're headed up to medical. It seems like we've got a few casualties."

We're moving up once Merek and Niah are in. Efa moves to sit next to me, and Fana does the same. Raey notices it and presses her lips together. What she's disapproving of, I'm not sure, and I don't really care. She's objected to a good deal of Fana's actions ever since she came on board.

"Where's Seren?" I ask. Efa and Merek drop their gazes to the floor, and my chest gets tight. "No!"

"We don't know for sure," Merek explains. "She freed us, and then we went to get everyone else but got separated along the way. Likely they caught her."

"Seren?" Niah half coughs, half chuckles. "They'd never catch her."

I'd like to believe that, just like I want to believe Niah sounds better than she looks. At least she's here with us so we can care for her. But when I think about how Seren and the others aren't, weariness returns to my body. I had forgotten about it when I saw Efa. I should have realized my elation would only be temporary.

With a bit of effort, the others get Niah and me into side-by-side beds in the main bay at the center of medical. Raey wastes no time raiding the cabinets with Merek's help—or possibly his surveillance—while Fana and Efa do their best to make us comfortable, which means laying Niah and me on our sides, facing each other.

The comfort of the mattress brings heaviness to my eyelids. Niah is fast asleep a few minutes later. I can't allow myself to rest yet, not while my crew remains in captivity.

"We need a plan," I say to Efa as she sits down on the edge of the bed.

"*We* need a plan?" she replies, eyebrows raised. "Have you looked at yourself recently? Don't forget I'm still hyuking angry at you." Then Efa sighs and drops her hands into her lap. "But what Sayer and I tried to do was foolish, too. We have to stick together from now on."

I reach out, my fingers just brushing across her back. This is my fault. I should have just accepted my position and led the crew like everyone expected me to. But I refused it for so long. They were right to be mad.

"You can't just go back there," Fana says. "Now that you've, uh, disturbed them, no one's getting through that airlock."

"Thank you for stating the obvious," Efa replies, flashing a glare at her.

Fana opens her mouth, then mashes her lips together and turns. "I'll get Merek. He'll probably needs to be part of this conversation more than I do."

"You didn't need to be so harsh," I say as Fana walks away. "She's trying to help."

"We don't need that kind of help," Efa replies. "Let her fix the ship, and then we can send her back."

"Or better yet," Merek says as he arrives to sit next to Efa, "let's let her fix the ship and then trade her for our crew. Raey too. They don't want to be here, and after what her people did to us, I doubt anyone would welcome them."

Raey may have a loyalty to her ship, but she's gone against her commander's wishes often enough to put herself at risk, and Fana...I smile. She's more like us than she realizes. Why she wants to spend any time on the *Stratford* is beyond me. Yet there must be something that draws her here. A challenge, perhaps. All I know is that I'm glad for it.

"I would," I correct.

Both of them spin on me, confusion on their faces. I set my jaw and do my best to appear serious. I must look like a complete fool, but I need to ensure that Efa and Merek understand Fana and Raey are allies and should be treated as such.

"Anyone who'd be willing to defy their orders and help us is welcome here," I state.

Merek shrugs. "I'm just saying the rest of the crew would have a hard time accepting them."

"I would make sure they do."

The edge of Efa's mouth curls up. "So now, when you're half dead and about to crash, is when you want to lead?"

My breath gets caught in my throat. How did I not realize it? Perhaps it's because I was busy trying not to die. All I was doing was what I thought was right. I never thought of it as leading. Now I see it was so much more than that. How long have I struggled to deny responsibility for the job I've been doing all along?

"It's what you want me to do." I smirk. "So I am."

Efa leans down and puts her face in mine with false rage, puffing her cheeks up. I'd laugh if I could and if I thought she was just kidding. Perhaps she is, partly. No one could be furious for long with a face like that.

"We wanted you to be our leader a long time ago, hyuk face," she hisses. "The only reason we tolerated your bish for so long is because we care about you."

"I know." I close my eyes for a moment, contemplating how they must have suffered through my time of denial. I caused them that pain. And they were as patient with me as they could be. How selfish I was to only consider my comfort and not the needs of the crew. I won't ever do that again.

Efa softens. "So then what's the plan?"

"Merek's idea is good," I reply. "We offer to return Raey and Fana in trade for our crew."

"And what happens if they want to stay here?"

That possibility makes my stomach twist. We'd be forcing them to go against their will. That'd be like sending Aidan and Mari to live on that ship. Permanently. Here, we'd have everything we wanted while they'd be subject to the whims of the *Devant*'s adults.

Adults. As long as they believe they're superior to us, they'll never earn my trust. We might strike a deal with them, and terms of a trade may be agreed upon, but the moment we have our backs turned, they'll just take whatever they wanted.

I push up off the bed to better look Efa and Merek in the eye and say, "We do the same thing we do before we make the offer. We prepare the *Stratford* for an assault. Whether or not the *Devant*'scommander agrees to an exchange, they'll be coming to take their crew back. We've got to be ready."

Efa and Merek share a glance, then turn back to me, nodding. Efa puts a hand over mine and squeezes.

"We'll be ready," she says.

OUTLAW

— • —

FANA

I WAS GLAD TO get away from Efa. She seemed ready to separate my head from my body just to make a point. How was I to know they already understood that? They're just teenagers. I never expected them to be crazy enough to infiltrate the best colony ship ever built or to know how.

Then again, I did some unsafe things when I was that age. Nothing life-threatening, of course, like squaring off against professional security agents. If that didn't terrify them, I can't imagine the horrific battles they've been through. Just the thought alone is enough to make me want to run to Raey. Which is why I am.

As pure white as this medical bay once was, it must have been more uncomfortable to be here. The stains on the walls—some dirt, some dried blood—add a comforting dull-ness to the sterile environment this used to be.

I take half a minute to find Raey. She's in one of the examination rooms, picking through a box of sterile-packed medical tools. Merek watches her with calm suspicion, his back on the wall and his arms folded across his chest. He glances at me as I enter.

"Hey," I say to Merek. "I think they wanted to talk to you."

He curls his lips in, his eyes sliding back to Raey for a moment before he pushes off the wall and walks past me with a look of warning. I press against the wall and duck my head to avoid his death stare. Maybe he's not as laid-back as I had thought. But I take his message as it's given. Raey and I will stay put until one of them comes back.

"Come here and sit down," Raey says as I approach. She points to an exam bench in the back of the room and pulls up a chair next to it. I'll follow orders. This is a good time to remain obedient and not cause any trouble. I've already done my fair share.

She takes my head in her hands and examines the scrapes on my face, then clicks her tongue and reaches for a pair of forceps and a cloth dampened with some kind of germicidal fluid. I tense, preparing for the sting that comes with applying it to a wound. This is hardly the first time she's done this for me. There's a scar just above my left eyebrow I got when replacing a filter unit on a shuttle a few years ago. The medical procedure to care for my wound was more painful than the cut itself.

"Thank you," I say as she works, poking me with the forceps to search for anything that shouldn't be a part of my face.

"For what?"

"For putting yourself at risk and helping Ceri."

"Did I have a choice?"

"Come on, Raey. Do you really think I would have shot you if you refused? I don't even know how to use a weapon. Well, save for that one shot. But it missed."

Raey hums a reply and refocuses to work on my face while I attempt to forget the mess it must be. Her motions are gentle, and she brushes the cloth across my cheek as carefully as a mother might with her frightened child.

I bet Ceri never expected to be caring for her crew and her passengers like a mom. It's got to be terrifying, especially when she's got no idea about how to do that. I don't either, so it's easy for me to imagine.

"She's only trying to protect her people," I say, thinking out loud. "It's Commander Azazhi who got aggressive. I bet if—ouch!"

Raey glares at me as she holds her cloth close to my face like a threat. *Make a statement like that again and I'll hurt you more.*

"You're mad that she's protecting her crew?"

"No," she replies. "I just think you have no right to criticize him after everything you've done."

My jaw drops open. I may deserve that, but to say it while she's trying to heal me...is...not right!

"Aren't medical staff supposed to have a soothing demeanor when treating their patients?" I charge. Raey just glares.

She continues to work, but her light touch returns. Maybe that's her attempting to make peace with me. If that's the case, I should try to do the same. Ever since we found the *Stratford*, Raey and I have been at odds. Or it could have been when I came out of stasis. Raey hasn't just gotten older in seventeen years. She's become a beautiful woman with a maturity I could only hope to ever emulate.

I'm trying to be more of an adult and do my best to act with responsibility. Which is why the two of us are here on the *Stratford*. They need my skills and knowledge, and I've realized taking risks to help others in need is the right thing to do. It's just strange that it took me this long to figure that out.

"I respect what she's trying to do," Raey says, drawing her sleeve across her forehead. "But violence is never an answer."

"They made her like that. The adults." I lean back to rest my hands on the back edge of the bench. "Ceri told me she had a normal childhood on Earth. Her family didn't leave the planet until she was twelve. And she was expecting to wake up on another planet. Not the ship. How horrible it must have been for her."

Raey rolls her eyes and snorts as she folds her arms.

I frown. "What?"

"You." She shakes her head. "Do you hear yourself?"

My frown gets deeper. *What's she on about?*

"You have no idea, do you?"

"What are you talking about, Raey?"

She smirks and leans forward to put her lips close to my ear, covering my hand with hers. Her breath is warm on my skin, and her nearness shoots a tingle through my body. I suck in a quick breath, feeling my heart thump in my chest and my face get warm. This is way more intimate than we've been in years, and yet she still can get my blood pumping.

"I see how you look at her, Fana," she whispers, caressing her finger across the back of my hand, "and how you're always as close to her as you can get."

I jerk away and stare at her. I'm just barely aware that my mouth is hanging open as our gazes connect. Raey's serious, and it only makes my heart beat faster.

I'm not sure which disturbs me more, that I've fallen for Ceri or that Raey noticed it first. Now I'll get awkward around her, wondering if she feels the same about me. Of course she wouldn't. Not after she's had to save me so many times.

But...could she grow to like me? No. It's a silly thought, and I'm not a schoolgirl anymore. I haven't been one for a long time. I shouldn't be acting like someone falling in...*No! Get that out of my head!* I'm here for the people of the *Stratford*, not for my own selfish desires.

"Hey, I understand," Raey says, poking my good cheek and smiling. "Ceri has a strength that's hard to deny. That she's beautiful doesn't hurt, either. But she's vulnerable, too. We should all be so lucky to get close to someone like that."

"Are you jealous?" I squeeze my fingers around my thumbs as I watch her reaction, not sure that I want to hear the answer. I'm already on her bad side.

Raey giggles. "A little," she replies, then shrugs.

I swallow. "Really?"

She stands up, her eyes dropping to the floor. "When you came out of stasis, looking just like the day you went in, I became a little nostalgic. I remembered what it was like to be a twenty-something, and I wanted to relieve some of that time. But when I noticed how you followed Ceri around as if she had some type of gravitational force pulling you toward her, I knew..."

She presses her lips together and ducks her head for a moment before continuing to clean the cuts on my face. I can't blame her for not wanting to complete her last few words. Making them audible turns them real, and that'd mean she'd have to accept the reality that so much has changed for her.

And for me. I never expected to like someone again after Raey and I ended it. Or, more accurately, after she dumped me. I deserved it, because I had some growing up to do, which I expected to happen during our long journey. I'd have nothing but time to consider my faults. But then I met Ceri.

My head lowers as I think about it. "I'm sorry, Raey."

"Sorry for falling for someone else?" She shakes her head. "We stopped being a couple a long time ago, Fana. Your heart doesn't belong to me anymore."

A tightness hits my chest in sympathy. I reach out to touch her face, hoping the connection will comfort her. Raey stops me before I can, taking my hand in hers and folding my fingers in to place my hand in my lap. But I can't accept her refusal. Before she moves her hand away, I snatch it and hold it in mine.

"I meant I'm sorry for the years you've spent missing what you once had," I say, "whether that includes me or not. And I'm sorry for dragging you into this. I hope we can still be close. I want to be your friend, Raey."

Her jaw tightens, and that quiet anger she had before comes back.

"Yeah?" she says, taking her hand back. "Well, listen, friend. That girl you've got feelings for? She's dangerous. And young. Ceri only knows how to attack. We've already seen how that works. Anytime you're near her, Fana, she'll put you at risk. Hell, she already has. She may not mean to, but she doesn't have much choice, and that makes me worry about you both."

"You don't need to. Ceri's...well..." I sigh. "There's no chance for me and her, Raey. You know that. Sure, we're taking a risk to help her crew, but once we're done, you and I will return to the *Devant*, where I hope you'll put in a good word for me, right?"

Raey stares at me for a long time, making me shift and fidget. Does that mean she won't? Am I that deep in trouble with the commander no words will help me?

"Fana, don't return to the *Devant*," she says, her voice soft but strong. "The only certainty that awaits you there is permanent stasis. Or worse. And I don't want that for you."

"Permanent?" I feel my eyes widen. "No! I've got a right to a trial!"

"There won't be a trial." Raey shakes her head. "Ceri nearly killed two senior crew. She's the enemy now, and you sided with her. Commander Azazhi will consider you nothing but a traitor. That's reason enough to forgo a trial and lock you away for good."

I laugh, but it's forced. "Come on, Raey. Stop trying to scare me. He wouldn't! I'm the chief engineer! The *Devant* doesn't run at peak performance without me!"

But Raey keeps still, and the hair on the back of my neck stands up. I get that tangy taste in the back of my throat, the same as when I get sick. Maybe it's just the vision in my head of being locked away in a stasis pod for good. Or maybe the virus inside of me is finally doing its worst.

All I know is everything has changed.

ATTACK

—— • ——

CERI

AN UNEASE FILLS ME as Fana rattles off the extensive list of steps required to connect a multiprocessor to the remains of the *Stratford*'s navigation system. She beams as she speaks, nearly jumping off her perch on the doctor's stool when she remembers another detail. She's been at it for three days now, using every spare moment to see me between her work to help Efa, Merek, and Niah prepare to defend the ship.

I smile at her energetic demeanor. There's something charming about it, though I haven't been able to apply much of my brain to figuring out what it is. I've spent most of the little time I've been awake considering strategy and the rest itching to get out of bed and make preparations alongside the others. Even when Raey cleared Niah as being able to leave medical, she was still coughing. I protested, but for once in many months, I decided it was best to listen to the adult in the room.

When Fana asks me a question that is far beyond my knowledge to answer, I just nod, and she continues offering alternatives to her idea. If it wasn't for her vast experience with computer systems, I might forget she's older than me. Perhaps it's the youthful aura around her that is so appealing.

"Have you slept?" I ask when she catches her breath. She blinks and stares blankly at me. I suspected as much. There's too much to get done. If we had the full complement of five Tarakh and six Fahrasi squads like there used to be, we'd have our defenses set up in a day. Of course, back when there were Tarakh and Fahrasi, we'd have been setting up defenses against each other.

"Not much." Fana shrugs and tugs on the white medical shirt Raey gave her to wear. "All my brain wants to do is run through lines of code, even when I'm lying down with my eyes shut and the lights off. And when it's not doing that, it just runs through every physical connection I'll need to make to the multiprocessor."

There's little I can complain about. Fana's sacrificed much to help us, and when I bring up my concerns about her, she denies any of it is an issue.

The wall comm buzzes, and Fana slips off her stool to press the answer button. Likely it's Efa or Raey looking for her. They probably have a question on how to access a circuit or kill power to a section of the ship.

"*Fana, Ceri,*" Efa says, tension in her voice. "*They're here. Get ready.*"

My pulse is already pounding hard enough to rattle my lungs as our eyes connect. I shake my head in anticipation of Fana's question.

"We're not ready," I say, throwing the sheet aside and dropping my legs onto the floor.

"No!" Fana raises a hand to stop me from pulling the IV line from my arm. "You need to stay here."

I lower my gaze at her. "Do you think your security agents will care if I'm wounded or not?"

Fana's shoulders sink. She's in as much danger as I am. The *Devant*'s agents have arrested her once. They'll do it again if they get the chance.

"Take the rail car down and meet Efa and Merek on level seventeen," I say as I limp away from the bed. "I'll climb down behind you."

"Won't you need the system to help you get down there?"

"No. My legs are good. My arms are good. That's all that matters." I motion to the rail car door. "Go. I won't be far behind."

Fana rushes me, throwing her arms around my shoulders. I stiffen in surprise, but she only touches her forehead to my shoulder and steps back.

"Please be careful, Ceri. You're still not healed," she says with pleading eyes.

I remain motionless as our gazes connect, the shock of her sudden action freezing my thoughts. It's only when my body warms, remembering the softness of her touch, does my head clear. Efa's hugged me a thousand times but never with such intensity. I almost wish it wasn't so brief.

"Don't worry, I'll be fine," I say and smile. But as she rushes off, my smile fades. I've lied to her. It was all I could think to do in order to get us both moving. She'll be safer with the others, anyway. I'll be lucky if I can protect myself.

Still, if that's all I need to focus on, I'll manage.

My destination is a brief jog down a side corridor—hull access. The ladders there are more basic than the ones between levels, but the *Devant*'s soldiers will be too busy securing the ship's levels to consider covering the hull interior. They may not even realize the entryways are there.

Cool air washes against my face as I open the hatch, and I hesitate. Since that time I nearly froze to death hiding from A Squad, I've avoided going in there. Just the memory of those torturous few minutes where I nearly succumbed to the impossible cold is enough to shake me hard. But this is the best path. There's no debate. I'm going even if I'm terrified to.

I grit my teeth as I slide down level after level, fighting the chill on my skin and the rawness in my side to hasten my descent. I need to be there before the agents can organize their attack.

At least level seventeen comes faster than I expect. I tap on the edge of the hull as I exit onto the level. Efa pops up from behind a makeshift barrier and motions me over. Fana is already there, peeking over the edge to watch me. Niah and Merek likely have taken up flanking positions along the corridor.

"They've just opened the airlock and are holding," Efa hisses and hands me a pistol and ammunition. "Likely not all of them have arrived yet."

"How many, you think?" I whisper.

"Seven now. Perhaps double that coming. Not that it matters. We're already outnumbered."

My stomach tightens, irritating my wound. Seven is a challenge for us, even with the advantage we have fighting in familiar territory. Fourteen is harder still. And any more than that will force our retreat.

I turn to Fana. "Go to level twenty-one and wait for us there. Use the ladder behind us."

She hesitates and purses her lips, then moves once Efa glares at her. Both of us want her far from potential capture, and we can't protect her if things get chaotic. Twenty-one is our fallback point. With so many places to hide on that level, she'll be safe, and the thought of her out of danger puts some ease in my tense body.

Efa tenses, and I hold my breath to listen. There. The *Devant*'s agents are approaching, nearly silent, but not enough to surprise us. Their footfalls are out of sync with the beats of ventilation fans, and the rustle of their uniforms is a recruit-level mistake. The darkness of the level may also be a factor, distracting them. Their eyes can't be comfortable in near black as ours are.

It's a slight advantage for us. Without proper equipment to compensate, they'll struggle to find targets. We can hit them with our eyes closed.

Efa puts a hand on my back and draws out the letters of her communication. *Don't shoot until they're all in view.*

I reach back and tap out a confirmation on her hand. She snatches it and gives a squeeze as my chest gets tight. We've no experience against this kind of adversary. Every rule of engagement we've mastered could be wrong.

The first pair of security agents comes into view. *Bish.* They're flooding the entire corridor with light. I should have expected that. We're in the wrong position to defend against that. Our advantage only exists when we've got the dark to work in. Time to pull back.

Efa taps me, and I nod, covering her as she moves. We slip away from our defensive line, hopping past each other in a staggered retreat. Merek and Niah will do the same, using the same tactics. At least I hope so. Merek had better be smart enough to follow her lead. He's the only one who didn't train as a Tarakh.

A deluge of light floods into the corner we just evacuated. They're pushing ahead faster than before—likely false confidence after finding no resistance. Despite the urgency to keep moving, I take a moment to breathe. Our retreat was wise and well timed. That imaginary bravado would have turned into an onslaught we couldn't defend against.

Merek appears as we arrive at the down ladder. He motions to it with a nod of his head, then offers me his arm for support. I refuse it. Even if I'm only moving at a weak shuffle, I can still move on my own.

I glance back at the lights. One is nearly on us. We need to move faster.

I hit the ladder first, sliding down as quickly as I dare. My body is sluggish, and I pant hard as I fight to hold on.

Niah drops next, her breathing raspy as she grasps around her throat.

"You okay?" I whisper as Efa and Merek touch down. Niah narrows her eyes at me.

"You shouldn't be up," she hisses, then turns to Efa. "This your idea?"

"I never said she should fight," Efa replies.

"But you told her, right? What you think she'd do?"

Efa tosses up a hand and looks away. It doesn't matter what she said, and Niah knows it.

Niah glances up through the port to the level above. Several light beams are already crossing over it. Her jaw tightens, then she motions for us to keep going.

"Since you've cleared yourself for battle," she says as we move, "what's the plan?"

I stare, dumbfounded, at her. Ten seconds ago, she was mad that I'd gotten out of bed. Now this? We were supposed to hold them at the airlock so that more of them couldn't enter, but we weren't ready. Maybe we can try the same at the ladder? No. That'd take the four of us, and the moment they discovered the rail car, they'd flank us.

Bish. Nothing I can think of will work. My head's still foggy from the medication Raey gave me. A better plan isn't coming. I need Niah's help.

"No." She raises a finger as if reading my mind. "You can make this call better than any of us. So make it."

My mouth drops open. Of all the moments to force me to lead, this shouldn't be it. But if she won't help, it'll be up to me.

I turn to Merek and Efa. "What level do you think is ready for a solid defense?"

They share a glance before Merek speaks. "Twenty. It's the one that had to be perfect."

I nod, taking some comfort in their confidence. After twenty, the stasis levels begin, and there lie thousands of weaknesses for us to protect and the *Devant*'s agents to exploit. If they get control of those levels, we lose control of the *Stratford*.

"Twenty it is then," I say, squeezing my fists. "Let's go."

SEPERATION

FANA

WHEN I STOP CLIMBING, I realize I don't know which level I'm on. My worry over Ceri and the others consumed my thoughts, and I forgot to check. I don't remember seeing any signs, either. Maybe there's some, but it's too dark for me to see them.

I should have stayed with them. They may be strong, but nobody can handle two squads of security agents with all the weapons and tools they have at their disposal. And Ceri would struggle to match even a single agent, wounded as she is. They'd kill her the moment she fought back.

Why did I listen to her?

But I couldn't have refused her. That deep gaze of hers and the strict tone of her voice. It was like she was my commanding officer, and that makes my willingness to obey even stranger. Commander Azazhi rarely gave me a direct order, and now that I'm a renegade, I don't need to listen to anyone.

Which leads me to my current problem. I could take the rail car and return to twenty-one, but I'd need to find where that is on this, too. This level is a big catacomb of storage lockers that aren't organized in any logical sense.

It's spooky down here, too. After they powered all the lighting down, there's only the dull amber glow of status lights every ten paces. I can barely make out the edges of the floor. And forget the ceiling. I get a chill down my back every time I glance up into that black hole above my head.

Maybe I didn't go far enough. It should just have been four ladders, but I can't recall that many. Everything looks the same in this moody light. I'm not even sure what's supposed to be on level twenty-one, though this seems like a good place to hold up a defense.

When it becomes clear there's no sign or any way for me to determine how lost I've become, I sigh and roll my eyes at my stupidity. Maybe if I can find the rail car, I can be where Ceri wants me.

I sigh again. Look at me, still trying to follow a teenager's orders. Raey was right. I've fallen hard for that girl.

As confusing as this level is, it can't be all that big. I saw the *Stratford* from the outside. The higher levels where I've been are smaller than the lower ones, often by half or more. All I need to do is search around until I find it. If my orientation's correct, I just need to aim myself down this corridor, and it'll be somewhere down at the end.

It's not.

A groan slips from my lips as I shake my head. *Fana, you're lost all capacity to think like the engineering chief you're supposed to be.* If Raey could see me now.

Wait. Where is Raey? She wasn't with the others. Did they tell her to hide? Or did she run to the *Devant*'s agents?

I haven't forgotten what Raey told me to do or, more accurately, what not to do. But I haven't thought about it much, and I'm not about to consider it now. My brain power needs to be reserved for getting off of this level and back to Ceri.

And that thought makes my heart beat a little faster. I really hope she's safe.

Stupid Fana. Now all you're going to do is think about her. I grimace and smack my head a few times to get her face out of my mind. It works. At least for now. I'd better hurry.

I think I need to go up that cross-corridor I passed a second ago. That'll get me closer to where I'm calculating the rail system to be. There's the minor problem of having someone I don't want to see on it when it arrives, but I'll deal with that when I actually get to the rail car.

As I travel down the corridor, I examine the doors I pass by, curious to understand the security mechanism that locks the doors. It's an odd combination of keypad and physical lock with mechanical tumblers, something that might be interesting to experiment with later.

Ooh! A storage locker is open! The door is slid wide, the dim portal beckoning me with the sight of several stacks of crates as tall as me. It'd be interesting to find out what's inside of one.

But no. I don't have time to explore. Ceri will be upset if I'm not where she sent me, and the last thing I want to do is create a problem for her. In fact, I should support her with whatever I can get my hands on. Weapons aren't the only thing that can stop a soldier.

And maybe there's something in there that could help with that.

I shake my head. *Stop it. Just get to be where you need to be.* My curiosity got me in trouble. If I keep giving into my impulsive desires, I'm never getting off of this level.

But what if I could do something useful for Ceri?

Just to test the reality of my thesis, I peek into the locker and see if I can find a label on any of the crates. That should tell me if they're worth opening. I'd still need to figure out how to open the molded composite, but it shouldn't be too hard.

If I could see.

There's an emergency light in the back of the space, but the tower of crates is blocking the light from shining onto the labels. I don't have a portable lamp. All I have are the clothes I'm wearing.

My eyes widen. *My shirt is white!* I glance at the light and judge the distance, then do the inverse calculation in my head. *Not much* is the answer I come to, which would have been my guess, anyway. Still, I'm going to try. Any light, even if it's reflected, is better than what I've got now.

I pull my shirt off and spread it wide between my hands, holding it as high as I can. Next comes finding the right angle. With a little trial and error, I find the best one and bend my head down until I can read the label.

But...what's an ultrasonic land imprinting calibrator? And what do these specifications mean? Amplitude? Frequency? Maximum sound pressure level?

I catch my breath. *This is an excavation tool.* Likely a powerful one. I won't know if it's useful until I get it out of its crate and look at it. And by the time my fingers are looking for a way to open the crate, I realize I'm putting my return to twenty-one on hold.

But only because I could help Ceri with this. As soon as I figure out how to get it out of its crate and learn how to operate it, that is.

Opening the crate turns out to be simple. There's an outer barrier wrapped around it, and once I tear that off, a pair of latches release the cover. I exhale as I peer into the case, a glint off the device's chassis catching a stray beam of light. It's not bright enough to get a good glimpse of the thing, and my shirt, which I should put back on, won't do enough to help. I'll need to find some better illumination. Maybe if I can get it into the rail car, I can see it well.

I run my fingers across the foam insert until I feel the cool chill of metal. Then I wrap them around the tool and give it a tug to pull it from the case. But there's resistance somewhere near the edges—of course there is. It's strapped in to avoid any rattling around in zero-g. A quick spread of my hands finds what I'm looking for, and with a last pull, the device slides from the foam. It's lighter than I guessed, but that could also mean it's not yet connected to a power cell. I don't even know if they had such things seven hundred years ago.

The so-called calibrator is long and thin, with a silver barrel extending from a black box with a grip. On the box is a screen—currently dark—with a set of recessed buttons around it. It's difficult to see, but I think the top right button is the power. When I press it, nothing happens, which I expected. Still, I can feel myself quivering to get it working.

I smile as I find a pair of power cells in the case, though both are dead. They go in a leg pocket of the military-style pants Efa loaned me.

My body itches to get off this level, and I slip out of the locker to hunt for the rail car again. With one correction, I find the doors of the system waiting for me at the end of a hallway, which was my second guess of where it would be. I hit the call button and examine my new prize as I wait for the car to arrive.

It looks way more like a weapon than I had thought, and the black and yellow diagonal stripes at the end of the barrel give the impression that it's dangerous to handle or at least point at someone. All of those specifications I read make me think this thing makes some really high-pitched and very loud noises. For what purpose, I'm not sure. I've never heard of a land imprinter before. It certainly sounds like something exciting.

Even if I can't get it to work, I've got proof in my hands that the *Stratford* has the excavation tools that Commander Azazhi wants. Showing him this could end the assault, which is all the more reason to get back up there. Or better yet, I should return to the *Devant* and show it to him. Then we can negotiate for the return of *Stratford*'s crew and the multiprocessor that I need to get the navigation system running. He'd deal for that, I think.

The rail system beeps as the car descends to my level, the lights of the interior making my eyes squint as they flood the area with bright illumination. To me, it's like my future, and Ceri's, just filled with shiny potential.

And the moment I step in, I know that's exactly what it is.

DEFENSE

CERI

A COOL BREEZE RUNS across my back as I crouch behind a barrier with Efa—one of a few she and Merek set up on level twenty. It's causing bumps across the skin on my arms, and while I'm thankful for the well-designed and well-built environmental systems on the *Stratford,* I wonder if this chill isn't my nerves getting to me.

They positioned our barrier fifty paces behind Niah and Merek's forward position. Theirs is a mere fifteen paces from the down ladder—just enough distance to allow them to aim and fire if a *Devant* soldier charges them. They've got clear sight of the ladder and enough ammunition to take out anyone who attempts a descent, but they're close enough to be overrun if they can't neutralize targets fast enough.

Which returns me to this icy feeling. Perhaps I'm just over-thinking our strategy. Or maybe my wounds have diminished my confidence in fighting. No matter what it is, I press close to Efa and watch the ladder for movement. The two of us are the second line of defense and the last. If we go, it's over. Our passengers on the level below will have no one to protect them, and the thought of my parents left to the whims of the *Devant*'s commander makes me wrap my arms about me and rub them warm.

"You okay?" Efa whispers, putting a hand on my back.

"Fine," I reply, even when I don't expect her to believe it. So I add, "I just want to hold up my end of things."

She watches me for a moment, then says, "You will. You're the best of us, Ceri. Without you, we would never have come this far."

I dip my head, tears threatening to cover my cheeks. Emotion is pouring over me, and I can't understand the reason for it. If we weren't about to fight a battle, I'd throw my arms about Efa's neck and press my face into her shoulder until the feeling went away. In another time long past, I could have done that, but I've chosen to be a leader, and I need to be the example of strength, so I grit my teeth and keep my feelings inside.

"Ceri?" Efa prods.

"I'm fine," I murmur in reply. It prompts her to put a finger under my chin and lift until our eyes meet. She smiles at me with a deep understanding behind her gaze. No one knows me better than Efa. We've entrusted our lives to each other, and I'm glad she's the one next to me in this critical moment.

Movement ahead catches our attention. Niah raises a hand, a single finger pointing upward. Her signal is clear.

They're here.

Efa squeezes my shoulder, then steadies her pistol against the edge of the barrier, ready for battle. At fifty paces, we're clear of the immediate action but close enough that we'd become a target should Niah and Merek fall. The lethal range of our guns barely reaches that distance. We'd be better off on a level where we could fight them point blank. But this is where we've chosen to take a stand. We must make it work.

A *Devant* security agent slides down the ladder and gets two darts in the back of his head for being first. Two more come down in quick succession. The first goes down, but the second finds cover at the edge of the ladder landing and fires back. His shot flies wide, shooting sparks down the corridor as it impacts the wall behind Merek and Niah.

I jump at the power of it. Nothing we have counters that. And the strength of their body armor offers limited targets. If we don't hit their heads, we'll hit nothing at all.

At least Merek and Niah are holding them. They've taken out four *Devant* agents so far, and only a pair have secured positions. It's a hopeful start. We've just got to keep it that way.

A bell rings from down the corridor, just like what'd happened during the massacre on ninety-five. Every muscle in my body goes tight when I recognize it.

"Ceri," Efa hisses. "The rail car!"

I wouldn't have expected them to find it so quickly or figure out how to operate it, much less know where to go. *Bish. Did they capture Fana?*

"We've got to cover it," I say. "One of us has to go."

Efa eyes the fight down the corridor, then turns to me.

"You." Efa motions with her chin. "I'm in better shape to handle things here. Go."

I stare at her, a refusal at the back of my throat. I'd pull rank if I thought I could do better, but she's right. My legs won't move me faster than a hard march. I'd be bish covering for Merek and Niah alone.

We smile at each other with pressed lips, and then I'm off, pushing hard to get to the opposite side of the level before the rail car stops. I check the ammunition in my weapon—full. A backup pistol sits at my hip should I need it, along with enough dart clips to shoot the entire crew of the *Devant*. I'm praying hard I won't have to.

The rail system's foyer comes up faster than I expect. I check my back to ensure no agents followed, then take up behind a barrier, ready to fight.

The weighty structure Efa and Merek put up is impressive. Three metal crates arranged in a semi-circle, with another stacked on top of two smaller boxes at the end. I can shoot through the space in-between with little need to take cover. It's exactly what I need to hold off any *Devant* soldier who comes through. If I'm lucky, none will, though I'm not counting on it.

The increasing sound of the rail car fills the corridor with an ominous hum, overpowering the distant screech of the security agent's weapons. I force my hands to stop shaking and take aim. I've never enjoyed hurting others just to survive. Only my desire to protect myself and my squad gave me the will to squeeze the trigger. This is no different and perhaps easier because I'm up against those I most despise.

Adults.

The rail car's light streams through the translucent windows of the system doors. I brace, my finger resting on the trigger, and imagine where the head of the first security agent will be.

Hyuk. The rail car's passing this level and heading lower. My stomach twists as I realize we'll need to defend two fronts. They've effectively trapped us on this level, and the only way off will be through them.

I race back to Efa, nearly smashing my face into the deck twice in my haste. My heart is in my throat as I turn the corner and dive behind the barrier to avoid the security agent's suppressing fire. Their fiery red beams fly from their position and pound the corridor around us. The impacts hurl molten composite in all directions, making bright afterimages in my sight and filling the passage with thick gray smoke.

Efa knows my report the moment she takes notice of me. She grabs my shoulders and lifts as I force myself up. When our eyes connect, I know she's waiting for an explanation. I'll give her one the moment my brain focuses enough to find the words.

But before I can, Niah and Merek vault over the barrier, dropping behind us as the weapons fire from down the corridor increases.

"What are you doing?" Niah snarls. "They're about to figure out we've retreated, and they'll be coming! We need to pull back to a new line."

Efa and I both turn to them, expectant for more detail.

"They won't make a frontal assault," Merek explains. "We've dropped too many of them for them to think that'll work, but we couldn't defend that position choking on smoke. They might wait it out, too. Let's hope we get lucky."

"We won't," I reply. "They've taken the rail car below. Now we're stuck."

But even as I say it, I realize that's not true. So does Merek.

"We can still retreat through the hull," he replies. "We can get to twenty-one and redeploy a defense line there."

A single shot flies over our heads, forcing us down and our weapons up. Everything goes silent, and against our better experience, we press our heads together to continue the discussion.

"Hyuk no, we can't set up a defense line between a bunch of stasis pods!" Niah hisses, her eyes shifting to glance at Efa. "You want our passengers to become targets?"

"Twenty-two, then," Merek says.

"No," I say and pause as an idea comes to me. "We need to draw them down. Way down. They won't be able to plan a flanking maneuver if we keep them guessing about our location."

The three of them share a glance. Merek nods at Efa, and she licks her lip.

"Okay," Efa says. "What level?"

"Ninety-six," I reply. Niah snorts and grins, then considers as she watches me.

"It's good," she says after a second. "I know it well."

There's a clank at the end of the corridor. The slap of boot soles hitting the deck follows, signaling our moment to retreat. I flex my legs and prepare to make the all-out sprint to the down ladder. We'll need to keep up that pace across twenty-one, and perhaps twenty-two as well, if we want to be sure we're clear of their trap. With the dull ache in my side turning into a sharper pain, I'm not sure I can do it. I can't become a liability. If they try to save me, we're all dead.

"Let's stop by twenty-five and get the comms. We're going to need them," I suggest, thinking of somewhere I can rest.

"We will," Niah says. "But you're not going with us."

I blink. "What?"

"I can see it on your face, Ceri." She points a finger at me. "You're worried you're going to slow us down, and even if you don't, we can't risk it. Take hull access down. We'll meet you there."

Even as I know it's the right choice, I hesitate. It's not the fear of the chill anymore. It's that I'll be on my own, and while that never used to bother me, the feeling I might die alone is locking my legs in place.

"Okay." I curl my lips in and nod. "But don't forget Fana's on twenty-one. Take her with you."

"No," Niah replies. "She'll be too much of a burden. You should get her. Maybe she can help you."

"But—"

"No time to think about it!" Merek hisses as more footsteps echo from down the corridor. "Let's go!"

He takes off, moving down the passage, swift and silent. Niah pats my shoulder and nods, then follows.

"Stop it," Efa says, then presses her cheek against mine. "We'll be back together again soon." Then she holds up her weapon and grins. "Go first. I need to remind them we're still here."

The edges of my mouth curl up. I can trust her words, but that will never stop me from worrying about her.

With a squeeze of her arm, I dash to the hull access hatch and slip inside, praying we all make it to our goal alive, and if not, that our end comes quickly.

RETURN

FANA

As I STEP OUT of the rail system onto level seventeen, there's a calm in the air. The lighting, save for what's splashing out of the car behind me, remains off, and other than the whirl of cooling fans in the ceiling, silence is the defining mood here. Not that I trust it.

I want to call out to Ceri. Or maybe Efa. They could have pushed the *Devant*'s security squads back, but I'm not taking the chance it didn't happen. Still, nobody came to investigate when I arrived, so either that's just poor soldiering on someone's part, or I'm truly alone.

The rail system doors close, and I jump, spinning on them as if it was anything but machinery in operation.

Now to...*what?*

That's right. I'm returning to the *Devant* and putting myself at risk of arrest again for the chance to bargain with Commander Azazhi. This calibration thing will do the trick. The commander is a reasonable man, and I know what he's after. He'll deal with me for sure.

I take two steps and then push up on my toes to slink down the corridor toward the airlock. I'll need a suit to get across, but one that fits should be there—no one would be stupid enough to wear such a bulky garment inside. Whatever oxygen's left in the tank will be fine. With the connector in place, it's a mere two minutes to the opposite side.

There's a small but tight ping in my chest as I wonder about Raey. Did she return to the *Devant*? Likely. She'll be angry with me for doing the same, but I hope she understands why. She might even support my choice, considering. Anyway, I'm too deep into this to back out, even if I wanted to. So sorry, Raey. *Maybe one of these days you'll understand what motivated me to choose a different ship.*

As I come to the airlock, there's not just one pressure suit. There's a pile of them! They're stacked in rows, their silver outer layer shining golden as they reflect the rays of the status lights. A grin hits my face as I take in the overabundance of them. I should find one that'll fit me rather than my horrible idea of folding thick fabric into sleeves short enough to get my hands through, which would never work.

I pivot to look behind me, scanning for any hint I'm not as alone as I think I am. The space is empty, so I'm not proven wrong. Now I can rummage at leisure for a perfect fit.

My breath gets caught in my throat when I spot the name badge of someone I recognize. They're nearly my height, so the size will be close enough, but they're male, which means the bottom half of the suit will be uncomfortable to wear. I'll manage.

I waste no time dropping to the floor to wriggle the pants and boots on. The top half requires a little dexterity, and I'm glad I've mastered the technique. In less than ten minutes, the suit is on, and all I need to do is top it off with a helmet.

"Fana!"

I freeze, my hands clutching the helmet as Commander Azazhi's voice blasts from down the corridor. Seconds later, a pair of security agents are jamming their weapons into my face. I swallow and stare as my commanding officer stomps down the passage toward me. I expect the rage on his face, but the way his boots pound into the deck, the thud echoing throughout the level, makes the hair on the back of my neck stand up. He's in no mood to talk business, but since he's here now, I've got to try. This will be my only chance to speak up.

"Commander," I say, forcing the edges of my mouth up. "I was just coming to see you."

"See me?" He narrows his eyes. "You mean surrender?"

The calibration device is resting on the wall, blocked from Commander Azazhi's view by the stack of pressure suits in front of it. I grin internally at my forethought.

"Well, before we talk about any of that, I think you're going to want to hear what I have to tell you about what I found on this ship."

He takes a step closer, his head tilting as he appraises me. His gaze is sharp as a winged predator's. I'd doing my best not to show him how much I'm shaking.

"What is it?" he demands.

"Something you're going to want," I reply, holding up a finger. "But first, I want you to return the crew of the *Stratford* to their ship and promise to leave them alone after."

The commander frowns and shakes his head. "Why would I consider any of that?"

I press my lips tight and duck my head a little. If we were discussing the *Devant*'s multi-layered coolant system, I could talk circles around him. Negotiation is his expertise. My only hope is he wants what I'm about to offer more than he wants me.

"And you'll allow me to fix their ship before I return," I add, putting force in my words.

It's a few seconds before he chuckles. It's okay. I didn't expect him just to drop to his knees and beg me to tell him what I've got. And we're still talking, so that's good, too.

"You are in no position to make demands of me, Fana." Commander Azazhi glances at his security agents. "Now tell me what you found, and I'll consider not pushing you out of the airlock."

My heart falls out of my chest. *Did he just threaten to kill me?* No way. He's just trying to scare me. Right?

"That's not funny," I reply.

"I wasn't joking."

Oh hell. Now what do I do? This is just...impossible. Commander Azazhi may bend the rules of inter-ship actions, but no way would he murder his own crew. I step back even though it's a useless action. No amount of distance I put between me and these guards will be enough to save me from getting shot if the commander orders it. I've got to do as he says or die, so I should get on with it. Yet my feet won't move. I can't accept he's holding my life over me for a bit of technology. Everything about it is wrong.

"Alright," I say, holding my hands up. "I tell you, but you can't kill me. I have a right to a trial."

Commander Azazhi smirks and looks down as if he's thinking about a joke only he knows. A second later, he sighs. "Oh Fana, do you really think you're still a part of my crew?"

The breath goes out of me. *How could he say that? I'm the chief engineer! He needs me!*

No. He doesn't. Raey was trying to tell me that, but I wouldn't listen. If I was confident I could get what I wanted, I was naïve to think so. I'll only be pleading for my life, and I hope I can be sharp enough to manage that.

"Listen," I say. "If you want me to tell you what I have, you'll take me back with you and hold a fair trial, as is the law."

"And I already told you, the only law out here is mine. Don't believe me? Watch this." He motions to the security agent on his right. "Shoot her in the hand."

There's a flash, and a searing pain rips up my arm. I drop, screaming and staring at the smoking hole in my palm. My head is spinning, and the agony coursing through me forces the air from my lungs. The mental shock is just as bad. How could he have such little value for my life? I came to the *Stratford*, thinking I was doing the right thing, trusting that my commander would support me on that move. What he just did, I...I can't even begin to consider.

"We're all we've got, Fana," he says, approaching just close enough to tower over me. "No one will save us out here. Which means we'll do whatever we have to survive. If you're not with us, then you're a threat that needs to be eliminated."

"What are you talking about?" I sob, holding the wrist of my wounded hand as I imagine it immersed in flames. "We came to help the people of the *Stratford*!"

"I don't care what happens to the *Stratford* or its people. All I want is the excavation equipment. So are you going to tell me where it is, or must I waste time and find it myself?"

"Go to hell!"

He stares down at me.

"Fine." He turns away to face his agents. "She's the enemy now. Kill her."

Panic screams through me. I freeze, every muscle in my body locking. But I don't accept death. Not here. Not by him.

Without thinking, I reach out and grab his ankle, yanking as hard as I can. As he steps away from me, he loses his balance and throws his arms up. The security agents drop their weapons as he crashes into them, too late to stop his fall.

I grab the calibration device and scamper for the airlock, rolling inside and pounding my fist on the cycle control. Before the door closes, I snatch the nearest helmet.

My breath is coming hard and fast as I fumble with the helmet, using my one good hand. Air is purging from the lock faster than I can think. I have to survive. That's all that matters. I've got to live and stop Commander Azazhi from murdering the people of the *Stratford. Just get the helmet on, Fana. Get it on. Now.*

I'm getting dizzy. The air is nearly gone. The helmet's on my head. *How do I lock it?* I've done it a thousand times. I can't remember. Why?

Push the slide, Fana! Push it!

My body collapses against the wall, oxygen returning to my brain. Only then do I catch sight of the security agent taking aim at me.

Commander Azazhi shoves the man away, shouting something at him. He was right to do it. The blast from his weapon would destroy the airlock, and the escaping air would have sucked the three of them into space, to their deaths.

I force myself up. They'll have their suits on in ten minutes. That's all the time I'll have to accomplish whatever it is I'm going to do on the *Devant*. Less if they warn the guards on the other side.

I'd better make those moments count.

RESISTANCE

CERI

I SLIDE DOWN THE ladders, one after the other, nearly losing count of the number of levels I've passed. Fatigue seeps into my muscles, threatening to stop my descent. Still, I press on, moving through a near dark that would send anyone unfamiliar with the hull's interior plummeting to their deaths.

Seventy-six levels are a long way down, especially in this oppressive cold. My head spins every time I check my progress by glancing over the side of the railing. But as it is, I'm moving too slow and my futile attempt to find Fana on twenty-one was a waste of time. I hope she's okay. There's no time to search for her. At my current rate, I'll arrive well after the battle is over. I'll hate myself if I'm not there to protect my friends and defend my ship.

I pick up my pace, even as the wound on my side continues to burn. Pain will not slow me down. I won't stop even if it bleeds. It's reminding me I'm still alive.

Niah, Merek, and Efa will harass the *Devant*'s agents every chance they get. That'll keep those bastards on the defensive and possibly take a few out of the fight. Then when we get to the last level, we'll turn their advantage against them.

And I'll be there to finish the job.

When I escape the hull on ninety-six, Efa is there, waiting. She throws an arm around my neck and squeezes me before handing me a comm device. I smile and nod. It's all the communication we need. There'll be little talking from here on out. We'll take up positions and prepare ourselves for the coming battle, already knowing what's on each other's minds.

Merek gives me a tight smile as we pass him. He's setting up his spot just down the corridor from the down ladder and will be the first line of defense. Efa and I will be at the rear again.

After a few steps, Efa puts a hand on my shoulder and squeezes. When I glance at her, she presses her lips together and pleads an apology. Then she spins, jogging back to Merek to wrap her arms about him. They spend a long moment gazing into each other's eyes.

I busy myself rechecking my two pistols and my ammunition levels. Let them take an intimate moment if they need it. It's not much for them to ask or to have. They may never have the chance again.

Efa's quiet giggle breaks me from my focus as she returns. I look up just as she pats my hip and motions for us to continue.

"One day you'll want that, too," she whispers. I just snort.

We move to Niah next as she's laying out her many weapons. Her position will create crossfire into the kill zone and hopefully take out a good number of the enemy. She acknowledges our approach with a nod, then stops me with a hand on my arm before we move by.

"Remember, I'm just a soldier." Niah levels her gaze at me as she speaks. "You're leader here, and I'm following whatever you command."

"Then I hope I can lead you well," I reply, swallowing my fear. "I still look to you for guidance, Niah. I cannot afford to lose you."

To my disappointment, she just nods.

Our last stop is Efa's position. I'll be behind her some twenty paces, giving her fire support, should the *Devant*'s agents get past our first line.

Before I leave, she grabs my hand and squeezes it, pulling me to her. Our eyes connect, and usually that's enough for the two of us. But as Efa opens her mouth to speak, my stomach gets tight. I don't want to hear anything serious. And I won't accept any kind of goodbye.

Perhaps realizing it too, Efa closes her lips, curling them in before she takes a breath and leans in to peck my cheek. I can only curl the edge of my mouth up before turning to head to my position.

But something compels me to stop and pivot back to her.

"Just remember I'm right behind you," I say.

Efa doesn't reply. She doesn't need to. She heard my words. That's enough. This isn't goodbye, after all.

As I settle into my spot behind a half-open door, a chill slides down my back, and I grit my teeth to force it away. So what if we're up against superior numbers and weapons? That we haven't experienced actual combat in months doesn't matter. We've had years of terror to survive through before now. This battle will be exactly the same as every other. I will pick my targets, shoot, and move. Then do it again. And again, until I eliminate every savage adult who's invaded my ship.

And that's what they are. Monsters. Their humanity left them when they abducted my crew and arrested their own for helping us. Perhaps if none of this had happened, I might accept them as people. Now they're only targets, and I will worry about the guilt I feel over pulling the trigger once they're gone.

I put my comm in my ear and the mic on my throat, keying it to speak. "Check in," I say.

"*Standing by*," Merek replies, his voice thin through the comm.

"*Standing by*," Niah adds.

"*We await your orders, squad leader*," Efa says, turning to glance at me.

Perhaps that's what she wanted to tell me, though behind those words is a much deeper message. I press my lips into a smile, just to let her know I've received everything she didn't put to words.

The pounding of approaching boots echoes through the level's corridors, obscuring their direction and number. I pull back inside the room and pivot. *Did they get behind us?* Unlikely. But I can't take the chance.

"All positions, eyes on your flanks," I whisper. "And watch each other's backs."

Only clicks of their mics come through my comm. Standard protocol now that we're in battle mode. Their acknowledgement is enough. Now I know they're all still alive.

Without warning, the air erupts in flashes of light, illuminating the corridor in a bloody red glow. Soldiers yell and charge. The scream of dart pistols counters the whine of the enemy guns.

The explosion of noise and light flood my senses. I shut my eyes to clear my head—a dangerous action in a fight. But I need situational awareness. Without it, I'm useless.

I peek out, scanning the battle down the corridor. Efa is engaged, hurling covering fire as Niah switches position. Two bodies lie on the deck before her. Neither is Merek.

Sparks fly off the door just above my head. I duck back into the darkness. A security agent skids around the corner behind me. *Hyuk. They've gotten behind us!* Another shot from his gun streams over my head, impacting the back wall of the room.

I fall prone and squeeze off three shots. Two bounce off his armor, but the final one finds its mark. The man drops his gun and clutches at his throat as he goes down.

"Squad!" I call. "Go mobile! Find any angle you can and keep them confused."

My pulse pounds in my ears as my feet push off the deck. I dash for the fallen agent's weapon, picking it up to remove it from the fight. I won't use it. It may be powerful, but it's a dead giveaway in this dark.

And in that is the root of a plan. All I need is time to think it through. If I can get it.

"Niah! I need support. I'm pinned down!" Merek hisses.

"Hold position," I reply before she can. *"I'm coming."*

Another agent rounds the corner, nearly smashing into me as she charges. I drop and kick out. She tumbles over me, crashing face-first into the deck. My jaw tightens as I aim for a vulnerable spot in her armor and fire. Shooting someone at this distance is personal. I'll never get over having to do it.

A volley of shots rips down the corridor, forcing me to keep low. There's at least two down there. Maybe more. I need to find out.

I fire the security agent's weapon back at them. The bright red beam shoots straight at the ceiling and burns a hole in it. Amazing. No recoil, and it's much lighter than I expected.

"Hold your fire! You're aiming the wrong way!" one of them says loud enough I can hear it from my position. A germ of an idea forms in my head.

My hand finds the head of the fallen agent, and I search for the comm in her ear. It comes out with ease, and I press it into mine, taking a moment to listen to their conversation as I lie flat on the deck.

"How many of them are there? Wasn't it just four?"

"They must have others waiting down here! That's why they drew us down!"

"All units, cut the chatter. You'll give away your position!"

A surge of energy fills me. We've got them confused.

The corridor goes quiet, and I smile to myself. Their weapons' fire lit up everything, destroying our advantage. Now we'll return to near darkness and the kind of fighting we've done since the adults first placed a weapon in our hands.

"*Efa, give me your position,*" I say in a whisper only the throat mic can pick up.

"*Stuck where you left me. I need fire support to move.*"

"*Pull back to the corner. I've got you covered.*"

As I wait for Efa, I scan the corridor, letting my eyes readjust to the dim light. Sure enough, there are three security agents at the end. Two of them are gesturing with some kind of vague hand signals while the other is hunched over, watching the passage before him.

"*Still stuck here,*" Merek says, worry creeping into his voice.

"*Hold tight, we're coming,*" Efa replies.

Half a second later, a tap on my shoulder signals her arrival. Her hand slides down to the middle of my back and draws letters in a query.

How many?

I reach for her hand and grab three of her fingers. She acknowledges with a shake of her arm and asks another question.

Plan?

Watch this.

I hand her the agent's comm to listen to. She stares at it and frowns before pressing it against her head—good enough. I crouch and shuffle across the corridor to a completely dark area on the opposite wall. Then, with a slow inhale, I rise, aim for one of the talking agents, and fire.

That one drops while the other jerks back, waving their weapon in wild arcs. I shoot again, and the second talker falls, inciting the third to unload his weapon at us. The corridor turns into a haze of crimson light and smoke. I dive to the ground, aiming for him, but Efa gets him before I can squeeze my trigger.

Weapons fire comes from behind us, pounding the wall and showering us in sparks. I cover my head with my hands as the tiny flares singe my arms, and I escape the attack. Efa's close behind.

"Split," I say, handing her the security agent's gun. "I'll get to Merek. Make them think their own team is shooting at them."

Efa grins and nods, then ducks down a side corridor to come around from behind on our new targets.

"*Merek, Niah. Give me a target count,*" I whisper.

"*Three,*" Niah replies a second after I make my request.

"*Two. Maybe more,*" Merek adds a moment later. "*I can't tell from my position. Are you coming?*"

"*On my way.*"

If we were facing fourteen before, and we've taken out at least a squad down here, there can't be many left. But I'll keep my hopes to myself. When they captured our crew, there was more, and I doubt that was all of them. Likely whoever's in charge has already requested reserves, which means they won't stop coming until they get us. Or until we get them.

I inhale and press forward, my hands tightening on my weapons. This fight will get a lot worse before it's over.

SPLIT

— • —

FANA

I'M GRATEFUL FOR THE self-healing fabrics in my suit. Without them, I'm not sure I would have had enough oxygen to make it across. The hole in my glove was on both sides, just like the one on my hand, and that caused an imperfect seal. By the time I fell through the *Devant*'s inner airlock door, I was gasping.

As I slip the glove off, the liner of the suit scrapes against my wound. I suck in a breath through my teeth and wince. At least it's not bleeding. The beam that drilled through my hand cauterized the wound. The design is purposeful that way. They call it a humanitarian consideration. Maybe just don't shoot people instead.

With one useful hand, the rest of the suit is a struggle. I writhe on the deck to wiggle the top off. The bottom half goes easier—I just kick it off my legs.

Once I'm done, I push myself up, cradling my wounded limb against my body. The agony shooting up my arm is making me see stars, and they won't just go away. I should head to medical and ask for something to relieve my pain.

On second thought, that's a horrible idea. They'd dose me with something I might never wake up from. I'm a fugitive now. Every member of the *Devant*'s crew is dangerous to me.

Which means I have to move. Commander Azazhi will be here any minute. I'm surprised there weren't guards already here, waiting to capture me. Maybe I'm already captive because I'm on the *Devant*.

Or maybe he just wants to kill me himself.

If he's truly labeled me as traitor, then the only safe place for me is the *Stratford*. I'll have to figure a different way to get back, hopefully one that doesn't include any EVA work.

First, I need to get to engineering and pick up a multiprocessor core to bring back with me. I can take the lift down and then hop on the conveyor to get all the way to the rear of the ship. The only walking I'll need to do is to get to the lift, and that's not far, which is good, because I'm feeling lightheaded.

I test my steadiness by taking a few steps. Not bad, but far from stable. I take a few more, just to get a better feel for my pace. As I understand how my dizzy plodding will go, I grow braver and speed up, then speed up some more.

And stumble and fall.

My body twists to protect my hurt hand, and I wind up landing hard on my side, my shoulder taking the brunt of the impact. I groan, curling up into a ball, but realize my error. Anyone that just heard that will come investigate. I've got to be up and moving before they do.

Getting to my feet is harder than expected. My sight is going blurry, and shutting my eyes only makes the ship spin around me. I'm getting more and more nauseous every time I try. But with some effort, I make it to the lift doors, leaning on the wall and sighing as I press the call key. Seconds later, the lift chimes.

The doors slide open, revealing a blonde woman. I freeze. Do I know her? Does she know me? She's got her head buried in her tablet. Maybe I can just slide by her and—

Nope.

The woman looks up and blinks, taking me in. Then her eyes go wide, and she gasps, her hand flying to cover her mouth. I stare back, my pulse quickening as I wait for the moment when she recognizes me and slams her palm against the alarm.

"Are you...okay?" she asks, frowning.

She doesn't know me!

I feel the warmth returning to my limbs as I allow myself to breathe again. This woman must be from second shift—the one I wasn't supposed to be a part of. That's why we've never met, though she'd know my name if I told her. And I won't.

"Sorry," I say and force a chuckle. "I look like a mess, don't I? Just came from outside doing routine maintenance on the optical sensors. You wouldn't even believe what kind of crud can get on the lenses after seventeen years."

Her eyes dart down to my hand pressed against my chest. "Did you hurt yourself?"

I swallow and hope she doesn't notice the huge void in it. "Oh, it's no big deal. I'm going to medical to get it checked out now."

"Oh." She gives me a sympathetic smile. "Sorry to hear that."

"Thanks." I nod and step in next to her. When she doesn't move, I panic all over again. She'll realize I'm not going to medical if I press the button for the engineering level. *Then what?*

"I'm Aada, by the way. Are you on second shift, too?"

"Yeah."

"And..." She leans closer in expectation of a reply with a name attached to it. I'm not giving her one, not unless I can come up with something dull and forgetful. Still, she's waiting for an answer. It'll be suspicious if I don't give her one, but my creative brain refuses to function.

Wait. None of the lights are lit up on the panel. *Where's she going?*

"Whoops!" Aada says. "This is my floor! I almost forgot!" She steps out, turning back to wave. "I'll see you, right..."

Oh hell. I can't think.

"Aisha," I reply, smacking the button as I attempt a smile. "And yeah, I'll see you around."

Once the doors close, I slump to the floor, covering my face with my good hand. *Thank you, Mother.* Her name was the only one I could think of in the moment. I guess parents will always be there to help. Maybe not so much with the *Stratford*'s crew. Their adults—

The Stratford*'s crew!* They're still here! But where? I could find out. All I'd need is a ship's terminal to break into the security system. And that'd be easy. I helped set it up.

The lift's doors open up on the engineering level. I slide forward to peek out before I exit. It's clear, so I'm going. The foot conveyor won't be empty for long, not if it's the middle of shift day. *Wait, is it?* With all that's happened, I've lost track of current ship time. But this is engineering. There'll be a clock around somewhere.

Yet as I step onto the conveyor, the corridor remains quiet. So was the floor above. That makes me think it's a dark hour, and maybe all the security agents that were flooding the ship before made it seem busy. Likely most of them are on the *Stratford* with Commander Azazhi now.

Wow. That'd be like fifty or sixty of them. Out of stasis, at least. Ceri can fight, but there's no way she can handle that many. Even with Efa and Merek and the other lady, it'd be a completely unfair fight. And if the commander is willing to kill me...

I've got to help them!

But how? Weapons? The security agents will still far outnumber them. What they'd need is...*of course!* I'll free her crewmates and send them over with guns. That'd even up the sides. I throw a leg over the conveyor's rail and move to dismount. This will work. I'll flood the tube with oxygen and heat like it's supposed to have and get them across.

Then I pause. I still need the multiprocessor, and I'm almost there. But it may be too late if I release them after I get it. The battle might be over, and then all I'd be doing is sending the *Stratford*'s crew into a massacre, though maybe I'd be doing that, anyway. Those kids could all be infected by now.

I mash my lips together and pound my good hand on the rail. This is impossible. What does Ceri say in situations like this? That's right. *Bish!*

Time's wasting, Fana. Hurry up and decide something!

With a sigh, I hop off the conveyor and head to the nearest terminal, pounding on the keys to call up security access. At least I can remember how to do that, even if it's slower with one hand.

And it turns out, I don't even need to hack the system. There's a public note on the main screen letting everyone know about a room on a stasis level that's under quarantine and forbidden. That means at least one security agent is outside that door. But so what? This is *my* ship. I don't need guns to remove a guard. I've got an abundance of tools and skills at my disposal!

First, I call up the medical roster and review the schedule. No sign of Raey. Is she still on the *Stratford*? As much as I want to find her, I have to hope that's the case, even if that means Ceri's using her as a hostage. Not that I'd believe that for an instant.

I get the information I need and return to the lift, wishing hard that no one walks out of it. Down here in engineering, people like Aada are nonexistent. Everyone knows their commanding officer. It's a requirement. Which is why I can't allow anyone to see me.

But I fail.

The tech who comes around the corner as I wait for the lift drops the container he's holding and freezes as he spots me. So do I, minus the container.

"Chief?" he stutters.

"Taye." I nod, fighting my body not to collapse in a fit of shaking. "You dropped something."

"Are...are...you back?"

"Temporarily."

My head is already racing with the possibilities of what happens next. Most of them are terrible. There's the slight chance only the officers know about the pending trial, not that there will be one now.

"I heard you were in quarantine...Are you feeling better?" Taye asks.

"Never better. You going to pick that up?"

He blinks, and I point to his container.

"Oh yeah."

The lift arrives, the doors opening. While he's distracted, I could jump in and close the doors before he had the chance to stop me. But then he'd sound the alarm, and my plan would fail.

Time's running out. The commander's got to be back by now. If I don't get away from Taye and save the *Stratford*'s crew now, everything goes bad.

Which is why I'm about to do something really stupid.

"Hey, Taye, have you ever met any of the crew of the *Stratford*?" I ask.

"The *Stratford*?" His eyes widen. "They're all quarantined on Stasis Two. Why would I go there?"

"That was just a precaution. They're fine. At least that's what I heard from medical. You want to come with me to meet them?"

I hold my breath, waiting for his reply. My heart is pounding so hard now I'd be surprised if he couldn't hear it through my ribcage.

"Uh." He shakes his head. "No, that's okay."

A jolt of adrenaline runs through me as I shrug. "Suit yourself. I'll see you later, okay?"

I'm home free now.

"Chief, wait!"

My muscles lock as he jogs toward me. I'm frozen in place. I stare at him as he approaches. His jaw is stiff, and his eyes pierce through me. This is it. He's figured my deception out. There's no way I can fight him or run. I'm feeling dizzy. My knees are weak. I'm going to faint. I know it.

Forgive me, kids. I messed up!

"Can you take this up there?" he asks, holding out the small box.

My eyes fall upon it. I should know what it is, but my paralyzed brain can't think.

"It's, you know, a power core for the stasis pods. I needed to restock the supplies up there."

Oh hell.

"Uh, sure?" For the second time in an hour, my shoulders slump. I reach out with my good hand and go to take it from him.

But when I grab the box, he doesn't let go.

"Chief," Taye says, lowering his voice, "I know there's more going on that you can't tell me, but just be careful, okay? We can't afford to lose you."

I force a nod. This is all too much. How does Ceri handle all this stress? Any more and I will fall over backward.

"Thanks for the support, Taye," I say, but as he smiles warmly, hope flows through my body, and I smile back. "Don't worry. Everything's going to be okay."

Ten minutes later, I'm standing in front of a door marked only by its code. If there was an agent here, they're now headed to the far side of the ship for a briefing, one they'll be waiting a very long time for.

I do my best to calm myself, and then, with a deep breath, I tap the code to open the door. With a ping, it clicks and unlocks.

And I open it.

ENGAGEMENT

CERI

MY EYES WELCOME THE dark. After so long in the light, I wouldn't have thought so, but the familiar touch of blackness everywhere fills me with ease. I'd forgotten how much comfort it brings me, even in moments of fear. And this is one of those moments.

In the shadows of the level, I make my way to Merek's position, sneaking past a pair of security agents who fail to notice me slip behind them as I hold my breath. I could have taken them out, but Merek's protection is what I'm after, so I need to remain stealthy.

It's not long before I find him taking shelter in a storage room just down the corridor from the ladder to ninety-five. There are three agents there, doing their best to keep out of the light on the landing. If they knew their opponent was in deadly range of them, they might do more than just stand there.

Merek slides the door shut as I slip in. As he steps back to make space for me in this literal closet, I lean over, placing my hands on my knees to catch my breath. My side burns as if under constant torching, making it difficult to think straight.

With such an advantage of intel and position, we should be attacking right now. Yet all I want to do is curl up and sleep.

"What's the plan?" Merek whispers, crouching in front of me.

"Getting you out of here," I reply. "We've confused them well, and their battle discipline is bad. We'll get past them and reposition for another attack."

"It's like they're waiting for something. Reinforcements, maybe?"

"All the more reason to move now."

Merek watches me for a moment as he flicks his thumb off his finger. "Can you?"

I take in a deep breath and remind myself that his challenge was just out of concern. He's not Sayer, nor does he want anything other than for the two of us to make it back to our own line. I'm the one being hard on myself. I've made too many mistakes, and the four of us are in a precarious position. Our advantage in the dark would disappear if they drowned the corridors in light.

"Let's go," I say, dropping to one knee. Merek draws his pistol and aims at the door as I slide it open, first just a crack so he can find his targets, then a little more for our eyes to adjust. By the time the door is halfway open, we're ready to go.

Except we can't.

I slip the door nearly closed as panic threatens to overtake me. Only a mere crack remains. Any more than that and the squad of agents climbing down the ladder will spot us.

"*Ten...no...twelve new enemy combatants just joined the fight,*" Efa calls. "*Did you find him?*"

"*Yeah. She's here with me. Standby,*" Merek replies.

"*What's the holdup?*" Niah hisses. "*The two of you need to move. Now.*"

"*That's going to be difficult.*" I attempt to calculate the possibility of Merek and me neutralizing all fifteen security agents before they locate us—something we've never done before. No one has. At least not on this ship. "Niah, rendezvous with Efa and find a place to hole up."

"*Aye. On my way.*"

Merek taps my shoulder and points, calling attention to another who has just joined this reserve squad. He's slightly shorter in stature than the agents and possibly older, too. Even with my eyes adjusted, it's hard to tell his age.

But he's definitely in charge. The way he jabs his finger down the corridor and waves his hands around as the agents surround him makes that obvious. Not military though. No officer would make themselves a target with such wide gestures.

"*Efa, listen to what they're saying over their comm,*" I say.

"*Standby.*"

The new squad breaks up, forming groups of four under the man's command—fire teams. So he knows something about military tactics, after all. If this squad knows how to use the formation well, it'll challenge us to stay alive, much less move.

"*Communications are referring to someone as the commander. Could that be him?*" I can hear her frown in the tone of her voice.

"*Commander of what?*" Merek asks.

I back away from the door, my jaw going slack. That's Commander Azazhi.

"*Of the* Devant," I whisper.

"*Why would he come here?*" Efa asks.

It's a question I don't yet understand the answer to. There's no reason for the ship's top officer to risk himself by coming here. Even if I've taken out his security captain, there would be another who could take his place.

Wait. No. Captain Yelekal's second is dead.I shot him three times. No one can survive that.

I shake my head. "*We've got no time to think about that. Efa. Niah. Stay alert. They're splitting into subgroups. Four to a team. You understand?*"

Efa's click of her mic is the expected reply.

"Stay together," I add, "and get off this level if you have to. We're in defensive mode again."

I trust Niah and Efa to be safe, but when I consider how outnumbered they are, my breath gets shaky. One slight mistake and they'll be dead. If we had a full squad to cover us, maybe we'd be okay. Maybe.

Ancestors protect you both.

"Look." Merek points at the commander. "Now that his reinforcements are gone, he's only got two guards. Let's hit them and take him captive."

"What?" I shoot to my feet, my body surging with energy. Our maneuver would be almost too easy. The two agents are just staring at the walls as Commander Azazhi presses his comm against his ear and paces. He lowers his head and pauses as if he's struggling to hear. We'd be out and back before any-one realized what had happened.

And then we'd bargain for the return of our crew with a prisoner swap. Seren, Tegan, Sayer. Even Rhys would be safe again. Plus, with the right angle, we may even get more than that. Equipment. Repairs. A doctor.

The opportunity is so tempting, I nearly rush out the door and capture him myself. But the moment I go to move, my skin gets cold. These adults have already proven our lives have no value to them. There's no telling what they'd do to our crew to force their commander's release.

"No," I reply. "We're getting out of this closet, finding the nearest fire team, and removing them from the fight. Then we're going after the next one. And the next, until they're no longer a threat."

"That's more crazy than capturing their commander!" Merek hisses. "There's at least five teams out there, all armed with those beam weapons! We've got—"

I throw a hand over his mouth and dip my head into the light coming through the open door so he can see the warning in my eyes. He nods and closes his mouth. We're silent from here on out.

"*Two teams approaching,*" Efa says. "*Should we engage them?*"

I slide the door open just enough to stick the top of my head out, pressing my cheek to the floor and scanning the corridor. It's clear. My hand goes up, motioning to Merek to get ready, and with one last check of Commander Azazhi and his guards,

I slip out, headed back the way I came. Merek follows, one hand on my back to keep close and in contact.

"*Ceri*," Efa queries again. "*Do we engage?*"

Bish. I grab my mic button and key it twice. She better have gotten that or at least not have lost her common sense.

Without warning, Merek grabs my shirt, jerking me to a stop. He presses on my back—*get down*—and I crouch, cursing myself for stupidity. I was so focused on Efa, I neglected to do my part at point. We're both lucky he was paying attention, because the scrape of boots on the deck is far too close and our eyes haven't adjusted yet.

I raise my pistol out, pointing into the blackness as I press on the cool metal of the corridor wall and listen, gauging the distance to our targets. Well within range, for certain. Why can't I see them yet?

Two shapes emerge from the wall, turning toward us. *They were in the room!*

I jerk back, squeezing my trigger as I try to aim high. Merek fires a volley. There's a cry. One shape tumbles backward. The corridor explodes in red light. Weapon beams fly down the hall over our heads. We move and fire again. Another agent goes down. More shots. Two strike the spot I just occupied. Flames shoot up from the deck, annihilating anything they touch. Smoke stabs into my nostrils, tearing up my sight. I'm blinded as I rub at my eyes.

Merek slams me forward as a single shot burns into the wall where my head was. *Hyuk! There's another team!* I throw my arms out as I land, firing down the corridor at our new assailants. I can see again, but now we've got a worse problem.

They've got us in a crossfire, with only one way out.

It's a trap.

"Here!" I grunt, grabbing Merek's arm and flinging him towards the side passage and likely the awaiting third team. My other pistol comes out, and I unload it at the second team, expecting to hit nothing. It's enough to force them into cover while we escape.

Merek's already firing at the third team. One goes down while the others line up a shot. I take a second one out and rocket toward the rest.

"There's too many!" an agent shouts, firing recklessly multiple times in our direction. It's hardly a stupid plan. Our advantage is the dark. They can't see what they can't hit.

Merek hits him with his blade as we plow through the last one. We break into a run and take a left and then a quick right, searching for an unlocked door. The other teams are after us, chasing us down as we show them our backs.

At the end of a passage, we duck into a room, shutting and locking the door. I fall to my hands and knees, my lungs burning more than my side. Merek is no better. He struggles to keep quiet as he wheezes for air.

"*Ceri! Status!*" Niah calls.

"*Alive and hiding,*" I reply between gasps. "*You?*"

"*Hit. Not bad, but it's my weapon arm. It burns like the hyuking sun. My aim won't be worth bish. I think I got two, though.*"

"*Efa?*"

She only clicks her mic once—they're close to her. Too close for her to risk even a whisper. Now she'll need rescuing, and we're in no position to help.

"You hit?" I ask Merek, who slides to rest his back on a cabinet and fold his arms over his chest.

"Grazed, twice. But Niah is right. It hyuking hurts." He gulps down a breath. "Bish, Ceri, how are you dealing with a direct hit?"

"Who says I am?"

I collapse on to my good side and just lay there, thankful for the few seconds I have to rest. Soon enough, they'll be blasting every door open to find us, and there's no defense of a room with one exit.

Once I've caught my breath, I run through what happened and realize how I just lost situational awareness like a junior still in training. Stupid. And I'm supposed to be the squad leader? How can I do that if I'm forgetting the basics?

We're lucky none of us are worse off than we are. And that's what it was, pure luck, not skill—and certainly not leadership—that got us through these past minutes.

I cannot fail my squad again, or they, like me, will be dead.

"*Orders?*" Niah asks. I'm not sure I have any.

"*Pull back,*" I reply. "*Get off this level if you can. There's no way we fight them and live.*"

COURAGE

FANA

I STARE INTO A room just large enough to fit the twenty or thirty kids that are in it. They stare back, some in recognition, all in confusion. My response is different. As I take in the sight and the smell before me, my good fist clenches in anger.

Other than the *Stratford*'s crew, there's just a bunch of flat mats with no blankets or pillows and a rigged-up portable shed that must be their toilet. That's where most of the smell is coming from, but judging by the grime and sweat on them, it's likely none of them have showered in days.

Most of the younger crew members sit cross-legged in a semicircle off to the side at the front of the room, while a few others lie motionless on their mats and stare up at the ceiling. Some of them have dried blood in their hair. All of them have cuts and bruises on their hands or face.

I recognize Sayer in the back, lying on his side. And there's Beka and two younger girls I don't know, who all have patches of gray skin anywhere that's visible.

The air in my lungs escapes through my open mouth as I slowly shake my head and a weight forms in the pit of my stomach. I may be a traitor to my crew and my ship, but what have these kids done to deserve this?

"Fana, you've got a hole in your hand," Seren says, coming up to me. "What happened?"

Seren's in better shape than most, but her cheek is puffy, and it's clear she tried to wipe blood off her face with the only thing she had—her sleeve. Its gray fabric is stained dark in more than a few places.

"I'm...here to—"

"Better come in and close the door," Tegan says, shuffling up and ushering me inside. "We're exposed with you visible to the entire corridor like that."

Sayer frowns as he pushes up from his mat. He's watching me with narrowed eyes as he comes forward, and even though he's moving slower than usual, his approach is sending a chill down my back.

"So," Tegan prompts, "you were saying?"

"Yeah," Sayer adds with a growl. "Why are you here?"

I pull back from him, any words I was about to say lost as my brain screams to run away. After my encounter with Commander Azazhi, I've got no strength to argue. Sayer's like another version of him, and if he keeps up this aggressive stance, I'm gone.

"Give her a break, Sayer," Tegan says, moving in front of me.

"Why?" he spits back, glaring at me. "She's one of them, isn't she? Her crew put us here, treated us like bish, and did a bunch of experiments on Beka!"

"Experiments?"

Shouts come from a few of the kids nearest to him. One boy stands, throwing his fist out as he bares his teeth. Others notice and turn their bitter gazes on us. I still feel sympathy for them, but any more of this and I might change my mind about setting them free.

However, before I turn and run, I should at least tell them why I'm here.

"I'm not here for experiments, or to hurt you, or any of that," I say, waving my hand as I gather what energy I have left. "I'm letting you out!"

"Why would your commander do that?" Seren asks as her eyebrows clash.

I shake my head. "He didn't."

"Wait." Tegan points at me and tilts her head. "You're breaking us out?"

The two youngest in the corner look up at me, their eyes filling with hope. A few others gather around, including the boy named Rhys, who I almost had to fight but didn't and was glad for it. He's giving me a hard stare. So are a few others who push close to stand behind Sayer.

Sayer notices the growing group of kids behind him and uses it as a cue to speak up.

"That's total bish, and you know it, Fana," Sayer says. "Don't lie to us."

"I'm not. I swear it!"

"That means nothing coming from you."

I look to Tegan for help, but she only presses her lips and lowers her head. Seren's the same, though she's way more weary. The security agents may have been a little rough to the other kids, but the poor girl looks like they took their anger out on her face.

"Why won't you believe me?" I ask Sayer.

He steps closer and leans down to push his face into mine. "For the rest of my life," he hisses, "I will *never*. Trust. Another. Adult. Again."

"She's an adult?" one boy asks.

"That's right," Rhys growls in reply.

A sigh escapes my lungs. Maybe I shouldn't have relied on the vision in my head where they were all cheering the moment I opened the door and stated my intentions. If I had known they'd be so resistant to my help, I would have tried to get them out another way.

So far, I've only got two of them believing in what I say. Sayer's backed by six, including Rhys, who is clenching his fists as if he wants that fight after all. It's all nonsense, but I've no clue how to manage children. Most of my engineering team is older than me.

The relief guard will come soon, and when he notices his partner is missing, there are going to be problems beyond the ones I've already got. My muscles are already tensing at just the thought of adding to this mess.

A sharp shock runs up my arm into my shoulder. I must be cramping because I've been holding my hand in the same position for too long.

Oh. My hand. Now that could help.

I raise my charred hand above my head, turning it flat to show them the hole in the middle of my palm. Gasps come from all sides along with comments expressing everything from wonder to disgust. Even Sayer is speechless.

"What the hyuk happened?" Tegan's mouth widens as she stares at it.

"Commander Azazhi did this to me," I say, gritting my teeth, "then ordered his agents to kill me."

The room buzzes with chatter, speculating about how it happened. I catch a few suggestions, and what shocks me isn't the level of detail they know about human anatomy, but how many causes for my wound they can come up with. I get these kids have witnessed things children never should, but this brings their experience to another, much more horrific level.

"He wants you dead?" Tegan asks.

"That needs to be looked at right away!" Seren says.

I shake my head. "Can't do that here."

My attention turns to Sayer, hoping this blatant attempt to shock him into believing me was effective. His face has softened a bit, but I don't know if that's enough.

"Even if that's true, we can't help you, either." He gestures to the room. "No bandages here. Nothing except for us and our infections."

I gasp. "Some of you are still sick?"

"Recovering," Tegan explains. "That medical specialist gave the two worst a few doses of something. Now Beka only has a sniffle."

"But Siân died," Rhys laments. "They took her away, and she never came back."

Two doses? That means there's one more med kit left. *Where's the third?*

Raey knows. And I'll find out the moment she's in front of me again. But right now I need to keep quiet about that. There'd be a riot if I brought that up, and I'd be the first target for their rage. All the more reason to get them out of here.

"I know you want justice for how they've treated you," I say, trying to appear as sympathetic as I can.

"Justice?" Sayer huffs. "Hyuk no, we want revenge!"

A cry rises from Sayer's squad. Even Seren and Tegan's gazes grow intense. Given the right target, these kids would kill, and they'd celebrate it. Likely they already have, more than once. And if this was any other moment, I would pity all of them for what they've been through. But I can't let Sayer take control of my plan.

"Listen!" I throw my hands up to get their attention. "Right now, Ceri, Efa, Merek, and Niah are defending your ship from the *Devant*'s security agents."

The racket ends almost as quickly as it began. If I wanted their eyes on me, now they are.

"How do you know that?" Seren asks.

"Because I got separated from them when the attack started. Ceri didn't want me there because there were too many for them to fight."

"And so you ran away? What kind of hyuking coward abandons others like that?" Sayer grabs my shoulder and shakes me so hard I slam into the wall. "You left them in a middle of a fight!"

I wail as fire shoots up my hand and across my body. My eyes roll back into my head as my knees buckle, but Sayer holds me up and pounds me into the wall again.

Two boys fly up and shove Sayer off of me. A boy and girl grab his arms and restrain him. Tegan and Seren race up to catch me as I collapse, letting me down gently. Then Tegan rips a length of her shirt off and wraps in around my hand. I might have told her not to bother, but I can't speak, and it feels like my entire body is being stabbed with hot metal.

"Stay out of this, Deryn!" Sayer growls and tries to break the lock on his arms.

"No! She's not a soldier!" Deryn shouts back. "Can't you see that?"

Sayer rages against his captors until his gaze falls on me, his eyes reflecting the horror behind them as he comes back to his senses. Tears moisten his eyes, then he shuts them and bows his head.

"I'm...I'm sorry. I just—" He grimaces. "I want no more deaths. We've lost too many already."

It must be twenty minutes before the agony running through me subsides and I can catch my breath. My thoughts come back to me gradually, along with my voice.

"Then go help them," I say and swallow. "I can get you off this ship and back to your own."

"How?" Seren asks, pushing her face close to mine. "How can you do that?"

I grin at her. "I'm the chief engineer here. Commander Aza-zhi may lead the crew, but this ship belongs to me. How do you think I got in here without getting caught?"

A small smile forms on Seren's lips. Grins come from other children, too, though some remain skeptical. I can still see pain on Sayer's face, but behind it, I see how much he wants this to end. For him and the other kids, I very much hope it does.

He catches Tegan's gaze, and they share some silent communication. Once they're done, he nods.

"Okay," Tegan says, with a fast glance to the others. "We'll follow you. Take us out of here."

DESPERATION

— • —

CERI

"Ceri!" Merek hisses, shaking me. *Bish. Did I fall asleep? In the middle of a battle? For how long?*

I jerk up to sit, my hands on the deck, sliding across its rough surface to find my gun. The absolute black of the room makes my head spin, and my search becomes a desperate attempt to cling onto the floor before I go flying off it.

But the moment passes as quickly as it came. A second later, my fingers touch the gun's barrel, and I sigh in relief.

"Why did you let me sleep?" I whisper.

"How was I supposed to know you were asleep?"

I grind my teeth at his obvious answer and my stupidity.

"How long?" I ask.

"Less than a minute."

Too long. I need to get situational awareness back. Now.

"Efa, Niah. Check in."

"Clear and moving to the ladder," Efa replies. *"Support would be very welcome."*

"We're coming. Rendezvous at the down landing. Niah? You copy?"

The silence on the comm makes me queasy. It's against our training to assume anything, good or bad, without intel. Yet I can't stop this eerie feeling from invading my body. The only way to fight it is with info, and right now, I've got too little of what I need.

"Let's move," I say.

"Get the door. I'll cover." Merek shifts in the darkness. I push up and follow the sound of his movement, reaching out to find the wall. I touch his shoulder instead and take hold of it as I stumble behind him. Fatigue is making my limbs heavy, and if I don't get some light soon, I'm going to crash.

This is all because we lived in the light for so long.

Merek takes my hand and leads it to the edge of the door, then signals me to open it with three quick taps on my arm. With a sharp inhale, I shake the drowsiness off and slide the door back so just a sliver of amber light comes through.

As dim as the illumination is from the tiny light source on the opposite wall, it recharges me, and I'm filled with determination to locate Niah and put distance between us and the enemy. It's the only way we'll gain enough time to regroup and create a new strategy.

With a quick check for movement outside the room, I wrap my fingers around the edge of the door and hold up my other hand, counting down three...two...one...

Go.

We slip through, our weapons up. I fly to the first corner and check it—clear—then crouch and scan down the corridor. Once I know it's safe, we turn right and glide down the passage, pausing at the next corner. The ladder is two turns away. I count down again as we prepare to cover the distance swiftly and silently.

Merek guards his side. I secure mine. We're ready. My last finger drops as we slide out and make the turns.

And find Niah.

"Cover, cover!" I hiss as I drop to my knees next to her. She's face down on the deck, her body still. My hands tremble as they check her over, hoping to find nothing but fearing the discovery of a gaping wound that announces her death.

This can't be the way her life ends. She's the oldest of all of us, yet she's barely begun her life. It'd be more than unfair. More than a tragedy. If Niah dies, I lose the one person I could look up to for guidance. My big sister will be gone.

I won't accept that.

With desperation pushing me hard, I press my fingers under her neck, then put my ear to her back. A weak thump is my reward. I nearly cry out in joy. But she's far from safe. Niah's breaths are shallow and ragged, and if she got hit like I did, she's in a great deal of danger. Evac from the level and back to medical is the only way we save her.

Without warning, Merek fires down the corridor. His dart strikes a light, and it bursts with a pop. He falls into a crouch and fires again. I drop and lift my gun, firing blindly.

The corridor floods with enemy fire. I flatten myself over Niah and cringe as it flies above our heads, slamming into the walls around us and lighting us up. We were lucky with that volley, but they won't miss the next time.

"We've got to go!" I say, grabbing Niah under the arms. "Pull back!"

"Pull back to where?" Merek cries.

He's right. Our destination is forward, not backward. Ten paces down the corridor—toward the enemy—is the ladder landing. We were so close to escaping this level. Not anymore.

The squeal of a dart gun opens up next to me. Efa. She's unloading darts as fast as she can, filling the air in front of the security agents with so much danger they're forced down. Merek too.

I yank Niah back around the corner, then the other. Merek follows. Then Efa. She reloads, then plants the barrel of her weapon on the edge of the wall and fires another volley down it.

"Not that way!" she says, her eyes wide. She thrusts a finger down another passageway, one I didn't notice before. It's got to be shallow, judging from its position on the level—a dead end. Efa better know what she's doing.

There's no time to consider. I grit my teeth and haul Niah down it, digging my fingers into the door to rip it open and pull her inside. Efa dashes in after, helping me turn Niah over and slide her away from the door to give Merek space to enter.

He's in a second later, sliding the door shut and locking it. Then he signals to Efa to help him shift a stack of crates in front of it while I power on a small light and pull Niah's body over my legs.

"Another closet," Merek moans. "Great."

"This closet might save your life," Efa retorts. "So shut up and stay quiet."

I push their bickering out of my head to focus on Niah. Two burn marks cover her chest, and another crosses her right arm. There's only minor blood loss, but that's no comfort. When I open her shirt to examine her wounds, I gasp. There's a hole as wide as my finger opposite her heart. That explains her breathing. The gap is black but cauterized. All I can do is cover it and hope we can escape this level in time to save her.

And I must. I cannot lose Niah. I will be hollow without her.

"There's no hiding!" a male voice shouts, the tone muffled by the bulk of the door and the crates behind it. "Come out, and I'll spare your lives!"

"Yeah, right," Merek growls. Efa glares at him and presses a finger to her lips.

I cradle Niah's head in my arms and press my brain to come up with a prayer for her. I've little else. Our only advantage is that they don't know where we are or how many of us are fighting. If they did, they'd be less careful about how they're searching.

Niah stirs, a weak moan escaping her lips. I brush her hair from her face, wishing I could do more than that, but I've used up all my bandages, and if I give her more for her pain...*No.* I shut my eyes, forcing away the negative thoughts. Still, I don't know what else to do. If she were conscious enough for me to talk to, maybe we could figure something out together. Some way through this.

Please stay with me, Niah.

"I'll say it again," the voice, which I think belongs to Commander Azazhi, says. "Surrender now, and I will grant mercy to your crew. They're all dying, you know. Only we can save them. Will you let them just suffer? They will, I can promise you that!"

His voice is getting quieter, which gives me a moment to panic over the vision that comes into my head. My entire crew, dead or dying. Seren, struggling for her last breath. Meri and Beka, lifeless on the ground. Even Sayer, fighting against infection with fading strength.

Efa connects her gaze with mine. Fear is deep within her eyes. Merek's too. His jaw is slack as his head swivels, searching for the answer we all desperately want yet are failing to find.

"My life for theirs is a good trade," Merek says. "Let's surrender."

"No," Efa pleads. "He's lying. He has to be!"

"If we fight and lose, they'll be dead, anyway!"

They look at me to break their stalemate, and instantly I get a lump in my throat. I can't make that choice for them. My hands shoot up as I shake my head, as if denying them will block the force of their insistence. Of course it doesn't. I'm trapped here with them. They've got forever to wait for my answer.

"Don't ask this of me," I say. "I can't decide your deaths."

"You aren't," Merek replies. "We were dead the moment they woke us from stasis."

A bang outside the door rattles the crates we've made our blockade, startling the three of us. That was close, maybe around the corner. They'll be here soon.

If there was a moment to decide, it would be now. The opportunity to choose our fate ends once they smash the door down.

Niah mumbles something I can't understand. I lean closer, but her head rolls to one side as her lips part and her body goes limp. A silent scream builds inside of me. If only I could ask her for advice. She'd know what to do.

But no. Niah has done as much as she could for us. Now the rest is on me to decide and for all of us to make happen.

Merek motions to Efa to listen for movement outside. She nods and presses her ear against the wall just next to the door, her eyes rolling upwards as she turns her focus to her ears.

Two seconds later, Efa shoves back from the wall, the edges of her eyes widening. Her hand comes up and moves in a flurry of signals. Merek glances at me for an answer.

They're here.

I crush my lips together and look at the two of them. If we're falling on their mercy, we'd better do it now.

I'd better make this count.

"We fight," I say, reloading my weapon. Efa sucks in a breath and holds it just long enough to consider the meaning of my words. Then she checks her pistols while Merek removes the top two crates and gets ready to slide the door open. I don't know how many we'll get in our first volley, but I hope it's all of them. Especially Commander Azazhi.

I make sure Niah is comfortable, then hold up my hand, fingers wide. Merek nods. Efa swallows. But I hold, taking a moment to let the cells in my brain burn the memories of their faces in. If any of us are to fall, I want to remember how we stood to defend our ship against the second horde of adults. I rub my tongue across the back of my teeth and raise my gun.

Now.

My hand clamps shut. I take aim. Merek grits his teeth and yanks the door open. Efa fires. I shoot. Darts fly and hit their targets. Security agents drop. Others scramble to evade. All of it happens slower than time should move.

An inferno builds inside me as I squeeze the trigger over and over. Never have I felt such hate. I don't just want to beat them. I want to erase every adult before me from existence. Their lives were forfeit the moment they attacked us. Now they will pay.

My gun goes empty.

"Shut it!" I cry. Merek puts his foot on the handle and kicks. Efa flies forward and enables the lock.

My hands fumble with my weapon to reload it, each breath coming fast. My body tingles with adrenaline as I prepare to do it all over again.

But next time, they'll be expecting us.

"Shoot and move, shoot and move!" I hiss, repeating the soldier's mantra.

Merek switches to the other side of the door. Efa builds a barrier with the remaining crates. I slide forward, ready to take out more of those adult bastards.

The entire room shakes as a massive weight slams into the door. A crate falls and lands on my leg. I wince and groan as pain shoots up my body. But there's no time to care. With a grunt, I shove it off, racing to reposition.

"Shoot out the lock!" someone shouts from the other side. *Bish and a half!*

"They're coming through!" I pull back, grab Niah, and do my best to cover her with my body. She can't die, even if I do. Someone will need to look after the younger crew.

The metal of the door whines as the edge by the lock turns white hot, lighting up the room in a horrific glow. Smoke pours in, filling the air before us. My heart pounds at a brutal rate. I can barely expand my lungs. I grip my weapon, my finger eager to squeeze the trigger. Death is close, but I will end as many of them as I can before I do. No adult will dictate my life to me ever again.

The melted lock falls out of the door, creating a hole. Shouts explode from beyond it. Multiple weapons fire. Men cry out in pain. A scream cuts through the chaos.

And then silence.

I tense and lower, listening.

Then a pounding on the door.

"Open up!" a voice demands. A male voice.

Sayer's voice.

SUPPORT

FANA

TEGAN HOLDS ME BACK as I try to shove my way past her and get to the room where they just found Ceri, Efa, Merek, and Niah. Seren called Raey in almost the moment they opened the door. No one could say who was hurt. I'm glad Raey was here, and willing to help, but the thought of Ceri, or any of them, seriously wounded makes my gut twist.

I need to see for myself.

"They'll be okay," she says, leveling her gaze at me. "And you shouldn't even be here. This is still a battle zone. Last I heard, you didn't know how to fight."

"I don't," I reply as I lower my head, though I know that answer will get me removed from the area. As it is, I don't really know where we are other than level ninety-six. Not as deep into the ship as I've been, but still deep. The air down here is thick, and when it mixes with the smoke from weapons fire, it becomes an effort to breathe. The *Stratford* crew glared at me every time I coughed. Maybe that's part of Tegan's reasoning for kicking me out of here.

"You want to help us, right?" Tegan charges. I curl my lips in and nod. "Then you should back off. That'd be the biggest help of all."

My feet stick to the floor. They'll only move forward, not backward. I want to see Ceri so badly the inside of my chest feels like it's burning. If I just see her face, just for two seconds, then I'd know she was okay.

"Come on," the girl Mari wraps an arm about mine. "I'll bring you back to our base point. You'll be safe there with the juniors."

"Juniors? Meaning younger than you?"

Tegan smirks. "Those juniors took out ten agents on their own."

My mouth drops open. *Kids? Like that? Beating highly trained adults? How is that possible?* Maybe going to sit with a bunch of preteen killers is not such a good idea.

Mari clears her throat and tugs on my arm. She's being polite, and I don't want to test her, not after she mentions something about training a few of those young assassins. Maybe they aren't so young anymore. Perhaps I'm the child being led away for my protection, when all I really want to do is—

"Wait."

I spin as I hear Ceri's voice, catching Mari off guard as I break from her hold. *Ceri's coming to see me!* But my breath gets caught up as she comes into view. Strands of her hair hang loose from her braid, while the sweat on her face causes the rest to stick to her cheeks and neck. Dirt and spatters of black cover her pale skin. She's been through hell and somehow survived it. I bet it's not even the first time, but I'm so glad for it, I'm having a hard time containing my joy. I really don't want to, and if she does anything more than say hello, I might just explode.

Behind her, Merek and Efa gather a handful of the older kids into a huddle, speaking in sharp whispers. I can only think they're getting an update on what just happened, the truth of which even I can't believe. Four squads of the *Devant*'s best routed by children.

Ceri offers me a small curl of one side of her mouth as she approaches. She's a mess, but alive, and that's all I care about. With relief pouring into me, I drop the calibration tool I'd been carrying and throw myself at her, wrapping my arms around her body and pressing my cheek to her shoulder.

"Woah." Ceri stiffens even as I feel my eyes getting wet. *Ridiculous.* I should laugh at myself for acting like this. I might be. But to be close to her like this is possibly the best thing I've felt in seventeen years.

She slides her hands up to my shoulders and pushes me back—gently but with insistence.

"This isn't over," she says, connecting her hard gaze with mine. "You should go with Mari. She'll take you somewhere safe."

I shake my head. "No. I'm staying with you."

"Not a good idea," she replies. "I can't worry about protecting you in the middle of a fight. No one can. It's better—"

"I'll take care of myself," I reply while wondering what the hell I'm saying. This is a serious battle, and I'm clueless about surviving one. But I know the safest place is next to her, and that's what I'm going to do.

Ceri crushes her lips together, tilting her head to the side.

"Okay. But stay in the middle of us, keep down, and don't lag behind. We'll move fast, and fights will happen without warning. If they catch you standing, you're dead. Got it?"

I shrink a little, the thought of me being caught off guard a near certainty. But I've made my choice, and I'll accept the risk.

Ten seconds later, the entire group moves out, faster and more silent than I could have ever guessed. Their footsteps are barely louder than the hum of the environmental systems, and they move with a precision that contradicts their age. The only thing that confuses me is how they know where they're going. I suppose they should, since they took a specific direction and—

Someone shoves me from behind. I fall and hit the deck as multiple weapons fire. The air whistles around me as I press myself to the deck. Cries come from down the corridor as shouts fill the air.

Then, pandemonium.

The passageway burns red as the security agents fire back, the beams of their weapons flying just above my head. They're firing at a relentless rate that's brutal. I wince, fearing a beam will hit me, but I can't get any lower.

"Get back!" a boy shouts as he shoves his hand into my shoulder, then screams and drops. I choke as his body falls next to me, lifeless, even as his eyes are open. He had to be only fifteen.

The breath goes out of me. *They just murdered a child!*

One of the *Stratford* crew shouts, and suddenly all of them are retreating at speed. Ceri rushes past, followed by Tegan. Hands grab my ankles and drag me back with the rest. I'm pulled around a corner and flung to the back. My arms cover my head as I smash into the wall.

And then the most sickening sound I've ever heard erupts from down the corridor. My entire body goes ill as an eerie beam of neon green shoots down the passageway. It's thick and intense, and if someone had been standing in its way, they'd be vaporized in an instant.

"What the hyuk is that?" Tegan shouts.

"Directed high-energy weapon," I say and shudder. "Don't go anywhere near that beam. It doesn't have to hit you to kill you."

She and a few of the younger crew look at me with widening eyes. But Ceri and Efa remain as steady as they were before. Merek and Sayer too. Only then do I realize that war has been the standard in their life since they woke up. They may have a strong desire to live, but they have no fear of dying.

Ceri drops in front of me, all business. "How do we defeat it?"

I blink and stare at her. *She wants me to give her a solution to this? What do I know about fighting or weapons?* I don't have any tactics or advice to give. *Why is she asking me?*

"I...I don't know!"

Another blast fires down the corridor, metal whining as it heats and melts. We duck and cringe as if dodging the shot.

"Bish, if they keep that up, they'll compromise the hull!" Mari hisses.

"It's not your problem," Efa says and gestures down the corridor. "Take three and cover the other side of this hallway with Merek. We can't let them flank us."

Mari's jaw drops open as if she just realized she made a serious mistake. Maybe she did, but I doubt it. She scans the kids around us and points at three, including Rhys, who's all but forgotten his mistrust of me. He's focused on Mari's commands, and the moment she moves out, he follows.

Ceri rubs my shoulders then. What I must look like for her to do that. Likely terrified. I'm not. I just don't want any more children to die.

"You know what that weapon is, right?" she says. "That means you know the solution to destroying it, or at least deflecting it."

"Deflecting?" I tilt my head as I look at her. The beam's in the visible spectrum, so theoretically we could reflect it, though to do that we'd need a very robust mirror to either scatter it into harmlessness or focus it back at them. I'd choose the latter, if I had a choice.

"They're moving up with that thing!" Tegan hisses as she pulls her head back from peeking around the corner.

"Fana," Ceri says, looking at me with more intensity. "I need an answer, or a lot of my crew will die trying to stop that weapon."

"Do you have a heavy mirror? One that can withstand a beam of high energy?" I ask.

She narrows her eyes at me. "No. Why would I?"

I shut my eyes and sigh. "Sorry, that was a dumb question."

Of course she doesn't. No one keeps an industrial-strength mirror in their back pocket.

A blast of sound and glaring light erupts from the corridor, battering the corner behind us. Ceri dives, pulling me down with her as the wall explodes, sending metal and composites in every direction. Tegan gets hit as she tries to take cover. She moans and crashes onto the deck, her face turning into pure agony.

Smoke—no—steam wafts into the corridor from the hole in the wall, filling the space with heat and moisture as vapor clouds form, covering over us and the entire area. Everyone tenses as if they're expecting something to happen, but when all remains silent, they become suspicious.

"Why aren't they firing again?" Efa hisses as she slides closer. "We can't defend—"

Both of them look at me when I gasp, realizing the answer.

"Stay down!" Ceri hisses, grabbing my arm.

"No! This is our chance to get away! Steam and smoke will scatter that beam and make it less effective." When they only stare, I add, "And I just figured out a way to deflect it."

"How?"

"Take me back to that storage room we found you in. I left something there that I've been playing with. If I can adjust the frequency and amplitude correctly, I can make a shield out of air."

Ceri and Efa wrinkle their foreheads. Of course they're trying to comprehend what I mean, but unless I give them an in-depth lesson about the engineering of directed energy processors, I can't explain it easily.

"Please trust me," I say. "This will work."

They share a glance, then Ceri taps the mic on her throat and whispers something so soft, I can't hear it even when we are nearly face-to-face.

"Okay," Ceri says to me. "Tegan will bring you back there, but she's wounded, so you'll have to help her walk. Once you get whatever that is, have her call Efa. Someone will escort you to where we've redeployed."

I purse my lips and glace at Tegan, who's being aided by another girl. Her face twists into a hard grimace as the girl patches her up. How she's going to lead me anywhere is a wonder.

"Don't worry, she'll manage fine," Ceri says when she catches my glance. "Now go, before you can't."

"And hurry back," Efa adds as she levels her gaze at me.

Despite her wound, Tegan moves fast. I've got to race to keep up. She throws a glare at me when my feet slap against the deck. But it's not my fault. I'm doing calculations as we run, one of which is to figure out how boys and girls more than five years younger than me can organize such a tough resistance. And how I, chief engineer of the best ship humanity has ever built, am taking orders from them.

Tegan groans and leans heavily on the wall. I put my frivolous thinking aside and slip my arm under her shoulder to help her the rest of the way back.

The calibration tool was right where I'd dropped it, along with its new power pack that was meant for stasis pods. I waste no time leading Tegan into the room with the junior crew and then going back to grab it.

"Fana!"

It's Raey, looking at me as she exits the room where she must have been caring for Niah. Blood smears her usually pristine lab coat, and her face is sweaty and pale.

She wipes the sweat from her brow as she stares at me. "What are you doing?"

I take an uneasy step back, bringing the tool around in front of me as if it will block her from attacking me. Raey may have just saved a life, but I don't know if I can trust her anymore, not after she made it clear she stands with a murderer.

"Fighting," I say and raise my chin.

Raey shakes her head and frowns. "Why? Why are you helping these kids?"

I shift on my feet. *So she's taking that angle. Well, I won't let her.*

"Because they still have their humanity." I turn to pick up my new guide.

"Fana!" Raey's voice turns pleading. The break in it stops me, and I look back. "Be careful. Please?"

She surprises me again. All I can do is smile and nod as a warm feeling comes over me. Raey may have chosen sides, but she's not one of those child killers. And I think she still cares about me.

The trip back goes fast. The boy who brings me to the new location is quiet the entire way, as if he's thinking hard about something. Most twelve-year-olds shouldn't have such a serious look. Most twelve-year-olds aren't in battles, either.

"What is that?" Efa asks as she sees me arrive.

"Your secret weapon. Where's Ceri?"

"Organizing a maneuver. You're here with me for the attempt. If that thing works. Are you ready?"

Efa is likely older than she looks, but I can't help but stare and smirk at the baby-faced girl giving me orders like she was the greatest military general to ever live.

"What?" Efa says, raising an eyebrow.

"How old are you?"

She rolls her eyes. "Eighteen. Are you ready?"

"Sorry. And yes. I think."

"There's no time for guessing. Either you're right, or a lot of us will die."

I swallow hard. In theory, this should work. It might also shake the walls apart. I've faced way too many experiences where the technology looked good on paper but failed badly in application. That's why they made me chief. I fixed all the stuff the designers couldn't.

"Where do you need to be?" Efa asks.

"In the lead. I'm no doctor, but I doubt it'd be good for anyone to be in front of this thing when I turn it on. Also, you'll need to fire over me and the beam, or your darts might not go very far."

Efa's eyes widen, but she acknowledges the danger. So should I. If it doesn't work, the weapon's first shot will vaporize me.

And now I'm shaking after realizing just how wrong this could go.

DIPLOMACY

CERI

I MOVE INTO POSITION just down the corridor and around the corner from the enemy. Seren's next to me, sticking closer than she ever has. I give her elbow a squeeze, trying to comfort her. She offers me a timid smile in return. It's enough. My stomach is as twisted and tight as anyone's in my squad. We're facing an enemy that outclasses us in armor and firepower, and an unfortunate side-effect of their weapons has severely compromised our ability to move around in the darkness.

After a short skirmish to test their tactics, our target has reformed their ranks back at the landing for the up ladder, their heavy weapon aimed down the main corridor where Efa and her small team prepare to neutralize it with some kind of thing that Fana has. Merek, Rhys, and their team are across the other side of the landing from me, ready to squeeze the security agents from their position.

And Sayer, back with the junior crew to protect Niah and the other wounded, will be all that remains of us should we fail.

"*In position,*" Efa says in her comm. "*Fana's ready but shaky.*"

"*She's not a soldier. That's normal.*"

"She doesn't seem too confident, Ceri. Are you sure you'll go, no matter what?"

I put my fingers on my mic and look to Seren, Mari, Deryn, and the others. Their lives might end in a few minutes. So could mine. And we could argue forever over if that was right or not. But just like me, they had a real life before the adults stole it from us. And now adults are once again trying to steal the little freedom we've had these last few months. It may not be much, but it's ours.

"For our ship and our families. We go no matter what," I say.

Efa clicks her mic. Then I hear others. More and more until it sounds as if the entire crew has acknowledged their commitment to protect all we have.

"Send her, Efa." And may the ancestors be on her side.

As I peek around the corner, I notice an immediate shift in the security agents. One man stands and takes a step toward the corridor entrance. Others tilt their heads. Most just stare.

Fana has to be there. That's the only reason they'd react this way.

Commander Azazhi steps forward, his jaw tight. His eyes narrow as he lifts his finger and points.

"What are you waiting for?" he shouts. "She's a traitor. Execute her!"

Bish. Did her device not work?

I key my mic, even as my body screams to run. "Get ready. We go on my mark."

An agent rushes forward, grabbing the handles of their big gun and swivels to aim it.

At Fana.

"No! Pull her back!" I yell. Too late. He bares his teeth and squeezes the trigger. The gun hums as a light forms inside of it. My hands squeeze my weapons, fearing the worst.

And then—nothing.

"*Something's burning,*" Efa says.

The security agents murmur as a stream of smoke wafts in from the corridor.

"How is she doing that?" an agent shouts.

The big weapon sparks and catches fire. There's a pop as smoke billows from the tube. The man who fired yelps and jerks back, his hands flying up as he falls into his companions.

I feel a smile come to my face. She did it. I don't know how, but Fana just saved us all.

"Forget that gun!" the commander cries. "Shoot her with your rifle!"

"*A team, go!*" Efa growls.

A volley of darts drops the three security agents closest to the corridor as the rest fumble to aim their weapons at Efa and her team.

I won't give them the chance.

"*B and C teams, go!*" I bark, charging into the landing and picking off as many as I can before my gun runs out darts. My blade comes out, and I pick my target. My body moves without thought. The memory of a hundred battles runs through my head. The whine of dart guns pierces the air, coming from two sides in a crossfire that sends the enemy into a confused panic.

Security agents scream. Some retreat. Many fall. We overrun the rest and subdue them.

By the time it's over, I'm sweating and panting. Dizziness strikes me as the rage and adrenaline dissipate. Somewhere in the back of my mind, I'm conscious of what I've done. What I prayed I'd never have to do again. But I had to protect my ship. I had to stop those bastards from hurting those I cared about. They left me no recourse, no choice of how I could do that. And now they know why we defeated them. Now they've experienced the terror we survived.

Commander Azazhi stands alone, his eyes shifting back and forth between each one of us as we surround him. I respect he's forcing his fear down and trying to hold strong against what is now an inevitable defeat.

"If you kill me, there's still another hundred security agents on the *Devant* that will seek justice on my behalf." He clasps a hand around the opposite arm. "And they won't show mercy just because you're just a bunch of kids."

"You had four squads," I reply, waving a hand at his fallen agents. "Look at what a bunch of kids did to them. Anyone that invades the *Stratford* again will suffer the same."

He scoffs at my words, but he's still calculating the possibility of another failure by his agents. Perhaps they'd be better prepared now that they have an idea about how we fight, but this is still our ship, and we will defend it even if he sent a thousand against us.

Efa enters the landing, her hands on Fana's shoulders as if the *Devant*'s chief can't direct herself. Her head hangs forward, and she holds a hand over her stomach as if she's about to vomit. I could almost grin. Every one of my crew that made it out of training has known that sensation. That sickness that hits after the first battle they experience.

"Traitor!" Commander Azazhi cries. "Your life is forfeit! I will end you the first chance I get."

"Not while she's on my ship and under my protection," I say.

"You have no authority to do that," he shoots back. "She's a member of my crew."

"Not after you tried to murder me," Fana says.

"Prove it," he challenges.

Fana lifts her hand to show him the big hole through it, her eyes narrowed. I catch my breath, staring at the grotesque, blackened wound. *How did I not notice?*

There's a wail from outside the landing. Raey rushes in, followed by Sayer. She heads straight for Fana and grabs her wrist to pull her hand closer and examine it. A whimper comes from her lips as she turns to her commander, her mouth dropping open.

"How could you?" she demands. "Not just one of your own crew, but a member of your senior staff!"

"She stopped being that the moment she chose these kids over us."

It's clear to me now what kind of man Commander Azazhi is. He'll be difficult to negotiate with, which means I'd better ask for a galaxy if I want even a star.

"We have some demands," I say. "If you want to be released, that is."

He puts his attention back on me then, once again assessing what he can get. His hand drops to his side, and he faces me square on—a poor fighting stance if I've ever seen one. That would explain his agent's failure to perform well in a battle.

It's a good thing I took Captain Yelekal out, even if it almost cost me my life.

"Go ahead, then," he says. "Amuse me."

"First, no one from your ship comes aboard the *Stratford* without prior approval. And I mean no one. Second, this attack is your doing. We were merely defending our ship. You will make no counter attacks, and none of us will accept any guilt in whatever law you claim. I don't care if it's real or not."

"That it?"

Before I can say anything more, Fana steps next to me and turns to face her former commander.

"We want a multiprocessor to repair this ship's navigation system."

My mouth drops open. *Of course. The multiprocessor!* Without it, we're back in the same bish we were in before. But now he knows that, too, and we have little to trade for it.

"We?" Commander Azazhi lets out a laugh. "Now that is amusing." He shakes his head, then his eyes turn hard. "No. You can all burn in hell for all I care."

"Commander," Raey says, biting her lower lip. "Maybe they have something we could exchange a multiprocessor for. Like...excavation equipment?"

Alert races through me as their gazes connect. Raey may act like she's on our side, but I wonder. She's likely protecting her own interests, whatever they may be. If she remains here, I'll be keeping an eye on her.

"Maybe." The commander shrugs, indifferent. "We'd need to see a manifest of the kinds of equipment they have. But no trade would happen without the return of Fana and Specialist T'ena to the *Devant*."

Fana turns to me, her eyes begging me to say no. I give her a small smile. I wouldn't have agreed to that demand. We'd be sending her to her death, and I'm done with killing.

Raey is a different story. Her medical skills have been critical to our survival. But as she just proved, having her on board might be a problem in the long term.

"If Fana requests refuge here, then I'll grant it. Raey is free to go if she wants."

"I request it!" Fana says, throwing a glance at the commander, who snorts.

"I appreciate your willingness to protect me as a member of your crew, Commander," Raey says. "But with your permission, I'd like to remain a little longer and complete my review of their stasis beds. No one has checked them in nearly a year, and there could be some issues."

"Fine, but the moment I call for you, you return, clear?"

"Of course."

Fana glances at Raey and lowers her head.

"But you're still not getting that multiprocessor without Fana returning."

My eyes narrow. He still thinks he's talking to a child, one who's throwing some kind of tantrum. But if he believes all he has to do is keep saying no to me, then he's going to experience a long solitary confinement aboard the *Stratford*. I know just the closet to throw him into.

"I think you're forgetting something, Commander," I say, stepping up to him. "All we've done is state our demands. None of which you've agreed to. And if we don't have an agreement in place, then you don't get to go back to your ship."

"You little brat! Do you think you can just threaten me like that?"

"She doesn't need threats," Efa says. "A single word is all she has to say, and we will follow that order to the letter."

"Did you forget you abducted my crew?" I challenge. "Then you invaded my ship and murdered my people. I think I've already been lenient with you. So go ahead. Keep up your fake outrage and watch me change my mind."

Commander Azazhi keeps silent as he glares at me. But even as he smolders in his hate for me, he's considering the few options he has. His hand comes up to his mustache, and he smooths it out with a long, slow press across its length.

"You want an agreement? Fine. I return to my ship, you get your multiprocessor. And I take all of your excavation equipment."

"Ceri, no," Sayer says. "The colonists will need that stuff when they arrive on-planet."

I catch Sayer's gaze to let him know I understand. There's no way I could strand my parents or any of our passengers on an unknown planet with no way to build shelter quickly. I'd be better off turning their stasis pods off now and saving them from a life of struggle.

"No excavation equipment," I say, "not unless you've got something better to offer. And if not, I'll take the multiprocessor for your release."

Commander Azazhi stares at me, attempting to intimidate, but he's played his last option out. Now either he says yes to the multiprocessor, or he gets locked up. As much as I'd like to see him suffer the way I did, I hope he sees reason. We desperately need that machine.

After a moment, he sighs and nods. "You can pick up the unit once I'm on the other side."

"No. Have Baati and Taye bring it across," Fana interjects. "Then once it's through the airlock, you can leave."

I grin. So do Merek and Sayer. Saving her life was the best thing I've ever done. Twice.

RESTORATION

FANA

I DON'T KNOW WHY my body is quivering. Maybe I'm just exhausted. These last two weeks have been the most trying moments of my life. And yet I couldn't be happier.

Ceri and I sit together, side by side, by the ladder on level two, waiting for what will hopefully be good news. If Baati and Taye do as asked, and Commander Azazhi gets sent back as agreed, we'll be on the right path.

We also agreed I'd be a liability if I was anywhere near the airlock down on seventeen. It'd be too easy for someone on the *Devant*'s crew to snatch me back to the ship, thanks to my pressurization of the access tube. So Ceri's here to protect me in case of trouble. I can't think of anyone I'd want more to be my guardian.

"Sorry you got guard duty," I say with an apologetic smile. It's for her. I'm not sorry at all.

Ceri shrugs. "Raey told me to rest, and Efa backed her up. She said I was too important to risk on a swap like this. As if I'm any different from her."

"You are different."

"What do you mean?"

"You're the leader. Everyone looks to you for direction. They'd be lost without you."

Ceri puffs out air in disagreement and looks up. The dim light from the single source in the middle of the room puts dramatic shadows on her face, highlighting wisps of her hair escaping her bangs, the streamlined edge of her nose and cheeks, the soft, strong curves of her lips and neck.

Oh, I am so lucky to have—

"Are you listening?" Ceri asks.

Oops. Was I just staring so hard I didn't hear her speak?

"Uh, yeah." I bite my lower lip like a schoolgirl and duck my head while she watches me, her eyebrows stuck somewhere between raised and furrowed. My cheeks are getting warm, and I'm suddenly grateful for the *Stratford* crew's preference for low light.

Raey, the one person who knows me best, really called it. She was the only one that made my pulse quicken. Now...

I slide closer to Ceri, our gazes connecting. Every fiber of my body melts as my breath gets caught in my chest. *Can she tell? Does she know?* I'm losing myself in her eyes, and I couldn't welcome it more. My body drifts ever closer to hers. I reach out to touch her face.

And drop my hand.

No. I blink and shake my head as I try to catch my breath. *We've got work to do.*

"What is it?" Ceri asks.

A bucket of guilt hits me from nowhere, and I deserve it. I'm older than her, and I've dated before. Ceri likely hasn't even looked at someone with the kind of desire that's threatening to cloud my better judgement, and if I don't come up with something to distract me, I will regret my actions.

"Thank you for being my protector," I blurt out, even as I hear how pathetic it sounds. "You've saved me multiple times, and I wouldn't be alive if you didn't."

"And you saved us," Ceri says, pressing her lips into a soft smile. "So I think we're even."

She clasps a hand on my shoulder, like she might with any comrade-in-arms. But then there's an awkward moment where neither of us says anything, so I lean forward to embrace her, and she follows suit. Hugs are often better than words, anyway.

I close my eyes and accept the moment as I rest my cheek on her shoulder. Her body is warm, her touch gentle. She rubs my back as if I was a child, and I let out a contented sigh and shut my eyes. This is perfection. I have to tell her how I feel. It's the only way to keep this going. And imagine if she felt the same...

Before I know it, my head arches back, and my lips brush against the base of her neck. Electricity shoots across my body, making my skin tingle with excitement. *Oh, no—I didn't mean to do that!* Yet all I want is more. So much more. I press closer and hold her like I'd fall off the level and plummet a hundred-plus levels to the aft of the ship if I let go.

"You're trembling," she whispers. "Are you okay?"

I am and I know it. It's too late now. I did my best...No, who am I kidding? I had no plan to stop. Not really. My head lifts from her shoulder. I press my cheek against hers. My heart pounds with anticipation as my skin caresses hers. With a soft, tender movement, I slide my hand to her lower back, the other to her shoulder. My lips touch her the edge of her mouth as it parts.

And Ceri gasps and pushes me back.

"What...why..." She stares at me, wide-eyed. "Are you trying to kiss me?"

I cringe and duck my head as I turn away, my hands clenching as they shoot up to press against my forehead. This has to be the worst miscalculation I've made in my entire life. And Ceri must be horrified. I took advantage of her appreciation to force myself on her.

I have to explain...No. I can't. But I should...I must. She deserves to know.

But if I look at her, I'm sure I will die.

"No!" I squeeze my eyes shut. "I mean...oh hell...I'm sorry."

The rail car chimes, signaling the arrival of the multiprocessor, as if someone had planned it that way, and I couldn't be more grateful for the sudden distraction. I shoot to my feet and cover the distance to the rail system doors in what feels like half a second.

Sayer and Merek step out, carrying a crate I recognize as being from the *Devant*. I can feel the corners of my mouth turning up as I stand before them like an eager child.

They grin back, as I must be beaming at them by now.

"Where should we place this?" Merek asks with a quick glance over at Ceri. I turn the opposite way, my cheeks flushing warm just at the thought of her. If there was a bulkhead I could hide behind, I'd have been there already.

"Right there. Next to the console." I point right where I think I'll need it. And where my eyes stay far away from Ceri.

The moment they drop it, I'm tearing the locks off and throwing the top of the crate open. And there it is, the nondescript metal box that I requested.

Yes. Exactly what I need to keep my mind off...*Oh, why, Fana? Why?*

In the next second, my hands are on it, lifting it from the crate and placing it just under the console. I hop over the box and pull the power lead behind the *Stratford*'s systems, searching for a place to connect it.

Merek and Sayer watch me jump around and then, deciding that they are no longer needed, return to the rail car, waving as the doors shut.

As much as I attempt to focus on my work, I can feel Ceri's eyes on me. I do my best to push any thought about her that comes up, especially the ones where I wonder what she's wondering.

I was such an idiot to...*Oh, this connection will work there...*give in to my yearning for connection. Ceri may act like someone twice her age, but she's barely escaped her teenage years. Raey once told me that no matter what we do, our physical maturity moves at the same pace it always has.

There. I've plugged the multiprocessor into all the couplings I think I need to make. *And not the ones I don't, like pressing my lips against someone else's when they're not invited.* Now to start up the operating system and pull the right bits of code together. The monitor I've got at my disposal is tiny, but it'll work for the moment.

With a last sigh of acceptance of my carnal stupidity, I power on the unit and watch as the BIOS code flashes across the screen. *This is good. Routine. I like routine.* It means nothing's wrong. Computers should be consistent and reliable, which is unlike the rest of my life, where I seem to constantly mess things up.

Then again, software has a way of smashing into the wall during the most basic of operations.

"Dammit!" I cry, pounding the edge of the console as the microprocessor throws up a glut of error codes.

"What?" Ceri pushes up...*Please, no, don't come over here. I won't be able to handle you so close*...and hurries over, only slowing when I make all sorts of angry movements. Not at her, of course.

How did I get to be such a dunce?

There will never be a moment in the rest of my remaining life that I won't regret what I just did. It doesn't even matter if I totally mistook if she likes girls or not. I don't want to know the answer. Not now. We're trying to save thousands of lives, and that's what I'll be focused on until this ship can navigate once again.

If I can.

"Is it working?" Ceri asks, her eyes tracing all the cables and jury-rigged connections I've made between the multiprocessor and the console.

"Not yet."

I drop in front of the unit, crossing my legs and leaning forward to tap on the keyboard to try a workaround that I'd already considered. The small screen on the box scrolls in response to my input. So far, everything that's happening is expected.

Until it's not.

I groan, leaning my head back as I open my mouth and stare at the ceiling. Systems should be more reliable than people. But this is far from a normal system. I'm patching modern technology to stuff that's seven hundred years old. It's a miracle that any of it works at all.

"What? What is it?" Ceri asks, crouching next to me. Her hip brushes against my shoulder, and I want to cry.

"The multiprocessor can't sync to the console's operating system," I answer as I force steadiness into my voice. "I've got a few ideas, but if they don't work, I may have to reformat the entire system."

"So? Just do that. Right?"

Explaining why I can't would be just as difficult as getting her to understand just how much I like her. Ceri's no program, but she hasn't had the benefit of the standard teenage software upgrade. If that can even be called an upgrade. I hated those years—I had to struggle to even get an idea of who I might be. It was only after I met Raey that my jigsaw life fell into place. It's why I still feel a connection with her now, even after our split.

"No, that might be a bad idea. Your navigation system is old. Really old. I don't...Just hold on, okay?" I say, knowing it likely comes off as rude. Ceri's only trying to save her people. She's got a right to push a little.

But I didn't. I just let my lust for her control me, and now either I become the adult and tell her how I feel, or I don't, though I might prefer permanent stasis over that. Ceri deserves to have someone who understands her and cares for her. Leadership is a lonely chair at the end of a long table. It's nearly impossible to get someone to see your point of view until they sit in your seat.

Bish, why did I try to kiss her?

As the multiprocessor's readout scrolls endless amounts of data down it, I get the feeling in my gut that this is a useless battle. I'll need to overwrite the entire navigation system to enable it to use the multiprocessor's resources.

"Alright." I take a breath and turn to her, still avoiding her gaze. "Here's the deal. The only way to get this to work is to erase everything in your system and start from scratch. The good thing is that I've got all the code we'll need to do that."

"And the bad thing?"

I press my lips together. This is why they made her boss. Ceri considers all angles before choosing a path. And she does it quickly. In a different universe, she would be commanding the *Devant*. And I, of course, would be her ever-willing subordinate.

"The bad thing is if the system doesn't accept the new code, or is incapable of running it, then we'd need to beg, borrow, or steal new hardware from the *Devant*, and I'm sure you can guess the trouble with that."

Ceri considers. "Still, the risk is easier to calculate there."

"True. So what do you want to do?"

"You're asking me?"

"It's your ship."

"It's not. But let's try the overwrite. If it fails, we won't be any worse off than we are now."

I salute. "You got it, Commander."

"Don't call me that."

"Sorry."

As I work through the mostly standard operations, my mind wanders, even when I fight for it not to. And of course, it keeps coming back to the same subject as if I was walking around in circles.

Ceri.

She has to be wondering how I feel about her, and I owe it to her to be honest. I'm just totally in fear of her response. Rejection will make me want to curl into a ball and hide away for the next millennia.

But if she feels the same...

I was never an optimist. Raey had the best part of that between us. Even then, we weren't an always positive kind of couple. We just understood each other well, and really, that's all we needed.

"So?" Ceri asks after I sigh and sit back.

"It's going to take a while, but so far, so good."

"Oh."

We sit in uncomfortable silence as we watch the readout. It's hardly thrilling because it's all one big procedural process—try this, test, try again, test, over and over again—until it works or until options run out. I've never experienced that, so I've never had to give up.

And I shouldn't give up.

The debate in my head clear, I swivel toward her, grabbing her hands and looking at her.

"Ceri, I really like you," I say.

She frowns, then mulls it over before she replies, "Well, I like you, too."

I should have expected that. It still makes me smile. Looks like I'll need to play adult for a moment.

"No, that's not what I mean," I say with a squeeze of her hands. "I like you. A lot. That's why I wanted to kiss you, because I like you. Get it?"

Her jaw goes slack, and she does her best to cover up any further reaction. I should be hopeful that she hasn't rejected me outright. And we're still holding hands. I'll take that to mean I should press her a little more.

"Do you...like me like that?" I ask.

"I..." Ceri curls her lip in and glances away.

"Hey, um, I know this might be new for you. And I feel terrible about...well, you know. I'm not the best at explaining how I feel. Raey was always the one—" I press my palm to my head. "Never mind about Raey. I just want you to know I think you're amazing."

She shrugs. "Thanks, I guess."

That was the best I could come up with? I might as well give up now.

But her indifference about my failed romantic gesture is odd. I just assumed, with the way Efa and Merek go after each other and Ceri's annoyance with Rhys, these kids knew at least something about holding hands. Maybe not?

"Have you ever been in a relationship?" I ask.

"A romantic one?" Ceri shakes her head. "No."

Ah-ha. Her reactions make perfect sense now. I think I need to slow the pace down. A lot. I rub my thumbs across the backs of her hands and then release them back to her side with a gentle caress.

"Have you ever thought about it?" I continue.

She shrugs. "It's not for me."

I wring the fabric of my shirt as my stomach twists. It's like Ceri just shot a dart right through it. I frown, trying to hide my dismay.

"Not for you? What do you mean?"

"The crew is my responsibility. I can't be distracted from that by focusing on one person. And I can't take favorites."

"But…"

"I just can't. Sorry."

The grip on my shirt gets tighter, even as I force a smile. I doubt I'm doing a good job of it. My face must look like a contorted mess. My shoulders slump, too. No question, she knows how I feel, even if she's not responding to it.

I've gotten my way so often, I'm a failure with rejection. Still, there's something in the way she apologized to me that makes me think there's more there than she's saying or maybe willing to admit. I'll take that as something to work with, because I'm not giving up on her so easily. Ceri really is special, and even if I'm the only one who sees that, I'll take it as a blessing that I met her.

I glance at the multiprocessor's screen. There's a prompt at the bottom of the screen. My jaw drops.

"It's finished!" I shout and jump over to it. "It's ready to synchronize!"

"Which means what?" Ceri asks.

"It means in a few days, we'll have a new direction to steer the ship to and a system to make it work. Congratulations. Your passengers are back on course."

The entirety of Ceri's face explodes in joy. In the next second, she wraps her arms around my neck and presses her head close, rocking me back and forth. Her attack hug stuns me so much I take many more seconds to hold her back.

"Thank you," she whispers in my ear. "You saved them. All of them. Thank you."

Well, maybe this is one way to reach her.

EPILOGUE

CERI

OUT OF THE LARGE port window on level one, I watch the ovaloid tip of the *Devant* as it continues to match speed with us for the start of a second month. They've kept to communications silence ever since we sent Commander Azazhi back to them along with their casualties. The looks on their faces when they saw how many there were is something I will never forget, because I've seen it too many times.

We had casualties, too. Not just from the battle. We lost three to the virus, which, for reasons Raey couldn't understand, fizzled out after a few days. It went through all of us, but most felt nothing other than normal. It doesn't matter to me if there's no explanation. I am just grateful for the health of my crew.

"Ceri!" Fana pops her head through the ladder hatch. "Navigation's up! Come on."

I smile before I even turn to look at her. Fana has been such a bright light on our dark ship. She acts like she's junior crew even though she's second in age only to Niah. It's funny to see her get scolded by Efa when she forgets to reset the water recycler. Only Beka forgets as much.

Still, between her and Raey, everyone has a new sense of purpose about them. And discipline. I am thankful to them for their influence on both.

"Be right there," I say.

Fana smirks, then nods and ducks back through the hatch. I let my eyes linger there for a few seconds longer as I remember that moment two nights ago. It was the first time anyone had ever made a confession to me like that. I was so lost for words, I failed to explain myself well. Or at all.

She must have been so heartbroken, and I feel horrible for hurting her when she's done so much for me and the crew. Still, I made the right decision, and I've got to stick to it, even if that means I wind up on my own. I can't be selfish. And I've been alone before.

I realize then my finger has been tracing over my lips while I've been lost in thought.

Hyuk.

With as much mental force as I can gather, I push the entire memory into the back of my mind and head to the ladder to follow the one person who has ever expressed an interest in me.

And made my pulse quicken.

Cheers and applause fill the space the second I hit the deck on level two. I spin to find the entire crew in celebration of this moment. Dru beams at me as she hops up and down. Seren, too, while Merek and Efa look on with pride. Even Raey is here, taking a moment from her care of Niah to play witness to what will hopefully be the moment where everything changes for our passengers.

Only Sayer and Rhys are solemn, if expectant. There's talk that needs to happen there, but at least for now, Sayer seems content to share in our success.

"Send the command, Ceri!" Tegan chants as she claps in rhythm. Others join in, then more, until everyone is shouting. Their voices are so loud, I cover my ears to stop them from hurting.

Fana beckons me to the navigation console, newly reconfigured to have the multiprocessor and its screen sitting in it. The keyboard rests just below it on the armrest that runs the length of the console. Off to one side, lights of all colors blink in a synchronized pattern, as if taking the moment to rejoice along with us.

"Quiet!" Merek shouts. "Everyone shut up for a moment!"

There's a few chuckles and giggles as the noise dies down. I'm adding to the laughter, too. It's seldom that we've found humor in anything, though we should find more joy, if we can.

"So," Fana begins, "um, just to let you know what we expect to happen once Ceri presses the command enter button. The system will search for any records in the backup memory down on level one-twenty-four. If it finds the original target, which it should, then the system will reorient the ship to that vector. And then we'll be on our way."

Another cheer erupts from the crew. After it goes on for a minute, I hold up my hands to silence them. Their quick obedience shouldn't surprise me, but as I catch their expectant gazes, I lose my breath, caught in the memory of the last time everyone gazed at me in such a way. It was when we first defied the adults and broke from their control. That one act brought us to this point.

Fana touches my arm, then leans forward to type in the command. Once she's done, she steps away to give me access. But before she goes too far, I snatch her wrist and tug her back.

"You deserve this honor just as much as I do," I say.

"We all do," Efa adds, then grins. "So just hit the hyuking button!"

Merek laughs. I smile. Fana does too. At me. On a different day, I might feel uncomfortable with that. Not today.

I take her hand, and together, we hit *GO*.

"What's it say?" someone calls. It's only been ten seconds.

"Yeah! Tell us!" Seren yells.

The screen displays a list of five likely candidate worlds. Each one has a list of statistics and the best resolution image that we could get hundreds of years ago. A light blue planet with patches of brown is highlighted with a green square around the image.

"The system is Seager-Ghez 1267b. The planet is called Asteria," I read aloud. As if any of that has any meaning to me. It will for our passengers—including my parents—and for that, I am glad to learn about it.

Fana purses her lips and ducks her head slightly.

"What?" I ask as my forehead tightens.

"That's the same target as the *Devant*," she replies.

My stomach twists so hard I nearly wretch. My hand flies up, ripping at the hair in my braid as the other one tightens into a fist.

"No," Efa gasps. "Why'd it have to be there?"

Beka and Mari share a worried glace. Tegan shakes her head. The junior crew looks to me for an explanation. I have none other than to say we must be cursed.

"Wait." Sayer rushes forward to scan the screen, finally pointing to another planet. "This one looks good. Why can't we just go there?"

Fana leans over to glance at the option Sayer's pointing at. "It looks okay. We've got the vectors right here, so it'd be simple to reorient the ship."

"No," Merek says. "It can't be that easy. There must be a reason they chose Asteria."

"Does that mean the *Devant* knew where we were going?" Efa narrows her eyes at Fana when she asks.

Fana's jaw drops open. "No! At least, I don't think so…I mean, we have all the data on every ship that's left Earth, but we wouldn't set our course based on the *Stratford*'s destination. We were leading another ship there. No one knew where your ship was or, honestly, cared."

"That's true," Raey adds. "I was there when we discovered your distress signal. Before then, we were just traveling along our normal route. It was Fana that convinced the commander to change course."

"Keep quiet," Deryn says. "Your words mean nothing here."

I take a step towards Efa's smoldering glare, putting Fana behind me. She just helped us achieve something incredible. There's no way I'm going to let anyone turn her into the target for their angst.

"It's not her fault," I say, then nod at Raey. "Or hers. So let's keep them out of this."

"Not completely," Sayer counters. "Fana, it'll be easy to change the vector, right?"

"Easy is relative. It can be done, but not without a lot of reprogramming, and given the age of the systems on this ship that still work, there's no guarantee it'll do what I ask it to. It was a miracle the multiprocessor worked at all!"

"So you're saying we might have to live on the same planet as those bastards that tried to kill us?" Deryn thrusts a finger at her.

Fana shrugs. "Planets are pretty big, remember? Your passengers wouldn't need to live anywhere near those on the *Devant*. It's not like they would even know what happened, and even if they did, nobody can keep a grudge going for multiple generations."

"Yes, they can," Sayer counters. "The *Stratford* is proof of that. The war here was going on for over fifty years, thanks to the adults."

As I listen to everyone's comments, the tension from my body releases. Perhaps it was Sayer mentioning how the war was over, or it could have been Fana putting reason to words. I feel like the truth's been spoken somewhere, but I don't know what it is.

Until it hits me.

"It should be up to them," I say over the clash of voices. "Our passengers will be the ones living on that planet, not us. Who knows how they will get along with the *Devant's* people, especially if they don't know what we went through? And I think we owe it to them to make sure they never find out."

The crew shares glances, considering my words.

"Let's take a vote," Merek suggests, "to see how we're all feeling about this."

Efa looks to me for approval. She doesn't have to, but I nod anyway. We should all agree on whatever we choose. Forcing ideals on others is how the people of the *Stratford* split into factions. And as long as I remain leader, I will never let that happen again.

"Before we do"—Sayer catches everyone's gaze—"remember what the adults of the *Devant* did."

Merek huffs and shakes his head.

"Your families might have to deal with those kinds of people. And for their sake, we may have to deal with them again, too."

"Alright, enough," Merek says. "You made your point. Don't try to scare anyone into siding with you."

Efa steps forward. "I'm not afraid. We stayed here for our families. I say we do whatever we can to make sure they get to the place they were promised."

"Me too." Merek slides his arm around her, and they share a warm moment.

"I'm part of this crew now, too, right?" Fana asks. I smile and nod. "Then I vote we keep on this course. Not just because it's the safer path. It seems they outfitted this ship to build a colony on Asteria. We go somewhere else, and the colonists might not be prepared for that."

"Who's trying to scare others now?" Sayer growls.

"It doesn't make it any less true."

"Whatever. Everyone who wants to change course, raise your hand." Sayer lifts his hand high. A few others join him: Rhys, Deryn, and Beka, who chews on her lip when she sees she's in the minority.

"Everyone who wants Asteria to be the final destination, let's see your hands," Efa says as her hand shoots up. Merek follows. Then Tegan, Mari, Dru, and the junior crew.

All eyes fall on me then, as I've yet to vote. Not that it will change anything. Our crew has made their preference clear. But I wonder if it's the best choice. We may risk everything by dealing with a known threat.

Which means I need to prepare my crew for disaster.

"Alright, we stay the course," I say. "And starting immediately, I want everyone back to combat training. If we have to deal with the *Devant* again, then we'd better be ready for a fight, because I guarantee there will be one."

Books by Marc B. DeGeorge

Origin Story Series

The Starship Sneak

The Reckless Rescue

The Traitors' Trial

The Conspiracy Clash

The Deadly Discord

Air Born Series

A Call to the Sky

A Challenge for the Sky

A Crisis in the Sky

Stratford Series

A Universe Upon Us
A Universe Against Us

About the Author

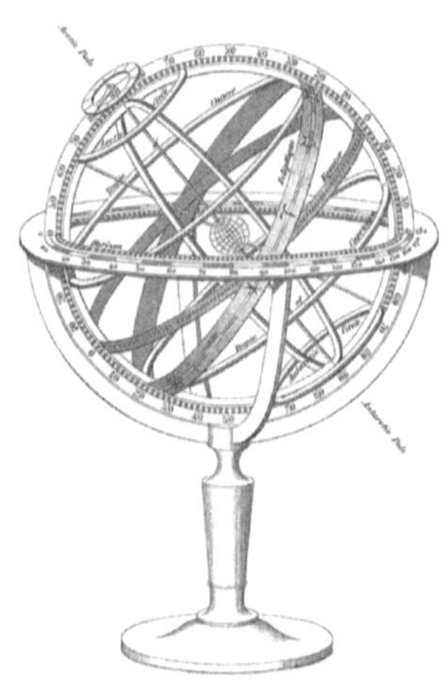

Marc B. DeGeorge has made every attempt in his adult life to maintain a balance between how much science and how much art he dabbles in. Sometimes, he's even successful. When he was young, he wanted to be an astronaut, and then an aeronautical engineer—he even went to Space Camp! But then he learned how to play guitar and his space dreams took a back seat. He spent a decade playing professionally in bands and studying music in college (university only took five years). These days, things have come round full circle, and Marc envisions the future by writing books that imagine what challenges humanity may face, and what we might accomplish together.

When Marc isn't writing, he performs traditional Japanese music on shamisen and writes, shoots, and edits performing arts photos and documentaries under the MuseMarc Studio name.

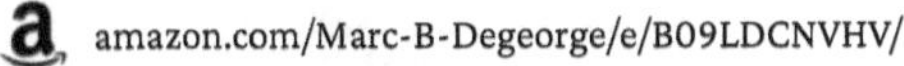

amazon.com/Marc-B-Degeorge/e/B09LDCNVHV/

facebook.com/MarcBDeGeorge

instagram.com/marcbdegeorgeauthor/

goodreads.com/author/show/22081012.Marc_B_DeGeorge